THE TROUBLE WITH KEEPING MUM

Annie Cochrane has it all up in the air: a demanding job in the Scottish Government, a teenage son with problems at school, and a mother whose behaviour is getting increasingly erratic. There just aren't enough hours in the day, especially when there are two men on her mind and a devious First Minister plotting to end her career. With the tabloid press in pursuit, and life-changing decisions to be made, how will Annie avoid dropping everything?

THE TROUBLE WITH KEEPING MUM

The Trouble With Keeping Mum

by

Rosie Wallace

Magna Large Print Books
Long Preston, North Yorkshire,
BD23 4ND, England.

British Library Cataloguing in Publication Data.

Wallace, Rosie
   The trouble with keeping Mum.

   A catalogue record of this book is
   available from the British Library

ISBN   978-0-7505-3744-5

First published in Great Britain in 2012 by Hachette Scotland,
an imprint of Hachette UK

Published in Large Print 2013 by arrangement with
Headline Publishing Group

Magna Large Print is an imprint of Library Magna Books Ltd.

Printed and bound in Great Britain by
T.J. (International) Ltd., Cornwall, PL28 8RW

Every effort has been made to fulfil
requirements with regard to reproducing
copyright material. The author and publisher
will be glad to rectify any omissions
at the earliest opportunity.

To the numerous honest, hard-working politicians, both local and national.

Thanks go to:

Bryony, Anne, Richard and Catriona for advice on community care, police procedures, dentistry and special care baby units respectively.

My agent, Lindsay Fraser of Fraser Ross Associates, Bob McDevitt from Hachette Scotland and all at Headline for help and advice.

All friends and relations who have offered support, advice and encouragement.

Chapter One

Annie Cochrane, Member of the Scottish Parliament and government minister, looked at
herself in the changing-room mirror. She had
taken the loud seventies-style creation from the
rail in the hope that it would make her look
slimmer. In vain, as it turned out. She undid the
zip and yanked the dress to the ground. Next, she
took a long black skirt from its hanger and paired
it with a satin blouse. Now she looked like her
mother at the pensioners' club Christmas night
out. Annie stuck her head out of the cubicle in
search of an assistant and encountered a small
lady with a badge pronouncing her the manageress. Pencil-thin and five foot three in her dainty
stilettos, she obviously bought her size eight
clothes from the petite rails.

'Very nice! Classic!' simpered Mrs Manageress.

'No. It's not me. Do you have something a bit
more ... glam, but not too racy?'

'Size?'

'Twelve,' said Annie hoping what might be
produced would have a generous cut.

Mrs Manageress reappeared with a long jacket,
camisole and trousers. It certainly looked better,
but the cut was not as favourable as she'd hoped.
She ventured out of the cubicle again.

'Very elegant, Ms Cochrane.'

Ah, Annie thought, that explained why the

manageress had replaced the junior assistant. She had been recognised – one of the perils of TV appearances.

'It's better than the other one, but it's a bit tight.' Annie gestured vaguely, first towards her chest and then to her hip area.

'I'll get you a fourteen. Better to go up a size and look slimmer, I always say.'

What looked like a huge pair of trousers and an enormous jacket were produced, but Annie had to admit that they were an improvement.

'Do you have anything else for black-tie occasions?' She might as well make the most of the help at hand. 'I seem to have grown out of my present wardrobe and, unlike my male colleagues I can't just get away with one dinner suit.'

'Must be a perk of the job getting to all these grand events,' gushed Mrs Manageress as she disappeared in search of suitable clothes.

Annie surveyed herself. Being Minister for Health and Wellbeing meant an average of two black-tie dinners per week, followed by at least two hours' work on her ministerial papers. Hardly very healthy. Her preferred option, an evening in the Edinburgh flat with a plate of scrambled eggs, was out of the question tonight. A gathering of orthopaedic surgeons awaited her.

She tried to find her waist. Despite picking at her food and refusing more than one glass of wine at these rich dinners, weight loss seemed to be evading her. Everybody said that your mid-forties were dangerous, weight-wise. The one consolation about this evening was that she wasn't very hungry. Annie shook her head at her reflection.

She should enrol at a gym, but there weren't enough hours in the day. And anyway – she couldn't bear the thought of all those treadmills.

'How about this?' said Mrs Manageress displaying a purple lurex ball gown with a long slit up the back. 'This designer believes that ladies should flaunt their curves. It's off the shoulder,' she added, unnecessarily.

Annie swallowed hard. 'No, I don't think so.'

'This?' Another sparkling confection was swished in front of Annie's nose.

'No, I don't do sequins.' She smiled weakly, regretting having prolonged this painful experience. She looked at her watch. She had to be at Edinburgh Castle by 7 p.m. to host the pre-dinner reception and it was now 6.45. 'Thanks. I'll just take the outfit I'm wearing and I'll keep it on. Can you put my old clothes in a bag?'

Dressed in her new finery, she emerged into the cold damp January evening, to find her ministerial car had disappeared. Eoin, her driver, must have been told to move on by the traffic wardens. Keeping an eye out, she looked at the illuminated window displays around her and tried to remember the last time she had 'gone shopping' just to have a wander and indulge in impulse buys. It must have been three years ago, before she became a government minister and personal time became something she simply didn't have. It wasn't that she didn't enjoy her job. In fact, she thrived on it and she knew she did it well. She juggled two full time political roles – those of minister and Member of the Scottish Parliament – and still managed to give her son a secure

17

family life. She was proud of that. On the eve of his departure, Kenny, her ex-husband, had announced that her priorities were her constituents, her party and then her family, and that he wasn't staying around to come third in anyone's life. Now, with her additional ministerial duties, she had four priorities. Well, she might lack a husband, but she had the help of her mother, the redoubtable May Laverty.

The toot of a horn brought Annie back to the present. She piled herself and her bags into the back seat of the ministerial car, just as her tame stalker rounded the corner.

'Drive!' she urged. 'I swear, that guy has this car on some kind of satnav.'

'Success?' her driver asked over his shoulder.

'I wouldn't say success, Eoin, but I am wearing an outfit which will have to do.'

The car-phone rang. Could only be one of her civil servants. Annie picked it up.

'Hello...'

'Mum!'

'Annie, got you at last!'

'How did you get this number? It's restricted...'

'It's written in my book with all your other numbers. *Annie Car* it says. You must have given it to me. You never answer your mobile. I thought I'd give this number a try.'

Oh dear. 'How are you, Mum?'

'I wanted to know how you got on with the cardinal today.'

'Ah... We had ... an interesting and lively exchange of views.'

'Did you go to confession before you met him?'

18

'No.'

Annie could hear tutting noises.

'Well, tell me what you talked about.'

Annie braced herself. 'We talked about the campaign we are running in schools to educate children about STDs and using condoms.'

There was a brief pause. 'You are telling little children about...' Her outraged mother whispered the last word, '...condoms?'

'Not *little* children, Mum. Big children ... fourteen and over.'

'And why do you need to tell them about phones? They all have these mobiles nowadays.'

Annie was lost. 'Phones? What are you talking about?'

'STD ... something ... something ... dialling ... I can't remember now, but it's to do with phone numbers...'

'No, Mum, STD means sexually transmitted disease.' There was no response. 'Hello? Are you still there? Mum?'

'...You mean to tell me, you were talking about VD to His Eminence?'

'I suppose I was,' said Annie. Eoin was doing some fancy manoeuvring to avoid a new set of roadworks on Princes Street.

'Did you talk about anything else?'

'Well, since you ask, we strayed onto gay issues, which wasn't on the agenda, and then I had to go to another appointment, so that was it. Somehow, though, he knew I was brought up a Catholic and kept using the pronoun "we" all the time.'

'I don't like this *brought up* bit,' said May sharply. 'You *are* Catholic! I said to Father McIver after

19

Mass on Sunday that you were going to be meeting His Eminence and he said he knew the cardinal's press secretary.'

'Well that explains it! I sympathised with some of his arguments, but we can't legislate solely for a Catholic point of view.' It was fun winding her mother up.

But May's mind had moved on. 'Did you get your photo taken?'

Annie smiled as the car drove up the road onto the Castle Esplanade. 'No, you've already got one of us together taken after his installation. Look, Mum, I've nearly got to where I'm going. Is Joe there? Can you put him on?'

'Had his tea at six and then off out to goodness knows where. He never tells me anything these days. Treats my house like a hotel, swanning in whenever–'

Annie cut her short.

'Mum, we'll talk about it tomorrow over tea when I'm back. Six o'clock as usual. Bye.'

She called Joe's number and left a message: 'Hi, Mum here. Just hope you're okay and had a good day. I might be late back to the flat tonight, but give me a text if you need to chat. Love you.'

As she was getting out, she paused.

'Eoin, you'd better get the number on the carphone changed. Mum can't be the only person to have it.'

He smiled and nodded. 'I'll see to it.'

'Are you picking me up? I should be finished about ten.'

'It's the contract-hire company to collect you tonight, Minister, but I'll be there to pick you up at seven-thirty tomorrow morning to go to the constituency. Just as usual.'

Having a driver made Annie's life so much easier.

She made her way towards the Grand Hall of Edinburgh Castle and found her private secretary, Tony, waiting for her in the ante-room. He handed her the after-dinner speech and started briefing her about those present.

'This is a world-wide conference for orthopaedic surgeons and this evening is the highlight of the non-medical events. The speech is the usual one for international conferences: "Scotland's health care is wonderful" etcetera.' He pointed at the speech. 'I've filled in the gaps for this event and there is even a small joke about hip-replacements.' He looked rather pleased with himself.

'Can I have a couple of minutes to read it through? It's a while since we last delivered this one, Tony.'

He looked at his watch, walked to the door and glanced into the corridor. He returned just as Annie was skimming the first page, the one about Scotland having a rich history in pioneering medical advances. She almost had that paragraph off by heart.

'Minister,' he said in a low voice, 'we are running really late and if you are going to work the room before dinner, you are going to have to go in now. The president is waiting to introduce you to people.'

Annie put on her polite conversation face, closed the folder and handed it to him.

'Okay then, let's go. Put the speech at my place.'

She was introduced to eminent surgeons from all over the world. She couldn't help wondering whether they might have saved themselves time and considerable sums of money by some sort of video conferencing. Surely these shindigs did nothing for their waiting lists? A Mr Norton had forsaken his native Scotland for a senior consultant's post in Timaru. He was waxing lyrical about the glories of Scotland over New Zealand when the drone of the pipes signalled the move to dinner. Annie excused herself and waited with the other inhabitants of the top table. Once hoi polloi had taken their places, the procession followed the piper into the Great Hall while everyone stood and clapped. It was just like a wedding – but with no bridegroom and no cake.

Dinner was much as she had expected – smoked salmon terrine, beef *filet* balanced precariously on a tower of potato and puréed something with a puddle of something else, then Crannachan. Why did someone have to ruin fresh raspberries and cream with horrible gravelly oatmeal? She picked at her food and sipped her glass of wine. Her audience was less abstemious. They had had their glasses refilled several times in that unobtrusive way caterers have perfected over the years. When she rose to speak, it took a moment for conversation to die down. Everyone, including Annie, viewed the next five minutes as a dull but necessary part of the evening's proceedings. She opened her folder and delivered the page about Scotland's medical heritage before moving on to the section relevant to the evening.

'I deem it a great honour to be able to address

the delegates and their partners of the International Conference on...' On automatic pilot, she turned the page and glanced down for the exact wording of the organisation and read the words *Advances in Genito-Urinary Surgery*. Nothing to do with orthopaedic surgeons. She flicked the page to make sure she hadn't turned two at once, but the large font page numbering confirmed her suspicions. Someone had managed to print off the previous speech – the one from the last medical conference – rather than the one Tony had carefully amended.

'...this international conference on orthopaedic surgery.'

A quick glance down the page revealed that the joke was about someone confusing opening waterworks with the commissioning of a reservoir.

She was going to have to wing this. The adrenaline surge kicked in. If in doubt flatter.

'Your skill as orthopaedic surgeons can turn lives around: my aunt who was trapped in her home has had a new lease of life since her double hip replacement; my nephew was involved in a car accident and is now able not only to walk but to captain his school football team, thanks to the skills of dedicated surgeons like yourselves. Advances in your field mean that the arthritic, the critically injured and those sportsmen and women with injuries which might deny them their sporting achievement are all in your debt.'

She looked up briefly. They seemed to be soaking it up. A joke would be good but only one came to mind, told to her by a medic years ago when she was nursing: *How do you hide a twenty pound note from an orthopaedic surgeon? Put it in a text book. No.* Tonight would have to be jokeless.

She paused while she turned the next page ... it was all about urinary problems and sexual dysfunction. It had been bad enough delivering it to the correct audience and there was no way she could adapt it for this one.

She turned another page and found she was back on script ... the merits of holding a conference in Edinburgh, the world's most beautiful and welcoming capital city, what the Scottish government was doing to improve the health service and research opportunities, and her hope that delegates would get to see other parts of Scotland while they were here. She sat down to polite applause. She took a sip of water and concentrated hard. Eventually, after the president's reply which was full of orthopaedic in-jokes about anaesthetists, and a recital by a harpist, she was able to make her escape.

As they drove away from the Castle, Tony was silent at first, then asked in a rather huffy tone why she had not read the prepared speech, as they had discussed.

'It would be helpful to have feedback, Minister, for the next time.'

Annie handed him her folder, 'Have a read at that.'

There was a short pause. Tony flicked over pages with increasing urgency. 'Ah! Sorry Emma must have printed the wrong one.'

'I don't care whose fault it was. Just try not to let it happen again. Please?'

'You managed fine,' Tony's tone was less accusatory now, 'and I didn't know your nephew had been involved in an accident.'

'He broke his leg when he was three. And to answer your next question, I don't have an aunt with a double hip replacement. Next time, either you or I read it over first.'

'Yes, Minister, sorry.'

Chapter Two

After he had left Annie at the Castle, Eoin had driven the ministerial Volvo to the government car depot. It was the driver's responsibility to make sure the car was clean and tidy at the end of the day. He put Annie's clothes in the boot ready to go to the constituency in the morning before removing his copy of the *Express* and an empty cardboard coffee cup. As he walked towards the bin, he passed the First Minister's Lexus. All its doors were open and the rear end of Patrick Liddell, the First Minister's driver, protruded from the back seat.

'Good thing I'm not into bums, Patrick.'

Patrick reversed out and stood up clutching a can of upholstery shampoo and a sponge.

'And I'm not into witty repartee today, Eoin.' He looked stressed.

'What's happened? First Minister wet her pants?'

'Fucking budgies!'

'Budgies?'

'I…' He jabbed his sponge at his chest '–have been transporting budgies from the FM's house to a bungalow near Edinburgh Zoo and one of the fuckers got out of the cage and crapped all over the car.'

'Transporting pets is not in the job description.'

'Tell me about it!' Patrick continued, 'I take the FM home to Glasgow and as I'm unloading all her paraphernalia, the husband comes to the door with a cage in his hand; next thing she takes it from him, trots down the path and puts it on the back seat. Without so much as a rug to protect the leather. Then she gives me her "woman of the people" smile and says, "Patrick, you won't mind delivering these budgies for Robert. It's on your way. The address is on the label." So I said I wasn't sure I was allowed to do this kind of thing and she says she's telling me to, and she's the First Minister, so off we went. Then when I was doing eighty along the motorway, one of them got out and started flying round the car. I pulled over to the hard shoulder and tried to catch it. That's when it got scared and started crapping all over the place. Then it flew into the windscreen.'

'Suicide?' Eoin asked, smiling.

Patrick saw nothing funny in the experience. 'It was still twitching so I bundled it back into the cage, replaced the cover and delivered the cage to the Edinburgh address as *commanded*.'

'Let's hope it was just mildly concussed or she'll be after you.' Eoin bent down and picked up the lid of the shampoo canister. He handed it to Patrick. 'FM doesn't usually go home on a Thursday does she?'

Patrick tapped the side of his nose.

'Got an appointment at the school in the morning, hasn't she? The obnoxious, sorry *misunderstood,* Jordan has been excluded for a week for swearing at his English teacher.'

'She tell you all this?'

'Not exactly, but, as you are aware, she doesn't bother what she says in front of the driver. We don't have ears, don't you know. Or lives. She was giving the school secretary hell, telling her she would be there *first thing* to see the headmaster. God help him, poor bugger. I wouldn't want the full force of FM's wrath descending on me. Not first thing in the morning.'

'I thought poor, hard done by Robert sorted out all things domestic.'

'Budgie man tried and failed, didn't he, so he'll be getting bollocked for incompetence. As usual.'

'That stuff about Jordan could be worth a bit if leaked to the correct quarters.'

'Could be,' Patrick sounded gloomy, 'but I bet no one will dare to touch it, especially if she browbeats the school into changing its mind about her little darling.'

'Going to give it a try?' Eoin asked quietly.

Patrick shrugged.

'Perhaps. Things aren't what they were. When the last lot were in power, that kind of snippet used to add up with all the other little snippets until it paid for our summer holidays; you know – Caribbean cruise one year and Florida the next. Last year we rented a cottage in Caithness and it rained all the bloody time.'

Eoin laughed. 'Well, as an Orcadian, I would

say it served you right. You should have kept going, got on a ferry to Orkney.'

'Yeh, yeh ... and you think the weather would have been any better?' Patrick shook his head. 'Being promoted to Marlene Watt's driver has certainly resulted in a loss of income.' Patrick attacked a new blotch of budgie poo with some violence.

'Why does she still call herself Watt?' Eoin pointed out another stain. 'She's been married to Chirpy for years and years, hasn't she?'

'Aye. Perhaps twenty years ago there were still enough people about who thought being called Keiller meant that you slept with politicians and the aristocracy on a daily basis – in return for a wad of notes and a few spy stories. Perhaps she didn't want to be associated with a jar of marmalade. Perhaps it's her feminist principles. Who knows?' Patrick noticed yet another stain and sprayed it fiercely. 'What about yours? You got any interesting snippets about Ms Cochrane?'

'Putting on the beef – had to go and buy a new posh outfit today. Her mother's very impressed the cardinal came to see her. Oh! That reminds me, car-phone.' He looked at his watch. 'I'll do it in the morning. Time to go home.'

'Lucky you.'

Eoin put a hand on his colleague's shoulder. 'Now, Patrick! You make sure you check it all carefully. Budgie shit may be small, but it could leave a nasty stain on the First Minister's backside.'

Patrick raised a friendly middle finger at his colleague's departing back.

Chapter Three

To say that First Minister Marlene Watt was angry was an understatement. For a start, she was sharing the back seat of her official Lexus with a budgie cage. And for another thing, her party press officer was not answering his phone.

She had started the day discussing her son's behaviour with his headmaster who felt that calling a female English teacher the C word was indeed grounds for a week's exclusion.

'Jordan thinks Mrs McNeil may have misheard him. He assures me he did not use the word in question. He was merely bantering with his friend, calling him "a stupid runt",' Marlene enunciated this phrase with military precision, 'because he had forgotten to bring a pen with him to class.'

The headmaster held her penetrating gaze without blinking.

'Mrs McNeil is a very experienced teacher, one who most certainly knows the difference between banter and abuse. I have already explained this to your husband, Ms Watt. Jordan had failed to hand in his homework for the third time in a month and Mrs McNeil informed him that unless his English folio was complete, he would not be able to sit his exams. He then called her a stupid ... we both know the word I mean – and left the room. By no stretch of the imagination could that be called friendly banter.'

Marlene moved to her next line of attack. She leant forward in her chair and lowered her voice.

'Mr Rutherford, you're probably right. But Jordan is a very sensitive lad and he's been having a tough time recently on account of my very public position.'

'There is no *probably* about it – Jordan swore at Mrs McNeil.' The headmaster was not to be swayed.

But neither was Scotland's First Minister. 'As I said, he's been having a tough time. You obviously don't realise how much bullying goes on in your school or I'm sure you would have addressed it, Headmaster. Robert and I have been finding it difficult to get Jordan to come to school at all. We've been telling him that he needs to learn to stand on his own two feet, but there are some very unpleasant children who have been taunting him – and worse. Before his English class yesterday, he was ambushed in the toilets, had his dinner money stolen and water poured into his bag. When Mrs McNeill criticised him, it was the last straw and he must have lost his temper. I will ensure that he apologises to her.' Marlene paused and looked at Mr Rutherford.

'I will ensure that he apologises to Mrs McNeill too, but as a result of the verbal abuse, she refuses to have him in her class and I feel she has good reason. From now on, Jordan will be in Mr Goodman's class and is on his final warning.'

Marlene considered this some kind of victory. 'Thank you, Mr Rutherford. I will make sure Jordan is back in school by morning interval.'

'The exclusion still stands, Ms Watt.'

Marlene gave her head a tiny shake. 'I don't think you quite understand, Mr Rutherford. Jordan has been victimised within your school and you and your colleagues have done absolutely nothing about it. I'm sure neither you, nor I, for that matter, want any negative publicity. Unfortunately, my family is of interest to the press and should it become known that Jordan has been excluded, then I would have to put the record straight as to the bullying which led up to the incident, and I would have to say that, very reluctantly, we are considering moving him to a private school. Somewhere like ... Glasgow Academy.'

Glasgow Academy was welcome to her ghastly son, the headmaster thought to himself, but he then made what he considered to be a conciliatory gesture.

'I think perhaps a compromise is in order. Jordan will be excluded for three days. He can return to school on Wednesday.'

Sensing weakness, Marlene went for the kill.

'Headmaster, I understand this school is in line for a major refurbishment. There is such a lot of competition for funding these days. Only yesterday I was speaking to our local councillors and they said that they had insufficient funds to carry out all the planned school refurbishments in the area.'

Mr Rutherford knew he was beaten.

'Jordan can come back to school on Monday.'

'Today!'

Oh, how he loathed this woman. 'All right; but he reports to me first, then he will apologise to Mrs McNeil – in my presence.'

'He will be back in school by eleven. I'm so glad we've cleared up this misunderstanding. I would be grateful if this could remain confidential. As I said, I wouldn't want to have to highlight the school's bullying problem if I had to explain things to the media.'

Marlene swept out of the school gates to the ministerial car and told Patrick to drive her home. Five minutes later, she was marching Jordan down the path while he attempted to tie his tie and walk at the same time.

'You will go to the headmaster and grovel. You will then go to Mrs McNeill and grovel. Make sure you sound as if you are sorry. Then you will keep out of trouble. For the rest of your life. I have better things to do than sort out teachers who cannot control their pupils. Is that understood?'

The boy raised an eyebrow at his mother.

'Patrick, drive him to school and come back immediately and pick me up.'

Patrick did as he was told, parked at the school gate and couldn't help watching Jordan sauntering into the playground. It was morning break and there were various groups of children outside the main doors. Jordan strolled towards a solitary bespectacled boy who was sitting on a bench reading. In a nanosecond the book was snatched from his hands, and a handful of pages ripped from it. The boy handed over several coins. Jordan pocketed them, threw the remains of the book into the bushes, and went to join his friends.

With her son's school career restored, Marlene and the budgie were en route for Edinburgh:

Marlene to a photo-call with some primary-school children who had won the MAKE SCOTLAND GREEN CAMPAIGN and the budgie to replace the one which had been found dead in its cage that morning by the new owner.

Robert had been despondent at the news. 'They just do that sometimes. They die. Shame I have to give her this one. I was going to keep it for myself. It's a real beauty.'

Marlene curled her lip at the memory. Finally, somewhere near Shotts, she eventually got through to her press officer.

'Where have you been? You'd better know that Jordan got in a bit of bother at school. He was being bullied and lost his temper. Any press interest, tell them the school has a major bullying problem which they refuse to address.' She cut the call and looked at her watch. They were going to be a bit late for the school visit but that was all to the good. The First Minister loathed small children.

Chapter Four

It was Friday evening, and Annie was in the living room of her mother's house in Corrachan, searching frantically for the remote control. This was the house in which she had been brought up and not much had changed, except it was no longer owned by the council and the television was now a large flat-screen – a far cry from the first she'd known in its wooden cabinet. Annie eventually unearthed the remote from under the local paper and turned the volume down to a manageable level.

May Laverty was in the kitchen preparing the meal. Annie could hear her moving about, opening cupboard doors and running taps. It was Friday so it would be fish, probably with a white sauce, mashed potatoes and some vegetable which had been boiled to extinction. That would be followed by something with custard. This evening, Annie would have settled for a glass of water, but she would try to eat a little and plead a diet in the hope of dousing the queasiness which had plagued her all day. Something she'd eaten last night perhaps? She wondered if all the orthopaedic surgeons were feeling sick too. So much for the grand Scottish welcome. One thing was certain – she wasn't going to mention it to her mother. The glass of Andrews Liver Salts was to be avoided at all costs. A whiff of boiled fish reached her. She took a deep breath and waited for the nausea to pass.

Glancing round the room, she noticed that the usual array of photos had been changed. Her wedding photo, in a drawer since her divorce, was back on the shelf, but Kenny had been obliterated with a bit of strategically placed parcel tape. The photo of Annie and the cardinal taken following his installation was still in pride of place, flanked by her late father in his national service uniform. But Joe's latest school photo and one of the American grandchildren seemed to have gone. In their place was a curious selection of religious statues.

May came into the room and started setting the table. She laid out three mats then put a knife, fork and spoon at each place.

'There's only the two of us,' Annie reminded her. 'Joe's off with his friends tonight.'

May picked up the spare mat and put it back in the sideboard drawer. 'He's always out. Here for his tea, then away out again. Says he's been going to your house to do his homework, but he could be anywhere. If I'm supposed to be looking after him when you are away, I need to know where he is.'

'Okay, I'll speak to him, Mum, but he's sixteen now so he needs a bit of freedom.'

'Or enough rope to hang himself! Too many out-of-control hoodlums in the town now. You don't see them, with being in Edinburgh as much as you are. Corrachan isn't what it was. You don't want him getting into bad company.'

'He's not in with a bad crowd, but I'll speak to him. Now, you tell me why my wedding photo is back on the shelf with Kenny covered up like that.'

'Don't you mention that adulterer's name in my house.'

'Mum! What's brought this on? I seem to remember you telling me that I spent too much time playing politics and not enough time being a good wife. Why is the photo on display again?'

May went and picked the photo up, gazing fondly at it. 'You are still married in the eyes of the church and you were a beautiful bride. Kenny ... I thought you had found someone to care for you, not someone who would run off and live in sin in England.'

'Mum! For goodness sake! He is not living in sin, he is married to Catherine. We can be perfectly civil to each other now, and there is nothing wrong with England.'

'I'll bet you he doesn't go to Mass any more.'

Annie was getting exasperated by this scatter-gun conversation.

'It's none of my business, Mum. If you really want to know, ask Joe what his father's church-going habits are.'

May replaced the photo and stood beside the table with her fists clenched. She looked suddenly small, as if the fight had gone out of her. Annie gave her a hug.

'Look, Mum, please don't get in a state about this. It doesn't matter to me, so it shouldn't matter to you.'

May shrugged her off.

Time to change the subject. 'Why are the Blessed Virgin and her friends on the mantelpiece instead of Joe and his cousins?'

'Our Lady is watching over me, keeping me safe.' May's tone was defensive.

'Yes, but you have always believed that, so why the statues? They're new, aren't they?'

'I just want them there, so I can see them. They give me comfort.'

'Where did they come from?'

'I bought them. All right?' The tone was verging on the aggressive now.

'Okay! Okay!' Annie changed the subject again. 'Do you want a hand in the kitchen?'

'No. I can manage fine,' May replied as she closed the kitchen door behind her.

After the meal, during which Annie had to go through everything that she had said to the cardinal and everything he had said to her, she sat through *Coronation Street* at extremely high volume, considering the weekend ahead of her – surgery with Mike Andrews, the local MP, tomorrow morning, then many hours going through her ministerial boxes and sorting constituency issues for the rest of the weekend. She also needed to find time to have a proper talk with Joe about his comings and goings. Perhaps he could shed light on the arrival of the saints. *Coronation Street* over, Annie stood up and put on her coat. She gave her mother a kiss.

'That was lovely, Mum. A really nice relaxing evening. 'Fraid I've got to go now. I've got work to do, but I'll see you for Sunday lunch. Come round at the usual time.'

May followed her to the front door. 'Will you come with me to Mass on Sunday?'

'No, Mum. I've got a heap of things to do and you know I don't believe in all that any more. I'll have your lunch ready for you at one. You can give me your version of the sermon then.'

Annie moved onto the step.

'Bye then.' She made it to the street without being called back and began the ten-minute walk home.

May looked at the closed door. She was worried about Annie – all the things in the newspapers saying she wasn't doing her job properly, not to mention the letters in the local paper. Rude and disrespectful, they were. She was worried, too, about Joe and about the teenagers who seemed to be rampaging about the streets. She was sure some of them were coming into the house when she was out. She'd forgotten to mention that to Annie. Nothing had been taken, but things had been moved around. She had found the TV remote in the fridge and someone had put the butter into the microwave. She would get Bob McCafferty from next door to fit an extra lock and chain on the back door for her. That had to be the way they were getting in.

The boiled fish was resting uneasily in Annie's stomach and as she neared her front door she knew it was about to make a return appearance. Luckily she located her key on the first trawl through her handbag and just made it to the downstairs toilet. When she emerged, the bass boom could be heard from Joe's room. She climbed the stairs and knocked on his door. There was a pause before she was invited in. There was a reek of chips and Joe and his girlfriend Ellie were sitting on the bed looking somewhat pink and tousled.

'Hello, Ellie. I thought you were going out for a meal, Joe?'

'Got chips instead. I have to eat Gran's food all week so I've come home for chips – and some sanity.' His tone became accusatory. 'Didn't think you'd be back for a while.'

'Obviously.'

Ellie's shirt had an extra button at the top and an extra buttonhole at the bottom.

'Well. I'm back now but I'm feeling a bit under the weather so I'm going to bed. Can you keep the music down please?'

'Too much boiled fish?' asked Joe, smiling.

Annie hated being disloyal to her mother. 'I've been feeling off all day actually. Something I ate yesterday. Make sure you put these chip cartons in the bin outside. I hate the smell of stale vinegar. Goodnight.'

She closed Joe's door and went to her room. She swapped her business suit for an outsize T-shirt and voluminous pyjama trousers and climbed into bed. It was wonderful to have a sanctuary like this where she didn't have to worry about how she looked or what she said. Switching off the bedside light, she luxuriated in the selfish pleasure of a king-size bed all to herself – no one snoring, farting or expecting conjugals. Friends had nagged her for years to find someone else, but she had had neither the time nor the energy – nor the desire – for a live-in partner.

Things, however, had changed slightly in that department in the past year, surprising her as much as it would have surprised anybody else, had they known. She was happy the way things were at the moment – seeing Andrew occasionally, but not too often. Despite her early misgivings that a sexual relationship would ruin an old friendship, things seemed to going well with him.

Andrew Fraser was her party leader, Deputy First Minister and Enterprise Minister. Annie had been close friends with both Andrew and Jane Fraser for more years than she could remember. Nearly two years ago, Jane had been diagnosed with a brain tumour and was dead within six months. Andrew had dealt with his grief by throwing himself back into work, but sometimes he needed to talk about Jane and, with his son and daughter now involved in their own lives, Annie was the one person with whom he felt able to do this. She too missed Jane badly.

Along with Andrew, Annie was in the habit of meeting some colleagues at Vittoria's on Leith Walk every Monday evening to discuss the parliamentary issues for the coming week over a pizza and a glass of wine. If Andrew wanted a private chat, he would make eye contact with Annie and leave the restaurant first. Annie would then refuse the chance to share a taxi, saying she wanted to walk home as it would be the only exercise she would get all week. She would walk the short distance to Andrew's flat where, over another drink, they talked about old times, about Jane.

On one such evening, about four months previously, Andrew had been telling her how guilty he felt about spending too much time on politics and not enough time with Jane, when he broke down and started to weep. Annie moved to put her arms round him and she held him till he stopped crying. Finally calmer, Andrew lifted his head from her shoulder, kissed her and then they were in his bed.

Afterwards Annie was the first to speak.

'That was a bit of a surprise.' What she meant was, *God Almighty! What have I done?*

'Not a bad one though?' The words coming out of Andrew's mouth were exactly what he was thinking.

He sat propped up on the pillows watching Annie dress. 'Perhaps we could do this again some time?'

Annie stopped buttoning her blouse and sat down on the edge of the bed. 'Perhaps not. I think Jane is still too near for both of us.' *Oh God! My dead friend's husband and my boss.*

'I don't think she'd mind,' he said.

How should she respond to this? After a short awkward pause she said, 'Perhaps, but I still don't think this should happen again.' *Oh Jane, I'm so sorry!*

She walked the mile uphill to her own flat in record time. What had possessed her to be so stupid? Not only was it far too soon for Andrew to enter into any sort of relationship, but, much more serious, she knew their friendship would never be quite the same again.

The following Monday, after a week in which Annie made quite sure that they were never alone together, Andrew had again left the restaurant first. Realising the unresolved issues would have to be discussed some time, Annie made the usual excuse of needing a walk and reluctantly made her way to his flat.

As she took off her coat, Andrew handed her a large glass of red wine, then sat down and patted the space next to him on the sofa.

'You've been distant all week. We need to sort this out.'

She chose to sit on the other sofa, hoping the distance would set the tone for the discussion. Andrew opened his mouth to say something but she held her hand up.

'Me first, please? Andrew, I can't deal with this. We have been friends for how long? ... fifteen years, it must be and Jane was my friend for nearly as long, the friend I saw most of. I keep thinking of her here in the kitchen, or that phone will ring in a minute and it will be her telling you what she did today and sending a message to me not to work too hard.' She paused to swallow the lump in her throat. 'Andrew, I feel like I'm cheating on her. I'm losing you as a friend and gaining some sort of different relationship which I don't want.'

He took a sip of wine and looked up at the ceiling.

'Annie, do you think *I don't* think I hear her in the kitchen? Do you think *I don't* sense her standing behind me and do you think *I don't* care when I turn round to find nothing? You think *I don't* long to speak to her again, to hold her? Of course I do! I tell her about my day, about my fears and concerns, but she doesn't answer. She has gone and, much as I wish it otherwise, she's not coming back. As the weeks go on, that sense of her presence is receding. Occasionally something brings her nearer, like last week when I found a dress of hers in the wardrobe, here in the flat. It was tucked away in the corner behind an old suit and it smelled of her and suddenly it was raw again.' He sighed then continued, 'Most of the time, though, I manage to get through the day. The pain, and it *was* such a physical pain, is diminishing.' He turned to Annie. 'In the short time we had when she was still lucid, we talked about what I would do after. She told me she didn't want me to sit and grow old alone. She told me to find someone else

42

and not to worry if that person came along sooner rather than later. Not to worry what other people think. Take your chances when they come your way, was how she put it.' He moved to sit next to Annie.

'I accept all you're saying, but I don't have time for any sort of new relationship at the moment.' Annie could hear her voice rising. 'There are just not enough hours in the day. You know that. I have ministerial work, constituency work, party work and the small amount of time and emotional energy I have left, I have to give to Joe. He gets little enough of my time and attention as it is.'

'We both need something other than our work and our children.'

'Your children are grown up. My boy isn't.'

'You need something and someone for yourself Annie. I'm not suggesting we move in together. I'm not even suggesting we tell anyone, but I think we are good for each other. We proved that last week.'

Andrew was looking at her intently. She found she couldn't hold his gaze.

'I'm not very good at managing relationships, Andrew. I don't do casual encounters. I have only been to bed with three men. My first boyfriend, then Kenny, then you.' She now looked directly at him, 'The first two didn't end well and I don't want to fall out with you.'

'Three men? What a slut!' The twinkle in his eye belied the reproving finger pointing in her direction. 'I think my tally is four. So perhaps we *are* suited.' He put his arm round her and she finally relaxed into his shoulder. 'Please don't dismiss this as a terrible mistake.'

Everything he had said was true. They knew each other well, they made each other laugh, they cared about each other and the sex had been good. Perhaps, just perhaps, it might work. She drained her glass and told him she needed a couple of days to think. They agreed to meet the following Wednesday evening.

Annie paused on the landing. 'I think, maybe, you should come to me. Half past eight?'

And so it had become a weekly tryst, but at her flat which held no possibility of a ghostly onlooker.

Tonight, though, she had returned to her Corrachan life.

Chapter Five

By Sunday morning, Annie was feeling much better and able to face preparing a meal. She felt strongly about the institution of Sunday lunch as it was the only time she could be guaranteed to sit down and eat with her son. Joe was at an age when he treated this not as Sunday lunch, but as Sunday breakfast, but she noticed that he too was careful not to let other engagements encroach on the occasion. May always joined them after Mass and she relished the time with her family.

Normally, Annie would wake Joe in stages at noon, twelve-thirty and finally at quarter to one to ensure he was dressed and downstairs by one, but today she needed to talk to him before May arrived, so she started the wake-up procedure at eleven and by noon he was dressed and slumped over the breakfast bar with a large glass of orange juice and a peanut butter sandwich.

Annie paused in her preparation of the chocolate puddings and looked at her son. Somehow, in the last few months, the boy had been replaced by a man. He now towered over her and seemed to be all testosterone and uncoordinated limbs. He was also in need of a haircut. She allowed several minutes for the rise in blood sugar to reach his brain, then, in a voice she hoped was light and non-confrontational, she said, 'Gran is worried about where you get to in the evenings. She thinks you may be falling into bad company.'

'Jeeeesus! I've told her I'm coming home to do my homework. And I am!' He put his sandwich back on the plate. 'It's impossible to concentrate there, Mum. She has the telly so loud that the walls vibrate and then she's knocking on the door to my room at every commercial break. Do I want a cup of tea? Would I like to see *Coronation Street?* Come and look at the weather girl. Would I like a cup of tea? Why don't I go to Mass? Why don't you, Mum, go to Mass? Why doesn't dad go to Mass? Would I like a cup of tea? She does my head in. I come here for some peace!' He picked up his sandwich again. 'And I am back there by ten. Always.'

'She worries. It's understandable.'

'She's worried about everything, Mum. I have better things to do than roam the streets mugging people. I am trying to pass exams I need to go to Uni. I *need* be able to do my homework in peace! I still don't see why I can't live here on my own when you are away. I'm nearly seventeen. It's quite legal.'

'It may be legal but I am happier knowing you are fed properly and keeping reasonable hours. We've been through all that before.' Annie offered him the bowl in which she had made the chocolate puddings. He took it, ran his finger round the rim and licked it.

'Fed properly? I don't think so! She's losing the place, Mum. Seriously, we had boiled mince on both Monday and Tuesday – no Bisto or anything in it. *Boiled*. It was all grey and bouncy. Boiled fish on Wednesday, bouncy mince again on Thursday and I bet you had boiled fish again on Friday. I asked her, why all the mince, and she said we hadn't had mince for weeks.'

Annie handed him a teaspoon. 'You shouldn't exaggerate. Gran has always been a good cook and you like mince and tatties.'

He waved the teaspoon away. 'Fingers are fine. I'm not exaggerating and I don't like bouncy mince every day of the week.'

'Well, I'm happier knowing that someone is keeping an eye on you and I don't want this house becoming an unsupervised venue for God knows what. That sort of publicity I can do without.' The minute the words were out, she regretted them.

'Glad you've got such a high opinion of my friends! It's not as if I'm friendly with Shawn McDuff or any of the other local lowlifes.'

'I didn't mean that. I just don't want you living here on your own during the week. That matter is not up for discussion. However, I agree that there is no problem with you doing your homework here – occasionally. We are, however, going to have to sell the idea to Gran.'

'Whatever we arrange, she'll forget.' He located another dollop of cake mixture with his finger and sucked it noisily. 'You don't know what she's been like. She's been really strange lately.'

'Strange?'

'She's ... different! She gets strange notions about things.'

'I did notice all the saints.'

'Them!' Joe burst out laughing. 'They're hilarious. She gets Minty Oliver to order them off the internet. Minty comes round and takes her to her house for the afternoon. They spend hours looking at all the stuff online, then the postman brings her another parcel full of religious tat a couple of days later.'

'I'll have to speak to Minty,' said Annie.

Minty had been Annie's unpaid agent and mentor for many years. She was a slightly eccentric old lady who lived in a draughty house outside the town, a good friend to many. She was more than ten years older than May, but still sharp as a tack, and she had embraced new technologies with a vengeance.

'Gran's not strange otherwise, is she?' Annie asked.

'Definitely, more forgetful.'

'Well, if we write it all down like a timetable, on a calendar, then she will know what's happening, where you are and when.'

She handed Joe a piece of kitchen paper, 'You've got chocolate all over your face, not to mention

47

your hands. Perhaps if you came here two evenings a week and stayed at Gran's for the other two?'

Joe sighed. 'Mum! It's only a ten-minute walk away. I am *always* back by ten. If you want me to get decent exam results, I *need* to come here every evening ... and can't I make my own tea here? *Pleease?* I can't face any more bouncy mince.'

Annie lit the gas under the carrots. 'Compromise. Tea at Gran's, homework here?'

Joe looked at her through his too-long fringe and said nothing.

'Well?'

'Suppose so!'

'And I don't think Ellie should be round here every evening either.'

'She's not here *every evening,* but we sometimes do our homework together. We do the same subjects. We're both on the Young Enterprise team.'

'This is a small town and it will not go unnoticed.' *Listen to yourself* Annie thought.

'We are both sixteen. Whatever we choose to do is legal.' Joe flicked back his hair and looked her in the eye. 'Yet again, my life is being dictated by your job.'

Annie pointed the peeler at her son, furious at having this thrown at her, just as she thought she'd managed to broker some kind of manageable resolution. 'Two items here! Firstly not everything you may choose to do is legal, namely alcohol and drugs. Secondly, the way you phrased that remark implies you're sleeping together.'

Joe coloured and looked at the floor.

Annie continued, 'I will not ask you directly, but I suggest you make sure you use condoms. I'll put a large box in the bathroom cupboard. If you are old enough to be sleeping together, you are old enough to be responsible about contraception.'

Joe stood up and ambled towards the door. 'Lecture over?' he enquired sarcastically.

'Not quite.' She softened her tone. 'What did you mean by *your life being dictated yet again by my job?* Is there something other than having to stay at Gran's that's bothering you?'

'No more than usual.'

'What does that mean?'

'Just the usual crap at school about everything the government does being your fault and that I only get good marks because you will get the teachers sacked if I don't, and that we are the richest people in Corrachan and other stuff along the same lines. It gets effing tedious after a while.'

'Do they really say that I can get teachers sacked?'

'Only Shawn McDuff and his cronies.'

'They're not even in your year!'

'Doesn't stop them ambushing me in the corridor.'

'Is this something you want me to talk to the school about?'

'No! That would make it worse. I can deal with it myself. I'm not a victim.'

'I hope you're not intending to sort them out?'

'Mum, it's not some soap opera in there. No. I just keep out of their way.' He gave her a withering look. 'I'm going to my room.' He thumped up the stairs and she heard his door shut, followed by the boom of his music.

Annie began to set the table. Joe had triggered

her guilty conscience. Her job did interfere with their lives. She wasn't the kind of mother she had intended to be. For the past twelve years she had been an active politician, first as a local councillor and for the last seven years as an MSP. It hadn't been too bad when she was on the council. The meetings had often been in the evening, fitting in with her part-time job as theatre sister at the infirmary, and Kenny or May had always been on hand for childcare. Joe had been nine when she was elected as an MSP and eleven when his father decided he would seek his comforts elsewhere. It was unfortunate that Kenny found his consolation in London when their marriage broke up. That was when Joe had started staying with May three nights a week, although he didn't seem to mind too much. May had a stash of bars of chocolate to which he had extensive access. She also let him stay up later than Annie would have allowed. The arrangement suited the recently widowed May too. The routine provided a focus to her life, but Annie could see that it was no longer the satis-factory arrangement it had been. For any of them. As a government minister she was now away from home from Monday morning till Friday evening for forty-nine weeks a year. Carbon footprints aside, the alternative, a daily hundred-mile com-mute, would mean she was only a token presence in a house where Joe pleased himself. She must remember to buy those condoms. Against all her political instincts, she was just beginning to wonder if a year at boarding school for Joe might be an option when May arrived.

Annie gave her mother the customary thimbleful of Croft Original and poured herself a small glass of red wine. While she made the gravy, she listened to the details of Father McIver's sermon and who had said what to whom outside the church afterwards. May had particularly enjoyed this Sunday morning as she had been able to tell everyone, all twenty of the faithful in attendance, that Annie had met the cardinal to discuss teenage pregnancy and abortion. Apparently they had all been suitably impressed.

'And I told them that you told His Eminence you fully agreed that abortion should not be allowed and that contraception was a sin.'

'Mum! I said no such thing! You can't go round telling everyone what you would have *liked* me to say. People are going to believe you.'

As she carved the roast lamb, Annie wondered if the false information her mother had disseminated at church might come back to haunt her. She placed the dishes of roast potatoes and vegetables on the table and called Joe. Because it was a summons to eat, he came clattering downstairs immediately and seated himself at the table.

'Mum, Joe and I have had a talk about his studying and everything, and I'm happy that he comes home to do his homework most nights, but we've agreed that you will still make his tea and he'll be back in with you by ten.'

May stopped helping herself to peas and turned towards Joe. She wasn't taking this lying down.

'What's wrong with my house, I want to know? Not good enough for you suddenly? After all these years I've looked after you while your mother was off doing whatever she does. Now all you want to do is treat it like a hotel.'

Annie opened her mouth to reply but Joe was quicker.

'Gran, there is nothing wrong with your house. It's just that I have so many books and files for all my subjects and I always find I don't have the right stuff for doing my homework. You know it's important that I do well this year if I am to get to Glasgow to do law.'

Annie couldn't help but be impressed.

May put her hand on her grandson's arm. 'I know that, son, but I'm worried about all the hoodlums in the town.'

'Gran, they are not my friends. I have nothing to do with them, honest.'

May took his hand. 'I just want you to do well. I don't want you falling into bad company.'

'I'll be careful. I'm a big boy now, Gran. I can take care of myself.' He squeezed her hand back and grinned, the same grin he had always used when he wanted an extra bar of chocolate.

Well done, Joe, Annie thought. Law should suit you. You certainly have the skills needed to argue a case. They ate in silence for a while.

'Bob McCafferty has put a new lock and chain on my back door. Remind me to give you the new key,' said May out of the blue.

'Why?' asked Annie.

'They've been coming into my house when I'm out and they've even been in once when I was watching TV.'

Annie paused, a forkful of roast potato halfway to her mouth.

'You've lost me. *Who* has been coming into

52

your house?'

'Hoodlums.'

'Hoodlums?'

'Yes. They come in and hide things and they've been taking money from my purse.'

'Has someone broken in?' Annie asked in alarm. 'When did this happen?'

'Started a few weeks ago. I came up the street from the tea dance at the community centre one Thursday with Phyllis Caldwell – you know the one who was married to Jack Caldwell who went off with all the money and his secretary who was no better than she ought to be. Phyllis lives in the flats up the road and as we got to my gate, two of these boys with their hoods up came from my back garden and pushed past us. When we went round the back they had done the toilet against the wall of the house. It was disgusting. I told you at the time.'

'You did not!' Annie was indignant. 'You never told me any of this.'

'Nor me,' said Joe.

May was indignant. 'I did so. I remember telling both of you.'

'I don't think you did,' Annie replied more gently now, 'but anyway, peeing against the wall doesn't mean they were in the house.'

Annie looked at Joe who raised his eyebrows and made a face. She turned in her chair to look at her mother properly.

'You say money was missing from your purse?'

'That was when they came back when I was watching TV.' May shot Joe a glance. 'He was here doing his homework. I was all on my own.

53

My purse was in my handbag on the hall table. When I went to make a cup of tea after *Coronation Street*, my purse was on the kitchen table and thirty pounds was missing.'

'How did they get in? Your house is always like Fort Knox. You never leave the door unlocked.'

'They must have copied the key that first time, but I've changed the locks so that's put their gas at a peep.' May seemed quite relaxed now that she'd got everything off her chest.

'Did you phone the police when the money was missing?'

'What's the point in that? When the McCaffertys had their break-in the police just came round and asked what was missing. They never found out who did it. Waste of time. I've sorted it myself. They won't be able to get in now.'

Annie turned to Joe. 'Did you know about this?'

'No! You think I wouldn't have told you?'

'Why didn't you tell us, Mum?'

'I did!' May paused and looked from one to the other. 'I'm sure I did, and if I didn't it's because it's very difficult to tell you anything, I hardly speak to you from one week to the next. And he's always out,' she pointed at Joe. 'As I said, I've sorted it.' She lifted the lid of the vegetable dish, 'Can I have another potato?'

Annie spooned one onto her plate.

'Now, did you know that St Eochod has something in common with Robert Burns?'

'Saint *who?*' Annie asked, blinking.

'Saint Eochod. He was one of St Columba's evangelists.'

'Good for him,' mumbled Joe.

Annie gave him a don't-be-rude glance.

'That's interesting,' said Annie politely. 'He has a connection with Burns?'

'So you've heard that too,' said May.

Annie was confused.

'Heard what?'

'Heard that there's a connection.'

'No, you just told me there was a connection. What is it?'

'You said you knew the connection!' May was getting annoyed now.

'I did not, Mum. Please tell me what the connection is.'

'They share the same special day.' The announcement was made in a tone which implied that everybody knew that.

Annie looked blankly at her mother.

'Tomorrow – twenty-fifth of January. St Eochod's feast day and Robert Burns' birthday. It was in my book.'

Annie was unsure what would be a suitable response but before she could think of something, Joe swallowed his last mouthful and quipped, 'Are you having a St Eochod's Supper instead of a Burns Supper then?'

'That would be novel,' said Annie. 'What would you have to eat? Gruel and unleavened bread?'

'No,' said Joe, 'nothing at all, because he would have spent his time fasting. Everyone would sit in silence and listen to everyone else's tummy rumbling before going out to find some Picts to convert.'

'They could sing "A saint's a saint for a' that" before they leave,' said Annie dissolving into helpless giggles.

Joe was not to be outdone. 'Someone could recite "Tae an evangelist" and everyone could get a relic in a goody bag when they go home.' He roared with laughter.

'Stop that at once! Both of you!' said May. 'I'll not have sacrilegious talk. It's not a joke. St Eochod spread the faith within Scotland and was canonised for it. I was merely pointing out a coincidence and you two just make fun of it.'

'Sorry, Mum.' Annie tried not to giggle.

'Sorry, Gran.'

The talk of Burns reminded Annie that she had two Burns Suppers to attend in the coming week. The first was a large black-tie do in Edinburgh when she had to reply to the Toast to the Lasses and the other was a local party fund-raiser where she only had to be the MC as Alistair, the MP for the Northern Isles, had agreed to stop over on his journey home to propose the Immortal Memory. Burns suppers also meant plates of haggis and mashed neeps. She hoped her stomach had fully recovered by then.

While Joe was clearing the plates, Annie dished out portions of chocolate pudding for him and May. There was no point in making herself feel sick again.

By three o'clock, May was on her way home and Annie would have liked to snooze on the sofa but there was a pile of work in her ministerial boxes which required her immediate attention and complicated constituency letters to be dictated. She took her briefcase to the study and, against her better judgement, decided to look at the Sunday papers online before she got stuck in. She never usually did this as she resented Sunday ruined by inaccurate and occasionally completely false articles. Any relevant press cuttings would be waiting for her in the office on Monday morning.

The *Sunday Clarion* was banging on about what school the members of the Scottish cabinet had attended. Who cares? she thought. At least she had nothing to fear on that front. The *Sunday Saltire,* never a fan of Annie's party, was keen to see the coalition disbanded. One article suggested that Andrew Fraser was not a competent Enterprise Minister, citing poor handling of a factory closure, ignoring the fact that it occurred the week after Jane had died when Andrew had been on compassionate leave. The article implied that he had been on holiday and had neither returned to his desk to save jobs nor given his junior minister proper direction. Andrew would be terribly hurt by the criticism. She couldn't help scrolling down to look at the comments below. The first had been posted at 11 p.m., the minute the paper had gone online, and they continued through the night. Most were the work of the army of the undead who were known to spend all night posting pro-Marlene Watt comments. This was a particularly nasty collection. She decided she would call Andrew on the pretext of discussing something on this week's cabinet agenda later in the week and see if he mentioned the article first. There was a lot of background noise when he answered.

'Hello, Annie! How are you? Just a minute, I'll get out of the melee and speak to you in the other room. I'm on Grandpa duty, babysitting Euan. Chief nappy changer and builder of railway tracks, that's me. I'd forgotten how exhausting toddlers are. So, what can I do for you?'

He had obviously not seen the article. Best not go there now.

'Just wanted to discuss how we play the funding issue at cabinet, but I'll speak to you tomorrow. Judging by the wailing I can hear, you're needed urgently.'

Chapter Six

The following Thursday, Annie changed into the 'black-tie outfit' that she had bought the previous week and left the office en route for the Burns Supper. She had two speeches with her; one was a version of what she had given many times over the years – erudite and in praise of the National Bard and his appeal to the lasses, and the other was a succession of anti-men jokes which could be strung together into a speech if that was the more appropriate reply to what had gone before. The bug, or whatever it was, seemed to be on the way out and her appetite had improved – she might manage a few forkfuls of haggis.

A seemingly endless selection of songs between each speech, sung by a modern-day Moira Anderson, and a proposer of the Immortal Memory, who had made the life and works of Robert Burns his specialist subject, resulted in the proceedings

58

being longer than expected. It was well after eleven by the time she escaped to her car where Eoin had been clocking up overtime reading the new Rebus novel. As she was driven through the outskirts of Edinburgh she wondered what Burns, who was known to like a good party and to dislike pomposity, would have made of the evening. She fished in her handbag and turned on her BlackBerry.

There were several texts and emails and then the phone rang.

'Annie? Annie? Is that you or is it the answering thing again?' May's voice was quavery.

'No, it's me, Mum. What's the matter?'

'I knew something like this would happen. I've been trying to get you for ages. I've left lots of messages and the car-phone isn't working. I tried that number I had three times and it just made a funny sound. I didn't know what to do. In the end, I phoned Minty and she said she would send an email to your phone and she sent you a text too, telling you to get in touch with the Corrachan police.'

'The police? What's happened? Are you at the police station?'

'Well I was, but I'm home now... I've had to take my angina spray.'

'Mum! What has happened?'

'It's Joe. I told you something like this would happen...' Annie took a deep breath. 'What has happened to Joe?'

'The boy's been arrested!' declared May.

Annie spent the journey back to Corrachan trying to piece together the events of the evening.

The duty sergeant at the police station was less than helpful. Joe was currently being questioned under caution following an incident. As Joe was not a juvenile, the sergeant explained, he was not in a position to tell her any more without Joe's permission.

'But I'm his mother! He's still at school! Surely you can give me some clue about what's happened.'

'Not without his permission.'

'Well, could you get his permission, please?'

'Not at the moment. He's being questioned.'

Stifling the urge to scream, Annie managed to say, 'Could you please tell him his mother is on her way. I'll be about forty minutes!'

It turned out that the unhelpful duty sergeant was the estranged husband of a constituent currently residing in a women's refuge in a neighbouring town. He knew Annie was up to date with his current domestic situation, so that explained his attitude. There would likely be a long wait before she could talk to someone useful, so she went back to the car and collected her ministerial briefcase and overnight bag.

'Big problems?' Eoin asked.

'I think so... This is going to take a while so you can get off, thanks. I know you like the overtime, but I don't want you falling asleep on the way back to Edinburgh.'

She went back inside the police station and waited in silence until the inspector eventually invited her into his office. It transpired there had been a gathering of young people at her house and a fight had broken out in her garden between Joe and another boy who had ended up with a space where his front teeth had been. One of her neighbours had phoned 999 and when the police arrived, the victim was doubled up on the ground and Joe, swearing loudly, was being held back by his friends. The living room window had a brick through it.

'Your son lives on his own in the house while you are away?' inquired the inspector.

'No, he stays with his grandmother. He goes to the house to do his homework some evenings, but he has to be back at my mother's by ten.'

'Well there appeared to be about eight young people in your house this evening. There were some cans of lager and alcopops, not to mention the remains of a joint. I don't know about you, Ms Cochrane, but that doesn't sound like homework to me.'

Many years of parliamentary and TV debates had given Annie practice in dealing with hostile questions and she was quick to come to her son's defence.

'Joe and his friends do not smoke cannabis – a can of beer at the weekend perhaps, but not dope.'

'You are away a great deal, aren't you?' The inspector's tone was patronising. 'It's difficult enough to keep track of what's going on when one's about all the time, and your mother's quite elderly, isn't she? Perhaps you've both had the wool pulled over your eyes?'

Annie was furious, but she knew never to admit a weakness or a mistake – or you were mince.

'I can assure you, Inspector, Joe has never

shown signs of anything like this. He and his friends are hard-working decent kids set on going to university. Which one of his friends had he been arguing with? Who did he hit?'

'It was a younger boy, Shawn McDuff.'

'Shawn McDuff? He's not a friend of my son! Shawn McDuff from the infamous McDuff family – the source of all trouble in this town?'

The inspector nodded, grudgingly.

'Do you really think that my son and Shawn McDuff move in the same circles?'

'Shawn has been taken to hospital and is going to require extensive dental treatment. Joe was the one who put him there,' replied the inspector.

'Shawn and his pals have been harassing Joe at school. They are obviously doing it out of hours now,' said Annie bitterly.

'That remains to be seen. We've taken statements from Joe and all the other young people present and when we have studied these, we will decide what to do. We could take no action other than telling him to behave himself in future, or we can send a report to the Procurator Fiscal who will decide whether or not to prosecute. In the meantime, I suggest you take him home and try to make sure he keeps out of any more trouble.'

Annie stood and wearily gathered up her bags. She had a brief conversation about May's security concerns and the inspector assured her that he would put someone on the job. He opened the door for her and she paused as she passed him.

'I'm afraid there may be press interest in this. I hope you and your officers will be as discreet as possible.'

The implication that his station might spring a leak was not well received.

'We are subject to the strictest confidentiality, Ms Cochrane. I do not tolerate any breaches in this station.'

'Thank you,' said Annie. But she knew there was no way this information would be contained. In fact, she would place a bet on the duty sergeant having been free with his mobile already.

Chapter Seven

Joe was seated at the kitchen table rubbing his skinned knuckles. Annie stood leaning against the worktop.

'Tell me what happened.'

'It wasn't my fault, Mum.'

'Well whose fault was it? You appear to have put a boy two years younger than you in hospital.'

'The fucker asked for it.'

'Don't use language like that! Whatever he did, he didn't deserve to have his teeth knocked out. Why was he here? I didn't think Shawn was a friend of yours.'

'He's not! He and Ryan Connerty turned up and began shouting and swearing. Then they sat in the front garden drinking cider and sharing a joint. We were inside minding our own business. Trying to ignore them.'

'Who is *we?*'

'Just the Young Enterprise team ... Paul, Craig,

Jenny, Keith and me and Ellie.'

'And minding your own business involves drink and drugs?'

'No one was smoking anything! They must have thrown the joint in the window after the brick. We were just having one drink after our meeting.'

'Great! Where did you get the drink?'

Joe looked at the floor.

'The beer came from the kitchen cupboard; Jenny brought the Smirnoff Ice.'

'This is all I need!' Exasperation was mixed with anger. 'The police are called to a fight at my house and it turns out that I have been supplying drink to under eighteens and allowing cannabis to be smoked on the premises. Remember what I said to you last year, about what would happen if you put a foot wrong? Your friends have their stomachs pumped, or even get arrested, and all they get will be a row and that will be the end of it. Unfortunately for you, the whole of Scotland is going to delight in your shame, because "Minister's son in drink and drug fuelled rampage" is not going to remain a secret. In fact, I suspect it might even make tomorrow's paper. It's not fair, but that's what is going to happen?'

Joe got to his feet and went to the sink where he filled a glass with water.

'Here we go again. It's always how it affects you, isn't it? It's your poxy job that caused all this. You're the one who stands for election, but your job affects Gran and me too. I'm never known as Joe Cochrane who should do well in his exams, or Joe Cochrane who plays for the First Eleven. No, I'm Joe Cochrane, Annie Cochrane's son. That's how I'm always described. And as for Gran, she varies between being so proud of what you do she could burst, and getting really upset when the newspapers or anybody criticises you. She thinks what the papers say is true!'

Annie flinched. She held a hand up, as if to admit defeat.

'Let's go back a little bit. Just how did my job cause this fight?'

Joe was silent for a moment, then looked up at her.

'Shawn and Ryan and some others have been bugging me for about two years now. They think it's "fun" to follow me about and put dogshit in my locker and "bump" into me in the corridor. It's a pain in the arse, but I ignore them and my friends ignore them. Tonight, they started off shouting about you, about how you were so rich 'cause you fiddled your expenses and were just out for yourself. Craig and I went and told them to bugger off or we would get the police. Then Shawn started shouting things about Ellie...'

Joe paused and Annie could see his now prominent Adam's apple move as he swallowed hard. She asked very gently, 'What sort of things?'

'Horrible things! That she was a slag. That all the boys in fourth year had had her before she started going out with me. That she was still shagging other people. So I hit the bastard and knocked his teeth out and I'm not sorry!'

'Did you tell the police this?'

'No, I told them that Shawn McDuff was my best friend... Do you think I'm stupid? 'Course I told them. And Craig told them, and Paul told them, and Keith told them, and Jenny told them, and Ellie told them.'

He put his hands over his face, then moved them downwards till only his mouth was covered. He looked a frightened little boy.

'What's going to happen?' he whispered.

Annie shrugged. 'Well, you might get off with a warning from the police or it might go to the Procurator Fiscal who might give you a warning. Worst case scenario, it goes to court.'

Joe mumbled something.

'What did you say?'

'I said, will I have a criminal record?'

'You could do, I suppose.'

Joe looked up at her, the tears visible in his eyes.

Annie went and wrapped her arms round him. 'But let's hope sense prevails and it won't come to that. Now, it's after half past one, I think you should go to bed. In the morning, we'll need to contact Dad before he hears it on the jungle drums.'

'I don't want to go to school. Everyone will be talking about it.'

'Well... It might be best if you had the day off. Things won't seem so bad after a sleep.'

'Want a bet?' he said.

Annie kept her arms round him.

'I know it's awful now, but it will be resolved somehow. You just have to hang in there.'

The following day, the police inspector looked at all the witness statements and the glowing report from Joe's headmaster. He could see precisely what had happened. He would have thumped Shawn McDuff too. But a decision had to be made about how to proceed. If the perpetrator of the assault hadn't been the MSP's son and the assaulted not a member of the most troublesome family in the town who knew the system, both legal and benefits, inside out, he would just have warned both of them to behave better in future and let the matter drop. However, the press was already alerted and Tracey McDuff had been enjoying her moment of fame, standing up for her little boy who had been so savagely attacked. So the inspector decided, on balance, he would refer the matter to the Procurator Fiscal and allow someone further up the line to make the decision. He phoned the duty sergeant and asked him to bring the lad in to be charged and he sent a referral to the Children's Reporter to bring Shawn to a Children's Hearing.

The weekend press had a field day. HEALTH MINISTER'S SON CHARGED WITH AS-SAULT, announced the *Daily Post,* while the *Sunday Saltire* screamed ANNIE COCHRANE'S SON IN VIOLENT HOME ALONE RAM-PAGE. Shawn had been photographed with a swollen face and a lack of front teeth and this, combined with ill-informed comment from all and sundry, implied Joe was a drunken, dope-smok-ing, violent layabout who assaulted a much younger boy to his life-time disfigurement. Shawn's ankle bracelet and electronic curfew were not mentioned.

Annie put out a short statement to the effect that her son had been involved in an incident following severe provocation and that there would be no further comment while the matter was being investigated. Joe wanted to put his side of the story, but Annie had been adamant – it was a matter for the Procurator Fiscal and the less said, the sooner the story would go away.

On Monday morning, Annie escorted a humiliated Joe into the headmaster's office to discuss the best way of handling the situation. The headmaster did not quite say 'Congratulations' to Joe but he might as well have done. He assured them both that measures had been put in place to keep Joe safe from harassment and that he had written a fulsome report for the police. He was hopeful that curfew-breaking would be the offence which finally sent the tagged Shawn off to some sort of residential school, greatly reducing the workload of the school management team. Joe was uncharacteristically silent and Annie watched him leave the room to go to his history class with a mixture of guilt and anger. Guilt that her position had put him there and anger at the unfairness of the situation in which her son now found himself. After Joe had closed the door behind him, Annie turned to the headmaster.

'You seem confident that Shawn is not going to get off with this, but I'm not so sure. He certainly isn't a pretty sight at the moment and he looks very much the victim.'

'He's on his last chance. Off the record, at the last Children's Hearing he was told that the next step was a residential unit. This should have done the trick.' The headmaster smiled brightly, then altered his expression to one of suitable gravity and continued, 'Of course, that's not your concern, Ms Cochrane. Be assured, we'll keep an eye on Joe. I've spoken to his friends and someone will walk to and from school with him. Is he going to be doing his homework at his grandmother's this week?'

'He certainly is,' said Annie, 'and I am going to try to get home from Edinburgh every night for a while to give him some support.'

Chapter Eight

While Annie was easing Joe back into school, First Minister Marlene Watt was in her office, a palatial room with a large desk, sizeable table and chairs for meetings, and some comfortable armchairs, one of which was occupied by Morton Hunter MSP. He was leafing through press cuttings from the Sunday papers.

Morton had started his political life ten years earlier as a junior researcher and had risen to campaign manager overseeing the election which saw Marlene move from Leader of the Opposition to First Minister, alongside his own election as a list MSP. He had the whole population of central Scotland as his constituents, but few of them, with the exception of the unhinged in possession of a green pen, ever bothered him with their problems. His role was to be both Marlene's political strategist and her eyes and ears about the parliament.

'Poor Annie Cochrane, not had a good week-end, has she?' said Morton. 'Child out of control ... tut tut...' He turned the page. '*Sunday Clarion* has even got an editorial about poor parenting of teenagers.' He picked up a piece of shortbread from the plate in front of him and bit into it.

Marlene looked up from the document she was perusing and took off her reading glasses. Anything which was unfavourable to Annie Cochrane was music to her ears.

'And online? What's going on there?'

Morton had just taken another bite of short-bread so Marlene had to wait for the reply.

'It's fine. The weekend shift took the "unable to look after your children unable to look after the country" line and there were even a few genuine punters in there with their comments. Not a thing in her support.'

Morton was in charge of his party's Media Reactive Monitoring Unit, the existence of which, if he were ever to be questioned, he would vehemently deny. It comprised several groups of individuals: those who would put their names to Morton's carefully crafted letters to newspaper editors; those who would participate in phone-ins on the radio, purporting to be a lifelong voter for another party now intending to vote for Marlene Watt and, perhaps the most sinister group, the Online Comments department, staffed by insomniacs who worked from midnight until dawn posting pro-Marlene comments on newspaper articles. Payment for their efforts came from a subsidiary company owned by a millionaire party supporter who knew he was buying some political influence.

Morton wiped a shortbread crumb from the corner of his mouth. 'Jordan got over *his* little bit of bother?'

Marlene continued noting things she wanted changed on the document in front of her.

'Uhuh. He apologised to the headmaster and to the English teacher with no sense of humour and it has been explained to both him and Robert that I do not have time to run around clearing up their mess.' She looked up. 'Any press sniffing around?'

'Just one. I said the school had a problem and if his paper chose to make something out of Jordan's involvement, then the competition would get briefed when there *was a* real story and he wouldn't.'

Marlene smiled. 'Morton, what would I do without you? Now, it's time for you to run along to the Parliament and listen at a few metaphorical keyholes. Meanwhile I shall try not to let boredom overwhelm me during my weekly conversation with Andrew Fraser.'

Morton made no move to leave.

'What's on today's agenda then? Apart from the week's parliamentary business?'

'Oh, let me see ... sympathy for *poor* Annie Cochrane, assurance that following my extensive investigations, the article about Andrew's failings during his bereavement had absolutely nothing to do with anyone in my party and I am confident that our coalition will last the next fourteen months till the election. That sort of thing.' She made a shooing gesture with both hands. 'Off you go. I'll speak to you tomorrow.'

Morton stood up reluctantly and walked towards the door. As he opened it, Marlene added without looking up, 'As you pass along the corridor, tell one of the staff to come in here and collect this document will you?'

Morton did as he was asked. The banter among the civil servants started as soon as Morton closed the door behind him.

'Summoned by the Praying Mantis! Your turn, Dave.'

'Don't let her stand too close...'

'Careful, you might get eaten!'

'Don't sit on the sofa with her...'

Marlene often made her male civil servants uneasy by standing just a fraction into their personal space. A surprising number of them suffered from travel sickness, necessitating the front seat of the ministerial car rather than the customary place in the back, next to Marlene. They all assumed Morton was more than a political aide to the First Minister and spent many an hour at the pub pondering the protective headgear he must wear in order to avoid becoming Marlene's post-coital snack. Consequently, he was known as Bob the Builder.

Andrew Fraser passed the exiting Dave on his way into the FM'S office.

Marlene rose from her desk and shook his hand. 'Andrew! Punctual as always. Come and have a seat and tell me how poor Annie is coping with all this. Such a dreadful thing to happen. It's so hard when one's children get picked on. Poor

72

Jordan has been having a difficult time too.'

Andrew fixed the usual polite smile on his face. What an unpleasant woman she was.

Chapter Nine

There was a line of ministerial cars parked at the back entrance of Bute House, the First Minister's official residence and venue for cabinet meetings. Eoin and Patrick were sitting in the First Minister's Lexus discussing Jordan Keiller's little bit of trouble.

'Absolutely nothing in the press at all! I fed it to all my usual sources and none would touch it. If any previous First Minister's kid had called their teacher a front bottom, it would have been all over the papers. The little creep just strolled back into school as if nothing had happened.'

'Why would no one use it?' Eoin asked.

'She's got some sort of hold over them.' Patrick sounded morose.

Eoin considered this as he opened a packet of mints. 'They scared of her?'

'Shit scared! If she thinks coverage is unfair, she complains and bullies until they apologise. So they opt for an easy life and don't annoy her.'

'Press scared of a politician? Never!' Eoin offered the mints to Patrick. 'Want one?'

'No, thanks. I told you, she scares them shit-less.' Patrick turned the radio off. 'Never did like that song. I see your one's boy's been in trouble too. They were happy to run that.'

'Perhaps Annie should do a bit of bullying. Least said, the sooner it becomes chip papers is how she sees it. Shame for the lad, though. He only took a swing because the wee bastard called his girlfriend a fucking slag.'

'Has he got to go to court?'

'Dunno. Powers that be are thinking about it.' Eoin looked at his watch. 'They're late.'

'Bet the FM has done it on purpose. She's going to meet little children next. Hates them.' Patrick opened the glove compartment, extracted a packet of chocolate digestives. 'Want a biscuit?'

Eoin pointed to his mouth. 'I've still got the mint, thanks.'

'Anything else new?'

'Annie's stalker has been showing up all over the place. Must be a full moon. He's more agitated than usual.'

'Annie has a stalker?' Patrick was intrigued. 'A spurned lover?'

'Hardly. He's the loony with the placard. The one you see outside the Parliament.'

'Him! Why is he stalking Annie?'

'His wife died on the operating table and he thinks that Annie should be able to bring her back to life. Not a skill she's mastered yet.'

'He been checked out?' Patrick asked.

'Verdict is harmless. You had to deal with any weirdies recently?'

'Don't start! I'm being sent on a course called How to be a Bodyguard or something equally stupid.'

'A bodyguard! You're just a driver!'

'I know I'm *just* a driver! I'm not Special Branch. Apparently, she wants me to walk behind her like Prince Philip, but instead of making inappropriate remarks like he would, I've to scan the crowd for trouble. I'm away for a whole week next month to be taught how to kill someone with my bare hands. I sit in the car and read the paper. I don't do the job of the police.' Patrick took another bite of his biscuit.

'You should be flattered she thinks you are up to it, you being a bit past your prime.' Eoin pointed at the packet. 'Can I have one now?'

'Cheeky bugger. I'll have you know, I am a honed fighting machine.' Patrick passed the packet across.

'Ta. And has the honed fighting machine been transporting budgies recently?'

'Fuck off, mate!' Patrick swallowed the last of his biscuit. 'No budgies since the replacement for the suicide victim, but she thinks I'm a fast-food delivery service now.'

'Eh?' Eoin was confused.

'She doesn't do cooking,' Patrick explained, 'so if there is no dinner engagement she gets a take-away. No, let me rephrase that, *I* get the take-away. I bring her back here, then she sends me out to pick up a curry or a Chinese or whatever.'

'You shouldn't have to do that, Patrick. After you've dropped her off, that's you finished. Why doesn't she just get it delivered?'

'Eoin, I drive for Marlene Watt. It's like the budgies. If she tells you to do something you jump. As for getting her tea delivered, word might get out that she can't cook.' Patrick glanced in the mirror. 'Here they come now. At last. You'd better get back to where you belong. Me and the FM are off to the multicultural nursery.'

At the close of the cabinet meeting, Annie was gathering up her papers when Marlene drew her to one side. What now? Every time Annie had opened her mouth Marlene's replies had ranged from hostile to downright unpleasant. Now the glacial tone had been replaced by honeyed concern.

'I just wanted to say how appalled I was at the press coverage of poor Jack's ... eh...' Marlene opted for, '...bit of bother.'

'Joe,' said Annie, 'Joe's bit of bother. Yes, I was appalled too and Joe is very upset. The so-called victim has been all over the papers, but we can't comment till they decide if they are going to prosecute or not.'

'Surely it won't go to court?' Marlene said smoothly. 'Can't you have a quiet word in someone's ear?'

Annie fastened the clip on her briefcase and looked Marlene in the eye.

'He might get off with a warning but, as for a word in someone's ear, I don't think that would be a good idea. Interfering in the legal process is not something I do.'

Marlene looked stunned. 'How awful for you. Jordan was very sympathetic. The boys got on so well when they met at the Celebrity Music Awards last year.'

Annie smiled politely. That wasn't quite how Joe had felt about his encounter with Jordan.

'Thank you for your support. I'll tell Joe that Jordan is concerned for him.'

Duty done, Marlene left the room and bumped into her private secretary who told her she was twenty minutes late for the nursery visit.

'What is the likelihood of anyone under ten getting within two feet of me?'

Her private secretary fidgeted.

'Quite high, I'm afraid. The scheduled photo opportunity is a finger-painting session.' He hoped he sounded suitably apologetic.

'Who arranged that?'

'Fiona thought it would show your caring side, FM.'

'You can tell Fiona she will see my caring side if she ever does this to me again. I shake hands with pregnant women and I admire babies from afar, I do not do poster paint. You'll have to give me ten minutes.'

Marlene went upstairs to her flat where she changed from her designer suit into a washable number from Marks and Spencer. As the cabinet had run on, she would cut the forty-five minute visit to the nursery to twenty at the most. She supposed she should be thankful for small mercies.

Chapter Ten

The waiting room in the Corrachan Health Centre was populated with the Monday-morning collection of coughing children, pensioners with heart conditions and teenagers in need of emergency contraception. Annie had chosen a seat in the corner and selected a copy of *Saga Magazine* rather than the elderly newspaper depicting a laughing Marlene Watt, paint-splattered and surrounded by small children, under the headline FIRST MINISTER SAYS CHILDREN ARE THE KEY TO A MULTICULTURAL SCOTLAND.

Having been unable to attend her allotted Well-Woman appointment because of parliamentary duties, Annie was lucky to have secured a slot first thing this morning. There was a muffled announcement over the tannoy.

'Blubiddy Blahblah to room three, please!'

No one moved. Everyone eyed everyone else. Annie was sure it wasn't her. The rhythm wasn't right. A minute later the order was repeated with more than a hint of exasperation.

'Mr Blubiddy Blah Blah to room three, *please!*'

The women relaxed and after a pause an elderly man got to his feet and hirpled off. Annie returned to travel opportunities for the over-seventies. When her name was called, this time coherently, she made her way to the allotted room.

Twenty-five minutes later, she climbed into her waiting car.

The doctor had chatted about the weather and the state of Scottish politics as Annie removed her knickers, climbed on to the examination couch and covered herself with a blanket. Holiday plans were discussed as the speculum was inserted, then conversation seemed to dry up until she was invited to get dressed. The doctor threw her what she thought was a reproving glance as she sat down by her desk.

'I know, I know,' Annie blustered, 'I'm horribly overweight. I have been trying to diet ... not with much success, despite a lingering tummy bug, but I *will* keep trying.'

'That wasn't what I was going to say.' The doctor assumed her best bedside-manner smile. 'You asked me to check your IUD.' Annie nodded. 'Well, it's still there.'

'That's good—'

'But there is something else there too.'

Oh God! She had cancer of the uterus. Hysterectomy meant time off work – two months at least, then chemo? How long had it been there? Had it metastasised? Was she going to die? The doctor was saying something to her.

'...about fifteen or sixteen weeks.'

'Sorry, fifteen weeks?'

'Like I said, you are pregnant. Nearly four months by my estimate.'

'Pregnant!'

'That's right.'

'No! No, I can't be pregnant!'

The doctor raised her eyebrows. 'No? Today's

79

the eighth of February...' She looked at her calendar. 'Did you have intercourse when would that be? ... towards the end of October?'

'Yes,' said Annie in a very small voice. She should have followed her instincts and kept Andrew as a friend. Then, with a rush of relief, she realised the doctor was mistaken.

'But, I can't be pregnant. I've had periods.'

'Like a normal period?'

'No. Only lasted a day or two. Come to think of it there has been nothing for about five weeks. I thought it might be the change.'

As she was speaking, she suddenly remembered the same thing happening when she was pregnant with Joe. She thought she was having yet another miscarriage and had taken herself to bed to lie immobile for three days. All the trouble and heartache over years to carry a baby to term and here she was, nearly halfway through, and totally unaware.

The doctor continued. 'IUDs do fail sometimes, especially elderly ones.' She consulted the computer again. 'Yes. You've had this one for seven years. Were you not told at the time, these particular ones are only effective for up to five years?'

'I can't remember,' Annie whispered.

'This is not a happy discovery?'

'Dead right!'

The doctor became business-like. 'If you are seeking a termination, time is not on our side. It has already become a much more serious and unpleasant procedure.'

'I'm being lobbied every day by pro-life activists. I know all the details!' Annie paused. 'Sorry,

80

I didn't mean to snap at you.'

'That's okay, I have a thick skin.'

Annie tried to sound measured. 'I'm not in a position to have a baby for reasons too many to list.'

'In your position, an abortion would be perfectly understandable.'

'Not to the media, it wouldn't. And I am about to launch a contraceptive campaign.'

'That does complicate things,' the doctor agreed. 'Do you want to go and think about this? Perhaps discuss it with the father?'

'*I'll* think about it.' Annie was emphatic. 'And *I'll* let you know.'

Now, as she strapped herself into the car, a flash of memory sent a chill down her spine. This situation might be even worse than she thought. She rummaged in her bag for her phone.

Eoin observed her in the rear-view mirror.

'Have you got a prescription? Do we need to stop at the chemist?'

'Don't need a prescription ... it's something which will get better in time. But I *am* tired. Think I'll have a snooze in a minute.'

She found her BlackBerry, scrolled back in her diary. The last week in October showed her visit to Aberdeen... The feeling of nausea that swept her from head to foot was unrelated to pregnancy. She had found what she was looking for. Oh Holy Hell! Perhaps Andrew wasn't the father.

Annie had met Tarik in 1987 in Dundee when she was a newly qualified staff nurse and he was a final-year medical student. He was her first serious

81

boyfriend and they had been together for nearly two years when he went to work in Leeds. Annie had been making plans to join him there, when he sent her a one-paragraph letter telling her the relationship was over. He had refused to give reasons and would not meet or even talk to her on the phone. She had been devastated. Tarik had been The One.

She had not seen him since. Not that is, until last October, when she was visiting a Special Baby Unit in Aberdeen. She had been asking the Chairman of the Health Board the usual questions about facilities and patient satisfaction when they reached the staff lined up to be introduced. First she shook hands with the charge nurse, congratulating her on the atmosphere she had created on the ward. Then Annie heard the chairman saying, 'This is our newly appointed consultant neonatologist, Dr Khan,' and she found she was holding Tarik's hand and looking into the same dark brown eyes she had fallen in love with all those years ago.

'Good afternoon, Minister. Nice to meet you again,' he said with what she felt was the hint of a smirk.

'You know each other?' enquired the chairman.

Annie pretended to scrutinise him carefully. 'Tarik Khan, that's right. Didn't we meet when you were a student? You went to Bradford or somewhere, didn't you? How nice to meet you again.' I sound like the Queen, she thought but she was pleased with her reply. She was damned if she was going to give Tarik the satisfaction of seeing that she remembered him clearly. She moved on swiftly to shake hands with the house surgeon.

Tarik sought her out over the statutory tea and biscuits.

'Annie! It's so good to see you again.' He looked round to make sure nobody was in earshot. 'I still owe you an explanation. It's been a long time.'

She smiled at him in what she hoped was a queen-like way. 'It was a puzzle at the time, but I can't say it bothered me for long.' She hoped her nose was not growing. 'You were not man enough to have a face to face conversation, so I didn't think you were worth getting upset about. After all this time I think reasons are irrelevant, don't you?' She looked around pointedly for someone else to talk to.

Tarik put his hand on her arm. 'It wasn't my fault.' He paused. 'Things happened...'

Annie removed his hand, but could not help herself asking, 'Things? What sort of things would they be then?'

He lowered his voice. 'Have dinner with me and I'll explain. Please?'

'I already have a dinner engagement.'

'Later? For a nightcap?'

Do I actually have to say piss off, she wondered.

'No, Tarik. It was a long time ago and I'm not interested in the whys and wherefores any more. It's been lovely seeing you again, but that's it.' Rescue in the shape of her private secretary appeared, so she continued in her best regal voice, 'I hope you'll be very happy in your new post here. It's a marvellous hospital. Now, I have to go. Another meeting in twenty minutes. So sorry.'

Later that evening, after dinner with the upper echelons of the NHS, Annie returned to her hotel, bade her civil servants goodnight and made her way to the lift. The doors were closing when someone squeezed through.

'Hello.'

Tarik! His reflection disappeared into infinity in the mirrored walls.

'Are you stalking me? Because I've got one of those already. Go away. I have nothing to say to you.'

That was the extent of their conversation before the lift doors opened at the first floor. She pushed past him and walked as quickly as she could along the corridor. She put the keycard into the door slot, removed it and pressed down the handle. The red light winked at her. Tarik was at her elbow. He pointed to the paper wallet which had contained the keycard.

'Give me that a minute.' He moved to the next door, inserted the keycard and opened it for her. 'Helps if you are at the correct room.'

Annie walked past him, then turned. He was still standing in the doorway.

'Remember the time you spent twenty minutes trying to get into the flat on the floor below yours after we had been to that party?'

'I was drunk then. I'm sober now,' she replied.

'So what's your excuse this time?'

'You are still as annoying as you used to be, you know.' She heard the lift doors open and the voices of her staff deciding which room was to be the venue for their nightcap. She couldn't be seen with Tarik at her bedroom door.

'Oh, for goodness' sake, come in and shut the door.'

He chose a Coke and she had a much needed brandy from the minibar. They sat in the arm-chairs on either side of a small table. Annie poured some ginger ale into her drink.

'Well, go on, then. Explain! Explain why a weekend spent in bed is followed two days later by a stilted paragraph telling me we're finished.'

'My parents had found me a bride.'

'Found you a bride?' Annie burst out laughing.

'My second cousin. She came from my father's village in Pakistan.' At least he looked embar-rassed.

'It was 1989 for God's sake! Why didn't you say "No thanks"?'

'Because it's our family's way.'

The penny dropped. 'Don't tell me – you knew all along that that was going to happen?'

His contrite look said everything.

'You bastard! What a shit you were ... *are!*'

Tarik looked very uncomfortable. 'I know I should have told you, but the more involved we got the more difficult it became. I'd sort of hoped that when I had to get married, our relationship might have petered out.'

'You're a coward, Tarik.' Annie couldn't dis-guise the disgust in her voice.

'You're right, I am.'

She had had enough. 'Stop agreeing with me! Just finish your drink and go away!'

He poured the rest of the Coke into a glass. 'You're still married?'

Annie stood up and started putting papers into her briefcase. 'Divorced.'

'Children?'

'One son aged sixteen. You?'

'Noor, my wife, was killed crossing the road two years after we were married.'

'I'm sorry.' There wasn't much else she could say.

'I didn't love her at first but I became fond of her. It wasn't like *our* relationship – no arguments, no making up again, but it was perfectly satisfactory.'

Annie filled the silence by closing her briefcase and putting it on the luggage rack.

'I know what you're thinking,' he said eventually.

'Mind reader now?'

'Why did they never find me another wife?'

'That wasn't what I was thinking, but you are obviously going to tell me, aren't you?' She sat down again.

'Noor didn't speak good English, didn't want to socialise. She was happy to stay at home. I told my parents that next time I would choose.' He stood up, pulled the curtain back and looked out at the car park below. 'I came to find you again.'

Annie's insides turned over. 'When?'

'I spoke to your flatmate, Karen. She told me that you had just got married.'

'She never told me!'

'There wasn't much point. I was too late.' He shrugged.

Annie remembered the awfulness of the two years she had spent trying to get over Tarik, and, looking at him now, she wondered if she ever had. There was still an undoubted chemistry, but they were no longer the people of twenty-something years ago. Time to move the conversation on. 'You may not be married, but I can't believe you spend your nights alone.'

'There is someone,' he admitted, 'but I'm not sure it's going anywhere.'

'Well, it certainly won't be if she discovers you are in a hotel room with an ex-girlfriend. So, time to go, Tarik.' Annie stood up to indicate the conversation was at an end.

'Tell me, what took you from nursing to politics?' Tarik was going nowhere.

'Various things. Now, what is it about the words "go" and "away" that you don't understand? What about "piss" and "off". Would that be more effective?' She needed him out of her room before he upset her equilibrium any further.

'I haven't finished my drink. You might as well answer my question in the meantime.'

Annie looked at him. He still had the power to get what he wanted from her.

'Okay then, it sounds clichéd, but a desire to change things. A very persuasive lady called Minty Oliver talked me into standing for the local council. She told me she needed a paper candidate in a safe Tory ward. I did no canvassing and I won – probably because the sitting councillor was subject to some unpleasant allegations concerning underage girls two days before the election. I enjoyed being a councillor and, to cut a long story short, the same persuasive old lady talked me into being the candidate for the Scottish Parliament and here I am.' She felt awkward standing, and sat down at the table again. 'You? What brought you back here?'

Tarik told her about his career – moving around the UK as he climbed the ladder to consultant level, never having a reason to stay anywhere long enough to put down roots. He drained his glass. 'Well, looks like I will have to go now.'

'So it does!' said Annie. Her stomach was turning cartwheels. She followed as Tarik moved towards the door.

'Thanks for allowing me to explain,' he said. 'I'll watch your career with interest.' He gave her a hug, then, still with his arms round her, he drew back a little and looked at her.

'Still my beautiful Annie.'

Don't do this to me, Annie thought. 'The years have not been as kind to me as they have to you,' she said.

'I'm not a fan of stick insects.'

Annie smiled. Tarik was going nowhere.

Lust had triumphed over the unresolved hurt, but when she awoke the next day Annie knew that that bit of her past was finally behind her. Despite assurances that he would be in touch, Tarik obviously felt the same. Neither had felt the need to contact the other since.

So ... what should she do? Half an hour ago she had been a middle-aged woman with a lingering stomach bug. Now she was an unmarried government minister with morning sickness. The baby might have sandy hair and freckles like Andrew, or it might be black haired and rather darker skinned.

No men for five years, then two in ten days. She was incubating a time bomb.

Chapter Eleven

After Eoin had delivered her to her office, Annie sat through two meetings, unable to concentrate. The first dealt at length with the cost implications of the current community care policy. Then, like an accusing finger, there was a meeting about the forthcoming contraceptive campaign aimed at teenagers. Finally she escaped and, pleading urgent paperwork, asked not to be disturbed. An hour later, with little achieved, she put on her coat, packed her briefcase, then told her staff she was feeling ill and would walk back to her flat.

As she left the building, her personal stalker, Mr T.H. Pittendreich, waved his placard at her. As always, he looked pleased to see her. The security report had discovered what T.H. really stood for but Annie had long since forgotten. To her T.H. meant The Haunter. He would appear wherever she went outside her flat, at the Parliament, outside hospitals she visited, and here at the Scottish Office, with his JUSTICE FOR EDITH placard. He never attempted to speak or create a disturbance. He simply appeared and he disappeared.

Even on this dank February afternoon, the pavement was crowded as she made the ten-minute walk to the High Street. Every second woman seemed to be pregnant, and as she passed the bus stop she saw a young mother struggling to manoeuvre a buggy onto the bus while attempting to hold on to a crying toddler.

Annie climbed the stairs to her flat to an internal chant of *no! no! no!* She decided on a cup of peppermint tea, and while the kettle boiled she found a blank sheet of paper. Taking her mug to the table, she wrote two headings. After half an hour of deep thought, she considered the list in front of her.

Termination	**Have it**
Don't want another child	Abortion OK for others but not me
Contraceptive failure	More than a blob of cells now
Father unknown	Might be a girl
Probably lone parent	
Job not conducive to baby	
Mother not up to child-care	
I'm old – abnormalities?	
Will be 62 when it leaves school	
Publicity if no abortion ... hunt for father!!	
Press intrusion	

She considered the reasons for having the baby: *Abortion OK for others but not for me* ... No longer applicable. *More than a blob of cells now.* Would her conscience trouble her in the future? *Might be a girl.* Don't be ridiculous, she thought. You take what you get and are glad it's OK ... which, given her age, this one might not be. Joe, her mother and the father would all be affected if she had it. Being an MSP, let alone a government minister, was not conducive to caring for a baby. Everyone knew that, even if they couldn't possibly say so. All in all, there was only one possible answer. Remove what was an unintentional error.

She put the piece of paper in the shredder and picked up her phone. Her name and face were widely known in Scotland – here someone would quickly realise they had valuable information. Her old flatmate Karen worked in a private hospital in London. *She sent her a text – p/s phone me asap. need to speak privately* – and immediately received the reply *what's up with u then? will have 2 b 6.30ish when i get home.*

Ninety minutes to fill before Annie could progress things. The contents of the accusing briefcase would pass the time while she waited. This was Day One of the 'go home to Joe' schedule. She phoned her office to change the time of her pickup from six to seven, then sat down and tried, unsuccessfully, to work. As half past six approached Annie could no longer pretend to concentrate. She began walking round the flat picking things up and putting them down again and by twenty to seven she was well through the contents of the ironing basket. Ten minutes later there had still been no call so she resorted to ironing a towel and some unflattering pairs of granny-knickers. Finally, at five to seven, her phone rang but it was only

Eoin telling her he was outside.

'Just waiting for a call on the landline,' she lied. 'Can you sit on the double yellow line for a moment or two? I'll be as quick as I can.'

She sent Karen *phone-me* vibes. Almost immediately her phone began to ring.

'Hi Annie! What's with the mysterious message?'

'Are you alone at the moment?'

'I'm in the kitchen and Pete is helping the kids with their homework, supposedly, but I think they are doing PlayStation or Wii or some other sort of male preserve.'

'Who's Pete?' asked Annie. Karen was divorced and without a live-in last time they'd spoken.

'A new possibility I was seeing him on my child-free weekends, but now I'm seeing him occasionally during the week because the boys and I come as a package. He's still on sale or return. But never mind me. What's up with you?'

'I'm pregnant.'

There was silence on the other end.

'Are you still there? I said I'm pregnant.'

'I heard you. Do I say "Congratulations" or "Oh shit?"'

'Shit!'

'Then *Oh shit!* Not like you to be careless?'

'Should have had my IUD replaced, but as I was celibate, I never got round to it.'

'Excuse me? *Celibate?* Is this an immaculate conception? Angel Gabriel come calling with the exciting news? I know your mother thinks you're destined for canonisation but this is taking it a bit far!'

'There was no one until recently.' Annie wasn't

92

in the mood.

'So, who is it? Do I know him?'

'I don't know!'

'You don't know who it is or you don't know if I know him?'

This was the bit Annie was not looking forward to. 'I don't know who it is. There are two contenders. But that's by the by because I'm going to have a termination.' She couldn't bring herself to use the phrase *get rid of it.* 'That's why I need your help. It needs to be privately, in London, and soon.'

'Hang on a minute, Annie, did you say *two?* You been running two men at once as well as running the country? You always were a multi-tasker, but you've excelled yourself this time. So, come on, the whole story – who are they?'

Annie could see Eoin in discussions with a traffic warden down at street level.

'It's either Andrew Fraser...'

'As in your bereaved party leader?'

'Yes, except his wife died about a year ago...'

'Like I said, bereaved. And the other?'

Annie watched Eoin, having lost his argument, drive off. Karen wasn't going to like this.

'Tarik,' she said in a small voice.

'Tarik? Please don't tell me it's the Tarik of old.'

'Yes.'

'Yes? Is that all you can say? Why, in God's name, did you let that bastard creep back into your life?'

'I met him on a hospital visit. He's a consultant in Aberdeen now ... Oh, yes – and he told me he spoke to you after his wife died. You never mentioned that.'

'That's right, he did. You'd just got married to Kenny and he comes to me saying you are the love of his life and wanting to know where you were. I told him two things ... first you were very happy and second to bugger off.'

'Why didn't you tell me?'

'What good would that have done? It had taken you long enough to get over him and you were married. So, back to the present – you met him on a hospital visit? Did you just nip into the disabled toilet for a quickie – an NHS version of the Mile High Club?'

'I seem to remember sex in hospital toilets was your hobby, not mine!' Annie snapped. She paused. 'He came to my hotel later. It only happened that one time.'

'Jesus, Annie, you're a nurse, that's all it takes!'

'It was supposed to be closure on the relationship.' How clichéd she sounded.

'Closure? What a load of crap! He always did have you wound round his little finger. Has he been in touch with you since?'

'No.'

'I thought not!'

'I didn't expect him to! We both knew it was a one night stand.'

'And what about Andrew? Was that *just the once* too?'

'No, that's more regular – once a week, sometimes once a fortnight. No one knows about it, though.'

'Does he know you're pregnant?'

'No.'

'So it's a bloody men like bloody buses scenario? None then two in the same week?'

'More or less,' Annie said wearily, 'I slept with both of them in the last week in October.'

'October?' Annie could hear the disbelief in her friend's voice. 'That's four months, Annie! Why have you left it so long?'

'Because I only found out this morning! I went to the GP for a Well-Woman appointment and I wanted to find out why I had been feeling sick.'

'Shit, Annie! Didn't you twig? It's not as if you've never been pregnant before! You know the signs – no periods, sore tits, very tired, off coffee, *feeling sick!*'

Annie was beginning to regret having chosen this particular friend as her confidante. 'Hindsight, Karen, is a wonderful thing. I was having a small amount of bleeding – I thought it was the start of the menopause or something, I thought I had a functioning IUD and, fuck it, I was busy!' She tried to compose herself. 'Look, can we cut the interrogation and work out how I can sort it out. Please?'

Karen's tone softened. 'Sure you don't want to have it? Sure you won't be crippled by Catholic guilt?'

'Yes, I'm sure I don't want to have it, and I'll deal with the guilt if and when it arrives. At the moment it's a time bomb in need of disposal. Does your fancy private clinic do terminations?'

'No, we specialise in bunions and hernias, but I know where it can be done. When were you thinking of?'

'Too many engagements to disappear off mid-week. It would have to be on a Saturday or Friday afternoon at a push. This week if possible.'

'OK. I'll see what I can do. How many weeks are you? They don't usually do it after eighteen.'

Annie had worked this one out already. 'Seventeen is the maximum. Could be less, if it's Andrew's.'

'Haven't you had a scan?'

'I told you, I only found out this morning.'

'All right,' said Karen. 'I'll play the urgent card.'

'It's such a relief to talk to someone about this. The past two weeks have been awful and now this...' Her voice cracked and she burst into tears.

'What else has been going on, Annie?'

She explained to Karen that her godson had been charged with assault.

When she came downstairs Eoin was back on the double yellow line. The Haunter raised his placard as she passed, then began to pack up, ready to disappear. She climbed into the back-seat, strapped herself in and opened her briefcase. She could do some work until they came off the motorway. After that the winding roads made her feel sick. When Eoin inquired if she was feeling any better, she told him she thought she needed a break and might have a weekend in London. Eoin didn't ask any more questions, but she knew her mother and Joe would.

Chapter Twelve

Late on Friday afternoon, the Procurator Fiscal looked at the reports in front of him. Minor assault was usually dealt with at a lower level than the Fiscal himself, but the owners of each in-tray in which this had landed had sent it up the line until it could go no further. Joe Cochrane was obviously a good boy and Shawn McDuff a bad one, but there was no doubt the assault had taken place. The common-sense approach would be to bin this and let the lad get on with his intended legal career without a criminal record. On the other hand, the case had already attracted considerable press interest and his previous dealings with the McDuff family made him extremely wary. He opened his desk drawer, lifted out a half bottle of vodka and added a generous slug to his coffee. Looking out the rain spattered window at the departing light, he wished, and not for the first time, that he had opted for a lucrative career with a corporate law firm.

Chapter Thirteen

As the taxi to the airport moved slowly through the Friday afternoon traffic, Annie reflected that by this time tomorrow it would all be over. When she had repeatedly miscarried all those years ago, each pregnancy had been mourned until she and Kenny decided they could no longer go on doing this. They would concentrate on the child they had. After tomorrow that was what she would be able to do, give all her energy to helping and supporting Joe.

It had been an exhausting week. Not only had she been travelling back to Corrachan each night but she had also to concoct a believable reason for going to London at short notice. Karen had suggested she tell people that Jan, an ex-flatmate, was passing through London on her way from Australia to Sweden. Jan had done this once before on the way to visit her husband's relatives so it had the tiniest grain of credibility.

May had not been impressed when Annie told her about the trip.

'So I've to keep an eye on Joe all weekend too? What if the hoodlums put a brick through my window?'

'That won't happen, Mum. The police are keeping an eye on your house now. See,' she said, writing in block capitals on the calendar, 'I've put it on the calendar.'

May peered at it suspiciously. 'I'll have to light a candle to St Paul of Verdun to keep us safe.'

'Don't think I've heard of him. Who was he?' Annie wondered if she should hide the book of saints.

May smiled wistfully. 'Your Great Uncle Paul, he died at Verdun. My mother always had a photo of him.'

'He's not a saint!'

'I never said he was!'

'You did so. You just said St Paul was Great Uncle Paul.' Annie was as indignant as May.

'I don't know how you manage in that job of yours if you can't listen. I said your great uncle died at Verdun and my book of saints says today is Saint Paul of Verdun's feast day. I have a picture of him.'

'The saint or the uncle?'

'The saint, of course!'

'Where are you getting all this religious stuff, Mum?'

May smiled.

'From the internet. Minty's going to show me how to skip next time.'

'Skip? You are both a bit past skipping aren't you?'

'You are behind the times, Annie. Skipping – it's a way to talk to people on the computer. You can see them. I'm going to practise talking to Minty's nephew in Athens. He's an ambassador!'

'Ah, you mean Skype!' Annie had caught up with her.

'That's what I said! You see, you don't listen.

Minty thought I could use it to speak to John in America. He'll be able to skip too.'

'Perhaps.' Annie had a shrewd idea that her brother, who only just remembered to send a Christmas card, would not be on for a weekly half-hour 'face to face' with his mother. But that was a discussion for another day.

This was typical of several recent exchanges. Her mother seemed to start in the middle of a story and it took ages to work out what she was on about.

As Annie and Joe walked up the road back to their own house, she asked if it would be okay for her to go away for a couple of days.

'Whatever. Done deal, isn't it?' The tone was sulky.

'Not necessarily,' she lied, 'but it's a good chance to see Jan.'

'Whatever.'

They walked in silence for a while, then Annie asked how his day had been.

'Okay.'

'No hassle from Shawn or anyone else?'

'No.'

'Your friends all being supportive?'

'Yeh.'

'Are you managing to concentrate?'

'Yeh.'

Annie linked her arm through his. 'I'm sure we'll hear soon the case is being dropped and then you'll be able to put it all behind you.'

Joe stiffened even more. She wanted to put her arms round him, to protect him from this situation and every other situation which might make him unhappy, but he removed his arm from hers and walked ahead of her in silence.

Now she was actually on her way to London, she felt in control again. She had to be at the clinic by 9 a.m. and would be back at Karen's by tea-time. She was ten minutes from the airport when her mobile rang.

'Hello?'

'Minister?' It was Tony, her private secretary. 'I don't like intruding into your private life, but I have to advise you not to go to London.'

Annie froze. Surely he hadn't found out. She was booked in the clinic under her maiden name. Had someone at the Corrachan surgery talked to the press? Was Tony, who she knew to have pro-life tendencies, calling to talk her out of it?

'What do you mean?' she blustered. 'I'm just going to London to see friends.'

'I know that, Minister.' There was a hint of exasperation. 'But something serious has happened and you need to be here, not London.'

Relief that her secret was safe was replaced with the fear she might not make her appointment in time. 'What's happened?' She really didn't want to know the answer.

'It's a community care issue. An elderly couple were supposed to be getting a care package. They didn't. The husband is dead and the wife is missing. Details are sketchy at the moment but I think you do need to be here, Minister.'

This was serious. 'Where did this happen?'

'In your constituency.'

There was no option but to return to the office. She tapped on the glass, told the taxi driver to turn round then looked for Karen's number. If she managed to sort things quickly she could catch the overnight sleeper and still be in time.

While Annie was travelling towards the airport, Robert Keiller was being driven from Glasgow towards Edinburgh, his prize female budgie in a cage by his side. He was looking forward enormously to the next day's caged bird show. As the car approached the outskirts of Edinburgh, he looked at the rain soaked bungalows and considered the evening ahead of him. Making small talk and playing Denis to Marlene's Margaret Thatcher held no appeal. Marlene regularly entertained the great and the good along with their spouses, in the hope that good food and free flowing wine would show her to be an interested and charming hostess. These dinners were usually held mid-week and Robert often avoided attending by pleading work and childcare, but today was Friday and he had no excuse. Vina, the new Bosnian au-pair, was in situ. He hoped she had the measure of Jordan and Stephanie before they got the measure of her. This was the third au-pair they'd had in six months.

Patrick was accelerating through an amber traffic light, when he suddenly slammed on the brakes and swore at the taxi doing a u-turn in front of him. The budgie cage was strapped in, but the budgie wasn't and it kept on accelerating. When Robert looked in the cage, it was obvious its occupant was dead. Patrick apologised profusely but

Robert said nothing. He took the bundle of feathers and cradled it in his hands for a moment, then placed it back in the cage. There would be no supreme championship silverware this year. Arriving at Bute House, he made his way to the private apartment where he found Marlene, wearing a towelling robe and painting her nails, a large vodka and tonic to hand. He put the cage on the bed and gave his wife a peck on the cheek.

'Hello, Marlie, how are you?' He tried to sound cheerful. She wouldn't be interested in his loss.

'I'm fine.' She glanced at the cage. 'Oh, for God's sake, Robert, take the bloody bird off the bed!'

He lifted the cage onto the floor. 'She's dead, actually.' He waited for Marlene to respond but she continued applying the second coat of Rubicon Red. 'We nearly had an accident at the end of the by-pass and she must have hit the side of the cage when Patrick braked.'

Marlene finished her pinkie, screwed the lid back onto the bottle of nail polish, then she looked up with what she hoped was a sympathetic expression. 'Oh dear! Is it the pretty green one?'

Robert nodded.

Marlene knew she shouldn't say it, but she couldn't help herself. 'Fell off her perch, did she?'

Too upset to reply, Robert took the cage to the kitchen. He would bury the little bird in the corner of the garden at home but, in the meantime, he needed to keep her safe. With great care, he wrapped her in several polythene bags and put her in the fridge. He then found a bottle of malt whisky, poured himself a measure and raised the glass in her direction.

Marlene was looking forward to the evening ahead. On paper, the guest list was unremarkable, but this evening differed from the norm as it doubled as a university reunion at the taxpayers' expense. One half of each couple had been in Marlene's coterie at Glasgow University in the eighties and she intended to extend this party well beyond the usual go-home time of 10.30.

Chapter Fourteen

When Annie reached her office, Tony was on the phone, but he made his apologies and replaced the receiver. 'Okay,' said Annie. 'Tell me what's going on.'

Tony looked down at his notes. 'An elderly couple were discharged from hospital three weeks ago following a car accident. He had several minor injuries and she was okay, but already had dementia. A neighbour found the man dead in his cottage at the head of Glen Perry this morning. Demented wife is nowhere to be seen. Police and mountain rescue are out looking. The hospital requested, then confirmed the need for, a care package with social services and assumed it was being implemented. Social services say they received a telephone request but no confirmation, so they did nothing. Evidently it's not uncommon for the ward to change its mind, so no one at social services thought they had to do anything. They are trying to piece together what happened.

Each side is keen to blame the other.'

'I'll bet they are!' said Annie.

Tony continued, 'There is a worrying possibility other referrals may have gone astray.'

Annie turned to one of the others. 'What's happening with the media?'

The press secretary handed her a piece of paper. 'There are requests from all channels; you name it, they want you. The car is booked to take you to the interviews.'

'Have we got a statement drafted?'

'Shocked and upset this has happened in your constituency, condolences to the man's family, hope that his wife will be found safe.'

'Yes! Yes! I can do that bit, but what's the line about the cock-up?'

'Cannot fully comment at the moment. Awaiting the report from the agencies involved. Systems will be looked at to make sure it never happens again.' Tony was on autopilot.

'Political implications?'

Tony pulled a face. 'Well, as you know, the meeting we had on Monday highlighted the danger of something like this because of cost cutting, and, slightly more embarrassing...' He paused.

'Go on, tell me!'

'Well, last May, in a reply to a question about community care from the leader of the opposition, you cited the successful partnership between health and social services in your own constituency as a model of how things should be done.'

'Great!'

But that was not the immediate consideration. Phone calls had to be made.

'Get me the chief executive from the health board and the director of social services.' She felt a wave of nausea. She hadn't eaten anything since noon. 'And get me something to eat and drink, please!'

'The usual?' asked one of her junior staff.

No, a double shot latte and a BLT sandwich was certainly not the answer today. 'I don't think so. Peppermint tea and...' She paused, considering her options '...and a packet of ginger snaps would be fine, thank you.'

Tony headed off to set up the phone calls.

Annie sank into her chair. There was no chance of being under an anaesthetic the next morning. Instead, she would have to give interviews after the interim findings were made public at 11 a.m. It *might* be possible to catch a plane around one, to be in central London by 3.30. She got up from her desk and made sure the door was firmly shut before phoning Karen who agreed to find out if this was a possibility.

The photographic backdrop in the TV studio made Annie look as if she was suspended several hundred feet above Princes Street. She checked her watch. Was there time to follow her stomach's suggestion that it would benefit from a ginger snap?

The interviewer, two MSPs from opposition parties and an academic specialising in community care, were in the Glasgow studio. She was not. She hated this sort of interview, because having heard what she had to say, those in Glasgow would then have a lively discussion amongst themselves. If she was lucky she might be allowed thirty seconds at the end to refute any misinformation. She took a bite of ginger snap.

The voice of the producer began the ten-second countdown, so, swallowing the biscuit, she looked into the hole in the wall housing the camera and adopted what she hoped was a serious expression. The red light came on and she heard the introduction.

'An elderly man was found dead today in his isolated cottage. The search for his missing wife who has dementia has been called off till first light. This vulnerable couple who were supposed to be receiving three visits per day from carers, appear to have received no care whatsoever for three weeks. Annie Cochrane, as minister in charge of Community Care, can you tell us how such a dreadful thing could have come about?'

'Good evening, Malcolm,' said Annie, employing the *if you are not going to introduce me politely then I will be overtly polite to you* tactic. 'Firstly, can I say both as minister and the MSP for this constituency, how shocked and upset I am that such a thing should have occurred, and offer my sincere condolences to Mr Johnston's family, and I know everyone will join me in hoping Mrs Johnston will be found safe and well.'

'Condolences are well and good, Minister, but they still don't answer the question. This is *your* constituency! This is a health and community care partnership which *you* have cited as being a model of excellence. I repeat the question. How could this have happened?'

Annie resisted the temptation to turn feral on

107

the interviewer and tell him she hadn't a bloody clue, that she wasn't the one who lost the referral. She kept to her script.

'There is an ongoing inquiry within health and social services and I understand they will be in a position to issue a statement tomorrow morning. It would be premature for me to comment at this stage why the care package was not implemented. All I can say is to repeat what the agencies involved have already put into the public domain: the hospital states that confirmation of a referral was sent to social services who say that no such confirmation was received. Believe me, I am as concerned as anyone to know what happened here and to make sure that it never happens again.'

The interviewer made a barely audible *hmph* noise, then turned to those in the studio, who cited lack of funding and Annie's failure as a minister in not foreseeing an event such as this. Annie's attempts to intervene were useless and the studio panel talked on. Presumably after his producer had said something in his ear about political bias, the interviewer addressed the screen and asked Annie for her opinion, only to say after three sentences, ''Fraid I'm going to have to stop you there, Minister, we're right out of time.'

The cameras were switched off and the connection to Glasgow cut. They wouldn't have been quite as cavalier with the First Minister, Annie thought ruefully as she took another bite out of the biscuit. Marlene would be phoning the controller at home by now to complain.

The waiting car drove Annie the short distance to her flat. An overwhelming exhaustion came over her and it was all she could do to drag herself upstairs to her front door. She sat on the edge of the bed and phoned Karen who confirmed that she had managed to get another appointment for 3.45 p.m. the next day, but that it could be no later. Annie had just got into bed when she received a text from Andrew asking if she was okay. She considered saying *no*, but realised he would phone. She did not want to speak to him before she had defused the bomb. She replied, *Coping, I think. Thanks for asking!* and turned off the light.

The First Minister's party was still in full swing at midnight. The staff had been dismissed and the company had moved from the grand drawing room to the private flat with sufficient bottles of drink to ensure continuing lubrication. Those who had been at university together were reminiscing, while their spouses were making polite conversation or, in the case of the partner of the professor of politics, snoring in an armchair.

Robert was listening to the wife of a millionaire businessman detailing the intricacies of needlepoint. He didn't realise that the lady in question was getting her own back for his lengthy treatise on the breeding of prize budgerigars. Her sewing skills were, in fact, limited to the occasional button. He surreptitiously looked at his watch and hoped Vina had managed to get his children to bed.

Vina had indeed managed to get Jordan and three of his friends into bed in the course of the evening. Having realised earlier in the week that the au-pair, who was a mere three years older than him, was anxious to earn extra money, Jordan had arranged a virginity shedding evening at his home for £50 per person. After his friends had gone, he had given her £75 out of the takings and was on his way to her bed rather than his own, when Stephanie came out of the lounge and blocked his way.

'Give me some of the money or I'll tell Dad.'

Jordan gave her a £10 note.

Stephanie wasn't impressed. 'Okay, I won't tell Dad, but I'll tell Mum.'

Jordan gave her another £15. 'That's your lot, now fuck off and mind your own business.'

'Your business is my business, big brother. Remember that, if you want this to be a secret.' Stephanie put the notes in the back pocket of her jeans and returned to the sofa. She picked up her Bacardi and Coke and flicked through the channels until she found one showing an adult movie.

Chapter Fifteen

The alarm penetrated Annie's dreams. Emerging into consciousness, she tried to work out what day it was. Then the events of the previous day came back to her and she was suddenly wide awake. She manoeuvred herself upright and waited for a few seconds, wondering if nausea was going to hit. She felt okay, so she padded to the kitchen and made some tea and toast. Full cup in hand, she called up the British Airways website and bought the only ticket available to London, a full price single on the 1.15 p.m. flight. This was going to be an expensive weekend.

By eight, she was in her office. The search for the missing woman had been resumed and the findings of the initial inquiry were expected at any moment. She hoped to be finished with interviews and free to leave for the airport before twelve. The phone rang. Tony listened for a moment, then replaced the receiver.

'It's just been emailed to me.'

'Forward it to me, please,' said Annie. She sat in her office and read. As expected, the disastrous episode was the result of unfortunate and unforeseen occurrences rather than negligence. The confirmatory fax from the hospital had arrived last thing on Friday afternoon during the care manager's baby shower to mark the start of her maternity leave. When she returned to her office to collect her coat, she failed to see the fax. Her temporary replacement started work ten days later and assumed that the care package had been implemented. No other referrals had been lost. The post mortem on Mr Johnston, who had been found face down near the back door, indicated he had suffered a stroke about ten days previously, but probably not a large enough one to kill him immediately. Annie's mind jumped to images of May, struggling to manage on her own.

The statement went on to detail the interim measures to be put in place pending a full inquiry.

Annie reckoned a similar mistake wouldn't happen again, but some other unforeseen circumstances would lead to some other tragedy and more procedures and red tape would be generated. An honest mistake was not part of today's culture. A scapegoat was required and she would be blamed for failing to provide adequate funding and appropriate monitoring of Health and Social Services. The pregnant lady who failed to check the fax machine would be hounded in the press too. Annie left her desk and went to find Tony.

'Can you check that there is some sort of support for the pregnant woman, the social worker? It was an oversight, not an intention to condemn someone to death.'

Tony raised his eyebrows. This was not the department's business.

'Just do it, please.' If he only knew, Annie thought. She looked at her watch. There were two hours to fill until she needed to make the statement. 'I think I'll have a power nap, I didn't sleep well last night. Could you book me a taxi to the airport for 11.45 please? *I'm* still hoping to get to London.'

Back in her office she stepped out of her shoes and lay on the sofa. Her own words were echoing in her mind. Pregnant woman… Oversight… Condemn to death… *No!*… It's a bomb in need of defusing.

As the morning wore on, the press and TV crews made their way to the Council Offices in Invercraig. The Chief Executive of the Health Board was trying to decide which tie was the most fitting for such an occasion. He had discarded the dark grey one when he heard that it was not a hospital

112

problem. He opted for the navy blue with the white dots. With his full head of grey hair it made him look distinguished. The Director of Social Services, who had aged ten years in twenty-four hours, sat in his office considering his resignation options, and the pregnant lady who had not seen the fax went into premature labour.

Just after eleven, Annie redid her make-up then placed her overnight bag beside the coat rack. She read and reread both the statement and her brief. Her mind was mince. She turned to the Sudoku in the paper. This might keep her occupied. She appeared to be managing the difficult one with ease until she realised she had two nines in the same row. She was about to abandon that in favour of the easy one, when her desk phone rang. The body of Mrs Johnston, dressed only in her nightie, and with her dead collie lying on top of her, had been found several miles from her home. The statement was being amended to include this information and consequently would be delayed.

'So it's two deaths now,' said Annie.

'Three!' said Tony. 'Don't forget Greyfriars Bobby! A dead dog adds another dimension to all this. *Faithful pet perishes trying to save dotty lady abandoned by the state.* Be ready for questions about that in your interviews.' He seemed to be enjoying this a little too much.

'When's the statement going to be?' Annie's anxiety levels rose further as she realised precious minutes were being eaten up.

'Noon they reckon.'

'I have to be away from here at 12.15 at the latest to get the plane.'

It was ten past twelve when Annie got into the waiting taxi, fastened her seatbelt and told the driver to take her to the airport. She had given three television and two radio interviews. She had again offered her condolences to the family, she had praised the police and mountain rescue services and commented on the faithfulness of the dog. Assurances had been given that all community care services would review their procedures and she had declined to comment further before a full inquiry into the role of the Director of Social Services.

'What time's your flight?' asked the taxi driver.

'One-fifteen, but I've only got hand luggage, so as long as I am there before quarter to one I'll be fine.'

'Not a hope, love.'

'What? Thirty-five minutes should be time enough to get to the airport on a Saturday.'

'Not today, it's not. There's been an accident on Queensferry Road and traffic's backed up in both directions so everything is trying to go out past Murrayfield. Rugby International today, so it was chocca anyway before this. It'll take forty-five minutes, perhaps even an hour to get you there. Can you get a later plane?'

The adrenaline which had been keeping her going all morning drained from her. This wasn't going to work. The time bomb with the shortening fuse was going to have to remain for another week. With effort, she managed to control her voice. 'No, I'd be too late. Could you turn round and take me back, please.'

Tony was leaving the building as the taxi returned.

'Forgotten something?' he asked.

'No, the traffic's more or less a gridlock. I'm not going to make the plane in time, so I've decided to go home instead.'

'Couldn't you get a later one?' Tony asked.

'I could, but after all this I would be crap company. I know you are just leaving, but could you please organise a car to take me home?'

She walked through the empty building towards her office. Everything had conspired against her. She dreaded to think what Karen was going to say when she asked her to sort it out yet again. There would be another week pretending all was normal. The organisation involved, the lies, the fact that time was running out overwhelmed her. Frightened she would meet Tony, she veered into the Ladies, locked herself in a cubicle, and howled.

Chapter Sixteen

Two hours later, Annie trudged up the path and unlocked her front door. The house was silent. Her first thought was to don her flannelette pyjamas and hide under the duvet, but she couldn't yet; her mother and Joe both needed to be told she was not in London. As she filled the kettle, she also added *Phone Karen* to her mental list. She had been less than impressed by Annie's change of travel plans. 'Appointments like this don't just grow on trees, you know,' she'd huffed in their brief exchange, while Annie was waiting for her car.

First, Annie dialled her mother's number but there was no reply. Then she tried Joe but that went to voicemail, so she sent him a text instead. She took her cup of tea to the living room and, for lack of anything better to do, switched on the television. The coverage of the Scotland – Wales rugby international was in full swing.

'Blocking the bloody road! I hate you!' she shouted at the TV. She disliked rugby at the best of times and, to make matters worse, the Scottish team was being annihilated. She switched it off. Her eyes fell on the box of discarded paperbacks for the forthcoming Amnesty Book Sale that Minty organised every year. Minty. Perhaps Minty was the right person to talk to.

She drove out of the town on the road to Loch Corrachan and, after negotiating the pot-holed track to Minty's house, parked beside the rusty ten-year-old Fiesta – a recent replacement for the 25-year-old Metro which had finally been consigned to the scrap heap. As she was retrieving the box of books from the backseat, Joe, with spade in hand, came round the side of the house. He did not look particularly pleased to see her.

'Thought you were in London.'

'Didn't manage to get there with all the stuff about the old couple. I texted you to say I was home.'

'No signal here.'

'What on earth are you doing?' Annie gestured at the spade. Joe cut Minty's grass during the summer months, but he did not usually do any digging.

'Minty thinks her old dog's going to peg it and she wants a hole dug. Says it's going to snow or something.'

'Poor old thing!'

'Who are you talking about? Minty or the dog?'

'Both I suppose,' said Annie. 'Where is she?'

'She and Gran are inside. They'll be buying things on saintsandcandles.com.'

'Mum's here too? That explains why she wasn't answering her phone.'

'Better get on.' Joe was already walking away.

Annie negotiated the abandoned wellingtons and elderly raincoats in the back porch and went into the kitchen where the soon-to-be-occupant of the hole was snoring in a basket beside the Aga. Once in the hall, she shouted, 'Hello!'

A door opened upstairs. 'Up here! Who is it?'

Annie turned to climb the stairs and was nearly knocked over by a black and white collie. Minty's head appeared over the banisters.

'Oh! Hello! May said you were off to London.'

'I was, but I'm not now,' Annie replied.

'There's a fire on in the sitting room, go and have a seat, my dear. We're nearly finished.'

By now the dog was leaping up and trying to lick Annie's face.

'Penny! Get down and come here!'

The dog scuttled back upstairs.

Annie went into the sitting room. She had been in here before, for election planning meetings, but she had never had a chance to look at the photographs and antique knick-knacks of which there were many. Both the Georgian tallboy and several small tables held silver-framed photographs. Some looked recent and Annie supposed they were great nieces and nephews, but others were older. She picked up a black and white wedding photo. The bride must be Minty and the naval officer must have been her husband who was killed on active service, not long after they were married. It was hard to match the young woman in the photograph with the elderly lady who was at present upstairs instructing Annie's mother in the art of internet shopping, but there was something in the clarity of gaze and the carriage of her head which had endured.

Annie picked up another frame, this one showing a group of people having a picnic on a heathery hillside, and identified Minty aged about twelve among the group. There was something familiar about one of the women in the picture and, on closer inspection, Annie realised it was the Queen Mother. She scanned the men's faces and found George the Sixth, and among the children there was a girl who could have been Princess Elizabeth. Annie had taken the photo over to the window to look at it more closely when Minty and her mother came into the room.

'You've caught me being nosey!'

'That's all right! They're there to be looked at,' replied Minty.

'Are they who I think they are?' Annie pointed at the relevant people in the photo,

'Oh! You mean the Duke and Duchess of York? Yes, and the Princess is there somewhere too. I love that photo because it's one of the most

118

natural I have of my mother. The Queen Mother was her childhood friend and they so enjoyed each other's company – my mother was her lady-in-waiting for a while.'

'Look, Mum,' said Annie handing her the frame. 'Minty having a picnic with royalty. Where was it taken?'

'Up on the hill, at Balmoral. The men were shooting – not one of the organised shoots, just walking the hill together with a gun and a dog – and we joined them at lunchtime. Such a happy day that was.' Minty looked into the middle distance and seemed momentarily to have returned to an Aberdeenshire hillside in 1933. After a few seconds she smiled briefly and pointed to a girl of about seven. 'That's Lillibet; Margaret Rose is not there. She would have been too little.'

'Lillibet?' asked May. 'You mean the Queen?'

'Bit younger than me of course, but I knew her quite well when we were children. Don't see her much these days – needless to say, our paths don't cross very often! Now, have a seat by the fire, May, and I'll put the kettle on.'

Annie couldn't help wishing that May was ageing as well as Minty was. 'Can I give you a hand, Minty?'

'You could give Joe a shout. He's doing a little job for me – digging a hole for the old dog.'

'He explained. I'm sorry,' said Annie. 'You've had him a long time, haven't you?'

'He is incontinent, deaf and tottery – bit like me really! It'll be a blessing. If he's not gone by the end of the week, I'll have to get the vet. Tried to dig the hole myself but I wasn't making much progress.' Minty threw two logs onto the fire. 'Getting old, you know – can't do things like that now. Joe has kindly been seeing to that while your mother and I complete our purchases.'

Annie turned to May. 'What have you two been buying now?'

Minty tapped the side of her nose.

'Not more religious ephemera?'

'We'll tell you all about it when the tea's made.'

Annie followed Minty to the kitchen and was making her way to the back door to give Joe a shout when Minty called her back.

'A minute, Annie. The boy's having a hard time at the moment. He thinks everyone in school is talking about him. He also thinks a criminal record will scupper his chances of being a lawyer.'

'He seems to be talking a lot more to you than he is to me.'

'Well, that's the way of it. Teenagers don't confide in parents. I never talked to my mother, I talked to Larry about things – that was my old Nanny. Miss Lawrence.' Minty had another brief look into the middle distance before continuing. 'Getting back to Joe; I listen if he needs an ear. And his girlfriend is helping him too. Will it be long before he hears if his case is going to court?'

'Should hear this week,' said Annie. 'Let's hope he just gets a warning, but knocking Shawn's teeth out makes it more serious, despite the provocation.'

Annie opened the back door and looked into the twilight. She could see Joe at the bottom of the garden. He was standing up to his knees in a hole shovelling the last of the earth onto a pile.

He raised a hand to acknowledge her shout and Annie went back inside.

She wondered why her mother was now seated on the other side of the living-room fireplace. Sitting in the chair her mother had vacated, Annie felt the warmth infuse into the right side of her body while the left was assailed by an icy draught. So that was why her mother had moved. Minty poured the tea into antique cups none of which matched, completely unaware of the competing thermal airstreams in the room.

'Two sugars isn't it, May?' She picked up a pair of silver tongs and dropped two lumps into May's cup, then added some milk.

It was a long time since Annie had seen sugar lumps. Did they still make them or had they been languishing in Minty's cupboard for years? 'Unusual tea-cosy,' she said, looking at a hand-knitted creation made from the remnants of old jerseys.

'Mrs Collins knitted it for the craft sale ages ago. Hideous – no one would have bought it. So I told her it was lovely and bought it myself. It does the job, and the lime green, purple and orange no longer impinge on my consciousness.' Minty shook her head sadly. 'She's a poor soul now, she can hardly see.'

'Wasn't it her cake that poisoned Mike Andrews last year?' asked Annie.

'Please, my dear, don't remind me. We are not allowed to sell home bakes any more in case history repeats itself.'

When the tea was distributed and biscuits had been handed round, Minty settled herself on the saggy chintz sofa and looked at Annie. 'So! You had a change of plan?'

'Yes, I was going to London to see a friend from Australia, but with the death of the Johnstons and all the statements etcetera, not to mention the Edinburgh traffic, it wasn't going to be worth it.'

'Poor old Jimmy. It gave me such a jolt, seeing him lying on the floor. Quite cold he was, and no sign of ma – or the dog.' Minty's tone was matter of fact.

'It was you who found him?' asked Annie in surprise.

'That's right. Their house is about a mile up the glen from here. Kept themselves to themselves – only ever saw them when they drove past on their Friday shopping trip to Corrachan. Realised I hadn't seen them for at least a fortnight, so I took myself up the road to see if they were all right.' Minty paused to take a mouthful of tea. 'When I got up to the house there was no car, so I thought they must be away visiting their son. I didn't know that Jimmy had driven it into a lamppost. Then I noticed the back door was slightly ajar and I went inside.'

'It must have given you a terrible shock.'

'Gave me a fright at first, because it was so un-expected. It was obvious he was dead. I looked around the house and garden for ma, then I covered Jimmy with a blanket and phoned the police.'

'A series of unfortunate circumstances which combined to make a disaster.'

Minty raised her eyebrows. 'But the world thinks it was your fault?'

'Something like that,' said Annie.

'Saw your interview last night. Such a rude man, that Malcolm Whatshisname – never let you put your point at all. Did my best to damp it down here. Lots of press coming round last night and a few this morning, so I pretended to be deaf and dotty.' She chuckled. 'I'm good at that.'

Annie glanced towards the window.

'It's okay, they've gone. Must have put the word out that I was senile, because no one has been back since.'

'Thanks, Minty, it's good to know someone is on my side.'

Talking of sides made her realise that one half of her was completely cooked. She went and peered into the growing darkness.

'I wonder what has happened to Joe. He must have trouble seeing out there.'

On cue, Joe stuck his head round the sitting-room door. 'That's it done, Minty. I'm off to get the bus.'

'Don't do that,' Annie said. 'We'll be going back as soon as we've finished our tea.'

'Meeting Ellie at six and I need to have a shower. You'll get into political discussion and take ages.'

Minty fumbled for her handbag. 'Just a minute, Joe, don't go without your money!' She handed him a ten-pound note.

Joe thanked her and headed off.

'Come and sleep at home tonight! See you later.' Annie addressed the closed door.

There was an awkward silence.

She sighed, 'I'm obviously not flavour of the month.'

'Give him time. He'll come round,' said Minty.

'Now let me top up your tea and May and I will tell you what we've been buying.'

'More saints?' asked Annie warily.

'No, no,' said May, 'much more exciting than that! I've bought my own computer!' She looked like a child who had just completed her first ever purchase in the sweetie shop. 'It's going to be delivered on Tuesday, so I can buy things and do skipping with your brother and goggle things if I need to find something out. I won't have to bother Minty any more.'

'May's really got the hang of it now,' said Minty. 'She should be able to manage fine. We've ordered a laptop with all the necessary, and a printer. We've practised speaking to my nephew in the embassy in Athens a couple of times now, so May should know what to do when she contacts your brother. And if she wants to buy something, she can do it from the comfort of her living room.'

'Or my bed!' said May, delighted. 'You said it would work in any room, didn't you?'

Minty nodded enthusiastically. 'We set up the internet connection yesterday, so that is all ready and waiting.' She and May beamed at each other.

Annie wondered if her mother having access to the world-wide web was necessarily a good idea, but settled for agreeing that it was exciting. May's penchant for ecclesiastical knick-knacks was quite far down her list of things to worry about at the moment. Minty lifted the teapot. 'Another top up?'

As Annie proffered her cup, Minty caught a fleeting side-on view and wondered about this recent weight gain.

Chapter Seventeen

While Annie was taking tea with Minty; Marlene Watt was at home in Glasgow with the remnants of a horrible hangover. When the party had finally broken up at 2 a.m., she had decided she needed something to eat to help soak up the Highland Park. Unwrapping what she thought was cheese, she discovered she was about to hack slices off a stiff budgie. The shock had necessitated another tumblerful of whisky, hence the lurking headache.

Earlier in the day, she had been the guest of the Scottish Rugby Union at Murrayfield for the International against Wales. As Robert had no bird to take to the Caged Bird Championships, Marlene had insisted he accompany her to the match where he had endured the whole proceedings with a face like thunder and the remains of the dead budgie in his pocket. He wasn't the only one with a thunderous expression. The official who had been forced to give up his seat to the unexpected guest was not best pleased either.

Sitting with her feet up on the sofa Marlene was talking on her mobile. Robert, following the burial of his budgie, was with the rest of his flock in his purpose-built shed in the back garden. Jordan, Stephanie and Vina the au-pair were out. As she had no hobbies or interests outside work, Marlene did not enjoy free time so she had called Morton to ensure he had fed the *Annie Cochrane is an incompetent* line to the Sunday papers.

She was assured it was all in hand.

'I've briefed the usual sources. Said I had it on good authority Andrew Fraser was going to sack her.'

'And don't I wish he would! Online comments organised?'

'Incompetent as a parent, incompetent as a minister is the line. I've arranged ten callers for the Radio Scotland phone-in on Monday morning. The first to get through will claim to be horrified at Annie Cochrane's inability to run the health service. Anyone else who is successful will change the message to her inability to control her child, followed by "you would be better off in a minority government, you are the only politician of any merit" etc.'

'This woman needs to be seen off, Morton. As she's not one of ours, I can't sack her. We either need to make her life so unpleasant that she cracks or we show her to be totally incompetent, then Mr Boring will have no option but to fire her.'

Morton was more relaxed. 'She seems to be making a monumental mess of things without our help at the moment. Her badly behaved child, the dead pensioners...'

'All the more reason to move in for the kill now. I hate incompetence, and Fraser is too weak to sort her out.'

The extent of the venom surprised him. 'What has she done to piss you off all of a sudden, Marlene? You never cared two hoots about her before.'

'I have *never* rated her, and the longer I have to suffer her round the cabinet table, the more I realise she has been promoted beyond her abilities. Make sure you put out something about her being slow on the uptake in cabinet.'

Morton suddenly wondered if Marlene actually thought Annie was too clever. Was she a threat? He smiled to himself.

'What did she ask for clarification on, last time? Health funding, that was it. It's her department, for God's sake. You would think she might just have grasped that.'

'It's all in hand, Marlene. You can leave it all to me. Just relax and enjoy your weekend.'

'I don't do relaxation, Morton.' Unwilling to terminate the call as she would have to find something else to do, Marlene attempted small talk. 'You having a quiet weekend?'

'Might go out later. Might stay in.'

He enjoyed winding Marlene up. Despite the gossip, they were not having a relationship. In fact, no one got emotionally close to Morton. A selection of female acquaintances were used to accompany him to official functions and he was able to manage some perfunctory lovemaking afterwards if the situation demanded, but he preferred solitary pleasures – those with more than a hint of danger. He knew just how far he could go.

'What about you? What have you got lined up?' he asked.

'An evening in.' The prospect was not exciting. 'Don't know what Robert's going to make for dinner, but I think I'll have an early night.'

Annie also opted for an early night, but she was unable to sleep. With the duvet pulled up to her chin, she lay in the dark and considered that by rights, she should have been recuperating in Karen's spare room with the problem solved. Her appointment had been rebooked for noon the following Friday. Six more days.

Karen had told her the clinic was suggesting counselling because she was always changing her mind. 'You do still want to go through with this?' she had asked when Annie rang to apologise once again.

Annie's answer was immediate, 'Yes, of course!'

'Okay, okay. I was just asking. When will you come down?'

'I have a dinner on Thursday night so I'll get the first plane on Friday. I'll be with you by about ten.'

'Last chance, you know.'

'I do know, I'll be there.'

Chapter Eighteen

Annie managed to plough her way through another four working days pretending everything was normal. On Monday morning she feigned a thick skin over the weekend's press cuttings which trumpeted her incompetence and warned of her imminent sacking. In the afternoon, she had to launch the condom campaign. At an Edinburgh secondary school, she extolled the benefits of sex education and decried unwanted pregnancy, fully expecting the hand of God to strike her down at any second. In the car back to the office, Tony suggested there could be some good publicity from their afternoon's outing. Provided I am not rumbled, Annie thought.

'Far too many girls, and women for that matter, getting pregnant when they don't intend to – not to mention all the microbes being swapped.' Tony, at least, had read the handout leaflet. Annie made a non-committal 'Mmmmm' noise, hoping he'd shut up. It didn't work.

'Take chlamydia,' he continued. 'Sounds like one of those made-up names children get called now. *Chlamydia, your tea's ready.*'

Please change the subject, she thought, but Tony was in philosophical mode.

'If this stops all these kids thinking it won't happen to them, if they get the message they are sleeping with everyone else their partner's ever been with, we will have achieved something.'

Dear God, would the man never shut up?

Annie suddenly stiffened. Microbes! Oh God! Perhaps she was harbouring something unpleasant! She knew Andrew's hadn't strayed far from his trousers but God knows where Tarik's had been. She fidgeted in her seat, trying to control the inevitable itch. She would have to ask the clinic to check.

On Tuesday, not only had she to appear before a committee to answer questions about the care débâcle, she was also the brunt of office teasing. The papers all carried a shot of a schoolgirl's hands putting a condom onto a cucumber with a beaming Annie clearly visible in the background, a shot also seen by her mother, who phoned up in a state for the second day running. The previous day

Annie had to assure a tearful May she was not about to be sacked. Now she had to defend what, in her mother's view, was pornography.

'Don't tell me it's educational! It's filth, not to mention a waste of a good cucumber! I hope Joe's not being taught that sort of thing.'

'Mum, I've explained this to you already. It's supposed to cut down unwanted pregnancies and STDs.'

'I had to light a candle to St Fiacre for the wasted cucumbers.'

Yet another one, Annie thought. 'Who the ... who is St Fiacre?'

'Patron saint of vegetable growers.' May was triumphant.

'Mum! Is he from your book?'

'No! My computer! Minty helped me set it up. Don't need the saints book any more. I goggled *saint* and *vegetable*. He's also the patron saint for venereal disease and taxi drivers!'

It was good to know the campaign had a patron saint. She would keep that for the cardinal if he lobbied her again.

On Wednesday, she had managed to get back to Corrachan by seven and as she opened the front door she could hear Joe's music, much louder than usual. She knocked on his door and went in, intending to ask him to turn the volume down, then noticed his red eyes. He passed her his summons to court for the following Tuesday.

She sat down beside him on the bed. 'Oh Joe! I'm sorry. I really thought it wouldn't come to this.'

His eyes looked huge. 'Mum, I'm scared.'

'I know you are.' She sat on the bed beside him. 'I think we need to get you a lawyer. We could go and see Bill Macdonald in the morning. You'll miss a bit of school but I'll phone and explain.'

'Teachers' in-service tomorrow and Friday. We're on holiday.' *He gave her a look which said, See! You're too involved in your life to keep up with what's happening in mine.*

She smiled an apology. 'So you are.' She put a hand on his shoulder. 'It won't be as bad as you think.'

He removed her hand and turned round to look at her. 'Don't think it could get much worse. I plead guilty, I have a criminal record. That's me fucked. No university will take me now. And as you are so fond of telling me, the whole of Scotland is going to know all about it.' He turned away. 'I might as well leave school now and get a job ... or I'll go travelling. Leave all the shit behind!'

'You have to go to court, Joe – otherwise, you'll be in much more trouble.'

He looked at her in exasperation. 'I'm not stupid, Mum!'

Annie managed to reschedule her Thursday morning appointments to allow for the legal consultation. Bill Macdonald, the local solicitor, was uncertain as to the outcome but promised to give it his best shot. As they left the office, Joe muttered that he was going to see Ellie. As Annie moved in to give him a kiss he turned away, leaving her embracing fresh air.

'See you Sunday then?' she said to his departing back.

The ministerial car was parked at her gate when she got home. Eoin was reading the paper. He rolled down the window as Annie approached.

'I'll be ten minutes,' Annie said. 'You want a coffee?'

Eoin held up a cardboard cup from the deli in the High Street. 'No thanks, I'm fine. Take your time.'

The phone call to Kenny could be put off no longer. Her previous call to tell him about the assault had been difficult, with Kenny taking the opportunity to point out that Joe was not being properly supervised while she was away. She had bitten her tongue. *You only have him for two visits a year,* she wanted to say, *don't criticise me for poor parenting.* Luckily his mobile went to voicemail so she left a message.

Because of her early plane the next morning she was staying in the Edinburgh flat that night so she packed what she needed for London. Then, before leaving the house, she undid the button and the top two inches of the zip on her skirt – sitting for an hour in the car with a tight waistband was becoming very uncomfortable.

As they reached the outskirts of Edinburgh, Annie congratulated herself on getting through to Thursday. Less than twenty-four hours now.

At 7 p.m., Annie was making pre-dinner small talk to some of those who would hear her speak later on, when Tony appeared at her elbow and said he needed a word. She excused herself and went with him to the edge of the room.

'I've just had a call from the office. Your mother

needs to speak to you urgently. Luckily someone was working late and took the call.'

'What is it this time?' Annie sighed in frustration. 'Has she discovered the patron saint of black-tie dinners?'

Tony made a I-don't-quite-know-how-to-react-to-that face. May's calls always kept the private office entertained. When they weren't driving them mad. 'I gather she sounded ... upset. She said it's about Joe; that's why we thought we had better tell you.'

Annie sighed. 'Could you lend me your phone, please? I'll be as quick as I can.'

She stood outside in the hallway and dialled her mother's number. 'Hello, Mum. What's the matter? I'm busy at the moment. I really can't talk now.'

'Annie! Thank God, I've got you! It's all these cucumbers! I knew it was wrong!'

Annie couldn't keep the irritation out of her voice. 'Mum! I'm at an official event. I'll phone you later.'

'No! You don't understand! It's the cucumbers ... they've made him think it's okay.'

'Made who think what is okay?' What was the woman on about?

'Joe! It's made him think it's okay to take Elsie, away for the weekend.'

Annie bit her tongue. Be nice, she thought. She's just got the wrong end of the stick again.

'No, Mum! You've got in a muddle. *I'm* away this weekend, not Joe.'

'I know that! That's why I know the cucumbers have made him do it.'

133

Tony was making deferential hurry-up gestures.

'Okay, Tony. Mum ... made him do what, for God's sake?'

'Go to Edinburgh!'

Annie was close to losing her temper now. 'But Joe is staying with you this weekend. He is going to Ellie's on Saturday evening. It's all written on the calendar. I *have* to go now. If I'm not too late, I'll speak to you before you go to bed.'

May was not going to be put off.

'He told me he was off to Edinburgh. I thought he was staying with you. When I was making tea, I looked at the calendar and it said *Joe Edinburgh, Annie London* on it. Then I knew it was the cucumbers ... they are still children, Annie.'

Annie felt a tiniest niggle of alarm but the odds were still on her mother getting it wrong.

'Mum, they can't be coming to my flat. There are only two keys. One is in my handbag and the spare is in my desk drawer in Edinburgh. I saw it today. I'll phone Joe and sort it out. Now stop worrying. It must be about time for *Corrie*. Settle down and I'll speak to you later.'

'I can't. I'm getting my angina again.'

This was all she needed. 'Go and get your spray.' Annie heard the phone being laid down. She turned away from the hovering Tony, and after what seemed like an age her mother came back.

'I can't find it! It's always in my handbag. It's not there!'

'Keep calm, Mum. Have another look.'

'They must have taken it. It's gone! The pain is getting worse.'

134

'Is it beside your bed?'

The phone was laid down again, and after some banging about her mother returned.

'No, it's not there.' The pain and breathlessness were audible.

'Mum, put the phone back on the hook and keep looking. I'll phone the McCaffertys and get them to come round.'

After the call to her mother's neighbours, Annie signalled to Tony.

'Can I have a minute? She's not well and I need to speak to Joe. I'll be with you as soon as I can.'

Tony retreated and Annie switched on her own phone and dialled Joe's number. It went to voice-mail. Then she phoned directory inquiries and got Ellie's home number. Annie asked the girl's mother if Joe was there. Irene Paterson sounded surprised.

'But they are staying with you in Edinburgh, aren't they?'

The niggle of alarm grew exponentially. Annie had no option but to tell Ellie's mother that they were not.

'Well, I put them on the Edinburgh bus this afternoon.' Irene's tone suggested more than mild alarm. 'They said they would be back on Sunday evening. Could they be staying with someone else?'

'I don't think Joe knows anyone in Edinburgh. Does Ellie?'

'Only her great aunt and she's in a home.'

Annie waited on the line while Irene tried to phone Ellie. There was no reply.

'Can you think where else they might have

gone?' asked Annie.

There was a pause. 'There is a rock concert on in Glasgow this weekend – a few weeks ago Ellie talked about wanting to go and I said no.'

'Keep trying her phone,' said Annie, 'and I'll keep trying Joe. My mother is not very well, so I have to check on her, but I'll get back to you.'

It was Bob McCafferty who answered May's phone. An ambulance was on its way, but in the meantime they had just found the spray in the tea caddy.

'I'll be as quick as I can,' she told him. 'I can't thank you enough.' She turned to Tony who was lurking as if on hot coals. 'My mother has been taken ill. I'm going to have to go. I'll give the speech now, before they eat. While I'm speaking, do you think you can summon up a car to take me home?'

Next Annie sent Joe a text. *Where r u? Please contact. love u. It will all b ok* xxx. Oh, Joe, she thought, don't do this. If you are not in court on Tuesday you will be in an even bigger mess than you are now. As she made her way to address her expectant audience, she realised she would now have to get up in the middle of the night and drive herself back to the airport for the first flight. Which was also the last possible flight.

On the drive back to Corrachan, Annie dialled her mother's number and May answered.

'Are you all right, Mum? Last thing I heard an ambulance was on its way.'

'It came. They were very nice, those ambulance drivers.'

'Paramedics.' Why do I always have to correct

her, Annie asked herself.

'What?'

'They are not called ambulance drivers any more ... they are paramedics.'

'Well, they certainly drove an ambulance to get here.' May was going to stick up for her terminology.

'Anyway, are you okay now?'

'I'm fine. Soon as I found the spray, I was fine.'

'Did they check you over?'

'Yes, they were very thorough. Then Jean made them a cup of tea and they went.'

'What are you doing now? Are you in bed?' Annie pictured her mother tucked up with a cup of tea and an ancient copy of *People's Friend*.

'No, I'm waterskiing in the living room.'

'Waterskiing?'

'Waterskiing the internet ... on my computer!'

'Surfing, Mum. Not waterskiing, surfing.'

Having reassured her mother with a big black lie that Joe and Ellie were staying with Ellie's aunt, Annie had gone straight to see Ellie's parents. They sat in the conservatory which, despite the efforts of a convector heater, was freezing cold on this February night. The angle of the surrounding hills meant mobile reception was not good in the centrally heated parts of the house. Much to Annie's relief, Irene and Steve Paterson had agreed it was not appropriate to report them missing. Annie was determined the police were not going to know Joe had gone until five minutes before the court hearing. Between bursts of polite conversation they sat in silence, imagining each in

137

turn their child at a rock concert, or sleeping rough in the middle of Edinburgh.

A few snowflakes fluttered past the windows, followed by more and more. Gradually, the lawns and shrubs in the garden became visible through the darkness as the ground whitened. The sleeping rough images were winning when both Annie's and Irene's phones signalled the receipts of texts. Finally, Ellie and Joe had turned on their mobiles.

Irene dialled Ellie but once again it went to voicemail.

Annie sent Joe a text. *Now snowing. v worried. r u both safe and warm.* And as an afterthought she added *if no reply going 2 go 2 police. xx.*

The snow was mounting up on the window ledge. Steve Paterson stood up.

'Anyone want a drink?'

Irene's phone began to ring.

'Ellie! Thank God! Where are you?' She bit her lip. 'What do you mean you can't tell me? ... Have you got money? ... Sunday? *No!* Tomorrow... Yes, I'll tell Annie ... Ellie? ... *Ellie?*....' Irene looked at Steve and Annie. 'She hung up!'

'What's going on?' Annie asked.

'She wouldn't say where they are, they've got £200 in cash and they will explain when they get back on Sunday. Joe wants you to know he's okay, Annie.'

'Well, at least we've heard from them,' said Steve. 'They've got money and they are not on the street. It could be worse.'

'Is he going to get a bollocking when he gets home...' A statement, not a question, from Annie.

Steve was more measured. 'It's unlike them to

do something like this. They're a sensible pair. I suppose we need to trust them and wait for a full explanation.'

Annie smiled gratefully at her hosts and picked up her coat. Nothing more could be done tonight and she needed to be up at four to drive to the airport. Steve offered to walk her home but she declined, although she accepted Irene's offer of a woolly hat. The snow was still falling – millions of big flakes fluttering down and piling up on top of one another. As she made her way gingerly down the road a car passed but came to a halt before the top of the hill, its wheels spinning uselessly. If the roads were like this after half an hour of snow, what were they going to be like for her early morning drive?

Chapter Nineteen

The alarm went at three-thirty and Annie reluctantly left the warmth of her bed and looked out of the window. The wind had got up in the early hours and the gentle flakes of four hours ago had been replaced by a total white-out. She couldn't even see the houses on the other side of the street and her car, now a large white mound surrounded by drifts, was just visible in the orange glow of the street light. One thing was certain, she wasn't going anywhere.

Wide awake now, she made a cup of tea and took it back to bed, glad of some residual warmth.

She propped up the pillows, pulled the duvet up round her shoulders and watched the snowstorm through the gap in the curtains. There was nothing else she could do.

Suddenly, there was a long-forgotten fluttering. She closed her eyes. The cartoon image of the bomb was instantly replaced by a foetus with little arms and legs – legs which were kicking, a hand up to the mouth to suck a thumb, a baby. She put her hand on her stomach and felt it again. Lying there, swaddled in the duvet, she felt not only safe, but serene.

'It's all right,' she said aloud. 'I'll not let anything happen to you.'

She finished her tea, then curled up in her warm cocoon and fell into a deep sleep.

She was woken by the muffled tones of her mobile ringing in her handbag. Through her sleepy haze she recalled the events of the previous evening. Joe! By the time she had got out of bed and found her phone, it had stopped ringing. Karen. Annie looked at the clock – ten past eleven! She climbed back into bed and returned her friend's call.

'Annie! Where in God's name are you? You said you would be here at ten. I've taken the morning off work to go with you.'

'I'm in Corrachan.'

'Corrachan? You told me you were in Edinburgh last night and getting the first plane south.'

'That was the idea, but I had to come back here and then it snowed. There was no way I was going to get to the airport this morning.'

'Why didn't you let me know?'

'I meant to, but I went back to sleep and the phone woke me just now. Sorry.'

'Back to sleep?' Karen sounded utterly flummoxed. 'So, when are you coming?'

Annie knew what the reaction would be to her next remark. 'I'm afraid I'm not.'

'What do you mean *not?* You might be okay for the beginning of next week, but you can change the appointment yourself this time. They were threatening cancellation charges.'

'I'm not doing it. I felt it move.' Annie heard Karen's exasperated sigh.

'Good God... Have you thought through all the shit that goes with having it? All the mess, the noise, the broken nights? People get over terminations, you know.'

'I don't think I would now.'

Karen let out a big sigh. She had known Annie long enough to realise when she meant what she was saying. 'It was ingrained into your psyche, wasn't it?'

Annie didn't reply.

'What next, then?'

'When I've worked that out, you'll be the first to know.'

'Well, phone me if you need a chat.' Karen's tone had mellowed. 'I'm a trained counsellor, re-member.'

'Thanks, I might.' Annie paused. 'Could you just do me one more favour ... please...?'

'Phone the clinic, I know. What would you do without me, Annie Cochrane? So, tell me. What took you back to Corrachan last night?'

As Annie was explaining, she climbed out of

141

bed and went to the window. The snow had finally stopped and although it was lying several feet deep, the drips falling past the window indicated a thaw.

Although thoughts about Joe and his whereabouts were ricocheting round her head, Annie had to use this engagement-free day to decide on the best way forward, before her expanding waistline made the announcement for her. The bath had always been a good place to think, and while it was running she tried Joe again. Once again she left a message.

She lowered herself into the scented water and considered her midriff, now breaking the surface of the foam, a molehill on its way to becoming a mountain.

'Well, Baby. What are we going to do now?'

As Annie was contemplating her navel, Karen was considering her friend's situation over a fresh cup of coffee. Annie was normally so cautious, someone who had succeeded in life by dint of hard work and very little social life. Now, after years of celibacy, she had managed to shag two men in one week. And two such unsuitable ones – a needy colleague and that bastard Tarik. Charity and exploitation.

The house phone rang. Annie again, no doubt. 'Hello?'

'Karen? Is that you?' The voice was Scottish and male.

'Yes, who is this?'

'It's Joe. Has Mum arrived?'

'No, she hasn't.' Karen was cautious. Something

142

told her this was not a straightforward call.

'Are you expecting her soon?'

'She's not coming now. Just phoned a few minutes ago. She's snowed in at home.'

'Oh!' There was an intake of breath. 'Why is she back in Corrachan? Is Gran all right?'

'As far as I know, your Gran's fine. She had some sort of angina attack last night but she's okay now. I think your Mum went back to Corrachan to find out where you had disappeared to.'

'Oh.' Joe paused.

'She hasn't a clue where you are.' Karen heard him hesitate.

'Is Jan there?'

Jan! She'd almost forgotten the Jan story, the one about her being on her way to Sweden from Australia. Karen thought quickly. 'She's had to change her plans – dash off to her parents in Belfast.'

'So you're on your own?'

'Yes, Joe, I am.'

'Can I come and talk to you?'

This so wasn't how she'd expected her day to unfold. 'Isn't that what godmothers are for? You must be in London, then?'

'We're in the Starbucks just down the road from you.'

'Well, I may not do flavoured syrups, but my coffee is free, so get yourself up the street.'

Karen was just about to phone Annie quickly before Joe arrived, when she remembered a conversation with him last summer when he had been staying with his father. If he ever had a problem, she assured him, she would listen. Depending on the nature of the problem, she explained, she might have to tell his mother, but she wouldn't do anything behind his back. As a teenager, she had had a divorced great aunt who smoked Russian cigarettes and was unshockable. Several times Karen had gone to her with what seemed insurmountable problems. A gin, a Sobranie and a frank conversation always put things in perspective. She was out of gin and she didn't smoke now, but it looked as if she was to play that role. The call to Annie would have to wait.

The doorbell rang.

'Come in – *both* of you! This is an unexpected surprise.'

She brewed more coffee and provided a selection of biscuits. After a bit of innocuous conversation, Karen leaned towards her godson.

'You want to talk to me about something, Joe?'

'It's a bit complicated.' He became engrossed in unwrapping his KitKat.

'Well, I know about the court case, if that's what you're worried about, but perhaps you should start at the beginning.'

Joe looked at Ellie, who nodded.

'Things have been shit at school. People getting at me 'cause of Mum's job – everything wrong that happens is all her fault. There's the letters in the paper saying she's not looking after her constituency properly...' He stopped and took a bite of the now unwrapped KitKat.

'Go on,' said Karen.

'Now she's doing a condom campaign – so I'm getting a heap of shit about that too. Last week there was all that stuff about her being a crap minister. Gran thinks it's true and she worries Mum's doing things wrong and won't get re-elected. It's making her go weird.'

'Weird?'

'She forgets things and she thinks people are coming into the house, taking things or moving them around. She's got saints everywhere too. *Everywhere*. There's even one on the cistern. Kind of puts you off.'

Karen smiled. 'I seem to remember she always did like to have one or two about the place.'

'This isn't one or two, believe me.'

'Is there anything else?' Karen offered round the biscuit tin again.

'People are saying Mum does fuck all and lives off expenses.' Joe started to unwrap a second biscuit. ''Cause she's a minister she's got a car and a driver. Everyone goes on about how rich we are 'cause we've got a chauffeur. I know Mum works really hard, but she doesn't realise how much it affects Gran and me.'

'That sounds awful,' Karen sympathised. She then asked him what had actually happened the night of the assault. Between them, Ellie and Joe explained.

'...and I now have to be in court on Tuesday,' he finished up.

'You'd better be there,' Karen warned. 'You'll be in a lot more trouble if you're not.'

'I've thought about skipping it,' admitted Joe, 'but it's okay, we're going home on Sunday.'

'You still haven't told me why you are in London. We could have had this talk over the phone.'

Joe lowered his eyes and made a ball out of the

145

silver paper wrapping. Finally he spoke. 'I came to see Dad.'

Karen raised an eyebrow. 'So why are you in my kitchen, not his?'

'We got the overnight bus and I phoned his mobile early to get him before he left for work. It had a funny ring. He's in Germany and won't be back till late tonight. He was in a hurry and said he would speak to me tomorrow. I never even got the chance to say I was in London.'

'Does your stepmother know you're here?'

'No.' Joe paused and looked at Ellie again for reassurance. 'I get on okay with Catherine but I need to speak to Dad, not her.'

'So what you're trying to tell me is that you would like to stay here tonight.'

He smiled for the first time since he'd arrived. 'Thanks. That would be great. We were going to look for a hostel or something.'

'There is one condition.'

Joe and Ellie looked at her.

'You must let me tell both your mothers that you are safe and under my roof.'

'I don't want her to know I'm going to talk to Dad,' said Joe anxiously.

'Okay. I'll not tell her at the moment why you are here, but perhaps you could tell me?'

'Go on,' said Ellie.

'I want to come and live with him.'

Not exactly the time to be changing education systems, Karen thought briefly. Then she realised the effect his decision would have on Annie.

'That's a major thing to do at your stage with exams and everything, and running away is not

146

necessarily the answer.' *Though it might be when you hear you're going to have another half-sibling.*

'I've been sort of thinking about it for a while, even before I hit Shawn.'

'Have you talked to anyone else about this?'

'Only Ellie.' He took the girl's hand and gave it a squeeze. 'And an old lady called Minty. She showed me how to look at all my options and consider each one carefully.' He looked sheepish. 'She did say I had to talk to Mum about it first. Then we had two days holiday and I thought I'd go to London and talk to Dad, and if it's not going to work, Mum need never know.'

'We thought everyone would think we were in Edinburgh for the weekend,' Ellie ventured.

'Well, you were wrong,' said Karen sternly. 'Okay. I'll only tell your mums that you are here and safe and that I'm helping you to sort yourselves out. That's all.'

They nodded.

'And after I've phoned, we'll talk about this plan of yours a bit more.'

Half an hour's thinking in the bath had only succeeded in using up all the hot water. Annie had no solutions. Being nearly five months pregnant meant the baby wouldn't be a secret for much longer; there was the inevitable political minefield and she was going to need good antenatal care. Andrew had to be told he might or might not be a father all over again. She hadn't forgotten his comments about how exhausting he found his grandson. Then there was her mother, and Joe. And Tarik.

147

'Bugger, shit, fuck!!'

Annie heaved herself out of the water and pulled a towel off the rail. Perhaps she should do a Reggie Perrin and go and live abroad. She glared at herself in the mirror. *Don't be ridiculous!* It was stay here and face it. Press interest was inevitable, and they would immediately want to know who the father was. They weren't the only ones. She supposed some sort of paternity test could sort that. She would have to find out what that entailed. Andrew would face up to his responsibilities, she was quite sure of that, even if he wasn't very happy with the situation. Tarik, on the other hand, was an unknown quantity. The word responsibility was not one with which he had demonstrated a close relationship. Could they rebuild their relationship for the sake of a baby, or would he bugger off into the ether like last time? She put on her dressing gown and went to her room, intending to get dressed, but she found herself back in bed, staring at the ceiling. She was still thinking round the impossible circle when Karen called. The relief that Joe was safe was overwhelming.

'But why on earth is he in London?' she asked.

'You have to bear with me on that one, Annie. I said I wouldn't tell you at the moment. He's got some problems – more than just the court case. I think that was the last straw.'

'Ellie's not pregnant, is she?' The vision of child and grandchild in neighbouring bumps at the antenatal clinic flashed through her mind.

Karen paused. 'Don't think so. It's something else.'

'Can you give me a clue?'

148

'Not yet. I'm trying to help him sort this out. He trusts me. That's all I can say at the moment.'

'He is my son, Karen. I've got a right to know what's going on.' Annie didn't much like the slight whine she detected in her voice.

Karen assumed a less brisk tone. 'I will tell you, but not yet. Sorry.'

'As soon as you can, then?'

'As soon as I can. I promise.'

'You're a very fine friend, Karen.'

'You're absolutely right about that. And by the way, now's a good time to tell you that you owe me £200 for the cancellation fee.'

Much as she was tempted, Annie realised she couldn't lie in bed all day. She dug out the trousers with the elastic waistband and a large baggy jumper. A concealed pregnancy, but she wasn't fourteen, she was forty-four. *She* was supposed to be the one in London having Karen help her solve her problem, not Joe. A problem-solver was what she needed though, one with political nous. In normal circumstances, she would have gone to Andrew, but in these exceptional circumstances there was only one person with the necessary political antennae combined with an enormous amount of common sense – Minty Oliver.

The thaw was continuing. The main roads would have been ploughed by now, but she might have to walk the quarter-mile track to Minty's house. She donned walking boots, a thick anorak, hat and gloves. With a shovel in the boot, Annie, not the most confident of drivers in snow, set off.

At Minty's road end, it was obvious the small

hatchback would not make it up the track. She parked in a layby and after a trudge arrived at Minty's back door. A Beethoven symphony could be heard from the kitchen. Leaving her snowy boots in the porch, Annie knocked on the door and let herself in. Minty was sitting at the kitchen table reading the *Economist* and listening to Radio 3. She looked up in surprise.

'Annie! Hello! I wasn't expecting any visitors today. Did you come by sledge?'

The collie ran to greet her but there was no sign of the old spaniel, just a space where the basket had been.

Minty laid down the magazine. 'Now... You look like the Michelin woman with all these layers on. Hang your anorak next to the Aga and let it dry off.' She pointed to the back of a chair. 'Very brave, venturing out here today – I do have a phone!'

Annie took off a number of layers and sat down. 'I'm here Minty, because I need to talk to you about something and it's not really a tele-phone-conversation sort of something.'

'Oh?'

'I have got myself into a complicated situation and I'm not sure how to handle it.'

Minty raised her eyebrows but said nothing.

Annie continued. 'It has personal and...' she paused, 'political implications ... in more ways than one.'

Minty leaned back in her chair. 'I'm intrigued. Go on.'

'Well, you just used the phrase Michelin woman and that sort of sums me up ... carrying extra

150

weight round my middle and I'm gong to be carrying a lot more. I'm pregnant, Minty.' There. It was out!

'Ah.' Minty nodded. 'I thought you might be.'

'You did?'

'I thought your waistline was a little thicker when you were here last week and there was something about you. Always had a knack of knowing someone was pregnant. Sometimes before they knew themselves.' Minty put a hand on Annie's arm. 'Perhaps I'm really a witch! Now, before we go any further, have you had lunch? Never a good idea to think on an empty stomach.'

The kitchen clock said ten to two. Annie had had nothing since her cup of tea in the middle of the night and she was starving.

Minty was already lifting the lid of a large saucepan on the Aga. 'There is soup here and I can make you a slice of toast.'

'Soup and toast would be wonderful, thanks.'

'OK, while I'm doing this, tell me all about it.'

'Where do I begin? Not at the conception, I'll come to that later. Well, about a week and a half ago, I went to the GP, as I thought I had a lingering tummy bug, and I also needed a smear test. That's when I find out the tummy bug was actually a sixteen-week pregnancy.'

'You hadn't suspected?' Minty had her head inside a cupboard as she tried to locate a soup bowl.

'No. It never occurred to me that my IUD wasn't working properly.' She paused. 'I decided I couldn't have a baby. I had to get rid of it – for all the obvious reasons – and I couldn't have a termination in Scotland. My face is too familiar.

151

So a friend arranged an appointment at a private clinic in London last Saturday.'

'And then there was all the business with the Johnstons?' Minty emerged from the cupboard with a bowl in her hand.

'That's right. I couldn't go on the Friday and was nearly in time for the plane after the interviews on Saturday, but the traffic defeated me. Then I was supposed to go to London today, but I had to come back here last night as Joe had gone AWOL and I got snowed in.'

'Joe's gone AWOL?' Minty asked in alarm, nearly spilling the bowl of lentil soup she was putting in front of Annie.

'Yes, he and Ellie told everybody they were going to stay in my flat in Edinburgh, but they weren't. We had no idea where they were. Mum thought they were off for a dirty weekend and had an angina attack, so I had to come back here. Then it snowed.'

'Poor May! Is she okay?'

'She's fine now, thanks.' Annie detailed the events of the previous evening. 'And now it appears that they are safe with my friend Karen in London – she's his godmother – but she won't tell me why he went there. He's in court on Tuesday, so I just hope he isn't running away.'

'I told him not to do anything rash, just to consider his options carefully and to speak to you about it,' said Minty, exasperation evident in her tone.

'So, do *you* know why he's gone to London?'

'To see his father perhaps?'

'Kenny? Fat lot of help he'll be. He's more

interested in his three-year-old daughter than he is in our son.'

Minty was unwilling to betray Joe's confidence. 'Well, Joe and I had a chat about things he could do in his life,' she said carefully. 'I told him he must speak to you about it.'

Annie looked at the space where the basket had been. 'Sorry about the dog.'

'Thank you. Had to get the vet in the end.' Minty started to butter a slice of toast, 'Enough about the dog. You were saying you were going to have an abortion.'

'For the last ten days it was all I could think about – time was running out. I had to make everything right again.' Annie took a deep breath. 'Then this morning I felt the baby kicking and I knew I couldn't do it.' Her eyes filled with tears.

Minty placed the toast in front of Annie and poured herself a cup of tea from the pot insulated by the hideous tea-cosy. 'Would you have gone through with it if you had managed to get to London last weekend?'

'Oh yes, I believe I would. I was refusing to think of it as a baby – it was a ticking time bomb.'

'I was just wondering...' Minty paused.

'Yes?' Annie halted a full soup spoon halfway to her mouth.

'I was wondering why you let another week elapse before your next appointment.'

'I couldn't just make up some excuse and shoot off to London! You know how much was going on.'

'You were making up excuses to go at the weekend. What's the difference between say, a

153

mythical aunt's funeral on a Tuesday and a mythical visit of a friend on Saturday. I assume the Australian friend wasn't really there?'

'You're telling me I was subconsciously putting it off?'

'Were you?'

Annie put down her spoon. 'Perhaps. When I realised I couldn't get to the airport, I was resigned. It was strange. There was no panic. Then when I felt it move, I knew the termination wasn't going to happen. I am dreading the fall-out, but I'm at peace with the decision.'

Minty refilled the kettle and put it on the hotplate, then sat down next to Annie.

'So, you are about four and a half months?'

Annie nodded.

'And do I know the father?'

'You might, but then again you might not. That's the problem.'

'Care to explain?'

Annie felt her face flush. 'Well, it might be Andrew, Andrew Fraser.'

Minty smiled, nodding. 'Is that a bad thing? Some folk might say it's too soon, but it's none of their business.'

'I wish it was as easy as that.' Annie pushed her empty soup bowl to one side. 'It could also be an ex-boyfriend whom I met again on a visit to Aberdeen.'

Minty's eyes widened. 'And your mother and I were worrying that you were working too hard to have a social life! Does she know?'

'No – not yet!' The scene was too awful to imagine. 'She'll be horrified.'

'For a while perhaps,' Minty admitted, 'but she'll get over it, especially when it's born. Do you have a favourite?'

'Sorry?' Annie hoped Minty wasn't starting to copy May's kangaroo-style thought processes.

'If you were a betting woman, which would you put your money on? As the father?'

'Andrew, I think.' She smiled at Minty. 'He's had more than one opportunity!'

'And is that who you would *like* it to be?'

This needed careful consideration. 'I don't know. One is safe and one is exciting.'

'Exciting? Is that a euphemism for unreliable?'

'You could be right.' While Annie retold the story of Tarik, Minty refreshed the teapot.

'So, there'll be no doubt about the parentage of the child when it arrives. You can have a test done. But this is a tad complicated, I agree. Either of them know you are pregnant yet?'

'No.'

'Well, Andrew must be told before any public announcement.' Minty put a fresh mug of tea in front of Annie.

'I know, I know.'

Minty briefly put a hand on Annie's shoulder.

'It's politically complicated too by the wretched contraceptive campaign. Good God, I wish I had never let either of them near me.' Annie put her head in her hands.

'My dear, a word of advice – don't waste emotional energy wishing something hadn't happened. Against the odds, you are pregnant – so perhaps it's meant. The ageing body will do everything in its power to have a last go at reproduction, and

155

that includes making you do things against your better judgement. Ovulation can lead the most respectable housewife to ask the milkman in.'

Annie burst out laughing. 'Oh Minty! You do put things in perspective. So, what should I do now – in the immediate future?'

'Your expanding waistline means questions will be asked soon, if they are not being asked already. I can't be the only person to have noticed your weight gain. If I were you, I'd speak to Andrew, put out a statement, endure a couple of weeks' gossip and conjecture, and then everyone will find something else to talk about.'

Annie nodded slowly. 'Do you think ... could you help me draft that statement?'

'I'll fetch my laptop. Much easier to delete or cut and paste than have to score it out and start again.'

Half an hour later, Annie rose from the table and put on her now dry anorak.

'I'll email that to you,' said Minty; 'and I suggest you arrange to see Andrew this weekend. Tread carefully though. He needs to know the whole truth. If it's his, he'll face up to his responsibilities, he's that sort of man. If it's not, you still need his political support.'

'I'll speak to him before Monday. What a bloody mess.' Annie was ready to cry again.

Minty gave her a hug.

'I have a saying – I think it came from Julian of Norwich originally – *All shall be well, and all shall be well, and all manner of thing shall be well.* However bad it is now, it will be all right in the end. It's seen

156

me through many a trial and tribulation in my time.'

Annie reflected for a moment on the words, committing them to memory. 'I'll try to believe you, Minty, and thanks for all the advice.' She started to move towards the door, but Minty put a hand on her arm.

'Before you go, can I say I'm all for a woman's right to choose and I would have supported you if you had chosen termination, of course, but I am glad you are going to have this baby.'

'Thank you,' said Annie swallowing hard.

Minty hesitated.' I don't know if you know, but we had a baby. She died.'

Annie frowned. 'I knew you were married and widowed in the war, but I didn't know you had a baby.'

'She was called Helena. Christopher, my husband, never knew I was pregnant, but we had one of these conversations on our two-day honeymoon about what we would call our children and that was a name we both liked, so Helena she was.'

'What happened?'

'She was very prem – about twenty-eight weeks. I'd come here, away from the bombs in London. She lived for a couple of hours. Of course, today she would have been in one of those special incubators and she would probably have been fine. She might have been a grandmother herself by now.'

'I'm so sorry,' said Annie.

'It was treated as if it was an early miscarriage. Everyone was brisk. It was "Pull yourself together, you'll get over it. You're only twenty, you'll get married again and have lots of children." Well, you pull yourself together, but you don't get over it. So, Annie, enjoy this baby when it comes.'

'I'll try, Minty, I will try.'

Chapter Twenty

Karen spent an evening in with Joe and Ellie. By ten o'clock, after an Indian takeaway and a DVD, her guests were asleep on the sofa – a combination of the previous night on the bus and relief that an adult was now in charge. Karen shook them gently and suggested it was time they went to bed. She led the way upstairs and stopped on the landing.

'One room or two?'

They both looked at the floor.

'It's okay,' Karen continued. 'I don't mind. As long as you are careful. Or one of you can sleep in the boys' room. Suit yourselves.'

They exchanged glances.

'One room, then?' Karen answered for them.

'Yes, thank you,' said Ellie. 'And we are always careful.'

'Wouldn't dare be anything else. Mum's always going on about it: *No excuse for unwanted pregnancies! Use a condom!* That was another thing. She got photographed with condoms and cucumbers. Now everyone keeps asking me if I like rubber salad.'

Teasing about rubber salad was going to be the least of his problems. Karen opened the door to the spare room and showed them in.

The next morning, Karen drove Joe and Ellie to his father's house. She and Ellie waited in the car. They watched him go up the path and ring the bell.

Kenny Cochrane was not pleased with the disruption to his Saturday morning plans. Catherine was also far from thrilled to discover *she* was now expected to take their little daughter swimming. She had planned on having the morning to herself. Kenny took Joe to the kitchen and without preamble got down to business.

'So what are you doing here? Couldn't we have talked on the phone?'

'I needed to speak to you without Mum knowing.' Joe's nervousness was obvious.

'Don't tell me you've got yourself in more trouble?'

'No!'

Kenny pulled out two chairs. He sat on one and gestured at the other. 'Okay, Joe. So what is this all about?'

He listened as Joe faltered through his account of the situation, but it was clear from his expression that he wasn't impressed.

'You are about to sit your Highers. You can't just float down here.'

'But I could do A levels here instead. I wouldn't have to sit them till next year. Please, Dad.'

'Running away is not the answer, Joe.'

'*Dad! I* can't stay at Corrachan Academy. I hate it. Please don't make me.' Joe was near tears.

Kenny remained unmoved and suggested an

alternative solution.

'Boarding school?' Joe was horrified. 'No! I'm not going to some posh school. If I can't come and live with you, I'll go travelling.'

'Travelling where?'

'Thailand, Vietnam, China? Somewhere far away. What does it matter?'

The thought of his sixteen-year-old son backpacking through south-east Asia finally concentrated Kenny's mind. 'Look, Joe, this had come out of the blue. It's not only up to me. It's Catherine's house too, so I need to talk to her about it – and we need to talk to your mother. Don't look at me like that! I know this is all her fault, but she *is* involved.' He put a paternal arm round Joe's shoulder. 'I can take a couple of days off next week. I'll come north for the court case and we can all discuss it. Okay?'

The fantasy of being welcomed with open arms had evaporated. Joe stood up. 'Better go. Karen's waiting.'

Kenny found his wallet and gave Joe £100. 'That should cover your costs. I'll see you on Tuesday and we'll all talk then.'

As Joe walked down the path, Karen assessed the body language. 'Doesn't look promising, Ellie.'

He slid into the backseat and as Karen pulled away from the kerb, she glanced in the rear-view mirror. All the fight had gone out of him. 'What happened?'

When he had told them of his father's reaction, Ellie took his hand.

'Perhaps Catherine will say it's okay.'

160

'She won't,' he said simply. 'I know, she won't.'

Karen was brisk. 'Let's wait and see. Now, what do you want to do for the rest of the day? I'll treat you to the London Eye if you like, then you can get the bus back to mine.' She could use the time to phone Kenny and acquaint him with a few extra facts.

It was late on Saturday afternoon when Andrew turned his car into Annie's driveway and switched off the engine. She had told him she had to see him, but refused to elaborate. That, combined with her seeming unwillingness to talk to him after the last cabinet meeting, was ominous. Either she was going to end their relationship or she was going to tell him she wished to resign as a minister or, worse still, as an MSP. He had hoped that for her, as it had for him, the relationship had folded all the advantages of a friendship into a new intimacy. When they were together, they not only talked politics, they talked about their families, Joe's problems, and their past relationships – his with Jane and hers with Kenny. It was close and it was comfortable. Relationship apart, she was his closest political ally. He did not want to lose her in either capacity.

With some reluctance, he removed the key from the ignition and got out of the car. Side-stepping the remainder of a snowdrift, he put his finger on the doorbell.

Annie looked dreadful – white-faced and exhausted. He tried to give her a hug, but she was unresponsive. He was going to be dumped, and, now that he knew, he realised how much he would have preferred it to be the resignation. She showed him into the living room.

He declined coffee or a drink, sat down and looked up at her. 'Okay, Annie. What's the matter? Spit it out.'

'You're not going to like it, Andrew. In fact, you are probably not going to want to speak to me ever again.'

He tried to take her hand but she pulled it away. 'What on earth could possibly make me do that? Come on, tell me.'

Annie walked to the window. 'I'm nearly five months pregnant.'

There was an awkward silence.

'I see,' he said finally.

She turned round. 'Is that all you are going to say?'

'What were you wanting me to say, Annie? *Oo, isn't that super? Congratulations?*' He was looking at the floor now. 'How pregnant did you say you were?'

'Nearly five months.'

'I see,' he said again. He fell silent for a few moments. 'About the end of October? For the conception?'

'About then,' she replied. He's so cold, she thought. I was sure he would be all concern and support. This was worse than she could possibly have imagined.

'How long have you known about this?'

'I found out about two weeks ago. Remember I told you I was feeling yucky. I just thought I had a tummy bug, I never thought I ... I decided to have a termination – in London – but now I've

162

changed my mind. I felt it move, so I'm going to keep it. The baby.'

Andrew was still looking at the floor so Annie blundered on.

'I've got a draft statement here. Minty helped me. Something will have to go out soon...' she looked at Andrew, but he didn't raise his head... 'or people are going to notice.' She walked over and put a hand on his shoulder but he shrugged it off. 'Look, I know this is a bit of a shock and there is something else I have to tell you.' She took a deep breath. 'There is a possibility you might not be the father. I slept with someone I knew a long time ago, a few days before we first ... first...' She felt sick. 'We'll have to do some sort of paternity test.'

He turned to look at her.

'You thought I might be the father?'

'More likely to be you than ... him.'

'Annie, it's not likely at all. I thought you knew! I had a vasectomy years ago.'

Her hands flew to her mouth. Everything in her mind rearranged itself. The potential caring attentive father vanished, leaving her with what? She could just hear what Karen would call Tarik – an unreliable narcissist. She saw Andrew's hurt expression.

'I'm sorry, Andrew. He was an ex-boyfriend. We met up again by chance. It was only once and it was before you and I...' The lump in her throat was taking over her breathing and, realising she could no longer control it, she gave in.

Andrew pulled her down next to him, put his arms round her and kissed the top of her head.

'Annie, poor Annie. What a mess. Have you told him?'

'I had convinced myself it was yours, rather than his.' She started to cry again.

'Would you have liked it to be mine?' he asked gently.

She nodded.

'That's nice to know. Okay, you need to stop crying and I'll try to put my party leader hat on while we talk things through.' He patted her hand. 'It could be much worse, you know. I thought you were going to tell me you were giving up. You're not are you? Giving up your portfolio?'

'You tell me,' she replied. 'I'm not the best advertisement for the contraceptive campaign, am I? I'm a liability. It would make Marlene's day if you sacked me.'

'Not as much of a liability as Peter, and that's who I would have to promote. You may be pregnant, but you are not a loose cannon.' He gave her another hug. 'And as for Marlene, making her day is not high on my agenda.'

Chapter Twenty-One

As Joe and Ellie travelled north that Sunday, the phone lines between Corrachan and London were buzzing. Kenny wanted Joe to come and live with him. Having found out about Annie's pregnancy from Karen, his attitude had changed and he took great pleasure in telling Annie that Joe deserved the chance of a normal life away from her misdemeanours. Joe would return to London with him after the court case to be enrolled at the local sixth form college as soon as possible. Seething at his autocratic approach to the problem, Annie told Kenny to take nothing for granted, at least until she had spoken to Joe. She slammed the phone down and rang Karen.

'Hi Annie, I was just about to call–'

'Well, you're too late! Kenny's just told me Joe's going to live with him. *And* he seems to know I'm pregnant! I wonder how he found *that* out?'

Karen was well able to defend herself. 'Wait a minute! This is Joe's idea. He went to see Kenny yesterday and was more or less told to go home and get on with it, so I phoned Kenny and we had a little chat.'

Annie was really angry now 'It's not your place to tell Kenny anything. Minding my business as usual! Interfering between me and my son! Whose side are you on, anyway?'

Karen remained calm. 'I'm not minding *your* business, Annie. I'm minding Joe's! I've spent the weekend talking to him. He's not a happy bunny. Let's run through the chronology here. Joe is teased at school. Joe assaults his tormentor. Joe ends up in court. Joe's mother is away all week so he has to stay with Granny who is losing the place. Joe's mother keeps appearing in the paper with rubber-clad cucumbers. Surprise, surprise! Joe decides life might be better with Daddy. And that's all before he finds out you're pregnant. And no, he doesn't know that yet.' Karen softened her tone. 'Annie, Joe has no intention of returning to Cor-

165

rachan Academy. If it's not school in London, he says he'll go travelling in deepest Asia. As far as he's concerned, boarding school is a definite no-no.'

'He's only sixteen! He can't expect everything his own way.'

'And because he is sixteen,' Karen replied patiently, 'nothing will work without his cooperation. Lest you forget, having a mother carrying all her indiscretions before her in the form of an expanding bump is not going to improve things. You have to let him go with your blessing, not with your anger or disappointment.'

Annie knew Karen was right. She couldn't force any solution on Joe. Much as she wanted to keep him at home with her, she doubted her chances of success. Promising Karen she'd keep her up to date with developments, she wandered round the house. The overflowing ironing basket accused her of maternal and domestic negligence. She might as well do something useful. She turned on Radio 4 and was treated to the final bars of 'Scotland the Brave'. What on earth was this?

'Scotland the Brave', your first musical memory. Now, Marlene Watt, tell me something about your early life...

Marlene on *Desert Island Discs!* The woman got everywhere. Her PR people must have fought hard for that slot.

That's right, Kirsty. We lived in a mining community and my father worked at the pit. My mother... There was a dramatic pause. *My mother had mental health difficulties. I was an only child but there*

166

was a sense of community, a sense of looking out for each other. That's what I am trying to foster in today's Scotland. I worked hard at school and...

And won a bursary to Glasgow University to study politics, Kirsty Young added.

Indeed. I am passionate about education being a way out of poverty. I want all able children to fulfil their potential and to make this a prosperous and successful country.

What a load of nauseating tosh. Annie made a face at the radio. Marlene was turning the programme into a party political broadcast. Annie folded a pillowslip and reached for the next one.

You are Scotland's first female First Minister. Do you see yourself as a pioneer?

Hardly, Kirsty. I am a mother, first and foremost. But I like to think I have shown that the glass ceiling is a myth as far as politics are concerned. The women in my cabinet are as able as the men.

Annie put the iron on its stand and pointed at the radio. 'I'll quote you on that next time you put me down.'

And your next record?

My grandmother lived outside Ayr, near the birthplace of our National Bard, so my next record can only be 'Ye Banks and Braes o' Bonnie Doon' beside which we had many family walks...

Annie switched off the radio in disgust and attacked one of Joe's school shirts. Talk about re-inventing yourself without actually telling any fibs! It was well known that Marlene's father was the pit manager and she had already admitted during Alcohol Awareness Week that her mother's mental health difficulties stemmed from the gin bottle. As for a 'way out of poverty' – that newspaper article a few weeks earlier had outed her as an alumnus of a Jean Brodie-type private school in Glasgow. Annie hung Joe's shirt on a hanger and pulled the next one from the basket. She bet Marlene's luxury item was a tin of shortbread but she was damned if she was going to turn the radio back on to find out.

By 12.15 the ironing was completed, but she had done nothing about cooking lunch. May's usual Sunday arrival was imminent; they would have to eat out.

The rain the previous day had seen off the remainder of the snow and there was a hint of spring in the air when they drew up outside a small countryside hotel which was fast establishing a reputation as a gastro pub. The expression on her mother's face when presented with the menu persuaded Annie she should have stuck to the Carvery at the Corrachan Hotel.

'What's a gouge-on?' May asked plaintively.

'Little bits of fried fish, but that's on the children's menu.' Annie directed May to the correct page.

There was silence while they both read.

'Is there any soup?'

Annie looked at the blackboard.

'Sweet potato and chili.' It was not a promising option.

'No lentil?' May asked hopefully.

'No lentil, Mum. Why don't you have the pâté? You like that.'

'It says it's served with marmalade.'

'Made with onions, not oranges, Mum. Like chutney.'

'Perhaps.' May was still doubtful. 'What's bowff burging-on?'

'Stew.'

'Not Sunday dinner is it?' May was unimpressed. 'Isn't there a roast?'

'Lamb shanks done in the oven. I think you would like that.'

'It's got wilted greens with it.' Suspicion was evident.

'Just leave them if you don't like them.' Describing it as hot lettuce would finish it as an option.

By the time they had waded through three courses, during which May had picked at her food, it was nearly three. At her mother's request, Annie drove the long way home to take in the views. May nodded off almost immediately and missed most of it, but the additional miles allowed Annie time to think.

When Joe arrived home that evening, she knew what she had to do. From the sitting room, she heard the thump as he laid down his bag, then he appeared in the doorway. The angry person of the previous week had been replaced by a reserved stranger. There were no pleasantries, no apologies, just an announcement.

'I'm going to live with Dad.'

She must stay calm. 'I know. I've spoken to your father and Karen.' Annie swallowed. 'You don't have to do this, Joe.'

'You won't change my mind.'

'Will you hear what I have to say?'

'You'll be wasting your breath.' He slumped on

169

the sofa, picked up the TV remote and began channel-flicking.

'Just hear me out, please. And turn the TV off.'

He shrugged and pointed the remote at the set.

'There is a way to change how we live. I can resign as a minister, then I'll only have to be in Edinburgh occasionally – for votes and things like that. You won't get the shit associated with me being in office. You won't have to stay with Gran.'

'Do you *want* to give up?' Joe asked.

'If I'm going to lose you, yes.'

'Had you considered resigning before I hit Shawn?'

Annie thought for a moment. 'No, I didn't realise there was a problem. Everything seemed to be going along fine.'

'Told you I was getting hassle!' Joe's tone was sulky.

'And, if you remember, you told me you didn't want me to do anything about it.' Don't get all defensive, Annie told herself.

'So, 'cause I'm going to London, you say you'll give it up?'

'Yes.'

'But if I hadn't said I was going, you wouldn't give it up?'

This was beginning to resemble a conversation with her mother.

'If we had talked about it and it was what you wanted, yes of course I would have come to this decision.'

Joe fiddled with the TV remote, passing it from hand to hand, avoiding his mother's gaze. 'Would you ever have thought, *I want be with my son and my mother, rather than sorting out everyone else's problems?'*

He had touched a raw nerve. Annie tried to keep her voice level. 'They are not mutually exclusive, Joe. I've tried my best up till now to make things work.'

'But something always gets in the way, doesn't it? There's always an urgent problem, always press wanting comments. That bloody Black-Berry is never silent.'

'I thought you were proud of what I do.' She sounded so needy.

'I am, Mum, but I can't hack the shit that goes with it.'

Resignation was the only option now. 'If I phone Andrew and tell him I'm resigning, will you stay in Corrachan? I'll help you through it.'

Indecision was written all over him. 'I don't know, Mum.' He placed the remote on the coffee table and put his head in his hands. 'I don't know.'

'You can sit your exams in May. You won't have to leave Ellie.' She was winning him over but knew she wouldn't for long. Not after the next bit. 'But, I do need to tell you something before you decide. What I have to say doesn't change how I feel about you. I love you very much and I don't want you to leave.'

'What is it?' He was fiddling with the remote again.

'Joe, I know you already think I'm an embarrassment, but I'm afraid I'm going to be even more of one from now on.'

He stopped fiddling and looked at her with a mixture of distaste and anxiety. 'Why?'

'I'm pregnant, Joe. The baby is due in July.'
Distaste triumphed. 'Pregnant? You?'
She wanted to say, Don't sound so surprised, two men wanted to sleep with me, but she didn't.
'Who's the father?'
A casual encounter with an old boyfriend could not be considered a good example. She took a deep breath. 'An old boyfriend I met up with again. It was only once.'
'Shit Mum! How could you?'
What did he mean? *How could you have sex with someone?* or *How could you be so stupid as to get pregnant?* Two questions Annie had already asked herself on more than one occasion.
'It just happened.' Who was the teenager now?
Joe turned on her, his fury evident.
'What happened to the condoms then? What happened to *no excuse for an unwanted pregnancy?*'
'It's not as simple as that. I had an IUD. It failed.'
He waved his hands in front of his face. 'Too much information! Jesus, Mum, it's revolting.' He went to the door. 'I see what's going on here! You're going to have to give up your precious job soon anyway. But don't worry, you don't have to give it up yet, because I'm going to Dad. I couldn't live here with … *you.*'

Chapter Twenty-Two

Dressed in his school uniform, Joe sat waiting for his case to be called. His top button was done up, the tie neatly tied. His mother and father sat on either side of him. No one spoke.

Tracey McDuff and her son Shawn arrived. He too was dressed in school uniform, looking the model pupil he wasn't. His neatly pressed grey trousers, specially purchased for the occasion, hid the ankle tag which monitored his movements, or lack of them, between 7 p.m. and 7 a.m. Dental treatment had not yet started, so the large gap for which Joe was responsible was evident to all. Tracey loudly informed the court official that Shawn was here to be a witness against the thug who had disfigured him. The court official explained that as Joe Cochrane intended to plead guilty, their presence was not required.

'You mean he's admitting he did it?'

The official nodded.

Tracey turned to her son in disbelief. 'You're right Shawn, he is a total wanker.' She turned back to the court official. 'If Shawn is not going to be a witness, I need a refund for these clothes I bought him. I'm on benefits. What's he going to do with clothes like that?'

'Perhaps he could wear them to school?' suggested the official.

'It's against his human rights to wear uniform.'

She pulled a packet of cigarettes and a lighter from her bag and lit up, only to be informed that smoking was not allowed.

Tracey took a deep drag and eyed the official as if he was something unpleasant she had picked up on her shoe. Still staring, she calmly offered another cigarette to Shawn and lit it for him.

'Thank God,' murmured Annie as the McDuffs sauntered towards the front door where members of the press entering the building had to fight their way through the smokescreen the pair produced.

Ten minutes after the appointed time, Joe's name was called. His parents went to sit on the public benches. Tracey and Shawn followed. Several members of the press, both local and national, were already there. Joe's guilty plea was noted and Bill Macdonald started to detail the degree of provocation and Joe's good character.

'You will see from the character references and the witness statements that Joseph Cochrane is an intelligent hard-working young man who hopes to pursue a legal career. He has never before been in trouble at school or with the police. You will also see from the statements of his school friends that he had been subject to continuous harassment over several years. On the evening of the assault his girlfriend's good character was seriously impugned. You should also have a letter in front of you from the Honourable Mrs Araminta Oliver for whom Joseph Cochrane works as a part-time gardener.'

As if on cue, Minty and May arrived. After she'd heard that Joe was going to live with his father, May had slept badly, so she wasn't ready when

Minty came to collect her that morning. Only after prayers to St Martin de Porres, the patron saint of justice, and to St Dominic Savio who was charged with interceding for juvenile delinquents, could May leave the house. Annie was shocked to see how pale she looked, how frightened she was. With bad grace, Tracey and Shawn stood up to allow Minty and May to shuffle past to sit next to Annie.

'Watch where you're putting your feet, you stupid old cow,' Shawn shouted.

Minty apologised profusely and noisily, but her not terribly surreptitious thumbs-up to Annie suggested that her ancient high heels had been worn with a particular goal in mind.

Bill Macdonald paused mid-sentence and looked to the public benches in order to draw further attention to the commotion.

'Quiet please on the public benches. Any more disturbance and you will be required to leave.' The Justice of the Peace, familiar with the McDuff family, would not tolerate any form of disorder in his court.

Minty and May sat down and Bill resumed his homily on the extenuating circumstances.

'Mrs Oliver details that he is an excellent worker, a good time keeper and that over the past few months he has confided in her about the harassment at school. The bench will see that my client is of good character and is unlikely to get in trouble again. Therefore, in light of all the extenuating circumstances, I would ask the bench to consider admonishing my client.'

Shawn was still staring at Minty in the manner

he had used many times to intimidate old ladies. Unfortunately, he had underestimated this one. Utterly expressionless, she held his gaze until Shawn was forced to look away first. And when he looked back, Minty was still staring.

Just before Bill reached the end of his speech, Shawn could stand it no longer. 'Stop looking at me, y' fuckin' old bat!'

'The complainer' was verbally abusing an old lady.

The Justice of the Peace had been considering a suspended sentence, but in light of the thug on the public benches he decided he would agree with Bill Macdonald's suggestion and limit the punishment to an admonishment. Joe Cochrane could get on with his life.

When the verdict was announced, Tracey rose to her feet and started shouting. Joe Cochrane was getting off because his mother had fixed it. There were two laws in this country, one for the Joes and another for the Shawns. She was promptly arrested, but, after being charged and released, she spent the rest of the day showing off Shawn's lack of teeth and telling members of the press that Annie Cochrane was a useless, freeloading cow.

Back at home, an hour after they'd finally left the court, Annie could hear Joe moving about upstairs as he got ready to leave. Kenny was sitting opposite her in silence, nursing a half-drunk cup of coffee. Polite conversation had dried up. This wasn't the leaving-of-the-nest that she had imagined for her son. There would be no settling him in to the university flat, worrying whether he would remember how to make macaroni cheese. Instead there was a handing over to someone she knew didn't *really* want him as a permanent resident. A succession of bumps indicated that Joe was manoeuvring a large suitcase down the stairs, so she stood up and went to help. She managed to remain calm as he arranged the contents of his room on the driveway, but she couldn't help making helpful suggestions about the best way to load the car. Kenny had always been hopeless at that.

Finally he forced the boot shut and opened the driver's door. 'Okay, Joe! Get in! We're late enough as it is.'

Annie managed to give Joe a hug. 'Text me sometimes?' she whispered into his ear. 'Good luck at your new school–'

He removed himself from his mother's embrace. As he closed the car door she heard him say, 'Okay, now for the hard bit. We need to stop by Ellie's.'

Annie waved till the car turned the corner, then she went inside, into the Joe-free house. An excruciating tiredness overwhelmed her. She needed to lie down. She paused at the top of the stairs to look into Joe's room. The bed was stripped, the duvet gone, along with all his DVDs, his computer, TV, iPod stand and speakers. A battered copy of *Dogger* – a story of loss and reunion which had been Joe's favourite when he was a little boy – was lying in the corner. A drawer was open. Annie's footsteps echoed as she walked across the room and felt the weight of the emptiness as she pushed it shut. She closed the wardrobe, empty except for a pair of elderly trainers and a skateboard, and with loss now overwhelming her she just made it to her bedroom. Joe was gone, and she couldn't help feeling that Andrew and Karen had moved away from her too.

Sitting on the edge of her bed, she considered how best to tell her mother she was to be a granny again. Two years ago May would have disapproved, but now, would she even take it in? Their roles had reversed. The mother she had known was gone and in her place was a confused old lady with an obsession with saints. And May was not the only person who needed to be told. The official announcement of her pregnancy would take place the next morning, so she could no longer put off contacting Tarik.

Annie fumbled in her pocket and found the scrap of paper on which she had noted the number from the hospital website. She stared at the phone for several minutes, then she punched in the number. A female voice told her Dr Khan was unavailable. Did she want to leave a message?

Annie opted for a tone of ingratiating friendliness. 'Thank you. If you could give him a message, that would be wonderful. It's actually a personal matter. My name is Anne Laverty and I knew him when he was a student. Our paths crossed again recently – albeit briefly. If you could tell him, I *really* need to talk to him about *our* reunion. He'll know what I mean. It really is important I speak to him as soon as possible.'

'Of course,' said the voice at the other end. 'That sounds like fun.'

'I'll give you my mobile number and my email, and if you could ask him to get in touch that

178

would be brilliant, thank you so much.'

After Annie had rung off she realised she had not asked when he would be back. She would need to make sure her mobile was to hand at all times. With some time to spare before she needed to visit her mother, she opted to hide under the duvet. Lying in the warmth, she considered her lost relationships one by one and began finally to cry. Then, just as it had the morning she had been snowed in, the baby moved – stronger and more pronounced this time. Another relationship.

Chapter Twenty-Three

The day after Joe's departure, Colin from the *Daily Scot/Sunday Saltire* stable sat with the other journalists waiting for Annie Cochrane's hastily convened press conference. He bet Lynn McKechnie from the *Daily Post* a fiver that Annie was going to resign her ministerial portfolio to spend more time with her teenage son, the one with the temper who was so free with his fists. Lynn was sceptical. Why a press conference? An email would have saved everyone a lot of time and bother.

Five minutes after the appointed time, Annie Cochrane, accompanied by Andrew Fraser and a press officer, walked into the room.

Annie tapped the mike in front of her and cleared her throat. She reminded herself that this had to sound as if it was planned and that everybody was ecstatic. Any hint otherwise would be

179

fodder for the press. Arranging her face into what she hoped was not a rictus grin, she began.

'Thank you all for coming today.' She looked round at the collection of bored faces before her. 'I have a short statement to make, then I'll take questions.' Think *happy*, she told herself. 'I am very pleased to tell you that I am expecting a baby in mid-July.' She didn't need to look up to know that she now had everyone's attention. 'I intend to remain as Health Minister and MSP for Corrachan Strathperry and Invercraig and will use the summer recess as my maternity leave. I am in good health and have the benefit of excellent antenatal care at Strathperry Infirmary. My family are all pleased and supportive.'

Annie let this lie fall from her lips. Most of the previous evening had been spent comforting a distraught May who asked repeatedly who the father was. Her mother had been unaware of Tarik's existence first time round, when his religion and skin colour would not have sent her looking for a wedding hat, and Annie saw no reason to tell her anything until she knew whether or not Tarik was going to be part of her life. He was living up to his reputation – she had heard nothing, despite a second call to his office earlier that morning, during which the now less than friendly PA assured her the message had indeed been passed on.

'I also have the support of my party colleagues.' She hoped they had all received the email sent ten minutes previously. She smiled at the journalists. 'Any questions? Within reason, of course.' She heard herself giggle nervously.

'Who's the father?'

Keep smiling. 'That is between me and him at the moment. Next?'

Colin wrote *can't tell/won't tell?* then drew several fancy question marks.

'You are presently heading up the contraception campaign. Was this a planned pregnancy?'

'I am pleased to be pregnant, Lynn, and very much looking forward to the birth of my baby.'

Colin wrote *mistake* in curly writing.

'You are going to be an older mother – do you think you have the stamina to be a government minister as well?'

'It is not unusual to have a baby in one's forties, and it is also not unusual for a mother to have a demanding job. I have not explored all childcare avenues as yet, but undoubtedly a suitable arrangement can be put in place.'

Colin added hasn't a clue how this is going to work below his efforts at calligraphy. Then he stuck his finger in the air. He had been emailed by his friend on the *Corrachan Times* that Kenny Cochrane had been seen driving his son out of town yesterday.

'You said your family is supportive?'

'That's correct.' Annie could feel the colour in her face. Look serious but not upset.

'I understand your son does not wish to live with you any longer and now lives with his father in London?'

As matter-of-factly as she could manage, Annie trotted out the prepared line. 'I don't think it is a secret that my son has recently found himself in a difficult situation. His father and I thought it would be best if he had the opportunity to make a new start. He is to attend a sixth-form college

181

in London. This decision was not related to my pregnancy.' Nearly true.

'Mr Fraser, how do you feel about this?' inquired another political hack.

'Ms Cochrane is a competent minister and constituency member. I am happy to support her in her decision to continue in these posts, both as her pregnancy progresses and, after a short period of maternity leave during the summer recess, when she recommences her duties in the autumn.'

Colin wrote *Andrew Fraser??*, then *too boring*, adding *zzzzzz* as an afterthought.

The press officer moved forward. 'Thank you ladies and gentlemen. Ms Cochrane now has to get back to work.'

Seated on Marlene Watt's office sofa, Morton Hunter filled the First Minister in on the latest political gossip.

'...and, of course, Annie Cochrane's making some kind of personal statement this morning. Do you know what that is about? Is she resigning?'

'I haven't a clue what it's about, but not resignation,' Marlene replied. 'Mr Boring has to tell me of any changes he wishes to make before they are announced. Probably be her dysfunctional son. Why are we wasting time talking about Annie? Haven't you any interesting news?'

'Why do you dislike her so much? She's not wonderful, but she's not as bad as some of ours in the cabinet.'

'She is not very bright, Morton. I would have thought that was obvious. She might have coped as a nurse, but being in charge of a government department is a different matter. Some of the things she comes out with are beyond belief. There are levels of competence and, as I think I have told you before, several times, she has been promoted beyond all hers.'

Feeling his phone vibrate, Morton fished in his jacket pocket.

'Fuck a doodle do! She's pregnant!'

'Annie?' demanded Marlene.

'Right first time!' Morton re-read the text and shook his head in disbelief. 'Well, well, well. Whoever's been inseminating her must have some kind of visual impairment. Not exactly top tottie is she?'

Marlene was jubilant.

'We've got her this time!! Pregnant and running the condom campaign?' She pointed a finger at Morton. 'Just make sure she's gone by the end of the week.' A tiny pause was followed by a slight sniff. Then came the change of tone. 'It worries me, Morton, that this news has taken you by surprise. Your eye was off the ball. Not good! Now, I suggest you try to redeem yourself by finding out who the father is.'

Looking meek but feeling anything but, Morton left her office and strolled down the corridor. He arrived at the lift just as the doors opened. One of the civil servants from Marlene's private office stepped out humming the *Bob the Builder* theme tune. Morton wished people with small children wouldn't bring banal ditties into the workplace.

Colin sat at his desk and considered the Annie Cochrane story. Everyone he had spoken to seemed surprised by the news, and no one had a suggestion as to paternity Annie was ... well not one of the MSPs he'd ever considered got up to anything much. She was too bloody sensible. Googling a pregnancy calculator told him conception must have been towards the end of October – too late for a summer holiday romance. He lodged a Freedom of Information request for Annie Cochrane's diary from mid-October till mid-November, then phoned his friend Gerry from the *Corrachan Times,* to see if he knew who was sharing the minister's bed. Gerry, however, had been about to phone Colin to ask the same question.

'Fucking immaculate conception then?' crowed Gerry. 'That'll please her good Catholic mother.'

'Isn't that a contradiction in terms, pal? Personally, I would put my money on the fucking bit rather than the immaculate bit.' Colin was pleased with this remark.

'Haha! Very clever! Seriously, have you no leads?'

'The government car service usually knows who is where they shouldn't be. I'll phone my contact.'

'Keep me in the loop, Colin. You owe me a favour for the tip-off I gave you when the gay minister came out in the pulpit.'

'If you're good, Gerry, if you're good.'

Patrick Liddell was in the car waiting to take Marlene to the Parliament when he took Colin's call.

'Don't know, but I'll ask her driver. Take it this is a financial transaction?'

'Could be, if the information leads to the answer I'm looking for.'

184

Patrick looked in his rear-view mirror. 'Got to go now. The Mantis approaches. I'll get back to you.'

'The Mantis?'

'Yes, the Mantis. Bites the male's head off after sex. You've heard the rumour about Morton Hunter, haven't you? Or Bob the Builder, as we call him around here.'

''Course I have. What about Mr Keiller, then?' asked Colin.

'I don't think he needs a helmet, do you? Speak soon.'

Colin put his phone back in his pocket and wondered if there was any way the Mantis could be made into a diary story, but he concluded not. Everyone was so scared of the woman. The nickname could be disseminated to other hacks over a pint, of course, but before he went to the pub for a bit of a laugh at the FM'S expense he had one more line of inquiry – his source at the Parliament. During a quick call he learned that Annie was friendly with Andrew Fraser, but, with him being both bereaved and boring, ruled him out as a serious contender.

Chapter Twenty-Four

Annie managed to smile her way through the rest of the week, repeatedly telling people how excited she was. In the early part of it she had told herself Tarik would contact her as soon the

185

pregnancy was public knowledge. Now she found she was making excuses for him – perhaps he didn't read the papers, perhaps he had been abroad at a conference and missed it all. The longer the silence, the more concerned she became. Surely he would call over the weekend.

After a busy week in Edinburgh, she had always relished going home to Corrachan on a Friday, but now she only had Joe's unoccupied bedroom, her mother's distress and her position as the focus of rampant gossip to look forward to. Every man of her acquaintance was a suspect. The press had been harassing her neighbours, and would have done the same to May, had not Minty taken her back to her house to stay. The coverage had been as expected – facts combined with innuendo, so that anyone with a reading comprehension age beyond eight had the impression that Annie was an over-promoted slut who should not be running a contraceptive campaign.

Morton's nocturnal army was busy with online comments. They had been told to concentrate on the following areas: Annie Cochrane doesn't know who the father is; Annie Cochrane is incompetent; Annie Cochrane may be telling children about contraceptives, but she has no idea how to use one; Annie Cochrane is so unattractive, the father must be short-sighted or desperate or both. They were having a field day.

Annie arrived home at six o'clock on the Friday evening to a dark, empty house. Minty had invited her for dinner, after which she was going to bring her mother back to stay with her for the weekend. After making up the bed in the spare

186

room she went to get changed. The choice was becoming more and more limited – she would have to give in and buy maternity clothes. Opting for an unflattering pair of tracksuit bottoms and the ubiquitous baggy jersey, she drove to Minty's via the supermarket. Annie had recently taken to doing her mother's shopping with her own and as she walked up and down the aisles, she carefully put May's things in the front compartment of the trolley. Arriving at the checkout, she put May's items – white bread, margarine, sugar, tinned peas, rice pudding, Spam, Carnation milk – between two dividers. The woman in front glanced at these goods disdainfully. This was not a healthy diet for a pregnant woman.

'For my mother,' Annie informed her. 'She likes a separate receipt.' Why couldn't she have just let it go?

The woman smiled frostily.

Annie made a show of placing the brown bread, fruit, vegetables, organic chicken, yoghurt and muesli on the conveyor belt, but the woman, engrossed in entering her pin number, paid no attention.

As Annie was loading her bags into the car, someone who had been in her class at school tapped her on the shoulder.

'Annie! Congratulations on your news! Imagine starting all over again at our age.'

Was this comment sincerely meant or did it come into the *so brave of you to wear red, so few women can carry it off* category? Annie gave her the benefit of the doubt. 'Thank you, Trisha. It *is* a bit daunting. Exciting though!' How many times had she trotted out this line over the last few days?

'I'm going to be a granny again next month,' Trisha trilled.

'How exciting for you! How many is that now?'

'This will be the third. I love it! You can give them back at the end of the day.' She put a hand to her mouth. 'Oops, shouldn't have said that to you, should I?'

Annie smiled in a *doesn't matter* sort of way and, explaining that she was late for her next appointment, managed to get into the car and shut the door.

As she let herself into Minty's unlit porch twenty minutes later, she bumped into something which fell over with an ominous thump. Minty emerged from the kitchen just as Annie located the light switch. Peering in the half light of the lowest-wattage low-energy bulb, she saw an ornate picture frame containing a portrait of a Victorian gentleman.

'Sorry, Minty, I didn't see it in the dark. Have I damaged it?'

Minty righted the painting. 'No harm done! Uncle Nathaniel and frame both intact.'

'He's a kind looking old man,' said Annie. 'He was your uncle?'

'No relation whatsoever! Mother saw him in a saleroom and was upset he had no relatives who wanted him. She bought him for next to nothing, called him Uncle Nathaniel and he hung on the wall all through my childhood.'

'Why is he in your back porch?'

'Your mother helped me get him off the wall.'

The image was frightening. Minty and her

188

mother up stepladders, manhandling a large painting off the wall, was an accident waiting to happen.

'I'm off to see my niece tomorrow. She's got a large house and she's always liked him, so I thought I would just give him to her. I'm nearly ninety you know, so I've been sorting out all my bits and bobs. That way, things go where I want them to go and the less you have, the less the tax. That's what my accountant says. Now, come away into the kitchen. I want to have a quick chat before we join May in the sitting room.'

They moved from the chilly porch to the only marginally warmer kitchen. Minty asked after Joe. Annie reported on the one short conversation she'd had in which he said everything was fine. Minty then asked about paternity.

Annie sighed. 'It turns out it's not Andrew. He had a vasectomy years ago.'

'What a pity. So no happy-ever-after there then?'

'No.'

'Is he okay about it?'

'On the surface, he's being kind and supportive, but he's hurt. Things will never be quite the same.'

'And the other party?'

'I've left messages but he's not got back to me. I only have his work number. His PA assures me she has delivered the message, so I expect he'll call over the weekend.' She could tell Minty was as unconvinced as she was.

'Well, good luck. Let me know how you get on.' Minty hesitated. 'Before we join your mother, I just wanted to let you know she's getting quite

189

forgetful – she has no memory of some things I've said to her, and this morning she thought you and Kenny were too old to be having more children. I let that one pass as she was upset yesterday that you wouldn't tell her who the father was. Just thought I should mention it.'

Annie suddenly found it hard to speak. 'She's about to be seventy-five. In fact her birthday's on Sunday. Surely she shouldn't be this muddled?'

Minty patted Annie's hand. 'I'm away next week, but when I get back, I'll keep popping in.'

'Thanks, Minty. People from the church keep an eye on her too. And the neighbours are great. At least she doesn't have Joe to worry about any more. I suppose there has to be something positive about his departure.'

Chapter Twenty-Five

As Annie and May were leaving the house the following morning, Minty drove up and parked several feet from the kerb as usual. Uncle Nathaniel was strapped into the backseat beside several cardboard boxes, one of which appeared to contain a Ming vase – the niece's inheritance was obviously generous. The collie occupied the front seat.

'Just brought a card.' Minty unearthed an envelope from the depths of her handbag and handed it to May. 'Many happy returns of tomorrow. I didn't realise it was your birthday till Annie mentioned it.'

'Thank you, Minty,' said May.

'Must get on my way now. I'm running late.' Minty zipped up her handbag. 'Should be in Yorkshire by teatime. Don't like driving in the dark now. Afraid to admit it, but the eyes are not what they were.'

'It's a very long drive,' ventured Annie.

'Don't worry, I'll be fine!' Minty was undaunted. 'Legs may not be what they were, but I can still sit on my bottom and steer. I talk to the dog if I get sleepy.'

May and Annie received a peck on the cheek, then, with only minimal grinding of the gears, Minty took off in a cloud of black smoke.

'Hope the car makes it,' Annie remarked.

Annie and May strolled down the hill to May's house. The purpose of this outing – to put May's shopping away and to allow her to get clean clothes – masked Annie's true purpose, to check if her brother had remembered to send his mother a birthday card. While May was in her bedroom, Annie sifted through the post. No American stamp. He really was the limit.

There was a knock at the back door and Annie found Bob McCafferty on the step holding a large bouquet.

'These were delivered earlier for May. It's her birthday tomorrow isn't it?'

'That's right. Mum! Come and look! Someone's sent you flowers!'

May appeared from her bedroom. 'Oh my! Who do you think they're from?'

'Why don't you look at the card?' Annie took back all uncharitable thoughts concerning her brother.

May ripped open the envelope. Her face softened. 'Oh! *Happy Birthday, Gran, Love Joe.* Isn't that lovely!'

Well, at least one of the men in May's life had done as she suggested. In fact Joe had excelled himself – Annie had simply reminded him to send a card.

'And here's a wee minding from Jean and me.' Bob handed over a small parcel and a card.

'Thank you.' May felt the parcel. 'I'll keep it till tomorrow.'

'Any more bother with the press?' asked Annie.

'Not since Thursday. I think the message got out that May wasn't here.' Bob cleared his throat and shuffled nervously. 'Jean and I offer you our congratulations on your news.' He looked down and shuffled some more. 'I hope it all goes well for you.'

'Thank you – and thank Mrs McCafferty too,' said Annie.

'I think you're old enough to call us Bob and Jean, don't you?' He was glad to move the subject on.

She tried the names out in her head. They'd been Mr and Mrs McCafferty for more than thirty years. Bob and Jean wouldn't fall easily from her lips. She would probably end up not calling them anything.

'Mum's going to stay with me for the rest of the weekend, but she will be back here on Monday. I'd be really grateful if you could continue to keep an eye,' Annie said in a low voice as May busied herself in the kitchen.

But there was nothing wrong with her mother's hearing today. 'I don't need anyone keeping an eye on *me!*' May was indignant. 'Do you think I'm losing the place or something?'

Chapter Twenty-Six

Alfred William Bigswell was a soldier in Morton's secret army. Despite his Victorian-sounding name, he was a twenty-year-old politics student recruited, following a fascinating summer internship in Morton's constituency office, to post on-line comments to newspaper articles. Ally, as he preferred to be known, was told it was top-secret work and that he was to tell no one. He worked three nights a week from 11 p.m. till 6 a.m., using several aliases per newspaper. His shift rotas appeared in an unsigned email from a hotmail address, and for his efforts he received £150 per week, with a discretionary bonus for effectiveness, defined as being as unpleasant as possible without pushing things so far that the post was removed by the site moderator. Ally enjoyed the clandestine nature of his work for the party.

During the early hours of Sunday morning, he created a rolling dialogue between his aliases.

Johnnyvoxpop was surprised that Ms Cochrane had found the time to take a lover, considering the shameful state of the health service. She

193

should have kept her attention on the job. Now it was her duty to resign and allow someone from Marlene Watt's party to take over her role. *Army-vet* had replied that no wonder no father had come forward – no one would want to be associated with such a failure. She should resign completely and her constituency could then elect somebody who put the community before self. Ally then produced what he thought was a subtle but devastating reply from *jennygeddes* – *I think you gentlemen are forgetting it is a woman's right to choose when she has her children and whether or not she keeps working. One can only assume that Ms Cochrane has chosen to get pregnant, chosen to keep working and chosen to keep the father's identity secret. You surely can't believe that a champion of contraception for the under-sixteens would get pregnant by mistake and not know the father's identity?*

Pleased with the exchange, Ally clicked onto a new paper and brought to life *bartonbob*, hardworking law-abiding Edinburgh resident; *mothers carer*, a lonely spinster; and *scalesofjustice*, a disaffected member of the legal profession.

Chapter Twenty-Seven

Following the previous Sunday's unsuccessful gastronomic venture, Annie prepared a birthday lunch of acceptable favourites – melon, roast chicken with all the trimmings, and a peach melba made with tinned peaches – all of which May ate with gusto. When she had finished the washing-up, Annie took two cups of tea to the living room where she found her mother holding a package.

'I know it's *my* birthday, Annie, but this is a present for you. I bought it on the internet. I'm really getting the hang of sailing now.'

Annie took the parcel. 'Thank you. And I think you mean surfing. Surfing the internet?'

'That's what I said! Go on, open it!'

Annie removed the wrapping. The box was labelled *St Gerard Pregnancy and Motherhood Collection*. What on earth was this? She struggled for something positive to say before settling for, 'Thank you, Mum.'

'He's the patron saint of pregnancy. It's got everything you need!'

Annie doubted it contained a letter from Tarik promising to be hers for ever more.

'Go on. Open it up!'

Annie tipped the contents onto the table. She picked up the small plastic statue of the saint holding a cross, a Bible and a bunch of flowers. His upturned eyes suggested he was approaching a climax of some kind and the bunch of flowers just made him look camp. Annie knew she mustn't laugh. Placing him carefully on the mantelpiece, she repeated what she had said before. 'Thank you, Mum.'

'There's more!' May pointed at a medal, a prayer card and a leaflet outlining why Gerard had patronage of pregnancy. 'You can keep the medal in your handbag.'

Annie dutifully zipped it into one of the pockets in her bag. The rest she put back in the box. 'I'll read all the bits later.'

'You do like it don't you?' May sounded suddenly apprehensive.

'Yes, Mum.' Annie gave her mother a hug. 'Thank you.'

Annie passed the afternoon working through her constituency correspondence while May, sporting the new cardigan Annie had given her, dozed on the sofa. By four o'clock Annie was beginning to hope for a call from her brother in Seattle. She had reminded him again both by text and email the previous evening, but he was never an early riser so she would allow him a bit longer before getting properly annoyed. One thing was for certain, he would not be going to Mass.

May woke up with a start. 'Was I snoring?' She picked up the TV guide and began leafing through it. 'What time is it with John?'

'It's still early. You know he's always slow in the morning. He'll phone soon.'

May put down the magazine and looked at Annie. 'So, are you going to tell me what you are going to do about this baby? Is Kenny going to be here more often ... not rushing off on business? He needs to face up to his responsibilities.'

Annie put down the letter she was reading and sat beside May on the sofa. 'Mum, it's not Kenny's baby. We're divorced, remember.'

May hesitated, then things seemed to click into place. ''Course I know you're divorced! Do you think I would forget something like that?' She paused. 'So who did you say the father was?'

'I didn't tell you who it was, Mum. I will, I

promise you, but I have to speak to him about it first. I'll explain it all soon, but there are too many unanswered questions at the moment.'

'Just the one unanswered question, if you ask me. Do you know the answer?' The old May was back with a vengeance.

'Yes, Mum. I do.'

They settled back to their activities – Annie to her paperwork, and waiting for a message from Tarik, and May to *Songs of Praise* and waiting for John to call.

It was seven o'clock before the phone rang. May reached it first. From the one-sided conversation, Annie realised it wasn't her brother. It was her son. She hovered at her mother's side, waiting for a chance to speak.

'Just a minute, your Mum wants a word...'

Annie held out her hand for the receiver.

May continued, 'Okay. I'll tell her. Bye.' She put the phone down. 'He's just rushing out somewhere. Says he'll speak to you another time. It was me he wanted to speak to, anyway.' The one-upmanship was obvious. 'He was only phoning you to see if I was okay because I wasn't in when he called my house. Such a thoughtful boy.'

Failure and rejection swept over Annie. She sat down and, for the millionth time, checked her BlackBerry before returning to her briefing document. By nine, neither she nor May had received the call they were waiting for. Annie was powerless regarding Tarik, but her brother was another matter.

Telling May she was going to make tea, she went to the kitchen and texted him again. She was pouring some milk in a small jug, her mother's standards being higher than her own, when her phone buzzed. The text said *oops!* and the house phone began to ring. This time Annie got to it first.

'John! Great to hear from you! Mum's been wondering all day if you were going to call. I'll just put you on to her. Don't ring off when you're finished, I want to speak to you.' She handed her mother the receiver and listened to the conversation.

'John! You shouldn't be spending your money on me! You should be treating yourselves to something. How are ... Marie and the ... sorry Mariana. How are Mariana and the children? Are they there? Will they come and speak to their gran?... At a baseball match? They must be getting so big now. Ritchie must be going to join...' May searched for the name, '...his sister at school soon? ... Twelve and fourteen? Where does the time go? Tell them I was asking for them. Thank you for finding the time to phone. I know you're busy, but it means a lot to me... Oh, did you get the thing for your computer, so I can see you?... Okay, well let me know when you have it... Yes, Annie's here, I'll let you speak to her. Bye bye! Bye bye.'

Her boy had phoned. With a look of pure joy, May handed Annie the receiver.

'Hi,' said Annie.

'What's up with Mum? She thinks Ritchie and Sonia are still little kids. Is she losing it?'

'Yes!' Annie walked towards the kitchen. 'I think that about sums it up. Any chance of you visiting this summer...?' she moved right into the kitchen so her mother definitely couldn't hear

198

'...while she still remembers who you are? She would love to see you all and you would be able to see your new niece or nephew. That was the other piece of news I was going to tell you.'

May was still somewhere up near the ceiling when Annie took the tea tray into the living room.

'John's sending me a present – says I'll get it in a day or two. He shouldn't have done that – waste his money on me.' She took a sip of her tea but decided it was too hot and set it down again. 'He can't do the picture thing yet. Said his computer is old and he needs a spider camera.'

'Webcam.' Annie wondered why she felt compelled to correct her mother all the time.

'Whatever it's called, he hasn't got it yet, but when he has I'll be able to see him and...' she paused. 'I've forgotten their names again...'

'Ritchie and Sonia.'

'Yes, Ritchie and Sonia, and they can show me what they're getting up to. This modern technology's wonderful isn't it? Mobile phones, emails and spiders' webs. There's no excuse for not keeping in touch.'

Chapter Twenty-Eight

The cuttings from the Sunday papers were waiting on Annie's desk that Monday morning. She leafed through them, astonished at the creativity. Journalists had attributed motives, opinions and aspirations which were not, nor ever likely to be, hers; there were letters to the editor about irresponsibility and the impossibility of combining such an important job with motherhood; some of the tabloids speculated that the father must be some high-profile married man whose identity Annie was desperately trying to conceal. She dumped the lot in the bin and reached for the pile of snail mail. A pink envelope marked PERSONAL was at the top. It contained a card with the words *CONGRATULATIONS* in curly writing above a bunch of balloons. The message inside was from Tarik.

Dear Annie,

Sorry not to be there when you rang. Was really pleased to read about your news! You'll get great antenatal care at the Strathperry Infirmary. (The consultant is a friend of mine – do mention my name.) Your message said something about a reunion? What reunion? Let me know the date and I'll do my best to be there. It'll be good to catch up with the old crowd again. Take care of yourself.

Tarik x

Annie re-read it three times with increasing disbelief and anger. Did he take her for some kind of idiot? She had used her maiden name and made it perfectly clear with the words *our reunion* what she had been referring to. Or was he the idiot? If this was a genuine mistake, it was time to put him right; and if he was, yet again, attempting to dump her, he certainly wasn't going to get away with it this time. After checking her office door was firmly closed, she dialled his office and announced herself as Annie Cochrane, Minister for Health.

The now obsequiously helpful PA told her that Dr Khan was on leave. 'In fact she added with girlish glee, 'he won't be back for three weeks. He's getting married tomorrow and then he'll be on honeymoon. Can I get one of his colleagues to help you?'

Annie felt as if she had been hit by a truck. Muttering, 'It can wait,' she replaced the receiver and stared at the wall. This explained the unwillingness to talk to her. She picked up the card and ripped it in two before putting it in her handbag. This was not for the office wastebin.

She rested her head on the desk for a few moments, willing herself not to cry. Then she sat back in her chair and took three deep breaths.

Yet again, Tarik had resorted to a letter. The man was beneath contempt. Why had she ever thought he might turn into an attentive father? He could get stuffed. She would manage on her own. Karen was right – once a bastard, always a bastard! And whoever the bride was, she was welcome to him.

Chapter Twenty-Nine

During the first week in March, while Patrick was learning to be a bodyguard, Eoin was temporarily promoted to drive the First Minister. It was a chance to drive the Lexus, but Eoin was not happy. Unlike Annie, who treated him as a colleague, Marlene treated him like a minion with limited intelligence. He had been back and forth along the motorway between Edinburgh and Glasgow more times than he could remember, including an extra trip to Marlene's home to pick up 'a very important document' that had been 'forgotten'. On collecting what felt like an empty envelope, he realised he was also expected to take Jordan, Stephanie and Vina back to Edinburgh.

Stephanie sat in the front, at first waving to anyone she knew, then inserting and ejecting CDs until Eoin thought he might hit her. His glances in the rear-view mirror confirmed what Patrick had told him – the relationship of the couple in the backseat was far more than that of au-pair and her charge.

After decanting his passengers, he set off to the car depot. He was nearly there when he remembered that the 'important document' was still in the glove compartment. He made a swift U-turn and drove back to the FM'S residence. He had to wait in the hall of Bute House for several minutes before Marlene appeared.

'What's this?' she asked.

'The important document you told me to collect from your house.' Eoin kept his tone and expression neutral.

There was a brief pause before Marlene rallied. 'So it is! Thank you.' She knew the little man's name was odd, but for the life of her she couldn't remember what it was. 'What's your name again?'

'Eoin. Spelt E-O-I-N. It's the Orcadian version of Ian.'

Too much information. 'E-O-I-N, how un-usual. Now Eoin, before you finish, go to the Taj Mahal and collect a takeaway. You don't need money, they bill me. And by the way, you left earlier without checking whether I required you for anything else. Don't do that again.'

Thursday had involved a day trip to Inverness to announce extra funding for green energy projects. The A9 was unexpectedly traffic-free, and by six o'clock they were less than an hour from Edin-burgh. The accompanying civil servant was dozing in the front seat while, in the back, Mar-lene was working on papers. Hopeful of getting home an hour earlier than scheduled, Eoin switched on cruise control and sat back. Nice car, shame about its backseat passenger.

As they approached the Forth Bridge, Eoin heard Marlene close her briefcase and pick up the car-phone. Good. At least she wasn't going to chat to him.

'Vina! It's Ms Watt here.' Marlene spoke slowly and loudly, waking the dozing civil servant who rolled his eyes at Eoin. 'Is Robert there?... Well, could you go out to the aviary and get him ... *aviary* ... the place where he keeps the budgeri-gars, that's right. I'll speak to Jordan or Stephanie in the meantime...' Her voice softened. 'Hello Stephie, have you had a good day?... What do you mean, you've not got any clean clothes? What has Vina been doing? I'll sort that for you, darling. Have you had your tea yet?... No, of course you don't have to eat something if you don't like it. Tell Daddy to make you something else. Now, is

Jordan there?' By the time she had finished assuring Jordan he could do as he wished and berating Robert for not being in control of matters domestic, they were on the outskirts of Edinburgh. She hung up and, with ten minutes to go, decided she would be chatty.

'Eoin?'

'First Minister...'

'Did you say yesterday that yours was an Orkney name?'

'That's right, I lived there till I was ten. Still got lots of relations on the islands.'

'My grandfather came from Orkney, but I have no relatives there now.'

I wouldn't be too sure about that, Eoin thought. He said, 'What part of Orkney did he come from?'

'I'm not certain...' Marlene waved her hand vaguely. 'He used to talk about a ruined palace and an island with a causeway.'

'Birsay?'

'Perhaps.' She sounded doubtful. 'I'm really not very interested. Only been there once, tidal energy or something like that. It was so windy, I couldn't stand upright. End of the world, if you ask me.'

It's home, if you ask me, thought Eoin, but Marlene had already moved on to item number two in her repertoire of small talk to her subjects.

'Any predictions for the Scottish Cup?'

Chapter Thirty

With some difficulty, Annie had managed to arrange her antenatal appointment for 4 p.m. on a Friday, allowing her to do a morning's work in Edinburgh. She was late leaving her office, though, and there was not enough time to go home first. By some fancy driving, Eoin, now back in his rightful place behind the wheel of the Volvo, managed to deliver her, complete with suitcase and official briefcase, to Strathperry Infirmary a mere five minutes late. The receptionist told her to take a seat.

Several women in the waiting area, the extent of their pregnancies varying from the svelte but nauseous to those at bursting point, looked up, vaguely recognising her. Annie cast a smile around the room before sitting down and checking that her urine sample was in her bag. A snotty-nosed toddler was alternating between throwing crisps into the air and running from one side of the room to the other. No one seemed to own him. She began to leaf through the pages of a magazine, pausing at a feature on how best to dress for your body shape. Unsurprisingly, there was no style option for fat and pregnant. She placed the magazine back on the table and lifted her briefcase out of range of the child, who was now having a tantrum because his crisp packet was empty. Out of the corner of her eye Annie saw someone grabbing hold of him. Good. Perhaps he would now shut up.

'Caleb! Are you wanting a smack?'

The voice was familiar. Oh God – Tracey Mc-Duff, up the duff again. This must be number four, surely. Was there a new 'uncle' in residence or had Tracey been out on the town again with a bottle of vodka inside her? Annie's inner-self heard the voice of her mother, the voice of the old May, *People who live in glass houses...* A nurse appeared.

'Anne Cochrane? Could you come with me please?'

Trundling her suitcase behind her like an ageing flight attendant, Annie started to follow the nurse.

Tracey got to her feet. 'Hey! We were all here before her! She only arrived five minutes ago.'

Waves of communal hostility wafted in Annie's direction.

'As the other ladies were here before me, they should go first.' Annie trundled the suitcase back to the waiting area and sat down. The hostility ebbed. The nurse disappeared for a moment or two before re-appearing. 'It *is* your turn, Mrs Cochrane. You're to see the consultant.'

Annie smiled sheepishly. 'Sorry! Looks like I've been summoned.' As she made her escape, she could hear Tracey again.

'I've never seen the consultant yet and this is my fourth! Just because she's a politician, she thinks she's better than the rest of us! It's a divided service, you know. She gets the consultant while the rest of us get stuck with the ones who can't speak English.'

Three-quarters of an hour later, Annie was standing outside the hospital, waiting for the Corrachan bus. She took the photo of the scan from her pocket and looked at it again. How could she ever have pictured it as a time bomb? She had refused when they asked if she wanted to know the sex. Now she peered at it, looking for signs, but the whole thing looked more like the map of a hurricane brewing mid-Atlantic than a baby. The consultant obstetrician, after taking the necessary details, had examined her, enquiring tentatively whether she had a partner who wished to be involved in the birth plan. Presumably he disapproved of her reply and had decided to punish her, albeit politely: having the health minister lying with her abdomen exposed was too good an opportunity to miss and Annie had been treated to a lecture on the funding shortfall faced by this and other hospitals. Justifying the government's spending priorities while flat on one's back is not easy. After she was dressed again, he launched into small talk.

'I understand you know my friend, Tarik Khan?'

'Yes, that's right.' Would that she didn't.

'He told me to take special care of you.'

Annie stood up. 'That was kind of him.' She started to put her coat on. 'We were good friends when he was a student. Unfortunately, our paths have only crossed once in recent times.' She did up the buttons. 'I hear he's just got married again.'

'That's right. Julia's a lawyer. A high flyer, only twenty-eight, but definitely one to watch – in more ways than one!'

'Have they been together long?'

'A couple of years. It was a lovely wedding. My wife and I were there.'

Annie smiled. 'I'm sure they'll be very happy.' She bent down to pick up her handbag. 'They sound as if they're well matched.'

Twenty minutes later there was still no sign of the Corrachan bus. Another lady joined the queue and introduced herself as May's friend Phyllis. Unfortunately Phyllis had just been told she had to wait several months for her hip replacement so she was keen to detail what she thought the government ought to be doing about waiting times.

Annie's phone rang. 'Excuse me a moment, Mrs Caldwell. Hello, Mum...'

The extent of May's excitement made it difficult to make out what she was saying but evidently John's present had arrived and help had been needed from Bob McCafferty to get it into the house.

'What on earth is it?' Annie was intrigued. Flamboyant gestures and her brother did not normally go together.

'I'll not spoil the surprise! You have to come and see. It must have cost a fortune.'

'I'm waiting for the bus at the infirmary at the moment. I'll come in on my way home.' Phyllis was making waving and mouthing greetings. 'Mrs Caldwell's here and she says hello.'

'Tell her to come too.'

It was forty minutes later when Annie let Phyllis in May's front door to be confronted by vast quantities of bubble wrap and several pieces of wood. She opened the living room door and stopped dead.

'Oh ... my ... God!'

Phyllis cannoned into Annie. 'Oh goodness!'

'Isn't it wonderful?' May moved towards the gift, beaming.

'It's huge!' Annie couldn't believe what she was seeing.

'I never thought I would own one like that. John is so thoughtful.'

Annie looked at the six-foot Madonna with painted pink face and blue and white robes, standing beside the table with her hands outstretched. She looked like an escapee from a nativity play who was now working as a part-time waitress. Words deserted her.

May, on the other hand, had plenty to say. 'It's Our Lady of Lourdes! Must have cost John a fortune! It's come all the way from America. It said Air Freight on the box.'

'It's very ... nice,' said Phyllis.

Annie raised her eyebrows at her and turned back to her mother. 'Why couldn't he have sent you one to go on the mantelpiece with the others?' What was John thinking of? She was livid for so many reasons. Well, *he* might be prepared to pander to their mother's delusions, but she wasn't taking this lying down.

'Can I phone John, to say thank you?' May looked at the wall clock above the Madonna's left shoulder. 'What time is it with him?'

'About ten in the morning in Seattle,' Annie replied. 'And yes, by all means phone. I'm very keen to talk to him too.'

'Can you dial it? I get all the numbers wrong.'

Her brother's cellphone was answered immediately. 'Hi Annie. What's the matter? Mum all right?'

'She's more than all right! Your gift has arrived!'

'Great! I hope she likes it.'

'Oh, she loves it! We're all overwhelmed at your generosity here.'

'Don't be so sour, Annie! Can't I send my mother something special for her birthday?'

Annie glanced at May who was showing off the finer points of the statue's garments to a still-startled Phyllis. Moving into the hall, she continued, 'What on earth possessed you to order something so enormous. It takes up the whole of the living room. It was designed to be on show in a cathedral, not in a little house in Corrachan.'

'You are making an incredible fuss about a bunch of flowers.' John was getting tetchy now.

'Flowers?'

'Yes, I ordered a deluxe bunch of flowers express delivery from the Channel Islands.'

'Flowers? Not a six-foot statue of Our Lady of Lourdes?'

'Don't be ridiculous. Look, I'm late for a meeting. Tell Mum I'll phone soon.'

Annie finally located the invoice among the packaging. It had been shipped from Sacred Artefacts Inc, Kansas, and the statue had cost a mind-boggling $2,300 plus $400 for express international shipping. There was another reference number with the words *temporarily out of stock, expect to ship within 2 weeks*. Oh God! There

210

was more to come!

She made an immediate international call, explaining that Our Lady of Lourdes had arrived in error at her elderly mother's house. The despatch address on the order was checked – 12 Hillside Avenue, Corrachan, Scotland. The postcode was correct and the billing address on the credit card was the same. The card used belonged to an M. Laverty. The lady in Kansas kindly spelled it out.

'I particularly remember this order, Ma'am, because we rarely ship outside the US.'

Annie was indignant. 'My mother doesn't have a credit card! This must be a fraud of some sort.'

'Pardon me, Ma'am, but if it was fraudulent, it would hardly have been delivered to her address.'

Annie turned to May. 'They're trying to tell me you have a credit card!'

May nodded eagerly and fumbled in her handbag. 'I have. Minty got me to fill in a form. Here it is.' She handed Annie a Visa card.

'Okay. It appears that she has got a credit card, and that she has used it...'

'Yes, Ma'am,' said the lady in Kansas.

Annie tried to cancel the second part of the order but she was told that it was already winging its way across the Atlantic. 'Could you tell me what it is?' she asked faintly.

'Just one moment, Ma'am.' There was some frantic keyboard tapping in Kansas. 'Yes. Here we are. It's a full-colour statue of the Holy Family.'

Jesus, Mary and Joseph! 'And how big is that?' Annie dreaded what was coming next.

'Eight feet high and six feet wide, Ma'am.'

Even bigger than this one. Annie swallowed.

'And the damage?'

'Pardon me, Ma'am?

'What did it cost?'

'This is a popular item on the lead up to the Christmastide, but doesn't sell so well in the first quarter. We just re-stocked, Ma'am, and it's on Lenten offer with a 15 per cent discount. A genuine bargain at $3,400, plus shipping.'

'Plus shipping.' Annie's voice was now a whisper. '$400 too?'

'No, Ma'am, this was bigger and heavier, so shipping was $600.'

Returns had to be received within twenty-one days of despatch, shipping to be arranged and paid for by the purchaser. There were only five days left on Our Lady. As Annie rang off, the Kansas lady instructed her, 'You have a nice day, now!'

May was adamant she had not ordered anything from America. It was those hoodlums again, using her card to play an expensive practical joke. But Phyllis, still clutching her bag in front of her like a hot water bottle, suddenly raised her finger, as if she'd seen some sort of light.

'Remember, a couple of weeks ago, on the way to the tea dance, you told me you had ordered some special statues on that world wide web of yours?'

May looked blank. 'Did I?'

Annie was already Googling. A glance at the Sacred Artefacts website jogged May's memory. She had thought £23 plus £4 shipping was quite reasonable for a six-inch high statue.

In the early hours of the following morning, Annie lay hoping the Holy Family was enjoying the in-flight entertainment. She had worked out that returning the statues would be as expensive as keeping them. Perhaps there was a market for religious statues on eBay? She went downstairs and switched on her laptop. It seemed that there was – but only for little ones. She looked at St Gerard on the mantelpiece and told him he'd better behave or she would auction him off. After pouring herself a glass of milk, a drink she used to hate, she sat at the kitchen table nibbling a ginger snap. Our Lady was giving May so much pleasure, it would be unkind to make her get rid of it, but the enormous Holy Family was another matter. Annie had cut the credit card in two and put it in her handbag to prevent any further on-line purchases, but her mother had been in possession of a computer and credit card for several weeks. What else had she bought?

A look at May's emails the following morning provided some answers, starting with an outstanding order for St Bernadette.

'Just the one,' said May with singular lack of conviction.

Annie rang an Irish number to cancel, but she was too late. Bernadette was already on her way. Fortunately, she was only three feet high and cost a mere €75.

There were also emails from several other organisations; one thanked her for her inquiry about a Caribbean cruise; another told her when

213

the salesman would call to discuss her new kitchen; a follow-up to that said they were sorry that she hadn't been at home when he called, and could she contact them about another appointment. There was correspondence in connection with a quote for double glazing, and confirmation that she had bid successfully on eBay for a bed which could lift and tilt in numerous directions. Annie remembered the sort of thing from her days on the ward. They used to joke that if people weren't careful they would turn into a sandwich filling, left toes to nose. There were also several emails demanding immediate payment for this masterpiece of orthopaedic engineering.

When questioned, May vaguely remembered someone visiting about new windows, but she had no recollection of anything to do with a kitchen or a bed. Several more telephone calls and abject apologies later, Annie began to open the large stack of mail she had found in the sideboard beside May's best tea set, the one she never used. There were letters from the bank regarding May's unauthorised overdraft, something the old May would never have allowed. There were final demands for payment of electricity and gas bills. And there was the credit card statement.

Annie stared at it in shock. In the last month alone, May had spent nearly £5,000 on saints and other sundries. It was obvious that her mother, who had always mended things, budgeted, saved and dealt with financial issues as they arose, was no longer coping. As Annie opened the cupboard under the sink to put the envelopes in the bin, she saw three ten-pound notes tucked under a bottle of bleach. Not stolen by the hoodlums, then. In the sink was a charred saucepan.

Annie had to face facts. She took the money to May, who was in the living room, gazing fondly at the Madonna.

'Look what I found in the cupboard under the sink.'

May turned. 'Money? How did that get there?'

'I think it's the £30 you lost a few weeks ago.'

'I haven't lost any money. I'm much too careful for that. What are you talking about?'

Annie sat on a footstool facing her mother. 'We need to have a talk.'

'What about?' May was defensive.

'About these things you've been doing and not remembering, about all these bills you haven't been paying.'

'I'm just a wee bit forgetful, that's all.' May looked away.

Annie took her hand. 'Mum, it's more than a *wee bit forgetful*, isn't it?... Isn't it?'

Her mother's belligerent expression changed to fear and bewilderment. 'It's like going into a thick fog, Annie. Sometimes I can't remember what I'm doing or where I'm supposed to be going.' There were tears in her eyes. 'It's awful, I nearly threw your father's photo away last week. I thought, who is this man? It isn't anyone I know. I had taken it out of the frame, then Jean popped in for a chat and told me it was your father. I was married to him for forty-five years and I didn't know him! How can that be?' May seemed to shrink in her chair. She blew her nose and wiped her eyes.

Annie squeezed her hand.

'Then sometimes I come out of the fog and it's okay. Sometimes it's just a bit misty and I'm only a wee bit forgetful.' She dabbed her eyes again. 'Things don't always make sense.'

Annie leant forward and gave her a hug. 'Perhaps I should make an appointment to see the doctor. Get you checked out?'

'Am I going doolally?'

'I don't know, Mum, but I think you should see the doctor.'

'I know I do silly things sometimes.'

'What sort of things?'

'Well, yesterday, I must have put a potato on to boil for my dinner, then I went to the town. Jean was hanging out her washing and heard the smoke alarm.'

'You could have burnt the house down!'

'I know, Annie. I know. And I think I went to visit Bob and Jean very early this morning.'

'How early?'

'Jean said it was only six o'clock.' The lost bewildered look was there again. 'I thought it was time for elevenses.' She paused. 'Can you make that appointment?'

'Of course I can.'

'Annie?' The voice was quiet and fearful. 'You remember how your granny went?'

Chapter Thirty-One

Ally Bigswell was not usually the sort of student who spent hours propping up the bar at the Union. He lived at home, earned well as one of Morton's online zealots, and saw no need to socialise with his fellow students. He had chosen to spend his Saturday attending an all-day seminar on *The Role of the Third Reich in Determining the Present Day Political Situation in the Balkan States,* an area of study round which he hoped to do his honours dissertation. Afterwards, a lecturer invited him and some other students for a drink and Ally decided to make an exception and go along.

After four pints of premium lager – three and a half pints more than he was used to – he returned home in unusually high spirits to start his night's work in front of his computer. He smiled as he scrolled down the emerging threads. The *Sunday Clarion's* story about Annie Cochrane queue-jumping was a gift, but, unfortunately for Ally, he had left his judgement in the pub. He logged on as *Babyjane,* a persona who specialised in complaining that life wasn't fair, and began to type.

She said she was coming and of course they all jumped. Fat cow needs to be noticed – as if you could miss her, the size she is now.

He then typed:

Who do you think she's been forming a coalition

with? Her colleagues are all w@nkers Can only cope with a blow-up doll.

There were a couple of swift responses. Ally then typed:

That MP used her flat to shag the student last year? She should be doing something for the poor sods in hospital.

He continued to work in a similar vein through the early hours. When he finally logged off he headed for bed, proud of a good night's work.

On Sunday afternoon, Andrew was at home in his constituency, staring at the computer screen. He was supposed to be making amendments to his party conference speech but his mind was elsewhere. Today was Mother's Day, a reminder of what he couldn't help but think of as Annie's betrayal. There was still an uneasy friendship, but unspoken hurt on his part and embarrassment on Annie's made their meetings difficult.

Against his better judgement, he clicked onto the *Sunday Clarion* website. HEALTH MINIS- TER GETS PREFERENTIAL TREATMENT shrieked the headline. Someone called Tracey McDuff was complaining that Annie had arrived late for an antenatal visit, then been taken ahead of the queue. The name was familiar. Wasn't it a McDuff at the root of Joe's problems? Ms Mc- Duff was quoted extensively and the article con- cluded with a bland statement from the hospital saying that no queue-jumping had occurred.

But the damage was done. Andrew scrolled down the page and was gratified to see that, for once, the moderator of the online comments had

218

been doing his job. Every second comment, from someone called *Babyjane,* had been removed as unsuitable, making the responses incomprehensible. What on earth had *Babyjane* said? It must have been poisonous, and, judging by the number of posts removed, relentless. He wondered if Annie's press officer had contacted her. In the past he would have had no hesitation in phoning her up to commiserate, but now he hesitated.

It wasn't that there was antagonism between them. The previous Wednesday, Andrew had found Annie still in her office at eight o'clock and cajoled her into joining him for a meal. After she had brought him up to date with Joe's move to London and her mother's increasingly bizarre behaviour, she had eventually managed to tell him that Tarik would not be a regular part of the baby's life after all. He was newly married, she said, so that was that. Andrew was horrified to discover she had not spoken to Tarik, had no intention of doing so, and did not intend to ask for financial support.

'The child will ask, Annie. They'll surely want a father's name on the birth certificate? There is also the issue of ethnicity. If this child has darker skin than you, people will want to know why.'

But Annie was adamant. 'I contacted him and he gave me the brush off. I'm not going to demean myself by trying again. This child will be like many others. No such thing as a bastard in a devolved Scotland – we did away with that in the parliament's first term, remember.'

Andrew heard the bravado but saw how drawn she looked. 'Well, you've still got a few months, but I do think you should contact him again,' he said gently.

Annie smiled wearily. 'Okay, boss, I'll think about it.'

They had gone on to talk about Marlene's recent hostility.

'I keep wondering what you've done to offend her, Annie. These last few weeks, she's been particularly unpleasant to you. She's never been warm or generous to anybody, as far as I know, but you seem to be getting the edge of her tongue more than most these days.'

'I haven't a clue. I think it started about the time Joe landed his right hook, or whatever he did that evening.'

'Perhaps she sees you as competition.'

Annie nearly choked on her ice-cream. 'Hardly, Andrew!'

But he was more measured. 'You don't knock a political opponent unless they pose a threat. Everybody knows that.'

Annie was grateful for the gentle compliment, but she wasn't prepared to pursue Andrew's theory. 'Well, whatever her problem is, I wish she'd go back to ignoring me like she used to do.'

Andrew decided against telling her about his most recent meeting with Marlene. She had been full of *far be it from me to tell you what to do* and *of course it's your call* phrases, but her message was clear. She was angry about the bad publicity and press ridicule and she wanted Annie replaced.

After paying the bill, Andrew escorted Annie to her flat where he collected some notes she had made for inclusion in his speech. Then he walked

220

home, mulling over the situation in which he found himself. The writing was on the wall. He had to move forward and if it wasn't going to be with Annie, then he needed to look elsewhere.

Now, several days later, he hadn't moved forward at all. He knew he had no right to feel jealous or slighted by her fling with Tarik – but he did. He'd been so cheered by Annie's company, and her quiet enthusiasm for their relationship. He'd allowed his imagination to go into orbit as far as their future was concerned. It had all seemed so positive, after the ghastliness of losing Jane.

Andrew made another vain attempt to concentrate on his speech, but gave up after a few sentences and gazed out of the window at his now overgrown garden. It had always been Jane's preserve. He should find a gardener before the summer. It was Annie who had shown him there could be a life after Jane, but how was he to achieve it? He was lonely. He'd enjoyed being married and he wanted to be married again. He went through the single women of his acquaintance. Perhaps Pam, a widow he had met at his niece's wedding recently, might be a possibility. He had to admit the prospect didn't fill him full of joy, but you never knew. She had certainly seemed interested in him.

He returned to his speech, knowing it had to be completed before the end of the day. Would anybody even notice if he repeated last year's version?

Like Andrew, Annie was not enjoying Mother's Day. Her press officer had rung that morning to warn her about Tracey McDuff's accusations in the newspaper. A rebuttal had been issued and a complaint sent that they had not asked Annie for comment before publication. The article made her first angry, then weepy.

She and May ate lunch together, carefully making conversation about anything but Joe, babies, forgetfulness or over-sized saints. Annie had presented her mother with a box of Milk Tray and a card. She had originally intended to buy flowers, but John's Channel Island Luxury Spring Bouquet, delivered the day before, outclassed anything she could afford. It had been placed on the table beside Our Lady who now looked as if she was giving a flower-arranging demonstration.

There was no card for Annie from Joe.

By the time they got to dessert, conversation had dried up. Annie chewed her way through her apple pie, silently recalling past homemade cards and presents while her mother rehearsed to herself what she had to remember for the doctor's appointment the following day. Suddenly May perked up

'John might ring.'

Her hopeful face almost reduced Annie to more tears. Not a chance, she thought. Apart from anything else, Annie hadn't prompted him. She went to the kitchen to put the kettle on and sent him a text – too bad if it woke him up in the middle of the night.

After a cup of tea under St Gerard's watchful eye, Annie accompanied May home. She said she wanted some fresh air, but in reality, she wanted to check that all was well in her mother's house. The statue in the living room still made her jump. She looked around. A half-burnt candle sat on a saucer and there were drops of wax everywhere.

'Mum, I don't think you should be burning candles,' she called.

'Why not?' May came through from her bedroom, brandishing a slipper.

'Because it's not safe. What if you forgot about it and went for a walk?'

'You're trying to dictate what I can and can't do in my own house?'

It was like dealing with an adolescent. 'I just want you to be safe.'

'You just want to interfere! You always were one for minding other people's business, now you're conspiring with Bob to stop me practising my religion.' She waved the slipper threateningly in Annie's face.

'I am not! And what has Bob got to do with this?'

May froze, she couldn't remember exactly, although it had something to do with the candle. Anger, frustration, but most of all fear, took hold of her.

The first blow to her upper arm took Annie by surprise, but she managed to deflect the second by grabbing the navy blue velour weapon.

'Mum! Stop this! Don't be silly!' She gently pulled her mother towards her and hugged her until she could feel the tension ebbing away. 'No one is trying to make you do anything. You know you've been forgetful recently. Neither Bob nor I want you to come to harm.'

Annie settled her mother in her chair and flicked

through the TV channels. She found *Breakfast at Tiffany's* and suggested that May watch for a while.

'Oh, I remember this one. I went to see it with your father –1961, it was – the first time he took me to the pictures. He was home on leave – so handsome in his uniform.' She looked towards the photo on the mantelpiece. 'He was one of the last to do national service.' She turned her attention back to the film. 'Your father used to say I looked just like Audrey Hepburn.'

Annie opened the chocolates and left the box on the coffee table. After a quick check in the other rooms for potential fire hazards, she put on her coat. 'I'm going home now. Will you be okay?'

''Course I'll be okay.' May popped an orange cream into her mouth. 'I'm sorry I got a bit muddled there, but I'm fine now. I'll just watch this for a bit. I'll need to keep an eye on the time, though, because your father will be back from the Bowling Club at half past five wanting his tea.'

Annie took off her coat and sat down again. She took May's hand and as gently as she could, reminded her mother she had been a widow for six years.

When Annie eventually arrived home, Minty's car was parked outside, but she could see no sign of its owner. There was nothing Annie would have liked better at this moment than a large gin and tonic to restore her equilibrium, but she knew better than to take a chance, and went to fill the kettle instead. From the kitchen she spied Minty in the back garden, doing her best to pick

224

up after her dog. Annie opened the window.

'I was wondering where you'd got to,' she called.

'The dog's been without a pit stop since Harrogate, so I let her into your garden. I hope you don't mind. It's all dealt with.' She waved a knotted carrier bag. 'I'll just put it in your wheely bin, shall I?'

Annie nodded. 'Would you like a cup of tea? I'm putting the kettle on.'

'Just what I need. I'll put the dog in the car.'

'Bring her in, I don't mind.' Annie shut the window and finished filling the kettle. The back door opened and the dog bounced through.

'Down!' said Minty fiercely. Semi-rebuked, the collie gave Minty a sideways glance, then went off to explore the house.

Minty helped herself to a ginger snap from the packet on the worktop. 'Just the thing.' She took a large bite. 'Mmm, that's good. Didn't realise how hungry I was. Now, while the tea is brewing, I need to have a chat with you about the next lot of leafleting.'

'Well, I need a little chat with you, too.'

There was a pause while Minty swallowed her mouthful. 'You do?'

'I do! A chat about Mum, internet shopping and credit cards. Perhaps we had better go and sit down.' Annie handed Minty a cup of tea and led the way towards the living room.

'Yes, the credit card. I thought it would a good idea if she had one so she could buy things whenever she wanted to.' Minty sounded just a tiny bit shifty and tried to deflect attention to the dog, now lying asleep on the sofa. 'Just look at that dog! Get off!'

The dog paid no attention.

'Off! *Now!'* Minty took hold of the dog's collar and yanked her onto the floor.

'Minty, this is really important. Mum has run up a bill of £5,000.'

Minty let go of the collar and gave Annie her full attention, her eyes huge. 'Five *thousand* pounds? Surely not? There must be a mistake in the account?'

'No mistake, unfortunately.'

Minty slowly lowered herself onto the sofa. 'My dear, how dreadful! What on earth has she bought?'

'Well, amongst other things, larger-than-life-size saints from the US of A.'

'America?' Minty was stunned.

'Yes, America. And, worse still, some of the order is yet to come.' Annie shook her head. 'If she's so confused, how on earth does she remember how to work the computer?'

Minty held up her hands. 'Mea culpa again, I'm afraid! I gave her a flow chart – how to turn it on, how to get onto the internet, and then how to find the website she wanted. She didn't need to remember anything. Just followed the diagrams. She's not completely without marbles, you know.'

'That piece of paper must be about the only thing she hasn't lost recently.'

'This is dreadful! Can I do anything in the way of sorting things out?'

Pay the bill, perhaps? No, that wasn't fair; Minty had meant well. She took a bite of her biscuit and chewed thoughtfully. 'You could turn your mind to what we are going to do with an eight-foot-high, six-foot-wide nativity scene due to be delivered any day now.'

Chapter Thirty-Two

Ally Bigswell began to get an inkling something was wrong on Monday, when he failed to receive the usual email detailing the week's shifts. A check on his bank account on Tuesday showed that he hadn't been paid for the previous week's shifts. He logged on to go back through his Sunday morning comments and was astonished to discover that most of them had been removed. It was okay to overstep the mark occasionally, but this was catastrophic. He tried to recall what line he'd taken, and was even more astonished to discover that he couldn't really remember. Panic stricken and ready to grovel, he phoned Morton.

'Hi, It's Ally Bigswell here...'

'I think you have the wrong number.' The call was cut.

Ally tried again and no one answered. He phoned Morton's office in the Parliament and left a message, then he phoned the constituency office and did the same. He waited for two days, his stomach churning continuously, then repeated the process, sending emails to back up the voice-mails. There was no reply.

Ally's desperation increased as the week wore

on. On Saturday, he decided to brave Morton's surgery. Carly, Morton's PA, told him he would have to wait till the end.

Sitting in his inner office, drinking a double espresso from the state-of-the-art coffee machine purchased on his office costs allowance, Morton could think of better ways of spending a Saturday morning. Today's list of appointments contained some familiar names and some new ones, no doubt in possession of the traditional green pen and shaky block-capital writing style. A glance at his diary confirmed his suspicions – tonight was a full moon. He drained his cup then made his way to the waiting room. 'Mr Pittendreich? This way please.'

It was only when Mr Pittendreich began to relate his tale that Morton realised this was the strange man who followed Annie Cochrane. He hadn't recognised him without his placard. Morton listened politely to the protracted tale of the late Edith's demise – *a routine operation for bunions – cardiac arrest on the operating table – risk not explained – medical negligence – I want her back.* The final remark focused Morton's attention. He had a high opinion of himself, but raising the dead was beyond even him. Before he could make this point, however, the Haunter had launched into Part 2 – *a post mortem – a letter to the hospital – a fobbed off reply – local MSP – unsatisfactory reply from the hospital – a letter to Annie Cochrane – fobbed off again!* Now he was going through the list of MSPs. Morton's ego was marginally dented to hear that he ranked fourth on the list of seven.

Normally, he would have promised to investigate and promptly escorted the man from the office, but with the downfall of Annie Cochrane on his 'to do' list, he enquired casually about why this strange little man insisted on following the Health Minister as assiduously as he did.

'Well, now,' said the Haunter in a *Jackanory* tone of voice, 'it's a strategy I devised after much thought, because I will not let her forget. I try to be in her line of vision as much as possible. I arrive outside her Edinburgh flat early – about 6 a.m. – and I wait on the pavement till she comes out. Then I raise my placard and sometimes shout out to her. She often waves back, she's very friendly. I watch which way the car goes – onto North Bridge and she's going to her office, or down the Royal Mile and she's going to the Parliament. Then I follow and wait for her to come out. Sometimes she goes on visits.' He leaned forward and adopted a conspiratorial tone. 'I have a mole, you know!'

A skin blemish or a furry creature? Morton wondered. Did he care? Not enough. It was time to move this one out and get on with the next one. He stood up and went towards the door. 'Well, Mr Pittendreich, if you leave details of your case with my secretary in the outer office, I'll write again to the hospital.'

The Haunter showed no sign of getting to his feet. 'I can't tell you who my mole is. Suffice to say, he too thinks there is a conspiracy of silence. He tells me where she's going so that I'm waiting for her when she arrives. I go on the bus – for nothing. I'm a pensioner, you see. I have a nice day out and she knows she can't get away from me. Sometimes it means a night away from home, staying in a bed and breakfast. It's like a wee holiday.' He beamed at Morton.

'And how long have you been conducting your ... vigil?' Morton was still standing near the door.

'Since the day after the hospital refused to accept responsibility for my wife's death, the thirteenth of September last year.'

So. Morton made a quick mental calculation and returned to his seat. The man was on Annie's tail around conception time. He smiled across the desk. 'I admire your tenacity and I'm really interested in your campaign, Mr Pittendreich. Why don't you tell me a little more?'

At 12.30, Morton accompanied the last person on his list to the secretary's desk, only to find a white-faced Ally still in the waiting area.

Morton ushered him into his office, pointed to the chair, then stood facing him. 'What can I do for you?'

'I'm sorry about the comments. It won't happen again. Someone spiked my drink.'

'Comments? What comments?' Morton adopted a puzzled expression.

'The online comments.' Ally sounded desperate.

'I have no idea what you are talking about. Now, I am a busy man. Time you went.' Morton moved towards Ally and with a sudden sideways movement kicked his computer bag into the corner. 'Oh dear, Mr Bigswell, how clumsy of me, was that your laptop? Let's have a look and see if it's okay.'

Ally retrieved the bag and made for the door. 'It'll be fine.'

'No, I would hate to think I'd damaged it. Let me have a look.' Morton held out his hand.

Ally held the computer bag to his chest. 'No! It's okay.'

'Oh I insist.' Morton took the bag, removed the laptop and examined it. 'Look! The screen is loose. Leave it with me and I'll get it fixed.'

'It's okay, I'll sort it. I need it. It's got all my coursework on it.' Ally attempted to snatch it back but Morton blocked him.

'Not backed it up anywhere? That's a shame. It's terrible when one loses all one's work. You can spend months on something and have nothing to show for it. Now, why don't you bugger off, and when I've got it fixed, I'll send it to you.'

'Please ... can I have it?'

Morton, his disdain plain to see, held the door open. 'As soon as it's fixed it will be returned. Goodbye!'

Ally made his way home, his mind spinning at Morton's treatment. He had known the politician was a ruthless operator, but this was beyond anything he had witnessed before. As his heartbeat returned to a normal rate he began to see things in a different light. Of course he had his coursework backed up – he wasn't a nerd for nothing – and he had other things backed up too, files that provided evidence of his online names, log-in details, and a complete archive of his rota emails.

Ally was already building himself a new laptop when a parcel arrived the following Tuesday morning by special delivery – a parcel which, when shaken, sounded like a 1000-piece metal jigsaw.

231

Chapter Thirty-Three

Following May's visit to the GP, a referral had been made for a full assessment at the infirmary. In the meantime, the McCaffertys had agreed to 'pop in' regularly in Annie's absence. Minty, trying to make amends for the computer lessons, made regular visits too.

Friday afternoon saw Minty in May's kitchen dealing with the accumulated washing-up when the doorbell rang. Drying her hands on her apron, she went to see who was there. The man on the doorstep was consulting a piece of paper.

'Mrs Laverty?'

'This is her house, yes,' Minty replied.

The man shouted towards the lorry parked at the gate. 'OK, Gordy! We've got the right place!' He looked at Minty again. 'Took us forever to get the bloody thing in there, so God knows how long it'll take us to get it out.'

May appeared at Minty's shoulder and they watched the two men struggle, first to unload an enormous wooden crate and then to manhandle it up the garden path.

'What on earth you got in here, missus? Lump of rock?' The paper was handed to May for a signature.

'Just a moment,' said Minty. 'You're not finished yet! Could you take it inside please?'

The delivery man looked at Minty in disbelief.

He pointed first to the crate then to the door-frame. 'I don't think so, missus.'

Minty was not going to let him off that easily. 'Well, you can help us remove it from the crate. It should go inside after that.'

'We don't unpack! Sign there!' He handed May a pen. 'Seriously, what have you got in there?'

'The Holy Family,' replied May, signing in the wrong place. The delivery men exchanged glances. 'Really? Well tell them it's time they all went on a diet.'

The two women watched the lorry disappear down the street. Unfazed, Minty went inside and returned with a hammer and chisel. After fifteen minutes and language one would not expect to hear from a well-bred lady approaching ninety, the packaging was removed and the contents revealed: Joseph standing, with the Virgin Mary seated, both gazing at a strangely pink Jesus in a manger complete with canary yellow straw.

'Isn't it beautiful?' sighed May.

Minty settled for, 'Very colourful.'

'Will we get it inside?'

Minty surveyed both the door and the statue. 'A camel and eye of needle situation, I'm afraid.'

'We can't leave it here. Someone might steal it.'

Minty thought that unlikely, but she patted May's arm reassuringly. 'Till we get some help, I don't think we have an alternative, do we? It'll be okay for a short while – bit difficult to carry it away in one's pocket.' She shivered. 'Chilly, isn't it! You go in and put the kettle on, May, and I'll tidy up the mess.'

Annie's route home from Edinburgh took her past her mother's house. A line of cars was moving so slowly along the street that Annie wondered if Eoin had inadvertently joined a funeral cortege. As they neared May's house, she could see a crowd on the pavement. Nearer still, she realised why.

'Oh, hell! The Holy Family has arrived! You'd better let me off here, Eoin.'

'Quite a tableau,' he remarked. 'Have a good weekend, Minister. I'll hear all about it on Monday.'

As Annie reached her mother's gate, the crowd parted. Mary, Joseph and Jesus were facing the street, but they weren't quite as Minty and May had left them. Joseph was now sporting a Celtic beanie hat and, not to be outdone, Mary had a Rangers scarf draped round her neck. Baby Jesus, in a manager now bedecked with a set of battery-powered fairy lights, was wearing a T-shirt emblazoned with *My Grandma went to Benidorm and all I got was this lousy T-shirt*. More worrying still was the real donkey chewing meditatively in the middle of the small flower bed.

'Merry Christmas, Annie!' someone shouted from a passing van.

She waved gamely at the onlookers, found her key, opened the door and escaped inside. All was quiet. In the living room she found her mother and Minty sound asleep, watched over by Our Lady of Lourdes and her dwarf companion, St Bernadette, delivered from Ireland two days earlier.

Minty woke with a start. 'What time is it?'

'It's five o'clock,' replied Annie. 'Have you been asleep long?'

'Ages, then! We must have fallen asleep after our exertions! Gracious, how dreadful! We were a bit tired after getting the statue out of the crate. It's big isn't it?'

'Big, yes. And it's been decorated! Come and have a look.'

Minty went to the window. May was still sleeping. 'Think we ought to go and sort it, don't you?'

Outside, Minty started to remove the garments while Annie attempted to shoo the donkey out of the flower bed. It moved on to the emerging daffodils, to the delight of those watching.

Minty thrust the bundle of clothes and fairy lights into Annie's hands. 'Take that lot inside! Leave the donkey to me!'

She marched through the crowd to her car and returned with a piece of rope. The donkey stopped chewing and looked at her. This elderly human was clearly not to be trifled with. It stood while Minty created a rope halter and meekly allowed itself to be tied to the gate. She gave it a pat, and offered it a fluff-covered pan drop she had found in her pocket. The crowd applauded.

Minty gave a small bow. 'Okay, folks! Show over! Away you go now.'

She stood waving as the crowd dispersed, then went inside.

Annie was finishing a call to the police station. A donkey had been reported missing and someone would come and pick it up. Fifteen minutes later, May was finally woken by the prolonged ring of the doorbell. On the doorstep was an irate

Barbour-clad lady who lacked both a sense of humour and any form of small talk.

'If I have to call the vet because Desmond has eaten something poisonous, I shall bill you. He's been maltreated in the past and has a very sensitive digestion.'

Annie made it plain she wasn't responsible for removing it from its field, but Barbour-clad lady was unimpressed. 'Desmond ended up in *your* garden! The louts who took him should be in an approved school, but I expect *you,* with your wishy-washy liberal views, would just give them a pat on the head and offer them counselling.'

Minty appeared behind Annie. 'Muriel! How are you? Not seen you for eons!'

'Oh... Hello, Minty.'

'Didn't realise that was your donkey. He's a fine fellow. Poitou, isn't he?'

Muriel thawed a fraction. 'He is, yes. Most people just think a donkey is a donkey.'

Minty persevered. 'A very under-appreciated animal, if you ask me. Now, shall we go and have a look at him and see if he's okay?'

'No need. Quite sure he'll be fine.' Muriel now seemed in a hurry to leave.

'Well, let me help you load him into the trailer.' Minty was putting on her coat. 'Have you got a head-collar? I'd quite like my tow-rope back.'

Five minutes later, Annie and Minty waved Muriel off. 'She has a whole menagerie, you know – horses, donkeys, cats, dogs, snakes even. They might go rather hungry without my monthly standing order.' She tapped her nose and grinned at Annie. 'Now, I could do with a small restorative nip before I go home. Does your mother have any whisky in the cupboard?'

Later, with Bob's help, the statue of the holy trio was manhandled into the back garden, and, with her mother's permission, Annie phoned Father McIver to offer him a gift for the church. A gift she would not allow him to refuse.

Chapter Thirty-Four

A party political conference is much enjoyed by the delegates, who enthusiastically listen to debates, vote on policy and spend their early evenings at any one of a number of fringe meetings before everybody repairs to the bar to exchange campaign stories. For elected representatives, a party political conference means yet another weekend not spent at home, yet another weekend making speeches in policy debates, addressing fringe meetings and listening to the same diatribes from the same people while queuing to buy an overpriced drink at the bar.

The weekend following the statue's arrival, Annie attended such a conference in Perth. She had spoken in the debate about funding for the health service, she had addressed a fringe meeting run by the Royal College of Nursing, and now she was sitting near the bar sipping a glass of sparkling mineral water, her condition denying her the comfort of something stronger.

An earnest young man who worked for a mental health charity was making the most of her company. Annie just hoped she hadn't inadvertently closed her eyes. She had long since lost the thread of what he was talking about. An occasional nod was much easier than attempting to terminate the conversation.

'...and that number doesn't include the elderly with dementia,' the earnest young man was saying.

'Really?' said Annie. Her mind turned to her mother and her increasing dependence on the neighbours who were now on semi-permanent alert. She was suddenly aware of being asked a question. 'Sorry! What did you say?'

'What have we as a party to offer young men at the next election?' The earnest young man was eagerly waiting for an answer.

'In what way?' Annie ventured.

'Help for the increasing number of young men with depression. The suicide rate is alarming, not to mention...'

Annie's mind wandered from young men with depression to her son. Joe had spoken to her once and replied briefly to a couple of texts. He was okay. His new school was good. He was enjoying himself. He was going to see Karen on Sunday. So, she thought, at least she, would get an unbiased report.

Andrew appeared at her shoulder. 'Do excuse me, but I wondered if I could have a word with you, Annie, about something in my speech tomorrow.' He turned to the young man. 'You don't mind if I borrow her for a moment?' As

Annie stood up, he put his hand on the small of her back and whispered in her ear, 'Don't make eye contact, keep walking, and we'll be out of here in no time.'

They reached the edge of the crowd and climbed the stairs towards their rooms.

'What's the problem? I thought our speech was done and dusted?'

'It is.' Andrew smiled at her. 'I thought you looked in need of rescuing.'

She nodded gratefully. 'Thanks. I was losing the will to live.'

'How have things been this week?'

Annie stopped on the first landing. 'Awful! Just awful,' she said quietly.

'Want to tell me about it?'

Annie realised she did. 'I'll lay odds you've been allocated a grander room than me. Come on then, make me a cup of tea and I'll tell all, but first I have to change out of these formal clothes.'

She returned to her room and removed her business suit and tights. Her ankles looked as if they belonged to an elephant. She rifled through her suitcase. Nothing looked comfortable so she pulled on the vast fluffy bathrobe provided by the hotel. Andrew's room was the next but one. She opened the door and peered into the deserted corridor before scuttling towards his door.

The kettle was just coming to the boil and Andrew gestured to the armchair.

'Do you mind if I sit on the bed? Swollen ankles! Need to put my feet up.'

'They do look uncomfortable. Right. Let me have it. What's getting you down so badly?'

Annie settled herself, then catalogued her woes about her mother, the press coverage largely thanks to Tracey's dogged determination to milk the situation in every way possible, and the unsatisfactory communication with her son. 'I sometimes feel I'm standing with a tennis racquet opposite one of these machines firing balls. I used to be able to bat most of them back, but now they are all smacking into me. It's relentless, Andrew, and I'm so tired.'

'Are you telling me you want to resign?' he asked gently.

'No, I'm telling you I am tired and battered. I need to sleep.' She turned to look at him. 'I'll be fine in the morning, don't worry.'

Andrew handed her a cup of tea. She put it on the bedside table and attempted to open the small packet of biscuits.

'Minty has a mantra – *all shall be well*. I chant it constantly to myself.'

'Minty's a wise old bird. She could be right. Give me those. I'll open them.'

Annie passed him the biscuits. 'One consolation: Marlene was back to ignoring me at cabinet this week. Is it too much to hope she has got over her hissy fit?'

No chance, Andrew thought.

They drank their tea and ate the biscuits. Then they watched *Newsnight*, during which Annie's eyes closed. Andrew shook her gently, then more forcefully. No response. She looked so much younger with the worry lines smoothed by sleep and he didn't have the heart to wake her. He undressed, climbed into bed and pulled the duvet over the top of them both. He thought for a moment before slipping a protective arm round Annie's nonexistent waist.

They awoke to the noise of the fire alarm. Andrew registered 02.56 on the digital clock. Annie sat up, trying to work out where she was. Meanwhile Andrew, clad only in his boxer shorts, went to the door. 'It's probably just a false alarm.'
    However, the night porter in the corridor was shouting at everybody to get out as quickly as they could. Andrew pulled on his trousers and a shirt and jacket. Annie finally found her shoes. She had no choice but to go outside bare-legged in the bathrobe. Andrew grabbed his overcoat and put it round her shoulders and, tousled and sleepy, they emerged together at the same moment as the political correspondent of the *Daily Post* came out of the room opposite.

Chapter Thirty-Five

Colin had been considering the information before him for half an hour. So Andrew Fraser was the father of Annie Cochrane's baby. The *Daily Post* had published a carefully worded diary story, and now it was universally assumed to be true. Case closed. But to Colin, something didn't quite add up. If Andrew Fraser was the father, why not admit it – neither of them was married to anyone else. After a bit of nudging and winking everyone would have said 'Isn't that nice' and forgotten about it. He lit a cigarette and blew two perfect smoke rings. There was no doubt they had been sleeping in the same hotel room, but that didn't mean they were sleeping together last October.

The copy of Annie's official diary for October told him there had been day visits to Glasgow and Dumfries, and an overnight visit to Aberdeen. Could it be one of her civil servants? Colin mused. Not Annie's style. But being pregnant and refusing to name the father wasn't her style either. Colin took a sip of his now cold coffee and removed some dirt from under his fingernails. There was more to this story, he was sure of it, but he needed a new angle. It was then that he remembered the funny little man with the placard.

The Haunter had been at his post outside Annie Cochrane's flat for two hours, and he had just reached into his knapsack for his thermos and Tupperware container of egg sandwiches, when he became aware of someone crouching beside him. The man introduced himself as a reporter from the *Daily Scot* who was investigating cases of medical incompetence. Colin accepted the offer of a cup of tea and a sandwich, then switched on his voice recorder and allowed the Haunter to detail the minutiae of his campaign. It went on ... and on ... and on... The guy's tenacity was extraordinary. Come wind and rain, he said, he would be here in the early hours of the morning, waiting for Annie to come out.

Colin bided his time, trying to ignore the cramp in his legs.

'Are there any other MSPs you lobby? Besides Ms Cochrane...'

The Haunter nodded. 'It pays to persevere,' he said. 'I have high hopes of Mr Hunter coming up trumps. People say he's a cold fish, but he couldn't have been more helpful. Andrew Fraser's always very decent. He waves back. I often see him outside the Parliament and the Scottish Office, and sometimes I used to see him going down the High Street as I was walking up to take up my post here.'

'At six in the morning?'

'At about five-fifty. I get off the bus at 5.48 and make my way up. It was always a Tuesday I saw him, because it was the first day of my week. Mrs Cochrane is in her constituency on a Monday morning.'

'Does he live around here?' asked Colin, although he knew the answer perfectly well.

'I don't think so.'

'Really? I wonder...'

'Well, since you ask, I think he sometimes stayed with Mrs Cochrane over the winter months – from about November to February, through all that bad weather. On a Monday night, she would arrive home and he would arrive ten minutes later. Then I would see him walking down the road when I came back in the morning.'

'Has he stopped visiting, then? Now that the weather's better, perhaps?'

'No, he still comes to visit sometimes, but he doesn't stay long.'

The man was wittering on, but Colin was trying to put things together in his mind. He tried to stand up and found he had a dead leg.

'Sorry? What did you say?'

'I was asking when this article will be in the paper?' The Haunter was happy his protest was getting somewhere at last. Mr Hunter was going to write letters for him, and now, out of the blue, there was this press interest.

'Not for a while yet,' said Colin briskly, trying to ignore the pain in his legs. 'I still have extensive investigations to carry out.'

Back in the office, Colin sat with his feet up on the desk, turning over the facts. Were Andrew Fraser's children the reason for the coy behaviour? Was it too soon after their mother's death for Daddy to have a pregnant girlfriend? Did they not like Annie? He checked Jane Fraser's obituaries online. She and Andrew had a daughter called Joanna and a son called Duncan. A few more enquiries told him 24-year-old Duncan was working in Dubai, but 26-year-old Joanna lived in Edinburgh with her partner and a two-year-old son. He was fairly sure he had discovered her phone number. If she was a stay-at-home mum, she just might be in at the moment.

After ascertaining that the woman who replied was indeed Joanna, he told her he was doing a feature for the Saturday magazine on the Scottish party leaders and he was looking for family background to give a picture of Andrew Fraser the man rather than the politician. He asked if she could spare five minutes to talk about her father.

'I suppose so. I have to take my son to toddler

244

group soon. What do you want to know?'

Colin started with condolences. 'Firstly, can I say how sorry I was about your mother's death. It was very sudden, wasn't it?'

'Thank you. Yes, it was very quick.'

'Your mother was involved in politics too?'

'Not directly. She was on the fringes. She held the fort at home.' There was a wobble in Joanna's voice.

'And how is your father now?' Colin was all concern.

'It was tough for a while, but I think he is working through it. He buries himself in his job. He doesn't have time for many friends or interests outside politics.'

'And who are his political friends?'

'Well, Annie Cochrane has been a family friend for years, and he's close to Peter Sutherland. Perhaps you should speak to them. Though if I were Annie, I wouldn't want to speak to anyone from the press at the moment.'

'What do you mean?' Colin tried to sound innocently puzzled.

'She can't do anything right at the moment, can she? Poor Annie. As far as you lot are concerned everything is her fault. Can't you leave a pregnant woman alone? It's not good for the baby to have to deal with maternal stress hormones.'

Colin rolled his eyes. It was now or never. 'I don't know if you are aware that there's a rumour circulating that Annie's baby is your half-sibling?'

There was a pause, then Joanna laughed. Not the response he was expecting. 'Nice try, but it's not my father.'

245

'You sound very sure.'

'Believe me, I am.'

'Any idea who it might be then?'

Joanna's tone of voice changed. 'If I knew, I wouldn't tell you. Now, whatever your name is, your time's up. I have to go out.'

He had to be quick. 'Your father and Annie were seen leaving the same hotel room at 3 a.m. at the Perth conference.'

'And I expect they were just having a nightcap and a chat. Now, I really do have to go out.'

'He's been seen regularly arriving at her flat in Edinburgh late at night and leaving first thing in the morning.'

A pause. Then, 'How dare you spy on my father! I have already told you that he is not the father of Annie Cochrane's baby. They are good friends, that is all!'

Good, she was angry. Now for a little journalistic untruth. 'That's not the word from those close to Annie.'

Joanna was fond of Annie, but a recent conversation with her unhappy father had left her slightly annoyed. 'Until recently she seemed to think it was an old boyfriend. She's pushing her luck if she thinks she can blame it on Dad.'

'Did you say old boyfriend?'

Realising she had said too much, Joanna put the phone down.

So perhaps Andrew *was* just a handy shoulder. This was turning out to be more complicated than Colin had hoped. Who else might Annie have slept with in her forty-four years? Were there just one or two or was there an army? She was a bit of a mystery was Annie Cochrane, come to think of it.

Colin swiftly tracked down Annie's Facebook page. He put in a request to be her friend, confident he would not be turned down – no politician offends a potential supporter. Within the hour, he had access to her page. There were various press releases and a posting about her surgery in Corrachan on Saturday. He knew postings such as these were usually made by staff, but further down the page he found some interactions between Annie and what were obviously personal friends. A recently added friend called Jackie Mason had commented, *Great that you are in charge of us all. I'm still at the coalface!* Annie had replied *Good to hear from you. Where are you now?* to which Jackie had replied, *Still in Dundee. In coronary care now.*

He phoned Coronary Care at Ninewells Hospital and, using the story about background for a feature article on her old friend and colleague, he arranged to meet Jackie when she came off shift at three. This meant a train journey to Dundee, but he always extracted more information from a face to face interview. As he watched the Fife countryside, he congratulated himself on being miles ahead of the others. If Jackie could name names, he might have all he needed to run the story.

At five past three he was nursing an Americano in the cafe in the hospital concourse, scanning the passersby. He imagined Jackie to be mid-forties, capable, blonde even, so he was surprised when a dumpy woman, nearing retirement, approached his table.

'Excuse me, are you Colin?'

247

He stood up. 'Jackie?'

She nodded.

'Have a seat. Can I get you a coffee or something?'

Jackie deposited herself on the chair. 'Phew... Good to get the weight off my feet! Been on the go since six. A cappuccino with sugar would hit the spot, dear ... oh, and a piece of carrot cake.'

On his return with the refreshments, Colin found Jackie in conversation with the man at the next table. She was assuring him that his wife was making good progress and would be transferred to the main ward soon.

'Never off duty, then?' Colin watched her decant three tubes of sugar into her coffee.

'All part of the job. People need lots of reassurance when their loved ones are so poorly.' She started to struggle with the cellophane on the carrot cake. 'Ooo, they do make it difficult don't they? Perhaps it makes you use up lots of calories, a sort of slimming aid.' She laughed at her joke – a sound reminiscent of the last of the water going down the plughole.

Colin steered her back to the point of the interview. 'You knew Annie Cochrane when she worked here?'

Jackie put down her cup. 'Are we starting the interview, then? I've never been interviewed by a journalist before, so exciting. Are you going to record what I say?'

'I might make a few notes.' He indicated the pad in front of him.

Jackie looked slightly disappointed.

'Annie Cochrane?' Colin reminded her.

'Yes, I knew Annie. She was Annie Laverty then – just a staff nurse and look where she is now. To think I used to work with someone who's famous.'

'Can you tell me what she was like? Was she shy? Was she outgoing? Did the patients like her?'

'Ooo, three questions at once. Let me think.' Thinking involved taking a large bite of the carrot cake and a slurp of coffee to moisten it. 'It's difficult to remember.' Morsels of cake were being fired from her mouth. 'She was a good nurse. Had time to talk to the patients. At least I think she did, or am I thinking of someone else?'

'I don't know, are you?' This woman was more than irritating.

'Yes, she was good with the patients. She was always polite to staff too. She helped me a lot.'

'In what way?'

'Well, I used to work in an office, then I decided I wanted to work with people, so I was new to it all. A steep learning curve, as they say. She was much younger than me, but she was like a mentor, if you know what I mean.'

'And what about socially? Did you see a lot of her outside the hospital?'

There was a pause while Jackie thought about this. 'I remember going on a ward night-out once. We went to a Chinese restaurant. I got food poisoning – bad prawns I think, sick for days I was, not to mention the other end!'

Please don't mention it, Colin thought. This lady had obviously been no more than a passing acquaintance of Annie's, but there was still a faint chance she could still be useful. 'I don't suppose you know who her *close* friends were?'

'Now that's a hard one.' Jackie sat back, casting her eyes heavenwards. 'She lived in a flat on the Perth Road or was it Dens Road? I think her flatmates were nurses too … or were they? My memory is not what it used to be.' She took another bite. 'This is good carrot cake.'

'Can you remember the names of any of her girlfriends? Or boyfriends?' Colin added hopefully.

There was a pause while the cake was swallowed. 'No boyfriends. She had been unlucky in love, I remember that. Nursing a broken heart she was.'

This was promising. 'Do you know what his name was?'

'No. Before my time, I'm afraid. She didn't like to talk about it. Too raw, I think.'

'What about her girlfriends? Can you remember any of them?'

'They were on different wards. There was one girl – can I remember her name? Did it begin with L? Lorna? No. Linda? No. Or perhaps it started with a J? Jessica? No…'

Colin gritted his teeth. 'They were your colleagues – are you sure you can't remember any names?'

Jackie was taken aback by his now steely tone. 'I suppose technically speaking they were my colleagues, but the nurses tended to keep themselves to themselves. As I said, Annie was very kind to me when I started, but most of the other nurses didn't socialise with the likes of me.'

'You're not a nurse?' Colin was confused.

'Oh no! What made you think that? Fancy you taking me for a nurse! My uniform is a completely

250

different colour from the nurses'! I take the trolley round with the tea and the meals. I was called a ward orderly when I started, but I'm catering staff now.' She popped the last morsel of cake into her mouth and drained her cup. 'Will you mention my name in the article? When will it be published? So I can tell my friends...'

Chapter Thirty-Six

Marlene Watt did not like dealing with things domestic – she had a husband and an au-pair for that sort of thing, but the noise of said au-pair throwing up in the downstairs cloakroom had interrupted her breakfast. When a white-faced Vina emerged ten minutes later, Marlene put down her slice of toast and asked if she felt better.

'Yes, Ms Watt. I feel better soon.'

Marlene turned a page of the *Daily Scot*. 'Something you ate?'

'Perhaps it is. I not feel well since I ate burger last week.'

'Sure this has nothing to do with it?' Marlene held up a polythene bag containing a pregnancy-test stick.

Colour suffused Vina's face. 'What is that? It is not mine.'

'Well, it's certainly not mine! It's a pregnancy test, a *positive* pregnancy test. Stephie found it. She asked me what it was.' Marlene stared at Vina who attempted to stare back but failed.

251

'It is not mine. Perhaps it is Stephanie's.' Desperation can lead people to say silly things.

Marlene stood up and leant down so that her face was uncomfortably close to Vina's. 'Are you suggesting Stephanie, who is thirteen, is pregnant? She has not yet started her periods.'

'She do have periods. I do the laundry.' The tone was sulky.

Marlene stood up and took hold of Vina's arm. 'Are you pregnant?'

There was no reply.

Marlene rephrased the question. 'Are you going to have a baby?' Vina mumbled something.

'I can't hear you!'

'Yes, Ms Watt. I am a little pregnant.'

'And do you know who is responsible?'

Vina was disconcerted by the question. 'Mr Keiller, he is responsible.'

'You and Robert?' Marlene sat down heavily. 'Robert is the father of your baby?'

Vina laughed. *'No! No!* He not father! Mr Keiller he a responsible man, but father of baby is perhaps Jordan.'

'Jordan...?' Marlene's mouth was hanging open.

'Or perhaps it is his friend Kyle or his friend Brian or his friend Marty. The boys have condoms but perhaps they not use them right. Anyway it does not matter, I need abortion. You pay.' Vina was quite sure her problem, now that it was out in the open, was about to be solved.

The First Minister was rarely rendered speechless, but it took her several seconds to find her voice. 'How dare you suggest my son could be

252

the father of your baby! You go out at the week-ends and come in at all hours and now you want me to pay for an abortion?'

'Your son or his friends *responsible* so you pay, yes.' Vina was emphatic.

'I don't think so, Vina.' Marlene stood up and pointed to the door, 'Go and pack your bags. While you are doing that, I will phone the agency and tell them why you are leaving.'

Vina had one bargaining chip left. 'I have photos on my phone. The boys want to show their friends.' She took her phone from her pocket and showed Marlene a picture of Jordan using Vina's ample breasts as a pillow. 'Brian take photo. There are others too. I show you?'

Marlene closed her eyes and pressed one hand across her forehead. 'You will not! Go upstairs now, pack your suitcase and get out of this house!'

'If you not pay, Mr Keiller will pay. Where is he? He is kind man.' Vina was sulky now.

'Mr Keiller left for work while you were throwing up. He will not pay either.'

Vina looked Marlene in the eye. 'So. I tell the newspapers.'

'Go ahead, but remember you are an adult. My son and his friends are still children. The law calls people like you paedophiles and puts you on something called the Sex Offenders Register. If I were you, I would get the next plane back to Serbia before the police come to arrest you.'

'Do not call me Serb! I come from Bosnia.'

'I really don't care which bit of Yugoslavia you come from – the sooner you are back there the better. You understand me?'

Vina hesitated. Her command of English was limited and she hadn't understood much of what Marlene had said, but she could read body language. Further argument was futile, but she wasn't entirely out of ideas.

'I owed two weeks' money. I need it for air fare.' She looked Marlene in the eye.

'When your bags are packed, I'll give you £50 and that's all!' Marlene held her glance.

Vina looked away first. Marlene pointed in the direction of the stairs. 'What are you waiting for? Go and put all your belongings in your suitcase, then leave this house. Do you understand?'

Jordan and Stephanie, dressed for school, came downstairs as Vina went out the front door. Marlene pocketed the phone she had just forced Vina to relinquish and poured herself another cup of coffee.

'Vina has left. We will get a new au-pair as soon as possible. In the meantime, you will have to manage. Stephanie, get your breakfast. Jordan, come with me, I want to speak to you.' Marlene picked up her cup and Jordan trailed after her into the living room. Stephanie poured herself a bowl of Cheerios and smiled to herself. That would serve her brother right for not giving her any more money after that first night.

Chapter Thirty-Seven

On Easter Saturday, Karen was sitting on Annie's sofa with most of a bottle of Australian merlot inside her. She poured what remained into her glass and pointed at the fizzy water. Annie shook her head. A girly evening putting the world to rights did not have the same dynamic when one member of the party was sober. Karen took another mouthful of wine and continued to explain why Pete, whom she had told Annie a month ago was on sale or return, had been returned.

'He was needy. It was okay to begin, but it always is, isn't it?'

Annie didn't feel qualified to answer that.

'But then I wanted to say to him, "For God's sake, go and kill a brontosaurus or something and stop a) telling me how unfair life has been to you and b) asking me what you should do next. I don't care!" Oh, I quite liked him, Annie, but, shit, I'm the needy one here. I told him to go and talk to his mother. Then he went – just like that. Got out of bed, dressed, told me I was a hard-nosed bitch, and shot out of the door. And I thought, You *have* got balls after all; but by that time he was gone.'

'I think I might have gone too, Karen.' Annie took a sip of water.

Karen appeared not to hear and took another large gulp of wine.

'So I'm back to square one. I'm going to a

speed-dating thingy next week and I've signed up on the internet – if you want a giggle we can look at some of the profiles. Some of them are really kinky, but most are just deluded.' Karen closed her eyes as if in slight pain. 'Tomorrow, though, too pissed at the moment.' She studied the contents of her glass with great concentration, before turning to Annie. 'Enough about me. I want to know how you managed to have two men and now have no men – just that enormous bump. Full story please, not the abridged version. I've come all this way, the least you can do is tell your birthing partner everything.'

'I've told you, I met Tarik again on a hospital visit,' Annie said, putting her legs up on the sofa. 'He said he owed me an explanation for his disappearance all those years ago. We ended up in bed. The next week, I ended up in bed with Andrew. Perhaps my libido was defrosted the week before, perhaps it showed me I could actually have a bit of excitement in my duty-ridden life. Whatever the reason, it happened. I thought, why not? Bit of closeness to another person, bit of a personal life, what's the harm, eh? Andrew wasn't exciting, but he was safe, easy to be with–'

'Needy, you mean.' Karen wagged an accusing finger in Annie's direction. 'I told you, needy is not good! It's boring! And a bereaved man is needy in the extreme.' Karen upended her glass above her mouth. 'On the other hand, oily bastards are not good either. Perhaps we should go to Greece and do a Shirley Valentine with a twenty-year-old waiter. What you doing for your summer holidays?'

'Having a baby, in case you had forgotten!'

'So you are!' Karen checked the wine bottle. 'Have you got any more? This one seems to be empty now.'

When Annie returned from the kitchen, a newly opened bottle of wine at the ready, Karen was examining St Gerard on the mantelpiece.

'Where on earth did you get the gay wee man?'

'I'll have you know, that is no less than St Gerard and he is the patron saint of pregnancy. He was the least of Mum's forays into internet shopping.'

Karen picked up the statuette and held it at arm's length. 'He looks as if he would faint if anyone mentioned the word pregnancy.'

'I've grown quite fond of him, actually.'

Karen offered him to Annie. 'All yours then. Swap him for that bottle of wine?'

'There you are. Don't drink it all at once.' Annie placed St Gerard back on the mantelpiece.

'You can be quite schoolmarmish, you know. Just because you aren't drinking. Now, tell me what Tarik is going to do for his baby. He may be married, but it's still his responsibility'

'Nothing!' Annie turned away and made a show of checking the curtains were closed properly. 'I don't want anything to do with him. I left messages saying I wanted to talk to him and guess what, he chose the letter option again.' She turned back to face Karen. 'This time, would you believe it, a card saying *Congratulations!* I don't want a father like that for my child.' She sat back down on the sofa. 'I used to think you were unfair to him, but you were right. The man is a complete bastard.'

Karen swivelled round, trying to make eye contact. 'Annie, I'm glad you agree with me on that point after all these years, but there is more than one bastard here!' She pointed at Annie's bump. 'And if there is a resemblance to Tarik, people are bound to talk. Sooner or later, someone is going to do the sums and realise that you and Tarik renewed each other's acquaintance nine months prior to the birth.' She sighed in exasperation. 'Have you told anyone else it might be him?'

'Just Andrew. He sort-of-knows who it is. Oh, and Joe – I told him it was an old boyfriend.'

'And I bet you he's told Ellie who will have told her mother who will have told her friend who will have told God knows who.' Karen leant towards Annie, her eyes struggling to focus. 'Your secret is out there! Sooner or later somebody's going to piece it all together. Won't take a journalist long to find someone who worked with us in Dundee.'

Annie closed her eyes and rubbed her forehead. 'Listen to me! You must speak to him about it.'

Annie poured herself more water. 'No! He's had his chance. And anyway, the world now thinks it's Andrew.'

'The world won't think that when it pops out!'

Annie grimaced. 'Don't nag, Karen. Please! You're supposed to be here to cheer me up.'

Karen topped up her glass. 'So, why's Andrew being touted as the father?'

'Being seen leaving his hotel room together at three in the morning resulted in talk.'

Karen raised her eyebrows.

'Don't look at me like that. Nothing happened!'

Karen pointed a finger at her. 'Ha, ha! No one

believes you!'

'You think I don't know that?'

'So. Is he happy to be gossiped about? Why doesn't he tell the world he had the snip?'

Annie had to think before she answered. 'No one has asked the question directly yet, and I think in some high-minded way, he's trying to protect me.'

Chapter Thirty-Eight

Marlene Watt was going to spend part of the Easter recess in New York attending Tartan Week, where she was representing the Scottish Government at numerous tartan-tinged events, and had decided the trip would be the ideal family holiday. This caused her civil servants some difficulty, as she expected them to make the family travel arrangements as well as her own.

Taking his courage in both hands, Frank, her private secretary, pointed out that she would have to pay half the cost if Robert shared her hotel room.

Marlene took off her reading glasses and looked up from her papers. 'What total nonsense! Robert will be working on behalf of Scotland while he's in New York. I see no reason why he shouldn't have his fare and accommodation paid for. I'm having to pay for the children, after all.'

'It doesn't quite work like that,' said Frank tentatively.

'I always get a large suite – makes no difference to the public purse.' Marlene turned her attention back to her papers.

'I realise that, First Minister, but it's the rules – all to do with public perception.'

Marlene did not look up. 'Book the cheapest family room available and he can pretend to go in with the children.'

'Thank you, FM.' Frank remained where he was, shifting from one foot to the other.

'What is it, Frank?' Marlene's voice was icy. 'You're hovering in a very irritating fashion.'

'Two things, do you want business class seats booked for your husband and children? And, er, could we have a credit card number please?'

The glasses came off again and she turned to face him. 'For goodness sake! Book them economy, and then phone the airline and negotiate an upgrade – and book it from Glasgow not Edinburgh. Much handier.'

For you perhaps, Frank thought.

When Marlene and her family arrived at business-class check-in at 7 a.m. on Easter Sunday, they were told that Robert, Jordan and Stephanie were expected to turn right on entering the plane before taking an extended walk to row 39. Frank's request for an upgrade appeared to have been ignored.

'Here's why...' said the cheerful tanned lady at the check-in desk. She pointed to the word 'Economy' on the paperwork. 'Business class tickets for you and your two colleagues, and Mr Keiller, Mr Keiller Junior and Ms Keiller have economy tickets, and business class is full, I'm afraid. A popular flight, this one.'

Marlene's smile and tone of voice became glacial. 'Could you use your telephone and ask the duty manager to come here.' She turned to Frank. 'You told me this was sorted.'

He shuffled on the spot. 'As far as I was aware, it was,' he muttered.

The duty manager started well. 'Good morning, Mrs Watt!' he chirruped. Then he did a lot of tapping at the computer as the check-in assistant muttered at him behind her tanned hand. 'Yes...' He pouted and shook his head. 'The plane is full. What can I say? Would you like me to check the availability in business class on this afternoon's flight from Edinburgh?'

Marlene leant over the check-in desk and in a low voice said, 'No, I would like you to tell three business-class passengers that there has been an unfortunate overbooking and that *they* are now flying from Edinburgh this afternoon.'

The duty manager moved his chair backwards, unused to having his personal space invaded like that. He raised his chin and pretended to look at the bookings on the Edinburgh flight. There was a great deal more tapping, before he moved even further back. 'I'm so sorry, Mrs Watt, I'm afraid that flight's full too.'

Jordan and Stephanie enjoyed their flight to New York. While their mother slept, they explored all the perks business class had to offer, as did a Mr and Mrs Watt and their son, who had been most surprised to find they had been upgraded. Back

261

in row 39, Robert sat between a seething Frank and disconsolate Amanda, the junior civil servant, eating their tepid dinner off plastic trays, overlooked by the toilet queue.

While Marlene and family were passing over Greenland, Joe and Ellie were sitting on a park bench in London. It was the last day of Ellie's Easter visit and they had taken to walking the streets in order to have some privacy. Joe had been in London for six weeks. For the first three he attended the local sixth-form college, but as the rest of his class had completed the syllabus and were revising for their exams, there was no point in Joe being there. With his father's permission, and on the understanding that he would go back to college in September for an accelerated A-level course, he quit. Now he worked night-shifts at Sainsbury's, stacking shelves. He had made no friends at college or work and it was only the thought of Ellie's visit that had kept him going. Now that visit was nearly over. He put his arm round her shoulder and she laid her head on his chest while he detailed his woes.

'Dad's away most of the week and Catherine just sees me as free childcare. I get texts asking me to pick Emily up from nursery. First time I did it, I got bollocked for not showing initiative and making the tea when I got in. I'm not a bloody mind-reader.'

Ellie moved away from him slightly so that she could see his face. 'Why don't you come back to Corrachan. Please? Shawn's been sent to boot camp, and now that Ryan's lost his commander, he's not so bad. You've not missed much school-work.'

He pulled her closer again. 'I can't! Mum's getting bigger all the time. Everyone's still talking about us.' He paused for a moment. 'And I can't live with Gran any longer. She's completely weird.'

'She is a bit,' Ellie agreed. 'I met her in the High Street last week. She couldn't remember the way home, so I walked up the road with her. I don't think she had a clue who I was.' Ellie took out her phone and scrolled through some photographs until she found the one she was looking for. 'That was her front garden recently. Talk of the town for days.' She giggled.

'How did that get there?' Joe was laughing so much he could hardly speak.

'She's supposed to have won it in a competition on the Vatican website. That's what people said, anyway.'

'Can't have been many entrants, it's awful.' He peered at the photo again. 'Did she win the donkey too?'

'No. Ryan's big brother borrowed it from Mad Muriel. Don't know how he got away with it.'

Joe flicked through the other photos.

'According to Mrs McCafferty, she's got a life-size Virgin Mary in the sitting room too.'

He handed back the phone. 'Told you she was weird. Is the nativity play still in the garden?'

'Word is, your mum sold it to Father McIver for £2000, but that might be Chinese whispers. Anyway, it's in his church now.' Ellie cuddled in towards Joe. 'It's cold. Let's get moving again. Where shall we go?'

'Suppose we could go and see Karen. At least her house is warm. I'll text and see if she's in.' They had reached the park gates when Joe's phone beeped with Karen's answer. 'Woo hoo!' he punched the air.

'What does she say?'

'*In Corrachan. House empty. Spare key under yellow bucket in shed. Alarm 6783. Enjoy Kx.*'

'I do like your godmother. Come on,' Ellie said. 'Only three and a half hours till my train goes.'

Chapter Thirty-Nine

Annie took the morning off to take May to her hospital appointment. They drove there in silence.

Annie could tell that the receptionist knew who she was. She leant across the desk and spoke as discreetly as she could. 'Um, last time I had a hospital appointment, I was taken ahead of the queue and ... er ... just wanted to say, we want to take our turn like everybody else.'

The receptionist bristled. 'I'm not going to bump you up the queue just because you're a politician. You *will* take your turn.'

Annie maintained a pleasant smile. 'Thank you.'

They sat down and waited. The time of the appointment came and went. Several people who arrived after them had their names called and disappeared down the corridor. Finally, over an hour after the appointed time, May's name was called. Annie shepherded her now agitated mother into the doctor's office.

'Mrs Laverty, come in. Take a seat. And is this your daughter you've brought with you?'

May ignored the social niceties. 'I don't know what you're going to ask me. I don't know what I'm going to have to do. We've been waiting such a long time.'

The doctor looked puzzled for a moment, then checked on the Post-it note attached to May's file. 'I'm sorry you had to wait but this note says you requested to be seen last.'

It was Annie's turn to bristle. 'No, that's not true.' She hoped she sounded suitably assertive without appearing to bully anybody. 'I simply requested that we be given no special treatment – as a result of the backlash from my last visit to this hospital.'

The doctor looked at Annie and the penny dropped. He nodded sheepishly.

'Your receptionist seems to have misunderstood me.' Annie paused then added more quietly, 'Whether deliberately or not, it's hard to say.'

'I'm so sorry, Mrs Cochrane. A misunderstanding, I'm sure.' The doctor turned his attention to May. 'Now, perhaps I should explain the assessment process, Mrs Laverty, or can I call you Mary?'

After three hours, Annie and May emerged from the hospital and walked to the car. May had undergone a battery of cognitive tests, an ECG and MRI scan had been performed and the diagnosis pronounced – mild Alzheimer's disease.

As Annie was backing out of the space, May

265

fumbled in her handbag, 'Wait a minute! I haven't got the pills. Where did I put them?'

'It's all right, Mum, I've got them.' Annie pointed to her handbag in the footwell.

'That's okay then.' May was silent for a few moments, then she frowned. 'Am I getting a miracle drug? I can't remember what the doctor said. There was too much talk.'

The doctor's suggestion that May participate in a drug trial had put Annie in a quandary. The drug in question, effective in treating the symptoms of Alzheimer's disease, was monumentally expensive. Some Health Boards prescribed it in the early stages, others only when the disease was advanced. This was a clinical blind trial to see if the benefits of prescribing in the early stages justified the cost. Annie had to decide. Should she allow her mother the possibility of getting the more effective drug in the test, rather than the normal one, or should she just say no and avoid possible criticism about preferential treatment?

She had looked at her once capable mother, suddenly a confused and anxious old lady. It wasn't a difficult decision.

Annie negotiated a daffodil-covered roundabout and took the Corrachan road.

'All the pills should make things better, Mum.'

They drove on in silence for a while. May looked out of the window at a field of lambs. 'So I'm officially doolally now?'

Annie took her left hand off the wheel and found her mother's right hand. 'Perhaps a tiny bit, Mum, but the pills will sort you out, you'll see.'

Over the next few weeks, May's condition did improve. Although she was still mildly confused, there were no more instances of bizarre behaviour, so whichever pill she had been assigned, it was doing her some good. Unfortunately, May's understanding of the finer points of a drug trial was still hazy and she delighted in telling everyone she was getting an expensive wonder drug. It was her favourite topic of conversation – to those at the pensioners' tea dance, to the McCaffertys next door, to Minty and to the man in the newsagent. Within a week the whole of Corrachan was under the impression that Annie Cochrane's mother was getting preferential treatment.

Annie, busy at work and happy that the press appeared to be hounding some other public figure this week, was blissfully unaware of the gossip until she received an irate letter from a constituent complaining that *his* father had been denied the expensive drug. At her surgery the following weekend, she encountered another huffy constituent who had been paying for the drug out of her own savings for her mother for the last year. The lady in question, Carol Martin, happened to be the wife of Gerry Martin from the *Corrachan Times* who not only wrote a sniping article in the next edition, but fed the information to his friends on the national papers.

Chapter Forty

Dressed in a specially designed outfit in Scottish Parliament tartan, topped with a beret complete with pheasant feathers, Marlene walked at the head of the Tartan Week Parade, waving regally at the crowd as she made her way down Fifth Avenue. The week had been a triumph, by all accounts, and her ego was well fed.

Walking beside her, dressed in a kilt, complete with velvet jacket and lace jabot, Robert felt like a poor man's Sean Connery. He managed an occasional self-conscious wave. As the week had progressed, he had found it increasingly difficult to monitor the whereabouts of his children who were roaming New York at will. At least Stephanie was with them today, walking on the other side of Marlene, dressed, he thought, like jailbait in a mini-kilt and high boots. Marlene had overruled his objections to the suitability of his daughter's outfit, explaining that as an ambassadress for Scottish teenagers, Stephanie was modelling the latest in cutting-edge designer tartan-wear for her age-group. Jordan, declaring that he had no intention of looking a tosser in a kilt, had remained in his mother's suite, watching pay TV and working his way through the contents of the minibar.

While Marlene was parading, Annie was standing outside a church in one of the smarter Glasgow

268

suburbs as the hearse bearing one of her colleagues left for a private cremation service. A bitter wind seared through her thin black business suit, making her teeth chatter.

Once the cortege was out of sight, conversations began. Old school friends renewed acquaintances, distant relatives decided whether they were second cousins or first cousins once removed, and those who were there for political reasons were liberated from the unwritten dictat, *No talking about successors till the funeral is over.*

The late Grant Paton had dropped dead at three-thirty in the afternoon in the shower in a house owned by a lady who was not his wife. Apparently he had been helping the lady who was not his wife get boxes of party leaflets from her attic, and was simply taking a shower to remove the dust from his hair before going to his next appointment. Grant Paton had won the seat at the last election with a tiny majority and a by-election caused by these doubtful circumstances was not good news.

'Okay then, Andrew. Who is the candidate going to be?'

Andrew Fraser glanced around. 'The husband of the owner of the shower would have been a possible, but a cuckold is not a good electoral proposition. So, it will be Marnie Shaw who has been a councillor since Eve was a rib, or we put someone in from outside. Either way, it's lost.'

There was a communal realisation that this might be true.

Annie tried to be positive. 'Surely, if we mobilise the whole by-election team, co-ordinate things properly, we have a chance?'

Andrew shrugged. 'MSPs having any sort of hobby outside work are thought to be short-changing their constituents these days. Whatever Grant's reasons for visiting the lady, the world is going to think the worst.'

Time to change the subject. 'So! When will the election be?' Annie doubted she would be much use on the campaign trail – walking miles and bending double to put leaflets in low letter boxes were not compatible with the third trimester.

'Last Thursday in May I expect.' Andrew spoke with little enthusiasm. 'Six weeks of non-stop fun!'

Later that evening, Andrew stood in the foyer of the Usher Hall in Edinburgh. Most of the concert goers had already taken their seats. He took his phone from his pocket, but there were no messages. This was his second outing with Pam. The first, a play followed by a meal, had gone better than he could have hoped. His sister had warned him that Pam was known as the Merry Widow and not short of admirers. She was having a much more exciting social life now that she had discovered the joys of internet dating than she ever had with her late husband. The message was clear – Andrew shouldn't hang about.

The two-minute bell rang. Andrew took a quick look outside, but there was no sign of Pam. Perhaps she had been put off by the rumours concerning Annie's baby. Every time there was a slow news day, the tabloids had another go at that story. An official approached and asked him to take his seat.

270

'Can I leave my friend's ticket with you? I can't think what's happened to her.'

'After it starts, there's no admittance till the interval.' The official looked at him. 'Your face is familiar – are you ... that bloke on TV?'

'Sometimes, yes, I am. I'm a politician.'

'Oh,' the official replied, obviously disappointed. 'So are you going in or not? Make your mind up time.'

Andrew hesitated. He didn't want to sit with an empty seat beside him, but neither did he intend to be left standing in the foyer. He decided to go home. 'No. I'll wait outside for a while and see if she–'

The door opened and Pam appeared, smiling. She kissed him on both cheeks and linked her arm through his. 'Andy, I'm so sorry. Time just ran away from me. Are we still in time to get in?'

Chapter Forty-One

Annie did her political duty and spent one evening per week helping at the by-election. The first was spent knocking on doors in the street with the largest houses and consequently the longest drives. By nine o'clock she had walked miles and canvassed only twenty houses. The response had been polite, but where the eye contact was not good, Annie told the party worker accompanying her to mark the householders down as a No. They needed to be realistic.

The following week, having requested less walking, she was sent to an estate owned by the local housing association. Here the response was less polite and equally unpromising.

'Nearly done,' Annie told the disconsolate party worker as she rang the final bell.

The door was answered by a young woman, more pregnant than Annie, with a toddler holding on to her leg.

'Yes? What do you want?'

Annie explained why she was there.

'Another one? I'll tell you what I told the last one – I don't vote. You're all the bloody same. Now, bugger off.' She started to close the door then looked Annie first in the face, then in the abdomen. 'I've read about you. You make me sick. Jump the queue just because you think you're important. If I did vote, I wouldn't put it anywhere near you.' The door slammed.

'That'll be a No,' said Annie, alarmed at how near to tears she was.

The following week, Annie asked for a task in the election office and found herself counting leaflets into bundles. That task completed, she took a blue pen and addressed pale blue envelopes in the hope that the recipients would think it was a letter from a long-lost friend rather than election literature – a forlorn hope, in Annie's humble opinion, but she was happy to toe the party line. She was nearly finished when the door opened and a beaming Minty appeared sporting a large rosette and carrying a supermarket carrier bag. By-elections were her hobby and she travelled the length and breadth of the country to assist at each one.

George, the election agent, glanced up from the canvass returns. 'I thought you went home ages ago, Minty. You went out at three.'

'Home? I'm here for the week, George! I've covered a lot of ground today. Must have done about a hundred houses, not to mention the shops at the traffic lights.'

'I only gave you a couple of streets to do.' There was a note of alarm in the agent's voice. 'About thirty houses.'

'Oh! I'd finished them by half past four. You weren't here when I came back, so I just took some leaflets from the box over there and did more streets. Oh, hello, Annie. Didn't see you in the corner.' Minty waved before turning back to George. 'Feeling a bit peckish by about seven, so I braved the pub near the station for a bite to eat. Do you know, there were only two people in there who intended to vote at all. The rest weren't going to bother! Outrageous! I told them in no uncertain terms that it was their civic duty to vote. What a good discussion we had! Difficult to say how many will vote for *us*, but they *will* vote!' She chuckled. 'If we get two votes out of five, we'll be fine. I've offered to give them a lift to the polling station.' She sat down heavily. 'Such fun!'

George sighed. He wished he had Minty's optimism. Forty per cent of the vote was beyond his wildest imagining. In the meantime he needed to find out where she had been. 'Minty; you said you canvassed some streets before you went to the pub?'

'Yes, I took leaflets and canvass returns from

273

that box and I went to–'

'You took them from that box over there?' There was a hint of panic in George's tone. 'Not the ones bundled up into streets?'

'Oh! Silly me. Never saw *them!*'

Luckily Minty could not hear George's muttered expletives.

'Just a minute. I'll get you the canvass returns.' As she searched, Minty pulled rolls of stickers and several leaflets belonging to opposing parties from her bag.

'Where did you get all these from?' asked Annie, pointing to the opposition literature.

'First Rule of Leaflet Delivering...' Minty wagged a finger, '...make sure it's gone right through the letter box, otherwise someone else can take it out!'

An irate party worker burst through the shop door. 'George, I'm happy to canvass, but I object to being asked to leaflet an area that's already been done!'

'I'm terribly sorry. My fault!' said Minty, smiling broadly.

It's difficult to be cross with a very old lady, so with a purse of the lips, the party worker changed the subject. 'And, who's been up lampposts putting *Vote Marnie* stickers all over Connor Clarke's posters?'

'Certainly not on my orders,' said George anxiously. 'We'll need to put a stop to that.'

'Such immature behaviour,' said Minty. 'Now, it's getting late for an old biddy like me. I'll see you in the morning, George. Annie? Want a lift to the station?'

'Yes, please.' Annie's heart just wasn't in it this evening.

They strolled round the corner to Minty's car, parked as usual several feet from the kerb. The dog was on guard in the front seat and there was a large stepladder attached to the rusting roof-rack.

Annie pointed to it, then raised her eyebrows, turned slowly and pointed to her driver. 'Minty Oliver, why am I not surprised? Apart from being very naughty, it's not safe – you are too old to be climbing up lampposts!'

Minty refused to look her in the eye. 'I have no idea what you are talking about. Just get in and buckle up.'

Chapter Forty-Two

Mid-morning on the day after the by-election, Morton knocked on the door of Marlene's office. He was late, but with good reason.

Marlene looked up from what she was doing and glanced at the clock. 'Thought our appointment was at eleven?'

'Yes, Marlene, it was, but something has come up. We have a problem.'

'Well, you'd better be quick.' She put the top on her pen and stood up. 'I am about to go to the Parliament to welcome our victorious candidate.'

'You might not be in such a hurry when you hear what I have to say.'

Marlene turned to face him. 'What do you mean?'

He pursed his lips. 'It would appear that our newly elected MSP, Connor Clarke, is not as squeaky clean as first thought.'

'Connor? Is this some sort of joke, Morton?'

'Unfortunately not.' He sat on the edge of her desk. 'Beside his extensive legitimate businesses, it would appear he has substantial interests in a string of saunas which have been linked with a widespread Eastern European money laundering operation.'

Marlene started to laugh 'Morton, that's nonsense! I've known Connor for years. Where on earth did you get that rubbish from?'

'This is serious, Marlene. It's come back to me from two different sources, both reliable. There is an exposé planned for Sunday.'

Marlene waved her hand dismissively. 'Journalists are always asking questions. That's their job. Connor is completely above board.'

Morton spoke very slowly to make his point. 'Marlene, it's set for Sunday. All they need to put the icing on this particular cake is a few pictures of you welcoming him to the Parliament.'

She walked over to the window, then turned back to face Morton. 'Which paper?'

'The *Saltire*, definitely, but my sources indicate the others have wind of it too.'

The potential fall-out began to dawn on Marlene. 'Have you spoken to Connor?'

'Yes. He denies any impropriety. Says he'll sue.'

'And I'm sure he will!' Marlene sounded robust, but then she hesitated. 'Anything else, over and above saunas and Russians?'

'Well, he chairs your Business Advisory Panel, he prints most of the party literature below cost and he's our biggest donor.' Morton didn't think that now was the time to tell her that Connor also financed the nocturnal activities of the likes of Alfred William Bigswell. That was a private arrangement which had not been run by the First Minister.

Marlene pushed her fingers through her expensively styled hair, which had been all ready for the morning's photo opportunity. 'The fact he's a donor is in the public domain.'

'And the fact that you have known him for years is going to be in the public domain on Sunday as well.' Morton paused and altered his tone. 'The fact that you have *known* him ... in the biblical sense?'

Suddenly Marlene was all bluster. 'We went out together at university – for a while!'

'And lived together for two years thereafter, I understand. Marlene, if I can find that out in twenty minutes, it's not a secret.'

She sat down at her desk again. 'This is obviously beyond your competency, Morton. I shall have to sort this myself! I need to speak to Connor and then the editor of the *Saltire*. Get me the numbers please!'

'Oh, I think that can wait.' Morton was now in charge of the situation. 'I have taken the liberty of putting out a statement to the effect that you have a virus and are going to bed for the rest of the day. There won't be a photograph of you shaking hands.'

Marlene looked up at him, trying to work out

277

what was going on.

He smiled. 'Apart from Annie Cochrane, who do you dislike most at the moment? Of your senior colleagues, I mean?'

'Why?'

'I would have thought it was obvious. We'll get one of them to do the handshaking.'

The trace of a smile passed over Marlene's lips. She thought for a moment. 'Calum enjoys the limelight. Get him to do it.'

'Consider it done.' Morton stood up. 'Now, Patrick is waiting outside to take you to Bute House. Try and look as if you are about to throw up if you can.' He handed Marlene her coat. 'I'll work something out and let you know.' He proffered her briefcase. 'Make your phone calls, then settle back and enjoy *Countdown.*'

Morton watched her leave the room. She really was looking a little queasy. His intimation of her ill health would be easily accepted. He knew she would fight the idea that the candidate with whom she had been so closely associated throughout his campaign was not a welcome addition to her parliamentary team. His short-term aim was simple damage limitation, but, long-term, Morton knew that he had to distance himself from this debacle. The Connor story wouldn't go away for long. If Marlene's popularity was about to take a dive, Morton had no intention of descending with her.

For the first time in many years, the editor of the *Saltire* was unavailable when Marlene called. And he didn't call her back.

Following the press exposé the following Sunday, a police investigation was launched, but Connor Clarke, with an ego and self-belief which exceeded even that of Marlene, denied everything and commenced an action for defamation. This meant that any journalist worth their salt was on the case, and Morton found that he did not have to leak the information on Marlene and Connor's past relationship after all. He merely had to confirm it.

Chapter Forty-Three

Colin sat in his office with a takeaway coffee, reading both his own and rival publications. Even with all his years of experience, he was still surprised how quickly someone's fortunes could change. Marlene Watt's error of personal judgement had been portrayed as a major character flaw, and a whiff of political downfall was in the air. Suddenly, her MSPs were prepared to speak – admittedly mostly off the record, but it was as if they too could see the end in sight, and were happy to do whatever it took to speed things up.

Colin leafed through the rest of the paper. ANNIE COCHRANE SAYS SHE WON'T HOLIDAY IN SCOTLAND THIS YEAR.

So Annie preferred to cruise round the Mediterranean in preference to a B&B in the Highlands. Colin smiled to himself. Wouldn't we all? But more fool her for saying so. She must be about seven months gone now, so for all her talk of foreign holidays, she wouldn't be going further than the local maternity ward.

All his rivals had the Andrew Fraser story written and waiting to go, but Colin was still certain they were wrong. There was something about the situation that didn't quite add up. Perhaps he could get the figures to make sense. Deciding there was no time like the present, he turned again to Annie's Facebook page.

Several hours, and 2,596 'friends' later, he had found three people who seemed – from the messages they'd left for Annie and her responses – to have nursed with her in Dundee. He sent Elaine MacLellan, Karen Warnock and Jan Larsen a message each, citing the Saturday feature story he was writing, and requesting an interview.

In Calgary; Elaine thought it best to check with Annie before replying to the journalist. She hadn't been in touch for a while, so her email gave Annie all the family news before getting round to Colin. She signed off with, *I know you are busy, so if I don't hear I'll assume it's okay to speak to him.* She then emailed Colin, asking what he wanted to know. If Annie said no, then she wouldn't tell him.

In Adelaide, Jan was in bed with a raging temperature and aching limbs. Facebook was the last thing on her mind.

In London, Karen turned on her laptop to check for responses from the previous evening's speed-dating. She was hoping the nice-looking city lawyer would be in touch. Damn! The screen resembled some sort of psychedelic tartan commissioned to commemorate something. What was going on? Blue and green horizontal lines crossed yellow and red vertical lines, leaving only two inches of desktop picture at the top of the screen. Then she remembered. The red-wine spill earlier that evening must have seeped into the workings. She looked at her trusty phone sitting on the coffee table and wished she had got round to arranging an upgrade.

Rachel, Annie's constituency worker, attended to the political aspects of Annie's Facebook page. She posted press releases and details of constituency engagements, and checked for messages and posts which required Annie's personal attention. The message from Elaine was obviously personal, so, without reading to the end, she added it to the list for Annie to go through.

The following morning, Elaine looked at the request from Colin for her phone number along with a list of questions. He suggested that it would be easier to talk than email back and forth. No messages from Annie yet, but she would give her a little while longer to reply.

A malfunctioning alarm clock meant Karen did not have time for a shower let alone time to check her emails on her son's computer, so it was well after seven the following evening before she finally looked at her Facebook messages.

Chapter Forty-Four

After the weekly meeting of all her parliamentary colleagues, Annie decided to walk back to her flat in the hope that fresh air would blow away the recriminations following the disastrous by-election results. There was also a faint hope the exercise would reduce her puffy ankles. This uphill walk, previously an easy ten-minute stroll, now involved frequent stops to catch her breath and she was less than halfway home when a taxi drew up beside her.

Andrew stuck his head out of the window. 'I'm going past your door?'

Annie clambered in, dismayed that the degree of bend necessary was now nearly impossible. 'Thanks, Andrew. I think my walking days are over till July.' The taxi continued up the Royal Mile, the opposite direction from Andrew's flat. 'Not going home then?'

'No. I'm meeting someone for dinner.' He was looking straight ahead.

Annie waited for him to elaborate. He didn't. 'That's nice. Where are you going?'

'That new place in Bruntsfield.'

'The Italian one?'

'Yes.'

It was like pulling teeth. 'I've heard it's good.'

'Yes.'

Had she annoyed him? They sat in silence at a

red light.

As they began to move, she could stand it no longer. 'Is everything okay? Are you angry with me?'

'Everything's fine, Annie. I'm not angry with you.' He was still looking straight ahead.

Everything's not fine, she thought. 'If it's about that tourism thing, they misquoted me. They asked where I went last summer and if I was going to holiday in Scotland this year. I said I lived in the beautiful Scottish countryside and worked in its historic capital, but that I liked a little bit of heat and sun each year. Totally misrepresented me – though I suppose I should be used to it by now.'

'Annie,' he said, still looking straight ahead. 'I'm not cross with you. Honestly.'

'Are you worried about the by-election then? Something's bugging you, Andrew. You're all ... buttoned up.'

'Nothing is bugging me. The by-election is finished with.' He turned to look out the window. 'That shower destroyed Grant Paton's reputation, and he was a good man. He probably *was* covered in dust from the attic, and even if he had been indulging in some relaxation therapy with his hostess, that was their business. Innuendo sticks.'

'And don't I know it!' Annie smiled.

Andrew said nothing sympathetic or encouraging.

Then it dawned on her that he was considering his own reputation, alongside that of Grant Paton. She lowered her voice to ensure that the driver couldn't hear. 'You must put out a statement saying the baby is not yours. You can't allow everyone to think otherwise. If I do it, it'll just fan the flames, but you should, Andrew.'

For a moment, Annie thought he was going to ignore her. He leant forward and tapped the partition, 'Just here.' The taxi came to a halt outside Annie's flat.

Andrew gave her a perfunctory peck on the cheek. 'Perhaps you're right. We'll speak tomorrow sometime.' He opened the door for her.

'I'm off to Orkney, but I'll phone you.' Annie manoeuvred herself backwards onto the pavement. The door closed and the taxi moved away. She found her key and let herself into the close. Not that she could blame him, but the relationship with Andrew was altered. She was surprised at how sad she felt about that. As she climbed the stairs, she could feel her phone vibrating. Why couldn't the world leave her alone? There was always someone trying to unload, be it a constituent, civil servant or family member.

Well this time they could wait.

She took her phone from her pocket, laid it on the table, then swapped her trousers with the elastic waist and the jacket which wouldn't button any more for her dressing gown, and sat down nursing a cup of tea. Her briefcase, containing work to be turned round by the morning, reproached her from the other end of the sofa, so she put it out of sight in the hall. A tiny rebellion, but it made her feel better.

The insistent ringing of the landline woke her. She heaved herself off the sofa and picked up the receiver. ''lo,' she said, still not quite awake.

'Thank God I've got hold of you. I've been leaving texts and messages for ages. Then Joe gave me this number. Where have you been?'

'Who's that?' She peered at her watch. It was nearly midnight! She had been asleep for three hours.

'Who d'you think it is? It's me! Karen.'

'Sorry. I was asleep. What's up? Is it Joe?'

'Not Joe, no. You are about to be rumbled, that's what's up. A journalist has been working through your Facebook friends. He wants to interview me about what you were like before you went into politics. Says he's doing an article on the person behind the political face.'

Annie slumped and yawned. 'I'm not aware of anyone doing that.'

'Wake up, Annie! He's contacting people from Dundee! Jan emailed me. She's heard from him too. Luckily she was ill, so didn't reply. Who else from Dundee days is your Facebook friend?'

'Sorry... Who is doing this?'

'Colin something from the *Daily Scot*.'

'Oh *him!* I didn't know he was one of my friends, but I do have thousands.' She laughed.

'I know you do. That's why I realised it would be quicker to speak to you. This is no cosy "Who's the real Annie Cochrane?" interview, my friend. It's a "find the daddy" exercise. Come on. Who else from Dundee is your Facebook friend?'

'Let me think. There's that funny little woman who was a ward maid ... Jackie something. And, oh yes, there's Elaine.'

'Elaine! How did I not think of Elaine?' Karen couldn't keep the contempt from her voice.

'I take it she is not your "friend" then?' Annie teased.

'You take it right. Despite her godliness, I don't think she is into forgiveness.'

'Well, it was a shock returning from looking at engagement rings in the jeweller's window to find you in bed with Holy Henry. Her Holy Henry.'

'I was doing her a favour – giving him a bit of instruction for their wedding night.' Karen became brisk. 'That means I can't contact her, so you will have to do it and check who else there might be. It won't necessarily stop the journo, but it'll slow him down.'

'Okay,' said Annie. 'I'll do it in a minute.' Her tone was flat.

'Have you spoken to Tarik yet?'

'Stop nagging, Karen. I'll do it soon.'

'Soon might be too late, if this Colin makes a breakthrough.'

Annie didn't reply.

'You okay?' Karen asked.

Annie sighed heavily. 'Knackered. I feel like I'm a hundred and I could do with my body back.'

'Everything okay at the last antenatal visit?'

'Blood pressure up a bit – ankles like an elephant, but otherwise okay.' She tried to sound cheerful. She didn't need a lecture on being positive.

'You need to look after yourself, not the rest of Scotland.'

'I know! Only another four weeks of work – I'll take the last three off.'

After Karen rang off, Annie looked at her computer, then at the clock. It was now gone midnight and she was going to have to be up before six to sort the contents of the briefcase and pack for the trip north. Facebook could wait.

It was just before eight the following morning when Annie climbed into the waiting car in which her private secretary was already ensconced. She was to give a radio interview on the newly published report on the care debacle concerning the elderly couple and the dead dog before the flight to Orkney where she was to attend the Health Board's annual meeting. Annie had read the care report at six and mentally prepared a few lines.

After she had fastened her seatbelt, Tony handed her a couple of the day's tabloids. 'You are in the news again, I'm afraid.'

Annie closed her eyes and exhaled. It was as if someone had hit her. The constant criticism over the past couple of months had worn her down and each onslaught left her feeling more battered. 'What is it now? Am I to be hanged because I holiday abroad?'

'No, they've moved on from that. I'm afraid it's your mother's pills, the cost of the delinquent's dental treatment and the private room at the hospital for your confinement.'

'Private room! What private room?' This was nonsense.

'Someone at Strathperry Infirmary has shown the press the room reserved for you – there is a picture of it.' Frank showed her the paper.

She grabbed it. 'I have *never* asked for, or, for that matter, been offered a private room.' She was furious now. 'And they are saying things about

Shawn and Mum?'

Tony handed her another tabloid. 'According to this, Shawn's getting implants for his missing front teeth at a cost of £5,000 to the public purse and your mother is getting an expensive Alzheimer's drug not available to everyone, again at the taxpayers' expense.'

She rapidly turned the pages and handed the papers back. As a politician, she was fair game, but her mother and her son were not. Surely Shawn's dental treatment couldn't cost that much? In the bit about her mother the words 'drug trial' were not even mentioned.

The car had covered the short distance to the studio and was now parked outside. Annie got out and Tony moved to accompany her, but she needed some space. 'I'll be fine. If you could stay here and try to find out the actual cost of Shawn's treatment that would be very helpful.'

As a well-practised interviewee, Annie had no trouble setting things up in the unmanned studio. She put on the headphones through which she could hear what was going on in the main Glasgow studio. The news headlines featured the care report after the Connor Clarke investigation and she was relieved there was no mention of her mother or Shawn's teeth.

Laura Anderson, that day's presenter, had a style which was both combative and shrill. 'And in our Edinburgh studio, we have Annie Cochrane, Minister for Health and Wellbeing. Good morning, Minister.'

'Good morning, Laura.'

'Before we discuss the report, Minister, I

wondered if you had any comment on Connor Clarke's refusal to resign as MSP.'

Nice try, Annie thought, but I'm not colluding in your guilty until proven innocent line. 'Certain accusations have been made and denied. I think we have to wait and see what the truth of the situation is before anyone starts demanding anything.'

Unsuccessful in generating an exclusive, Laura returned to the matter in hand. 'Minister, the report of the tragedy resulting from failure to implement a care package has just been released. It cites a catalogue of errors and dereliction of duty by staff who, it has to be said, were operating in what was clearly an underfunded and stressful environment. In an earlier interview, the spokesman for social services complained staff had to deliver a five-star service on a one-star budget. What is the Scottish government going to do about the underfunding? And what is it going to do to prevent such a tragedy happening again?'

Annie started on her prepared lines. 'Firstly, Laura, can I say that several unfortunate circumstances combined to create this tragedy. No one was deliberately negligent. A group of care workers—'

'The negligence surely is on the part of the government, and yourself as Health Minister, for expecting those who deliver care to function on reduced budgets?'

'If you could let me finish my original point, I will then address the issue of funding. No one was deliberately negligent. A group of care workers held a small party for a colleague going on maternity leave at the end of a working week.

It was common practice–'

Laura wasn't letting Annie got away with a simple listing of what everybody already knew. 'But surely, parties should not be held during working hours? That was negligence!'

'In workplaces all over Scotland, it is common for employees to hold such events in office hours, but if you have read the report–' and I bet you haven't, Annie thought '–you will know this will no longer be allowed to happen in public sector departments. *As I was saying,* it was common for the hospital to flag up the need for a care package, only to have discharge arrangements change. A fax sent at the last minute went unnoticed. It was a most regrettable human error.'

Laura, however, was determined to name, shame and blame. 'Surely a system should be in place which eliminates human error.'

Annie was annoyed now. The interruptions and attempts to dig pits for her were nothing unusual, but the last comment was stupid, to say the least. 'Laura, I'm sure those who work at the BBC are above human error, but unfortunately, unless we hand everything over to a tribe of robots, human error will very occasionally occur. This particular human error is unlikely to occur again, but we cannot foresee every circumstance – and even with a tribe of robots we would be liable to mechanical failure.'

Annie realised her tetchiness had crossed a line. The interviewer's task is to make the politician look stupid, not the other way around.

Laura's voice became louder and higher. 'And is funding to community care to be increased?

What are you personally going to do about this, Minister?'

'As you know, Laura, the budgets are reviewed annually. The finance minister will be considering funding issues over the summer.' She realised her pitch had risen too. Low and slow, she reminded herself.

'But Minister, waiting till the autumn increases the risk of similar tragedies. There must be a way of increasing funding in the meantime.'

You understand the process of government funding perfectly well, Annie thought. This is a clear attempt to make me sound heartless and unreasonable. She continued. 'The need for extra funding will be urgently reviewed in light of this report, but as you will realise, it is important that funding is targeted appropriately and that cannot be achieved without careful consideration.'

'So you intend to leave the elderly and vulnerable for months while civil servants review options.' Before Annie could reply, Laura went for the kill. 'In the meantime, can you comment on reports that you and members of your family have the benefit of preferential treatment from the NHS.'

'I beg your pardon?' Annie played for time. Her heart was racing.

'I'm referring to newspaper reports today that you are receiving preferential treatment regarding your own antenatal care, that your mother is receiving a drug to treat her Alzheimer's which is not available to the general public, and the cost of dental treatment to the victim of an assault by your son is of the order of £5,000.'

Slow down. Be calm and measured. 'I have never requested preferential treatment–'

'Do you deny you were taken ahead of the queue at an antenatal visit, that you were seen by a consultant and that you are to have a private room when the baby is born?'

Annie tried to speak slowly. 'I have never asked for preferential treatment for myself and I am not prepared to talk about my mother's health issues, or issues relating to my son.' Firm and assertive, that was the way to do it, but her voice had the hint of a shake.

Laura was just getting into her stride. 'Can you not see that people will think you, a government minister, a member of the Scottish Parliament, are using your position to get services not available to everyone?'

Something snapped. Annie's judgement and self-control deserted her. 'Right! I've had enough of this!'

Laura started to interrupt, but this time Annie was not giving way.

'Be quiet, will you! Let's get a few facts straight! One – yes, I was seen by a consultant on my first antenatal visit, but I did not request this. Two – I have not asked for a private room, and had no idea that it was the hospital's intention to give me one. Three my son hit someone under severe provocation and was later admonished. I have no idea about the extent or cost of the dental treatment required. All I know is that the delinquent in question is now in a residential unit – I think the colloquial term is "junior jail" – and lastly, because you have forced me to air my mother's medical issues on national radio, I will confirm that she has been diagnosed with Alzheimer's and is on a drug trial – and for those like yourself, Laura, who obviously do not understand what a drug trial is, let me explain. Some people get the drug being trialled and some people get the usual drug. No one, not even the doctor, knows who is getting what. Therefore I don't know, and my mother does not know, which drug she is getting – is that clear enough for you? And while we are at it, why don't I clear up the matter of the whispering campaign regarding the paternity of my baby. Andrew Fraser is not the father–'

An arm had reached past her and disconnected the microphone. 'Minister!' Tony said sharply. 'I think you've said enough.'

Annie closed her eyes. Tony must have covered the distance between car and studio in record time.

She heard Laura saying '–and we seem to have lost the link to Edinburgh. Let's go to the traffic news.'

Annie removed the headphones and sat quite still. Resignation was now inevitable. She must have made Marlene's day! Trying to pass this off as a hormonal rant was unfair to pregnant women everywhere. Shawn's anonymity as a child offender had been compromised, and her remark about Andrew was unforgivable. Tony helped her with her coat and escorted her from the building as if she might fall at any minute. As the car moved away, she reached for the phone. 'I need to put my resignation to Andrew now.'

Tony took his best 'let's be reasonable' tack.

293

'Minister, we have a plane to catch in just over an hour's time. You are going to be away from Edinburgh for a couple of days. Can I suggest you think about this, for a while at least?' He added, 'You'll be interested to know that Shawn is not getting implants – just a bridge costing about £500.'

Annie thanked him for that news, but she was adamant. As the car continued towards the airport she repeatedly tried Andrew's landline, mobile and office, but he was not to be found. She would have to carry out the day's engagements even though she knew no one really wanted to see or be seen with a soon-to-be ex-minister.

Marlene lay in bed with her eyes closed as the morning news programme emanated from the clock radio. Never an early riser, she was allowing herself a leisurely start. Annie was droning on about the report into the care debacle, so Marlene turned over for another ten-minute doze.

The change in tone of the discussion brought her back to consciousness and she listened with growing delight as Annie gradually signed her death warrant. What a result! She hugged her knees with glee.

Morton had already enjoyed a five-mile run, followed by a workout in the gym with his personal trainer and had been in his office for over an hour by the time Marlene reached him on the phone.

'Did you hear it? The woman has seen the light and committed suicide! Hallelujah!'

'Morning, Marlene! I take it you are talking about Fat Annie's interview?'

'I most certainly am! I like to start the day on a high. The only thing I missed was the bit about Andrew Fraser? I didn't hear it properly.'

'She said *Andrew Fraser* ... then it was cut off. Is the father of her baby? Is not the father of her baby? Is a complete plonker? Likes making love to hamsters? Who knows?'

'Is the father, surely? The stalker assured you, Andrew stayed over every Monday. It must be him.'

'That's right. He did! So you are probably right, Marlene.'

'I am so looking forward to the moment when he tells me she is resigning. I'll remind him of all the occasions when he has assured me of her competence. Leak that, will you, Morton – that I have been trying to get him to get rid of her for months, but that he has been inexplicably stubborn on the matter. They'll read between the lines.'

'I'll do my best. At least this takes the heat off us, regarding Connor.' Morton put his mobile back in his pocket and returned to his croissant and coffee. He hadn't let Marlene in on a snippet of new information he had received from the Haunter. Annie had had a male visitor in her hotel room in Aberdeen in late October last year. The Haunter was sure of it, and Morton now had a good idea who that man might be. Things were falling into place.

There was, however, one outstanding puzzle. Why did Marlene hate Annie with such ferocity? The strength of that hatred had increased of late. Morton was keen to get to the bottom of that one. Perhaps he would give Mr Keiller a call.

From the Flybe lounge at Edinburgh airport, Annie eventually managed to discover that Andrew was at his office, but in a meeting and unable to speak to her. She felt sick. Not the pregnancy this time, but shame, embarrassment and the realisation that so many things could not be undone. The sooner she resigned and could go home and hide in Corrachan the better. She was pouring herself a glass of orange juice, when she remembered the conversation with Karen. She hadn't checked her Facebook friends. Why bother? What was one more scandal now on top of all the others? Tarik deserved to be found out.

But the thought of what Karen would say made her find her phone and go on line. Wearily, she called up her page and saw that people were already posting comments on her wall about the interview. Most were unfavourable. She saw she now had 2,889 friends. I wish, she thought. She typed in a couple of names of Dundee friends but got no joy. She could not be bothered. She switched off her phone and checked she had her boarding card ready.

Chapter Forty-Five

After a day of meetings in Orkney where some congratulated her on defending her privacy and others avoided the matter, Annie found she had some free time before dinner. The sick feeling had stayed with her all day and she had found it difficult to concentrate. When she emerged from the Health Board meeting, there was a TV camera and various photographers waiting. She refused to comment.

So far she had only managed a brief stilted conversation with Andrew.

'I'm resigning.'

'And what if I don't want to accept it?'

Why was he making things more difficult? 'Andrew, I lost my temper on air, I have compromised the identity of a child offender and I've brought you into it too. I have no option but to resign.'

He wasn't going to give up easily. 'I'm being told there is more than a little public sympathy.'

'Yes and a lot of public ridicule. What's the point? Can't you just accept it now?'

'I'm in the car at the moment. We'll discuss this properly this evening, Annie. Call me after seven.'

She looked out of the window of her hotel room and watched a small ferry approach the slipway. She had an hour to fill before speaking to Andrew, and, with the baby turning somersaults, she decided on a walk round Kirkwall in the hope that some fresh air might help put things in perspective. There was no sign of the media as she strolled up the narrow paved street until she arrived at the pink and yellow sandstone of St Magnus Cathedral. Eoin had told her about this Viking building but, with the large wooden doors firmly closed, she was obviously not going to see inside on this trip. She walked up the path at the side of the

297

building, intending to look at the old gravestones. On the off chance, she tried the handle to a side door as she passed and it opened. Just as she stepped in, the organ began to play and then the singing began. Realising she had gate-crashed the choir practice she sat down near the door, closed her eyes and let words and the music wash over her.

When peace like river attendeth my soul – wouldn't that be nice, *she thought. When sorrows like sea billows roll* – sorrows like a bloody tsunami! *Whatever my lot, thou hast taught me to say, it is well it is well with my soul.* It is well – Minty's mantra! – or nearly. Looking up into the vaulted roof, she wondered how many people over the centuries had sat in this place. Perhaps, if it was a boy, she could call him Magnus. Magnus Cochrane conjured up an image of a tall blond Viking – perhaps not, then. She checked her watch. In less than an hour, she would no longer be a government minister. As with the vast majority of politicians, her career was going to end in failure – and she realised she didn't care. The choir were singing the chorus – *It is well, it is well with my soul* – and although she couldn't say why, she felt it just might be. She shifted her weight in the chair to get comfortable and felt the baby grip her bladder with both hands. Much as she would have liked to stay longer, she let herself out as quietly as she had come in.

Back in her hotel room, with her feet up on two pillows, she phoned her mother who professed to be fine but couldn't remember how she had spent the day. Annie made several suggestions. Had she gone next door to visit the McCaffertys? Had she gone shopping? Had she been with Minty? Had she spent the day at home? The answer to all of these was the same: 'I don't know.'

She did remember that she had heard Annie on the radio. 'They were asking you lots of questions. Has something gone wrong?'

'No, Mum. Everything's fine. I've had a lovely day here in Orkney and just been for a walk to see the sights. I'll be home tomorrow and I'll be over for tea.'

A call to the McCaffertys told her May had spent the day with Minty. Yet another call provided the details. 'I gather you had Mum today, not that she can remember anything about it. The miracle medicine doesn't seem to be working too well.'

'She was fine with me,' said Minty. 'We had a lovely time – lunch in the garden, then she had a snooze on the sofa while I did my Amnesty letters. Pity she can't remember it. By the way, heard you on the radio, giving that snippy piece what-for about your mother's right to privacy and the rest. Are you okay?'

'Not really. Much as that woman deserved to be put in her place, I've gone too far. I'm about to phone Andrew about my resignation. Ranting women and efficient government ministers are not the same thing.'

'Please, don't do anything rash!' Minty appeared to be shouting over background noise.

'I can't hear you properly, Minty. Where are you?'

'I'm in the supermarket car park. Always do my shopping at this time of day, you get all the reductions. I got a pound of mince for forty pence last week. You wouldn't believe the crowd round the reduced stuff – people you wouldn't expect. Joyce Macdonald from the Tory committee lifted a quarter of cold ham from under my hand.'

Annie was unsure of the relevance of Joyce's shopping habits to what had gone before. Minty then returned to the point. 'Most of them had heard you on the radio and agreed with everything you said. I'm telling you, your popularity is on the up!'

'Don't think so, Minty. I'm glad of your support, but I'm on the way out.'

'Well, dear, your decision, not mine, but I do think it would be a shame.'

'I'll come and see you at the weekend. When things have calmed down.'

'Any time, my dear. I'm always here.'

What would she do without Minty? Always there with a word of support. 'By the way, I was in St Magnus Cathedral earlier and I thought about your mantra – *all shall be well* – and I realised that it could be in the end, but the getting there is awful.'

'Perhaps you're further along the road than you think.'

Annie was weary 'Well, I must go now. Have to ring Andrew before dinner.'

'I'm not an early bedder, call me later if you want an ear.'

'Thanks, Minty. Bye.'

Annie looked at the phone in her hand and, in order to delay the inevitable a while longer, she phoned Joe. Over the past few weeks he had been taking her calls, and, while their relationship was not back to normal, it was improving. He answered after four rings.

'Hi, Mum.'

'Hi. How are you doing?'

'Fine. You?'

'Okay. I'm in Orkney.'

'What you doing there?'

'Meetings.'

'Oh.'

She had better warn him to stay away from the press. 'I had a bit of a run in with a radio interviewer on air. There may be a bit of fallout.'

'Oh? Why?'

'Health funding, Gran's medication, my fatherless baby, and the £5,000 cost of Shawn's dental treatment to the taxpayer. I put them straight and I said Shawn was in a residential unit. That is a real breach of his rights. Unfortunately, I didn't know till afterwards that his new teeth only cost £500.'

'Good for you. Stuff Shawn's rights.'

'I'm about to resign.'

'I'm sorry, Mum.'

'Not your fault.'

'It was me who hit Shawn.'

'And I lost my cool on air and said things I shouldn't. It is most definitely my fault.' She paused. 'If the press get to you, I would rather you didn't comment.'

'I'm about to go on nightshift, stacking shelves. No one even knows my name there. Got to go now, but speak to you soon.' He paused. 'And take care, Mum. Bye.'

'Bye?' He didn't sound as if work was much fun.

She would have to phone him again at the week-end. There were only ten minutes before dinner, so the call to Andrew could be delayed no longer.

His phone rang several times before a woman's voice answered. 'Andrew Fraser's phone.'

'Hello?' Annie didn't recognise the voice. 'Is that Joanna?'

'No. It's Pam here.'

Pam? Pam who? He doesn't have a civil servant called Pam.

'Pam Miller. I'm a friend of Andy's. He's not here at the moment. Can I take a message?'

'It's Annie Cochrane. He asked me to phone about now. Do you think he'll be long?'

'About ten minutes or so. He's just popped out to the off licence to get a bottle of wine to go with our dinner. Can you call back?'

Annie looked at her watch. 'Could you just ask him to ring me, between ten and eleven? I have an early start.' She paused. 'So sorry to intrude on your evening, but it's important I speak to him tonight.'

'Did you say it was Annie Cochrane?'

'That's right?

'We were just talking about you.'

'Oh?'

'Yes. I said to Andy that you don't have your troubles to seek, do you? I must say, I admire what you said this morning. Your personal life is your business and nobody else's. I've been telling Andy he needs to speak out to clear his name.'

'Well, that's all sorted.' Annie was short. Who was this woman who was discussing her with Andrew?

302

'I don't think it is, actually.' Pam was equally short. 'It's caused even more speculation.'

Annie adopted the falsely pleasant tone women use when talking to other women they dislike. 'I know he wanted to keep the heat away from me. *Andrew is* always the gentleman. Thanks so much ... Pamela was it? I won't keep you, but if you could give him my message...'

She put the phone down on the bedside table. So Andrew had a girlfriend. That explained the taxi ride, and it probably explained why she couldn't get hold of him this morning. She ought to be pleased for him, but she wasn't. In fact she was surprised at how strongly she felt about the news. Reluctantly, she forced her feet into her shoes then re-applied her lipstick. As she surveyed her reflection in the bathroom mirror, she decided Jane wouldn't have taken to Pam either, and that Andrew was never called Andy by anyone. Who did this Pam think she was?

Downstairs in the bar, she found her civil servants making small talk with the council delegation. She accepted a fizzy water and began to talk about joint community care funding.

By nine, having passed on the starter, and picked at the salmon and new potatoes, Annie was toying with a 'trio of ices'.

'...and we cannot deliver a seamless efficient service with the current level of funding. It can't be done; the director of finance was saying.

A creeping warmth in her nether regions, similar to the sensation resulting from a heated car seat, distracted Annie. Oh my God! She hadn't felt any urge to go, but she was peeing herself.

'...We want to achieve this, but we can't. Do you have an answer for us, Minister?'

She had to get to the Ladies. 'Well, there might be an answer, but you'll have to excuse me first. Drawbacks of pregnancy! I'll only be a moment.' She pushed back her chair and stood up. There was a dark patch in the middle of the beige upholstery. She draped the napkin as decorously as she could, and pushed in the chair. Luckily she was wearing black trousers, and the wet-pants walk could be passed off as a pregnant waddle.

As she sat on the loo with an empty bladder but continuing leak, it became obvious that her waters had broken. She put her hand on the bump. There was no pain, only tightenings which each passed off after a few seconds. What did she know about premature rupture of membranes? Not very much, but she did know she needed to see a doctor immediately.

Eoin had spent the afternoon driving north on the A9. He was to have the people-carrier on the pier in Caithness at eight the following morning when Annie and entourage disembarked from the ferry from Orkney. He was then to convey them to a succession of meetings in Caithness, Sutherland and Inverness. As he drove north, the radio news bulletins all featured Annie's outburst. He knew he would not be driving her for much longer. He would miss her. Unlike some politicians, she was still a member of the human race.

As he neared his hotel at the edge of Thurso, he could see the Orkney ferry berthing at Scrabster harbour. The last ferry of the day back to Orkney had not yet sailed. Why stay in a hotel here when he could be on the ferry, heading home for the night? He bought himself a return ticket as a foot passenger. A visit to his Granny, a pint with his cousin and he would be on the same boat as Annie in the morning.

Chapter Forty-Six

Annie was waiting in a side-room at the hospital. She wasn't in labour and she had stopped leaking, but the reaction to her suggestion that she get the first plane to Edinburgh in the morning made her realise things were potentially more serious than she thought. She was told in no uncertain terms that she would be compromising the health of her baby if she did not agree to an immediate air-ambulance transfer to the nearest place with a special baby unit, Aberdeen.

The sick feeling returned. Dear God. Not Aberdeen. Just when she thought she had reached rock bottom, there was yet another hole to fall into. A hole containing Tarik. A transfer to Edinburgh or anywhere but Aberdeen would have to be arranged, but first of all she needed to be on the Scottish mainland. *Oh, baby, please stay there long enough for me to sort things.*

She summoned Tony and began to detail what had to be done. 'You'll need to cancel tomorrow's visits. Eoin must be in Thurso by now, so all of you can go home by road. I have to contact Andrew Fraser too.'

'All in hand, Minister. Don't worry. Just concentrate on yourself.'

'Easier said than done, Tony.' She managed a smile. 'Any hint of tomorrow's coverage of my outburst?'

'Not yet, I'm afraid.'

She noticed that he didn't meet her eye.

There was a knock on the door. It was the midwife who was to accompany her on the flight. Annie held out her hand to Tony. 'I've enjoyed working with you. Thank you for all you've done. After I have spoken to Andrew tomorrow, my resignation will be public knowledge. Tell the staff in the office that I'll pop in as soon as I can to thank them personally.'

Any hopes she might have had that her admittance to hospital would remain a secret were dashed as soon as she failed to return to the dinner table. Local media, both press and radio, were alerted and, by the time she was airborne, the national press and BBC Scotland were fully informed.

At Aberdeen Maternity Hospital she was scanned, then poked and prodded by increasingly senior members of staff who in turn ascertained that her membranes had ruptured, she was not in labour and the baby was fine. So far so good. She asked to be transferred to Edinburgh in the morning, but this was not as straightforward as she had imagined. Edinburgh's special baby unit was full, she was told, before being treated to a lecture on the nationwide shortage of neonatal intensive-care cots.

Attached to drips containing antibiotics to prevent infection and steroids to promote foetal lung development, she was put in a side-room. As she was resigning, she no longer cared if this was reported as a special privilege. She was told to get some sleep but her mind buzzed. Everything was such a mess. Her baby might be very premature, she had stuffed up her job, she had a batty mother, an unhappy son and she had lost Andrew. Tears began to run down her cheeks and when a midwife looked in ten minutes later to check on her, she was red-eyed.

'What's the matter?'

Annie sniffed. 'Bit worried about things, you know?'

The midwife patted her hand. 'You shouldn't worry, Ms Cochrane. Thirty-three weeks is not bad. Lots of babies smaller than that do just fine.'

'I know. I just wasn't quite ready for it yet.' She reached for a tissue.

'Well, it may not happen for a while, but if you go into labour, we've got a great team here. Doctor Khan is just amazing with all the prems.'

It was more than Annie could take. The cause of the problem being cited as the solution! The tears started again.

The midwife handed her the tissue box. 'Come on, now, dry your eyes. You really should try to get some sleep.'

'I know.' Annie tried to pull herself together.

'Perhaps a cup of tea or a glass of milk would help?'

'Yes, please. A glass of milk, thank you.'

As the midwife left the room, Annie remembered she had not contacted Elaine – now that she had fetched up here, a journalist 'outing' Tarik was not the attractive prospect it had been earlier in the day. She rummaged in her handbag for her phone and found instead the St Gerard Medal. She gave it a squeeze, sent a mental apology for all her uncharitable thoughts and politely asked him to indulge in some intercession on her behalf. With the phone finally unearthed, she had just managed to call up Elaine's Facebook page when an auxiliary returned with the milk.

'No mobiles allowed, I'm afraid. This wonderful thing beside you–' She pointed to a contraption with a phone and screen on it '–allows you to phone, internet and email as well as watch TV. We'll get it fixed up in the morning, then you'll be all set, but for now, you need to switch your phone off.'

Annie dutifully did as she was told.

'You can have the phone trolley if you need to contact anyone tonight

'No, I'll be fine. Thank you.'

As soon as she was alone again, she switched the phone back on and sent Elaine a message – *do not answer any questions please* – then she switched it off and closed her eyes. She felt a kick. *Stay there, baby. For your sake and mine, please don't come out yet.* Another kick answered her. She tried to relax, silently saying *all shall be well* each time she breathed out until she drifted into an uneasy doze.

A sharp pain brought her back to consciousness. She breathed through the contraction then lay in the dark, waiting to see if it was followed by another. She reached the ten-minute mark and was beginning to hope it had been a one-off when another started. She rang for the midwife and, after explaining what was happening, requested the phone trolley. It looked as if she would need her birth partner sooner rather than later.

Chapter Forty-Seven

It had taken Annie ages to get to sleep and she could have done without being woken up to have her blood pressure taken. After several contractions around two in the morning, all had gone quiet, but she had remained awake until after five, trying to figure out what to do about Tarik. Now wide awake again, she considered her situation till breakfast arrived. Having abandoned the soggy cornflakes, she was chewing on a piece of toast when an entourage of medical and midwifery staff piled into the room. Annie focused on only one person – consultant neonatologist Tarik Khan looking suave and totally in control.

Suddenly she realised the consultant obstetrician was saying something to her. 'Sorry? What was that?' she asked.

'I said, how are you feeling this morning?' He looked at her over the top of his glasses.

'Oh, yes. Okay, I think.' Annie patted her bump. 'Everything seems to have stopped.'

'Good, good. Better in than out at the moment.' He turned to the registrar. 'A summary please, of what has been done since admission? I gather there were some contractions during the night.'

As the results of the prodding and poking were detailed, Annie glanced at Tarik. He was listening intently to what was being said, not looking in her direction at all. The long-winded summary led to a discussion amongst the staff about probabilities and possibilities till Annie could stand it no longer.

'Hey! Could you include me please?'

The consultant obstetrician apologised. 'I'm sorry. How rude of us! To put it in a nutshell, we will continue to give you steroids for the baby's lungs and antibiotics to prevent infection and hope the baby stays where it is for as long as possible. However, if you do go into labour, you can't get a more experienced man than your friend Tarik when it comes to caring for premature babies.'

Perhaps, but she wasn't having him anywhere near her. 'Isn't there a problem with us knowing each other?' she ventured. 'Shouldn't someone else be in charge?'

'No, no!' the obstetrician was happy to inform her. 'It's only a problem when there is a family relationship involved.'

Too right. Annie's thoughts raced. It was now an either/or situation. Either a transfer to somewhere else or she would have to tell Tarik. She decided to try the transfer option again.

'If nothing is happening, could I be transferred to Edinburgh? Or perhaps Glasgow? It would be much easier for my family and my civil servants. Also, as this isn't my home area, I don't like taking up one of your beds.'

The consultant shook his head. 'The special

310

baby unit in Edinburgh doesn't have any spare cots at the moment and I understand Glasgow is reaching capacity.' He paused and looked paternally over the glasses again. 'Even if there was a spare cot, it's a three-hour drive and you wouldn't want to give birth to a baby as small as this in a lay-by, now would you? I strongly advise you to stay here.'

Tarik was smiling at her. 'He's right. You could go into labour any time and you need to be in a special unit. We'll take good care of your baby. I promise.'

Bastard, she thought. I'm going to have to tell you.

Marlene's staff knew that she did not receive calls before eight-thirty, so when her phone woke her at eight she was ready to be rude to whoever it was.

'Yes?'

'It's Morton.'

She peered at the clock and sat up. 'What do you want at this hour? It had better be important.' And not more bad news concerning Connor Clarke she added to herself.

'Thought you would be interested to hear the latest on your favourite coalition partner.'

The Cochrane woman again! 'What has she done now? Resigned, I hope.'

'Not yet. The official word is that Annie has been air lifted from Orkney to Aberdeen as a precaution after having a few contractions. Unofficial word is that her waters have broken and she is in premature labour.'

'Is that all? I'm not really interested in her

311

gynaecological details. The least the woman could have done was resign immediately. I told you she wasn't bright. Hanging on like this. It reflects badly on the whole coalition.'

There was the briefest of pauses. 'Marlene, it distracts press interest from Connor and is likely to continue to do so. Hospital vigils, statements about babies, and revelations about potential fathers are far more interesting to the general public than money laundering. I'm surprised that you hadn't worked that out for yourself.'

'Well, let's hope she is in labour then!' Marlene hated it when Morton talked to her in that tone of voice. 'Find out, but don't phone me back till after nine.' She hung up immediately, determined to have the last word.

Chapter Forty-Eight

It was not unusual for May to wake early nowadays and it was just after six when she went to the kitchen to make her morning tea. While the kettle came to the boil, she set off for the bathroom, making a detour into the living room to open the curtains. The local paper was on the coffee table, so she sat in her chair and began to read. After a few minutes, she became aware of steam in the air and went to investigate. She eventually located the kettle, with lid off, boiling merrily. She managed to open the window first, then tried to turn the key in the back door before realising it was already unlocked. May's heart began to race. She always checked it was locked before she went to bed. The hoodlums must have come in during the night! They would be hiding in the house, waiting to attack her.

She picked up the phone and speed-dialled Annie. A voice told her that *the Vodafone you are calling is switched off, please try again later.* She looked at the clock. She couldn't go to Bob, it was too early. What could she do? There was nothing for it. She would have to sort this herself.

A few minutes later, armed with a large frying pan, May crept through her house. Our Lady Of Lourdes and the midget St Bernadette had been moved into what had been Joe's room, creating a private chapel of sorts. As she opened the door, the fanlight window, open to remove the smell of candles, created a through draught and the back door shut with a bang. Now certain she was not alone, she managed to drag the chest of drawers across the doorway and began to pray for help.

After she had gone through every prayer she could remember, she stopped and listened. Were they gone or were they lying in wait for her? Then she heard footsteps. She tightened the grip on the flying pan. They were still here, going through her things; they would find her engagement ring and her mother's brooch! She stifled a scream.

'May? Are you in there? It's Minty! Open the door.'

'Minty! Have they gone?' May whispered.

'There's only me here, May. Open the door.' Minty rattled the handle.

The strength May had summoned to move the

313

chest of drawers across the door in the first place had now left her. It was only with some energetic pushing from the other side that Minty managed to move it a little further and squeeze herself through the gap.

May flopped down on the bed. 'Oh, Minty. I've been praying for someone to come and help me and here you are.' She glanced at the bedside clock. 'You're up very early this morning.'

Minty sat down and took May's hand. 'You phoned me. Don't you remember? About half an hour ago. You told me someone was in the house.'

May looked confused. 'Did I? I tried to get Annie. Did I phone you too?'

'Yes, you phoned me and I said I would come. Have the police been yet?'

'Police?' May was completely lost.

'Yes, I phoned them to say you thought you had an intruder.'

On cue, the doorbell rang. Minty struggled through the gap and went to the front door where two uniformed police officers waited on the step. She led them into the living room.

'I think everything's fine, but perhaps you had better check.' She looked at her watch, 'Took your time. I had to drive from Loch Corrachan and still got here before you.'

'We came as quickly as we could, Madam.' The tone was frostily polite. 'Are you the householder?'

Minty rolled her eyes at the officer's skills of deduction. 'No. I told you I *drove* here. Mrs Laverty phoned me and I phoned you.'

'She'll be the other one,' one of the policemen muttered to the other.

314

'Other?' said Minty. 'Did someone else phone you?'

'Mrs Laverty phoned us. Not for the first time either.' He consulted a piece of paper in his hand. 'It's the third call in ten days. All false alarms apparently.'

'Even so, I would be grateful if you could check the house,' Minty said briskly.

The policemen looked at each other and shrugged.

Minty knew she was now about to sound like her nanny, but she said it anyway. 'The sheep belonging to the boy who cried wolf were eaten, you know.'

Ten minutes later, as Minty was pouring tea, Bob and Jean McCafferty appeared at the back door, having seen the police car. May was tearful and flustered. Her living room was becoming rather crowded.

'I tried to get Annie,' she kept repeating. 'My daughter. Where is she?'

'Annie Cochrane, the MSP,' explained Bob to the policemen who exchanged a look which indicated that they knew exactly who May's daughter was.

'Well, your daughter won't be answering the phone if she's in labour,' said one of the policemen, his voice kinder now.

'Is the baby coming?' May reached for her beads. 'Is she in the infirmary? In Strathperry?'

'According to the radio, she's in Aberdeen,' Minty explained. 'I heard it on my way here.'

'No. Annie wasn't in Aberdeen!' May had a rare

315

flash of almost clear thinking. 'She was in Shetland, in a hotel.' She looked at Minty, daring her to contradict, then added, 'Your buttons are done up the wrong way.'

Minty examined her blouse. 'So they are! I got dressed in a hurry, my dear, without my glasses on. Probably lacking in some undergarments too!' She adopted a wistful expression. 'That takes me back...'

May pointed at Minty's feet. 'You're a case this morning. One shoe's brown and one's black.'

The policemen closed their notebooks and made for the door.

Chapter Forty-Nine

With her MP3 player plugged into her ears, Annie was trying to find Radio 3. She needed something calm, something to promote logical thought. All the tracks she had were too upbeat. She settled for a moment on Radio Scotland, where the announcer was saying, '...and following Annie Cochrane's angry outburst yesterday, our programme this morning asks: Do we expect too much from our politicians? If you have a view, call on the usual number...'

A hasty press of the button took Annie to Brahms. She lay back on the pillows and closed her eyes. When she opened them again, another half hour had passed, another thirty whole minutes for her baby to mature. She was just drifting

316

off again when the door burst open and Karen appeared, with Tony on her heels.

'Look at you! Sleeping!' Karen wagged a finger at her. 'I thought you said it was urgent!' She gave her a hug.

Annie manoeuvred herself upright. 'Everyone thought it was urgent, last night.' She looked to Tony for confirmation. 'Didn't they?'

Tony nodded. 'Air ambulances, the lot! How are things today, Minister?'

'Bit of a drama at two this morning when I summoned poor Karen, but quiet for now.' She pointed to the chairs. 'Have a seat.'

'Well, you're in the right place.' Tony took off his coat. 'It must be a comfort to know all the proper expertise is at hand.' He made himself comfortable.

'You could say that, I suppose.' She exchanged a glance with Karen. 'I've to stay right here – at the moment – till all this stuff is inside me.' She pointed to the drip. 'Then if nothing has happened, they will think what to do. I need a transfer to Edinburgh, I keep telling them, but that's full at the moment.' She suddenly turned to Tony. 'Hey! How did you get here so quickly? You can't have come with Eoin!'

Tony beamed. 'No, Minister, I came on the first plane. The others all went on the ferry. Karen, here, was next to me in the taxi queue and we realised we were both going to the hospital, then on the way we discovered we were both coming to see you.'

'Well, I'm very glad to see you both. I was feeling rather abandoned.' Her eye fell on the phone

317

contraption. 'Tony, it looks as if I'll be here for the rest of the day at least. Could you fix up the phone account for me? I need to check up on Mum and speak to Andrew.'

'Not a problem, Minister.'

Karen raised her eyebrows appreciatively as he left the room.

Annie scowled. 'Leave him alone. He's married!'

'Happily?'

'Karen!'

'Okay, Okay!' Karen looked round the room. 'So, here we are, in the bastard's lair, eh? Only you could manage that! Have you seen him yet?'

Annie fell back onto the pillows again. 'Just on the ward round.'

'And?'

'And what?' Annie brushed some toast crumbs from her front.

'You know bloody well what! *Have you told him?*'

'Not yet.' Annie shook her head. 'I decided after everything that happened yesterday I didn't care if he was named, and I still don't, as long as I can get a transfer out of here.'

'After yesterday? Did something else happen yesterday?'

'Oh yes, I forgot it didn't go out over the English airwaves.' She recounted the tale of the previous day's radio interview.

Karen attempted a high five. 'Glad to hear you've stopped talking shit and are giving some instead. But transfer or no transfer, Annie, you are still going to have to tell the bastard. There is no perhaps. Tarik is going to find out, because at some point a journalist is going to tell him!'

318

Annie was fiddling with the sheet.

'Earth to Annie! Hello!' Karen forced her friend to make eye contact. 'You need to sort out a line between you, before some hideous tabloid makes it up. Not only for your sake – try thinking about the effect on Joe and your mother if this goes public.'

'Suppose so.' Annie knew she sounded like a sulky teenager.

Karen was now in parent mode. 'I hope you've spoken to Elaine?'

'I sent her a Facebook message. Using a mobile is a hanging offence in here, you've no idea. I'll check when Tony's sorted the phone and internet.'

But Karen was not going to be diverted. 'So, when are you going to tell him?'

'Soon, I expect. Now, give it a rest, please. How on earth did you get here so quickly?'

'Soon as I put the phone down I was off! Booked a flight, packed, then woke my mother up in the middle of the night. She'll be on the train to London by now. Woke my neighbour at five to ask her to see the boys to school. Mum'll be there when they get back. Sent a text to my colleague at work saying I won't be in today and here I am. Don't you think I deserve a medal for efficiency?'

'You do. Thanks, Karen, you are a true friend.' Annie surveyed the bump. 'After all that, it might just be a false alarm.'

'And it might not! Now I'm here, I'll stick around for a while.' She wagged a finger. 'If only to make sure you and the bastard have the necessary conversation.'

Annie raised her hands in defeat. 'Mum may have lost the capacity to organise me, but you make a good substitute.'

'And don't you feel the better for it? Handing over a bit of control?'

'I do, actually. I've been very lonely recently.' She could feel the tears starting.

'Hey there! It'll be okay.' Karen gave her another hug then handed her a tissue.

Annie blew her nose and tried to smile.

'Better now?'

Annie nodded.

'As you don't need your hand held right now, I'll go and dump my stuff at my sister's house. She's been warned I'm on the way. Is there anything you need while I'm out?'

Annie thought for a moment. 'I could do with a nightie, this hospital gown is awful. Knickers and something elastic-waisted to wear in case I'm allowed to get up later would be good too. I've only got my business suit.' She pulled her bag from the cupboard by the bed and located her purse. 'Here's a card. The pin is the last four digits of my mobile number.'

'Anything else madam requires?'

'Some goodies from the M&S food hall would be lovely, and—' Annie paused '—a trip to a chemist for anything I might need, if the baby decides to be born. You are a wonderful woman, you know.'

Karen took a bow and picked up her coat. 'Okay! I'll be as quick as I can.' She opened the door then turned back to look Annie in the eye. 'So are you going to speak to the bastard while I'm out? You might find he's as keen as you are to

320

effect a transfer.'

'Okay! I'll do it now! Look, I'm pressing the call button.'

Ten minutes after she had requested to see Tarik, a woman whom Annie remembered from the early morning entourage stuck her head round the door.

'Hello, I'm Dr Buchan, the senior registrar in the neonatal unit. I understand you have some questions?'

Annie smiled apologetically. 'They're not that easy for you to answer. I was actually wanting a chat with Dr Khan about a few things.'

'He's busy at the moment, but I can try to answer any queries you may have.'

Why wasn't life easier? 'Thank you, but I want to speak to him about a ... personal matter. Could you *possibly* ask him to pop in for a minute or two when he has time? Sorry you had a wasted journey.'

As she left, Dr Buchan held the door open for Tony.

'You now have a personal telephone number and access to the internet – and I brought you these.' He laid a pile of newspapers on the bed.

Annie couldn't bear to look. 'Have they crucified me?'

'It's an interesting mix. Some sympathetic, some not so. Online comments are similar – just checked them out. Try not to worry, Minister. I think the tide might be on the turn.'

Annie shrugged. 'Can't go any further out can it?'

The newly connected phone began to ring. They both stared at it, before Annie picked it up.

'Annie? Is that you?'

'Hello, Minty! The phone's only just been connected. How on earth did you get the number?'

'I phoned about eight o'clock, but they wouldn't tell me anything, even though I said I was phoning on May's behalf. Just said you were comfortable. I told the woman if you were in labour, you wouldn't be in the least comfortable.'

Why had Minty been with her mother at eight in the morning? 'Is Mum okay?'

'She got herself into a bit of a state earlier on, thought she'd an intruder, but it's all sorted now.'

'An intruder?' Annie dreaded what she might hear next.

Minty was reassuring. 'Don't worry! It was a false alarm. She's fine.'

'What happened?'

'Bit of a muddle. She's going to stay here with me for a few days. You're not to worry.'

'You still haven't told me how you got this number,' Annie reminded her.

'I got May to phone this time and she ended up speaking to your civil servant. Tommy? Tony? Hey presto, we have your number! She wants to talk to you of course, but before I put her on ... Annie, I think you should hang in there, not resign over all this fuss. It's the rules of the playground, you see? The bully – in your case it's the media – kicks you till you're on the ground, then, when you bite back, they decide that it's no fun any more and they find someone else to kick. A tipping of the scales. In Marlene Watt's case, she was the bully and the press the victim, but now–'

Annie didn't want to think about Marlene this morning, and before Minty could let rip, she interrupted, 'Is Mum there? Can I have a word?'

'Of course! Certainly, my dear. Here she is.'

The handset bumped and whistled at the other end.

'Hello?'

'Hi, Mum, are you okay?'

'Hello?'

Annie raised her voice. 'Hello, Mum.'

'Hello? Hello? I can't hear a thing, Minty.'

Annie heard Minty suggesting May move the phone to another part of her ear.

'Hello?'

'Hi, Mum. Can you hear me?'

'I can now.' May's tone implied that Annie had been at fault. 'Minty says the baby might be coming. Have they got a hospital in Shetland?'

'Mum, I'm in Aberdeen and they have all the high tech things for premature babies, so don't worry. I hear you are going to stay with Minty for a bit?'

'No! Why should I stay with Minty? I've got a perfectly good house of my own. We bought it – from the council. What's that, Minty?' Annie could hear a muffled exchange. 'Oh, I *am* staying here. Why? Oh yes, I remember now. Is Kenny with you? I would never have wanted your father near me when I had you and John, but it's all the thing nowadays, isn't it?'

'Kenny's not here, Mum,' Annie took a deep breath, 'but Karen is. You remember my friend Karen?'

'Oh?' The Karen part of May's memory obviously had a large hole in it.

Annie felt the beginnings of a contraction. Tony looked in alarm at her sharp intake of breath and screwed-up face. She mouthed at him to find a midwife. 'Karen's getting me all the things I need. I'm fine and I'll phone you later at Minty's.'

'She wants to speak to you again.'

Annie closed her eyes and waited.

'Annie, I've been thinking, you're going to need some help when this baby is born. My great-niece has just finished a Norland Nanny training. I'll get in touch with her–' Minty stopped in full flow as she heard Annie gasp. 'Everything all right, dear?'

'Not sure, Minty. Things ... starting to happen ... have to go now ... the midwife's here.'

A couple of hours later Karen returned to the hospital, weighed down with carrier bags. She'd had a lovely time at the shops with Annie's credit card. As she came out of the lift, she found herself face to face with Tarik, who was standing at the nursing station.

'Well, well. Look who it is.' She dropped the bags and put her hands on her hips.

Tarik glanced up from the notes he was reading. The last time he'd seen this woman she had told him what he could do with himself. He looked back at the notes, but said, calmly, 'Karen. Not seen you for a while. What's brought you here?'

'I'm Annie Cochrane's birth partner, as if you hadn't guessed already.'

'Nice of you to come and hold her hand.' He

flicked over a couple of pages. 'I gather there's no daddy on the scene.' Karen's eyes narrowed. 'There most certainly *is* a daddy, Tarik.'

'Really? And when are we expecting him to show up?' Tarik closed one set of notes and picked up another.

Karen had had quite enough. She took him by the arm and moved him forcibly out of earshot of the staff. 'Have you spoken to her this morning?'

He shrugged off Karen's hand. 'Just at the ward round. She had some questions, apparently, so I sent my registrar.'

'Can I suggest you find some time in your busy, busy schedule to talk to her? On your own – not with an entourage. It's personal and very important.'

'What on earth is all this about, Karen?' He picked up another set of notes. 'I'm very busy today. Annie's is not the only premature baby threatening to make an appearance.'

'Cut the crap, Tarik!'

The venom in her voice finally broke through. 'I beg your pardon!'

'Don't give me that! I know you two got together again last October. I know she tried to contact you and I know you *deliberately* misunderstood her message! Dumping her once was bad enough, but walking away by letter for the second time is inexcusable!'

Tarik looked around, as if hoping somebody might rescue him from this mad woman. Then his expression changed to one of mild amusement, before he started to laugh. 'Surely, she doesn't think it's mine?'

Chapter Fifty

Twenty minutes later, his equilibrium restored, Tarik knocked on Annie's door. She was now in labour and any hope of a transfer had gone.

Karen, sitting in the armchair munching some of the food she had bought, put the sandwich back in its container and stood up. 'Think I'll go and get myself a coffee.'

They watched her leave then both started to speak at the same time.

'You first!' Annie made a mock gesture of deference.

'Annie, there seems to have been a big mis-understanding.'

Here we go again. It's never his fault. 'Really?'

'I spoke to Karen, in the corridor.'

'I know. She told me.'

'You think this baby's mine!'

'Ten out of ten!' She leant forward and stared at him. 'I don't think it's yours, I *know* it is. But don't worry, I'm not going to name your or sue you for maintenance.' She lay back again. 'I wouldn't have told you at all, except for the fact that a journalist is making inquiries ... and anyway, you should not be in charge of your own baby's care.'

Tarik sat down in the chair Karen had vacated. He seemed to have nothing to say.

'Well?'

He looked up at her. 'Annie, was I the only

person you slept with around that time?'

Here we go. 'No, but the other person has had a vasectomy. It *is* your baby, Tarik.'

He was silent again for a few moments. 'Annie, you have no idea how much I would like this baby to be mine, but I don't think it can be.'

A liar as well as a bastard. She looked at him in disgust. 'Why am I not surprised to hear you say that? Facing up to your responsibilities never was your forte.'

'No, Annie.' He moved to sit on the edge of the bed. 'This baby isn't mine because I'm sterile.'

Annie stared at him. This couldn't be happening again. 'What? Sterile?'

'Yes.' He paused. 'After my wife died, I went to work in Pakistan for six months. While I was there, I caught mumps. Fertility comes back for most men, but not me. I have regular tests, but I am still infertile. If you want the full story, Julia – my new wife – and I are now actively investigating the options of sperm donors and adoption. Do you understand what I'm saying, Annie? To the best of my belief, it is impossible for me to father a child.'

Annie was speechless. She looked at him and realised he meant it.

'You have a zero sperm count?' she managed to say.

'More or less.'

'Well one of the buggers just won a Paralympic swimming medal.'

'I can hope,' Tarik replied. He paused. 'You said the other guy had a vasectomy?'

'Yes! Twenty years ago! It's hardly likely to have reversed after all this time.'

'Unlikely,' Tarik agreed, 'but not impossible. Or perhaps he just hasn't been with fertile women.'

Jane's early menopause surfaced in Annie's memory as another contraction started. Tarik handed her the gas and air and took her hand as she breathed her way through the pain.

'Stronger one, that time?'

'Definitely.' Annie removed her hand from his. 'Either I am favoured by God thanks to my mother's incessant praying, or I am about to give birth to a baby fathered by one of two infertile men. Moreover, that baby defied the presence of an IUD. What do you think the odds against are?'

'Huge.' He smiled. 'Sounds like you might have offended someone up there, rather than being favoured.'

Annie shook her head.

He stood up and looked out of the window. 'Now I know I'm not the only infertile one, I can hope that the baby just might be mine. I so want a child of my own.' He turned to face her again. 'If it is mine, Annie, I want to be part of the child's life.'

One look at his face told her he was being sincere. 'I can't believe your wife will be thrilled.'

Tarik shrugged. 'She knows how much I want my own child. She will understand.'

I wouldn't bet on that, Annie thought wearily. 'Anyway – what now? Do you intend to remain my consultant?'

'At the moment. No point in creating speculation, if it's unfounded?'

'And if it is "founded"?' She watched his face light up at the possibility.

'I expect I'll own up and hand you over to one of my colleagues.'

'You don't have to go public. It's not fair on Julia,' she added.

He nodded grudgingly, then paused before saying, 'That message you sent about the reunion – you know, I honestly thought you were talking about a real reunion of the old crowd. Were you very angry when you got my card?'

'Angry comes nowhere near it, Tarik. Incandescent, then betrayed and, abandoned would just about begin to sum it up. I decided my baby was better off without a father than someone who could treat me like that.'

'Oh, Annie, I'm sorry. I really am. There was nothing in the way the message was relayed to make me think you needed an immediate reply. You should have contacted me again.'

'And disturb your honeymoon?'

Another contraction swept over her. When it had passed, he took a cold flannel to her face, then handed her a towel.

'Annie, Annie...' He took the towel from her and returned the flannel to the basin. 'If it's me, I won't abandon you this time, I promise.' He glanced at his watch. 'Now, I'm afraid I have to go, but I'll be there at the delivery. Will you be all right till Karen gets back, or shall I get the midwife?'

After Tarik had gone, Annie considered the situation. So the father of this child could be either him or Andrew, and each of them now had a potentially disgruntled woman in tow. This was too bizarre. Could there be another explanation?

Had someone spiked her drink at some constituency bring and buy? Was it possible she was a hermaphrodite?

The door opened and Karen was back. 'Well?'

Annie put her hands on each side of the bump. 'You'll love this. My baby's father is either the man with the vasectomy, the man whose balls have shrivelled up as a result of a bout of mumps, or has some exciting sexual encounter slipped my mind?'

Outside Annie's room, there was some speculating going on amongst the auxiliaries and midwives.

'Is that Annie Cochrane's birthing partner?' asked Annie's midwife as Karen walked past.

'Yes. She's come up from London.'

'She's a friend?'

'Yes. Friends from way back, so I hear. She knows Dr Khan too. Saw her talking to him earlier. Why d'you ask?'

'There's no man about. She won't say who the father is.'

'You don't think…?'

'Well, it's not beyond the realms of possibility. Would explain a lot, wouldn't it?'

'But why doesn't she just come out? No one cares any more. Even in Aberdeen.'

'She's got an elderly mother. The one that keeps ringing. And she's a public figure.'

'I suppose so … so a lesbian daughter with a sperm donor is worse than a straight daughter with no man?' They giggled.

A light flashed on the console. 'Look! Annie Cochrane's buzzer! She's your lady, off you go –

and keep your eyes open.'

As the midwife entered the room, she observed Karen holding Annie's hand during another contraction.

'Things seem to be hotting up,' Karen informed her. As the contraction passed off the midwife observed that Karen kept hold of Annie's hand. 'Well done, honey,' she said in a mock American accent. 'We'll have a lovely baby by the end of the day.'

Annie took a sip of water and lay back. 'Less of the "we"! I'm the one doing all the work.'

'It's very stressful for me too, you know,' Karen replied. 'I have to mop your brow and hold your hand. I take my responsibilities very seriously.'

'Can I just have a little look and see how things are coming on?' the midwife asked, smiling at them both in a non-judgemental way.

Chapter Fifty-One

Andrew Fraser had been up since six, working on his ministerial papers. Not having received a call from Annie, he had tried her number at about ten the previous evening, but her mobile was off. It couldn't have been that urgent after all. It was now nearly eight and he intended to make one quick call before trying Annie again. He checked the call log on his phone, looking for the number he needed, and was surprised to see that Annie had indeed rung him the previous evening, and that the call had been answered. Answered while he had been out buying a bottle of wine.

Andrew considered his position. The sound of the hairdryer indicated his overnight guest had completed her shower. He rang Annie's number, but the phone was still switched off. Telling himself that mobile coverage was patchy in the far north, he went to the kitchen and started to make breakfast. While he waited for the kettle to boil, he put one slice of bread in the toaster, then paused. What about putting a slice in for his overnight guest? He decided to wait. Breakfast preferences had not yet been discussed. He popped two teabags into the pot. Judicious use of alcohol the previous evening had taken the edge off his nervousness, enabling him to proceed smoothly to the second part of the evening and, all things considered, it had been a pleasant experience. He missed the easy intimacy he had shared with Annie, but still, this relationship had considerable potential.

Pam appeared at his side. She slipped an arm round his waist and gave him a quick kiss. 'You weren't there when I woke up!'

The toaster popped.

She took the hot slice and selected a plate and knife from the drying rack. 'I'd hoped for a more exciting way to start the day than a slice of toast.'

Andrew put more bread in. 'Sorry, but I had work to do.' He smiled at her. 'Didn't get any done last night.'

'Any butter and marmalade?'

'Certainly.' Andrew opened the fridge door for her.

'Oh! Golden Shred. I didn't know they still made that!' Pam's nose wrinkled.

Andrew lifted the pot, ready to pour her tea.

'Do you have any coffee? I need a caffeine shot in the morning.'

He put the pot down, opened the cupboard and took out a jar of instant.

The nose wrinkled again. 'Perhaps I will have tea after all.'

Andrew poured milk into his tea and sat down at the breakfast bar. He flicked the switch on the radio to catch the eight o'clock headlines.

Health Minister Annie Cochrane has been flown by air ambulance from Orkney to Aberdeen. It is understood Ms Cochrane, who is nearly seven months pregnant, was in premature labour. A hospital spokesman in Aberdeen said she was comfortable and her condition was being monitored.

The state of Scotland's economy will be the subject of a debate today in the Scottish Parliament–

Andrew pushed the off button and put down his cup. 'Oh my God! Poor Annie.' He stood up. 'The baby will be tiny! It must have been the stress.'

Pam put a hand on his arm. 'Hey, Andy! It's all speculation. You know what they're like. It's probably a false alarm.'

'I'm worried about her. She's a good friend. She was going to phone me last night...' He paused and looked at Pam expectantly.

She held up her hand as she swallowed a mouthful of toast. 'Sorry! I forgot to tell you! She did phone last night while you were out. Asked you to call later, which you did anyway, didn't you? She'll be fine. She's seven months isn't she?

That's not a problem nowadays.'

Andrew wasn't listening. 'I need to find out what's happening. She was on an official visit, so her private office must know.' He scrolled down the numbers on his phone as he made his way to the living room. Her officials knew very little – Tony hadn't yet reported in. He called the hospital, and they told him Ms Cochrane was sleeping. He relaxed slightly. She couldn't be in full-blown labour.

Pam came to join him. She nestled in against his chest. 'Is she okay?'

'She's sleeping.'

'See, I told you it wasn't all gloom and doom.' Pam nestled in a bit further. 'What are we doing at the weekend, then?'

Andrew put his arms round her. 'Don't know about you, but I am doing a party dinner on Friday, constituency business on Saturday and seeing my daughter and family on Sunday.'

She looked up at him. 'Oh poo! Don't you ever take time off? I fancied going to that French restaurant in the New Town. It's got two Michelin stars, apparently. I thought you could just drop your name and we'd get a table.'

'Sorry, Pam, not this weekend.'

'So when *are* you able to give me some attention?'

Andrew checked the diary on his phone. 'How about next Thursday? I'll see if I can get a table.'

'Fine. And afterwards we can go to my place. I have proper coffee and decent marmalade.'

Chapter Fifty-Two

Colin had caught the mid-morning train to Aberdeen. Adrenaline and naked ambition made it difficult for him to sit still. He knew he was onto a good story. Everything had fallen into place the previous evening when Elaine in Calgary had obligingly let slip a name – Tarik Khan, a doctor who had vanished out of Annie's life without explanation in 1989. A bit of Googling produced a Tarik Khan, now consultant neonatologist at Aberdeen Royal Infirmary. Annie had visited the maternity and special care baby unit in October and the codger with the placard had seen someone whom he thought was Asian, looking out of the window of Annie's hotel room.

Colin had found the daddy!

When he had woken up this morning and discovered where Annie was, he couldn't believe his good fortune. What a story! And no one else anywhere near. Having checked the train times to Aberdeen, he made an appointment with the Corporate Communications Department at the hospital for four o'clock. Once he had all the details of the special care baby unit, he intended to do a bit of hanging around, listening to staff gossip, before writing it all up.

Lynn McKechnie from the *Daily Post* was also on a train. She had the Annie/Andrew story written and ready, but her editor had told her to wait for the birth and to concentrate on the Connor Clarke story in the meantime. Now she had been pulled off that and told to go immediately to Aberdeen. Lynn's contacts there were limited, and as the train sat in Perth station she tried to think of the best way to get the information she needed. Three ladies, hoping to sit together, paused to ask if the seat covered with Lynn's coat, handbag and overnight case was taken.

''Fraid so.' Lynn smiled sweetly.

'Back the other way, Sandra,' said one of the trio wearily. 'We'll see what's in the next carriage.'

Sandra. The name triggered something in Lynn's brain. She fished out her phone. There was a Sandra who worked as a PA in the Glasgow office. Didn't she have a sister working as a midwife in Aberdeen?

Bingo.

Chapter Fifty-Three

Throughout the day, as Annie's labour progressed, Karen had held her hand, mopped her brow and kept Tony, who was on his way back to Edinburgh, and Andrew up to date with her progress. Joe wasn't to be told till it was all over. Towards the end of the afternoon, Annie, who had been determined to cope without, begged for an epidural, but was told it was too late.

She was entering the transition phase and,

woozy from the gas and air, was becoming belligerent. 'It's so unfair. I should be running the fucking country, not trying to push out a baby I never wanted.'

'Shh,' said Karen, eyeing the midwife.

'Don't shhh me! Here am I, trying to crap a football, and you just sit there holding my hand and telling me to shhhhh. If it was you in this position, we would have bloody well heard all about it.'

Karen calmly wiped her friend's face. 'I couldn't be in your position – I had a hysterectomy if you remember.'

The midwife silently clocked the information. So that was why Annie was carrying the baby.

A few minutes later, Annie felt things change. 'I think I want to push.'

'Let's have a look.' The midwife bustled over to inspect. 'You are fully dilated, so go ahead. I'll just keep the neonatal team up to speed.'

The contractions were getting closer together, the baby's heartbeat slowing with each one before normalising. After a particularly strong contraction, it remained slow for what seemed like an age, then very gradually recovered.

'Good. That's better.' The midwife's relief was obvious.

The next contraction produced a similar result. The midwife watched the monitor and tried to sound matter-of-fact. 'I think I'll just get the doctor to come and have a look. Won't be long.'

Annie grabbed Karen's hand. 'Something's the matter, I know it is! The heart rate shouldn't stay slow like that. Oh shit, another one...'

The midwife reappeared with a registrar as the

contraction passed. The heartbeat was again slow to pick up. Their mumbled conversation in the doorway infuriated Annie.

'Can you tell me what the hell is going on!'

'Your baby's heartbeat is a bit slow. Move onto all fours and see if a change in position helps.' The registrar was businesslike.

Annie obliged, getting into position just in time. The heartbeat was no quicker to pick up after the next contraction.

'Think we need you on your back again.'

Annie turned over with difficulty.

'Hmmm...' The registrar turned to the midwife. 'Alert the team, please. ASAP!' He moved round the bed so that he was talking directly to Annie. 'Your baby is not getting enough oxygen. We need to get it out as soon as possible.'

'A section?'

'Perhaps, but we may be able to do a forceps delivery. We'll decide as soon as the team gets here.'

'Will it be okay?'

No one answered.

The room began to fill – the consultant obstetrician, the neonatal team, Tarik – and by the time she had pushed her way through three back-to-back contractions everyone was in place. Then everything became a blur. Her feet were raised. She heard somebody say '...just a little prick...' as they gave her local anaesthetic, to which Karen muttered, 'That's usually the cause.' Annie vaguely remembered the midwife quipping, 'But not always, eh?'

As the next contraction started, Annie was instructed to push and the doctor began to pull.

A few seconds later, it was over.

'You've got a little girl!' said the midwife, holding something purple resembling a skinned rabbit in front of Annie face before disappearing to the side of the room where there seemed to be a great many people.

'Karen, what are they doing?' Annie groped for Karen's hand. 'She should be crying. What are they doing?'

Karen was unusually uncommunicative. 'Just the usual procedures – stimulating her breathing…'

After what seemed like an age, there was a cry, faint at first, then stronger. Annie and Karen exhaled. The midwife brought the baby, now wrapped, to the bed. A minute face, pink now rather than lilac, peered at her mother.

'Hello,' said Annie.

Karen had tears in her eyes. 'She's so tiny.'

'Yes. We're taking her to the neonatal unit now.' Tarik's face floated into Annie's line of vision. 'Don't worry, you can come and see her later when they've sorted you out.'

'Will she be okay?' She tried to read his face.

'I hope so,' he said. 'We'll take good care of her.'

Chapter Fifty-Four

It was early evening when, like a geriatric Thelma and Louise, Minty and May arrived in Aberdeen. Minty had driven north at a steady 35 mph, oblivious to the hole in the exhaust pipe and the irritation caused to other motorists. The dog, relegated to the back seat, had panted in May's ear all the way.

Minty had decided that Aberdeen was the place to be in the circumstances, so with an overnight bag each, they had set off. Stopping at Glamis Castle en route, May was disappointed to find herself in a self-service café with a bowl of soup and a sandwich – where was the Queen Mother? – but Minty made up for this by re-living previous visits to the castle and elaborating loudly on her connections with the Bowes Lyon family. May was not the only one in the cafeteria to be enthralled – all sixty-six of those on the *Splendours of Scotland* bus tour fell silent and allowed their food to go cold. Lunch was followed by a walk in the grounds for the dog, and a restorative snooze in the car followed by another cup of tea which meant that it was well after four before they were on their way again.

Having reached Aberdeen, Minty had no idea where she was going. She drove towards the city centre and, seeing no relevant signpost, pulled up on a double yellow line, got May to roll down her window and asked directions from an elderly man.

He gave her an incomprehensible series of lefts and rights, and for reasons best known to herself, Minty did a U-turn, narrowly missing a bus.

'That bus nearly hit us!' Minty was irate.

May, her eyes shut, said nothing.

Several more sets of directions and several U-turns later, they arrived at the maternity hospital. There was a lack of available spaces in the car park, so Minty parked on a yellow line next to a notice which said *Parking Permitted Only Within the Designated Spaces.* 'Right then May, let's go and see what's happening.'

When Colin left the Corporate Communications Department, he had been fully informed about the workings of the neonatal intensive care unit. Word had come through just before he left the building that Annie had had a little girl who was now in the neonatal unit on account of her prematurity. Outside, he bumped into Lynn, who had just had a coffee with Sandra-from-the-office's sister.

'Well, look who it is,' she said.

'You been sent to cover the Cochrane birth?' Colin thought he had better check there wasn't an even better story about.

'Yes. You?' Lynn was doing the same.

'Uhuh. She's had a daughter. Baby's in intensive care. Suppose that's newsworthy.' Colin decided to test the waters. 'Any sign of Andrew Fraser? Or any other possible daddies?'

'No.' Following her coffee with Sandra-from-the-office's sister, Lynn was now confident that no daddy was involved. Annie Cochrane's was a turkey-baster baby. 'You think it's Andrew?'

'There doesn't seem to be anyone else in the picture. There was that business on the radio yesterday. Sure it's him.' Colin hoped he sounded convincing.

Lynne nodded. She wasn't going to give the game away. She took a cigarette from its packet and offered Colin one. 'Baby going to be okay?'

'Thanks.' Colin accepted a light and took in a

341

lungful of smoke. 'I don't know what the prognosis is. Suppose we'll have to hang about here for daily bulletins.' He rolled his eyes at the prospect.

'Probably.' Lynn nodded. 'In the meantime, fancy a drink?'

'Why not?' said Colin. 'Let's try and find a pub full of off-duty medical staff.'

Chapter Fifty-Five

Once she had been stitched up and had some tea and toast, Annie was taken to see her daughter. She looked so tiny lying in the incubator. She was on a ventilator, wired up to numerous machines. Tarik appeared and stood beside her.

'Will she be okay?' Annie asked.

'She's finding it a bit difficult to breathe on her own at the moment, but the odds are in her favour. She's a reasonable weight and she's obviously a fighter.'

Annie looked at the tiny girl whose veins showed clearly beneath her skin. 'I've been trying to work out if she's yours. I thought it would be obvious, but I'm none the wiser. Are you?'

Tarik took her hand. 'You know I really wanted her to be mine.'

'There's a but?'

'I'm afraid there is.' He let go of her hand. 'I've done some checks. My blood group is 0. Your blood group is 0. We could only make babies with blood group 0. This baby's blood group is A.'

342

Annie looked at her daughter. 'Simple as that.'

'It's not me, Annie.'

She heard the genuine regret. 'I'm sorry, Tarik.' Was she? She was sorry for his disappointment, but at least her daughter would have no resentful stepmother. But then she recalled the phone call with Pam. She stared at the baby. Andrew's baby. She was Andrew's after all.

A nurse approached and told Annie her mother was outside.

'Where did she spring from – as if I couldn't guess? Is she allowed in?'

'Yes, grandparents are allowed.'

'And if there's another old lady there, could she come in for a peek too? She's an honorary grandparent.'

A few minutes later, May and Minty appeared beside the cot.

May was nearly in tears. 'She's so small. All these tubes and things, poor wee mite.'

Minty put her hand on Annie's shoulder. 'I'm sure she'll be fine. They have all this now.' She pointed to the surrounding equipment. 'It's so different.'

'I'm trying to convince myself that *All shall be well*,' whispered Annie.

'It will be, you'll see.' Minty gave her a fierce hug.

'She looks like Kenny. Where is he?' May looked round the room.

'Mum, said Annie gently, 'Kenny's not the father.'

May looked momentarily appalled then confused. 'Well, who *is* the father?'

343

Minty raised her eyebrows, and tilted her head.

Annie lowered her voice and leant towards her. 'New information has come to light,' she said quietly.

'Is the priest coming to baptise her?' May asked anxiously.

Annie took her mother's hand. 'No, Mum. I don't have a name for her yet and besides, she's not in any danger.'

May was unconvinced. 'I'll need to say a prayer to St Brigid. She's the patron saint of babies, and of children whose parents aren't married.' The disapproving tone was obvious. Then as an after-thought, she added, '...and of chicken farmers.'

Later, back in her room, Annie took the opportunity to speak to Minty while May was snoozing in the armchair. 'I hope all this isn't bringing back bad memories.'

'No, my dear, it's fine.' Minty patted Annie's hand. 'I haven't forgotten, not at all, but it was a long time ago. I was at home with just the district nurse, and Helena was much tinier than your baby. She was viewed as a lost cause as soon as labour began.' There was a pause. 'The worst thing was that she was my last link with my husband.' She swallowed hard, then, with an almost imperceptible shake of the head, returned to the present. 'But all this high-tech equipment gives these tiny ones a chance, and that's wonderful.'

Annie checked May was still asleep. 'Minty, Tarik isn't the baby's father. It must be Andrew after all.'

'I thought he'd had a vasectomy.'

Annie shrugged.

'I don't understand.'

'No, I don't either. It must have reversed itself or something. Apparently these things can happen. She doesn't have the right blood group for her to be Tarik's, and Andrew *is* the only alternative. Jane had a very early menopause, so he's probably had live ammunition for years but not known.'

Minty sat down on the bed. 'Have you told him?'

'I've only just found out. I've made such a mess of things. After what I said yesterday on the radio, he can't own up to it now. The press won't rest till the whole story comes out.'

Minty was totally confused. 'What happened yesterday? Did I miss something?'

'I announced on the radio that Andrew wasn't the father.'

'No you didn't,' Minty told her. 'You just said, "Andrew Fraser–" I must admit I wondered what in God's name you were thinking about, and then you got cut off. It was most peculiar.'

Annie sat, stunned for a moment. 'So ... nothing, apart from the name?'

Minty shrugged. 'Not a peep. Sounded like one of those lost line things. Happens more than it should, in my opinion.'

Annie smiled. 'Good old Tony.'

'The father's somebody called Tony?' Minty blanched.

'No! Definitely *not*. Tony, my private secretary, dived across and disconnected the microphone.'

'Good grief,' said Minty, then she paused. 'So

does Andrew even know she's been born?'

'Karen phoned him.'

Minty glanced quickly at May but she was still snoring gently. 'You need to tell him as soon as possible. He'll be okay about it, I'm sure.'

He might be, Annie thought. 'I was all set to be a single parent, Minty. Perhaps we should just leave it like that.'

'Annie, he's not stupid. Or are you going to pretend there was a *third* man involved?'

'There is a reason why I don't want to tell him.'

'Yes?'

'He's got a girlfriend, a cosy-dinner-for-two sort of girlfriend, who calls him Andy. He's moved on. It's not fair to come crashing back into his life with a baby in my arms.'

'A stay-the-night sort of girlfriend?' Minty asked.

'Possibly.' Annie hesitated. It stuck in her craw to have to say it. 'Probably.'

Minty looked hard at her. 'If Andrew and this lady – does she have a name, by the way?'

'Pam.'

'If Andrew and *Pam* are sharing a bed, he may find that your baby is not the only addition to his family. You might think it's unfair to tell him, but not telling him isn't fair either.'

The thought of Pam with fat ankles and stress incontinence was the one bright spot in Annie's day, but Minty was right, it wasn't fair on Andrew. 'Depends if she's still of child-bearing age. If not, then it doesn't matter.'

'Have you met her?' Minty wasn't going to let the matter go.

'No. Only spoken on the phone. It's hard to know how old she is.'

'Just tell Andrew, Annie.'

Annie closed her eyes for a few seconds. First it was Karen nagging her to tell Tarik, now it was Minty insisting she tell Andrew. She was a grown woman, she would make up her own mind. 'I'll find out how old she is. If I have to tell him I will, but not otherwise. Not now, anyway,' she added.

There was a knock at the door and Karen joined them. 'They were giving her a tube feed. I left them to it.' She rifled in the bag of Marks and Spencer food and unearthed a packet of millionaire's shortbread. 'Don't know about you, but I'm starving. I've just had a very strange conversation with one of the nurses. She commiserated with me that my parents weren't here to see the baby.' She took a large bite of shortbread. 'I know my mother likes you, Annie,' she continued with her mouth full, 'but she's hardly likely to come visiting. It's one thing May coming, for goodness sake ... and you, Minty. But my parents?'

Annie looked at her watch. Joe must be up and about by now. She dialled his number and he answered almost immediately. 'Hi, Joe. Have I woken you up?'

'No. Been awake a while.'

'I've got some news. You have a little sister. About two hours ago.'

'*What?* What happened? You weren't due till July. Are you okay?'

Tears filled Annie's eyes at the sound of his concern. 'I'm fine. Bit of a stressful day, though.'

'Are you still in Orkney?'

'No, Aberdeen. It's a long story. Because she's premature, she's in the neonatal intensive care unit, but she's doing okay. You're not to worry.'

'What's she called?'

'Don't know yet. Got any ideas?'

May woke up with a start. 'Where am I? Why am I in hospital?'

Minty reminded her about her granddaughter.

'You need to get the priest to come and do it now,' said May, agitated. 'She's such a wee thing and all these tubes and wires on her. You need to get her baptised in case ... I need to know she's safe.'

'Is Gran there? That's all you need!' Joe said.

Annie laughed. 'Yes, Minty, Gran and Karen. All the women in my life.' She welled up again. 'Wish you were here too.'

There was no reply and Annie was immediately furious with herself. Why put pressure on him? This was none of his doing.

'Joe, Gran is getting in a state. I'll speak to you again in the morning.'

She put the phone down and took her mother's hand. 'Mum, it's okay. Limbo has been abolished, if that's what's worrying you. Once the baby's home, we can talk about whether she will be baptised, but not now.'

Chapter Fifty-Six

The following day, when it became obvious the baby wasn't in a critical condition, most of the press interest waned. There was nothing left in the story now until Annie took the baby home – probably weeks hence, when there just might be a man accompanying her. Colin had caught the last train back to Edinburgh the previous evening and was now in his office following a meeting with his editor. He had been told that if he could get another piece of corroboration, the paper would be delighted to run the Tarik story. He sat wondering how best to proceed, and was about to call Gerry Martin on the *Corrochan Times* when the phone rang. Patrick Liddell, from whom he hadn't heard much in some time, explained briefly that one of the other drivers in the government car service had a very interesting snippet of information for sale. When Colin heard it was Eoin Drever, Annie Cochrane's driver, his spirits lifted.

An hour later, Colin was seated at a corner table at his favourite watering hole with a pint in front of him.

'Ah. There you are, Colin. We'll both have a pint of Belhaven.'

Patrick was standing with a man Colin presumed was Eoin behind him. 'Hello, Patrick. Long time no see. You got something for me too?'

'No, not this time, but this man's a novice, so I'm here to make sure he doesn't get screwed.'

'Fair enough.' Colin headed for the bar.

When he returned with the tray of drinks, he laid his cards on the table. 'I don't pay for what I already know and I already know a lot about Annie Cochrane. Be warned, a pint might be your fucking lot!'

Eoin took a mouthful of beer. Then he leant in towards Colin. 'I'm sure you know a lot of things about lots of people, but I bet you anything you like, you don't know this.'

Colin left the pub knowing he would have to move quickly. It was Friday lunchtime and this needed to be in Saturday's paper because Eoin had surely told someone other than Patrick and that someone would tell someone else. These guys were never able to keep their mouths closed. He sat at his computer and wrote the story – a few hundred words and a headline. It worked like a dream. No subeditor was going to change a single word in *this* story. Now he needed to get a couple of photos within the next two hours, and he knew just the man for the job.

Marlene Watt was more than a little uneasy. After many years of successfully bullying the press following coverage which was in any way critical of her, she was used to saying and doing whatever she wished, but the Connor Clarke debacle was still the number one news item. Things had to be brought back under control, immediately.

Morton perched on the edge of her desk in

such a way as to give him a psychological advantage. 'So! What's the problem, Marlene?'

'What's the problem?' She was incensed that he even needed to ask. 'Connor Clarke and all the unfavourable press coverage is the problem! It's your job, Morton, to control what they say and what they print.'

Morton looked calmly at her but made no comment.

Marlene continued. 'Annie Cochrane's shortcomings seem to be forgotten too, since she had her ... calf. You can't even get *that* piece of media manipulation right.'

Morton's face was expressionless.

Marlene stood up. 'What the fuck have you been doing these last few days?'

In fairness, Morton had been far from idle. He had spent the time distancing himself from Marlene, making sure that all those in the media who needed to know were aware that she was a bad-tempered bully, and hinting that, far from her relationship with Connor Clarke finishing twenty-something years ago, it was still ongoing. He had also had an illuminating conversation with the First Minister's husband regarding Annie Cochrane.

He smiled, as if he was addressing a child. 'Marlene, I have spent twenty hours a day on damage limitation since this story broke. You have to understand, this is more than a criticism of your handling of the economy. You are seen to be closely connected to him – from his election communication, in which you wrote, *I know Connor Clarke will bring talent experience and integrity*

351

to the parliament, to the fact that it is now widely known you had a relationship with him.'

Marlene jabbed a finger towards his chest. 'Well, perhaps you should have been working *more* than twenty hours a day – because whatever you have been doing has achieved fuck all!'

Morton stood up. This was the moment he had been waiting for. He fixed her with his eyes. 'Are you suggesting I have not been putting enough effort into my job?'

She glared back. 'If the cap fits.'

Morton said nothing. Then, with the hint of a smile, he turned away and picked up his briefcase before turning back to face her. 'Well, Marlene, it is obvious I no longer have your confidence. Consequently, I can't continue running the Media Reactive Monitoring Unit.'

Marlene looked blankly at him.

'I don't have to take this shit and I no longer need your patronage. I'm sure there are people in the press office who will be happy to help. Now, if you'll excuse me, I have another meeting.' He turned and walked towards the door.

'A bad mistake, Morton. You are nothing without me.' Her voice was almost a whisper.

Morton stopped and slowly turned to face her. 'Marlene, patronage has its uses, but there comes a moment when the patronised on his way up passes the patron on her way down.' He walked across the deep-pile carpet, then paused by the door, tapping the side of his nose. 'Oh! By the way, I also know why you hate Annie Cochrane as you do.'

Chapter Fifty-Seven

Andrew usually enjoyed a long drive. He would turn his phone off and make the most of uninterrupted solitude in his moving bubble. If he was in good spirits, he would sing along to CDs, and if he needed time to think, he drove in silence. There was no musical accompaniment today. He was heading to a constituency dinner in Aberdeenshire, but he intended to take a detour via the maternity hospital.

When Karen had phoned him to say all was well, he had been surprised not only at the extent of his relief, but at the tears in his eyes. Now as he drove, he thought about Annie. If this doctor was the cold-hearted bastard she had described, he would probably deny his involvement anyway. He glanced at the empty passenger seat. If Jane was still alive, it would have been the two of them en-route to offer support. She would have talked sense into Annie. His chest constricted. These moments of loss were fewer now, but they still took him by surprise.

As he drove round the edge of Dundee, the heavy traffic occupied his attention and it wasn't till he had negotiated the final roundabout on the ring road that he started to think about Annie's political career, an easier subject than their personal relationship. He knew she would resign as soon as she saw him. It was probably the correct decision, but ironically she now had the grudging respect of the nation. A bit of fire in the belly when dealing with journalists had been perceived as strength. He tried not to think of today's press offerings. All the *sources close to the First Minister* stuff suggesting he was unwilling to fire her because of their relationship. Think thick skin. Don't let it get to you. Perhaps a loss of temper might be the solution for him too. Being consistently reasonable and polite was seen as dull at best and not even worth reporting at worst.

Once into the Angus countryside, he allowed himself to think about Pam. She had given him a new way of looking at things. With no interest in politics other than the *what's-Marlene-Watt really-like* sort of questions, outings with her, were – what was the word? – *carefree,* that was it. She made him laugh, made him happy. Was it love or merely lust? Not that it mattered; it was good. He turned the radio on, inserted the *Abbey Road* CD and sang along to 'Something'.

Annie was still enjoying the privacy of the side-room. Let them criticise her all they wanted; she no longer cared. As soon as she could speak to Andrew, she would be free. She had tried his mobile several times that morning, but there was no reply.

It was now early afternoon. Annie was sitting on top of her bed, admiring her now trim ankles while Karen, sitting in the armchair, was studying *Name Your Baby.*

'Felecia? Means lucky,' Karen suggested.

Annie made a face. 'She would get called faeces. It was bad enough being Laverty. Lulu was the

354

best of my nicknames.'

Karen turned a page. 'Louise? Means warrior? Oh! So does Tracey. How about that?'

Annie took her new Marks and Spencer leisure-wear from the bag. 'Louise, perhaps. Does Tracey really mean warrior?'

Karen nodded.

'Very apt when you consider my pal, Tracey McDuff.'

'Oh, look, Karen means pure!'

'Well that book is clearly unreliable,' Annie replied.

'It grows back, you know. Not had a man for over three months; I must be halfway back to virginity already.'

Annie was too busy attempting to put on a pair of tracksuit trousers to respond. The pain from her stitches made it a complicated operation. 'Couldn't you have found something better than these?'

'It's the latest in gym wear. Put the T-shirt on top and you'll be fine. It's so hot in here, you don't need anything else.'

'I suppose they're more useful than the pink fluffy mules.' Annie picked up what she thought was a rather revealing T-shirt and put it on.

'Stop being so sensible! A girl needs a bit of froth now and again.'

Annie laughed. 'Let me see the book.'

'In a minute.' Karen continued to turn the pages. 'Haven't you *any* idea what you want to call her?'

'Not had time to think. It was on the to-do list for the final three weeks when I expected to be sitting with my feet up.' The T-shirt was too small and she wasn't too taken with the shade of green either.

'Eunice means good victory.' Karen looked up, obviously impressed.

'Be serious! There must be something better than that.'

'Okay,' Karen returned to the book. 'Abigail means father rejoices.'

'That'll be a no.' Annie tried unsuccessfully to tuck the T-shirt into the waistband.

'Andrina? Andrea?'

'No!' Annie sat down heavily on the bed.

'I agree with Minty. You should tell him.'

'Don't you start! I only have to tell him if I think he might get Pam pregnant. That's the deal. I have enough to think about now without complicating things further.'

She glared at Karen who shrugged and flipped a few more pages. 'There's no telling you, is there?'

Annie stuck her feet into the fluffy wedge-heeled slippers. 'Minty has been an important person in my life. Perhaps I could call her Minty.'

Karen put the book down. 'Unless you intend sending her to a posh school, I wouldn't call her Araminta. Her life would be hell and Minty sounds like a flavour. What about Mary or May?'

'May would have to be a first name. If you put it in the middle it sounds like a conditional statement. Araminta May – on the other hand, she may not.'

'Karen's a lovely name.'

'Isn't it just.'

There was a knock at the door and an auxiliary

appeared. 'There's an Andrew Fraser here. He says he can come back tomorrow if it's not convenient.'

He hadn't hung around. Annie took a deep breath. 'No, it's okay. Ask him to come in.' At last, she could shed her responsibilities.

Karen gave Annie a meaningful look and stood up. 'Well, you know what Minty and I think.'

'Yes, but I know what I think, too!' Annie held her arms out and gave Karen a hug. 'I know I don't always take it, but thanks anyway for the advice.'

Andrew appeared in the doorway. He was clutching a bunch of flowers and a supermarket carrier bag. He looked slightly flushed.

Annie made the introductions.

'Good to meet you at last,' he said, shaking Karen's hand. 'I'm glad you have been here with Annie.'

Karen didn't think the handshake or demeanour suggested needy. 'So am I.' She smiled at them both. 'Now. I've got a few things to catch up with, so I'll leave you two in peace.'

Andrew kissed Annie on the cheek. 'Congratulations! How are you feeling?'

'Tired, but okay.'

'How's the baby?'

'She's in the neonatal unit, on a ventilator at the moment, but they are pleased with her.'

He paused, unsure what to say next. 'Has she got a name?'

'Not yet.' Annie smiled at him.' I do have a few thoughts, but nothing definite.'

He was still holding the bag and the flowers,

and now thrust them awkwardly at Annie. 'These are for you. Not very exciting, I'm afraid.'

'Thank you, Andrew. Take your coat off and have a seat.' She pointed to the armchair. The bag contained a box of chocolates and a first-size Babygro which might fit the baby in about three months' time.

'They're lovely, thank you. Want a chocolate?' She opened the box and offered him one. 'Thanks for, coming all this way to see me.'

He waved the box away. 'I'm speaking at a dinner in Banchory, later.' He realised that didn't sound good. 'But I would have come to see you anyway.'

'Got your speech written?' She selected a strawberry cream and popped it in her mouth.

'It's the usual rallying of the troops one. Got any good jokes?'

She raised her eyebrows and swallowed the chocolate. 'How about me?'

'You're not a joke.' He looked down at the floor.

'I am, you know.' Now was the moment to offer her resignation, but before she could begin, Andrew interrupted with more small talk.

'Do you know how long you are going to be in hospital?'

'I think I'm being discharged tomorrow, but the baby will be here for a while, till she can manage on her own. There's a place I can stay.' There was an uneasy silence.

'You look as if you're off to the gym.'

Annie plucked at her T-shirt. 'This is Karen's idea of what a new mother ought to be wearing.'

'It suits you.' He examined his fingernails. 'Is

358

this where Tarik works?'

'Yes.'

'I hope you've got round to telling him.'

Before she could answer, the door opened and Minty and May barrelled into the room.

'So sorry!' said Minty, trying to go into reverse. 'Didn't realise you had company.'

'Hello, Minty,' said Andrew, giving her a kiss. 'How are you keeping?'

'I'm fine, Andrew. Fine.'

He then shook May's hand. 'Hello, Mrs Laverty. Congratulations on your new granddaughter.'

May stared at him.

Minty glanced at Annie who gave a small shrug. 'Look, Annie, I can see you and Andrew are in the middle of a conversation. We'll go away and come back later.'

Andrew looked at his watch. 'It's okay. I have to be on my way soon.'

'Oh no you don't, Andrew! Not before I resign.' Annie wasn't going to see him disappear out of the door without achieving her aim.

'Annie!' Minty looked horrified.

But Andrew held his hands up in defeat. 'Okay, Annie, I hear you, but it's now Friday afternoon. We don't need to issue anything formal till Monday. If you're being discharged in the morning, can I take you to lunch? We can chat about it then and work out what the statement should be.'

'I can manage an hour tomorrow – as long as the baby is okay. I warn you though, you won't talk me out of it.'

'I'll phone the ward in the morning, but let's assume I'll collect you at noon, outside the main door.' He picked up his coat and gave her another peck on the cheek.

May watched him intently as he left the room. 'Who's that man?'

'That's Andrew Fraser, Mum.'

'It's not fitting.' May's fists were clenched.

Here we go, Annie thought. What's it about now? 'What's not fitting?' she asked.

'Going out to lunch with another man! What's Kenny going to say about that?'

Annie wilted. She was exhausted. 'Kenny's not going to say anything, Mum. I'm not married to Kenny any more.' Perhaps she could get her mother a crib card – *Annie is not married to Kenny any more. Kenny is not the baby's father. The baby does not need the priest. Your grandchildren are called Joe, Richie and Sonja.*

May changed the subject. 'Is the baby okay?'

'Yes. She's doing fine. I was with her all morning. They're going to try her off the ventilator later. We'll go and see in a minute or two, but first I need a word with Minty.'

'With me?' Minty was clearly itching to find out what had gone on between Andrew and Annie.

'Yes, I need to ask your permission about something.'

'How intriguing.'

'I know what I would like to call the baby. I would like to call her Helena, Helena Mary. But only if you don't mind. I don't want to upset you.'

Tears were running down Minty's cheeks.

'I *have* upset you. I'm sorry.'

'Not upset, my dear, I don't mind at all, and Mary is a good choice too. Do you hear that

360

May?' She located the hankie tucked up her sleeve and blew her nose. 'Goodness me – at least you didn't consider Araminta! Ghastly name!'

'Is the baby okay?' May asked Minty.

'Yes, Annie just said she's doing very well. The baby is to be called Helena Mary. Helena was the name of my baby and Mary is after you.'

When they arrived at the nursery, Helena was breathing unaided. A nurse offered to show Annie how to hold the tiny baby against her chest.

'Mum, come and see,' said Annie, 'Isn't she just amazing?'

'Can I have a drink of water?' May asked.

Annie looked down at the little person she cuddled to her. 'It *is* hot in here, isn't it? Go and ask the nurse. I'm sure she'll find you some.' She gently rocked back and forwards. It was so good to hold the baby at last. Hello, Helena Mary Cochrane. 'Will I be able to breast feed her soon?' she asked the nurse.

'You'll have to keep expressing for a while – till her sucking reflex is better.'

May came back with a plastic cup of water, muttering.

'What is it, Mum?'

'Her name. I'm saying her name so I don't forget it. Heather Mary.'

'Helena Mary,' Annie corrected her gently.

'That's right. Helena Mary.' May dipped her fingers into her cup then touched the baby's forehead, 'Helena Mary, I baptise you in the name of the Father, Son and Holy Spirit.' Helena crumpled up her face and gave a cry.

'Mum! What on earth are you doing?'

'You wouldn't get the priest. Anyone can do it. Father McIver told me that once. If anything happens now, she'll be okay.'

'Oh Mum, I'm sorry. I never realised you were so worried.'

'Heather's OK now,' said May.

Later, after Minty and May had left, Annie began to gather her few belongings together ready for discharge in the morning. What should she wear for her lunch with Andrew – tracksuit or business suit? Neither was exactly suitable. She placed a pillow on the armchair, and gingerly sat down. This must be what it was like to sit on a circle of barbed wire. To take her mind off the discomfort, she began opening her cards. Some were from friends and colleagues, others from people she had never met, all wishing her and the baby well. She heard a baby crying in the next room and felt the pull to go back to the unit. It was nearly impossible to stay away, now that she and Helena had been properly introduced. She was looking round for a magazine to take with her, when she heard a quiet knock at the door. She turned round and there was Joe. She held out her arms.

'Joe! How did you get here?'

'In one of these metal tubes that go up in the sky; it's called a plane.' He gave Annie a careful bear hug then looked round the room. 'How are you, and where is my sister?'

'Your sister, whose name is Helena by the way, is still in the special baby unit.'

'Helena is the heroine in *All's Well That Ends*

Well, isn't she? I saw that on the school trip to Stratford.'

'So she is,' said Annie. She hadn't felt this happy in months. 'So she is! I'd forgotten that. Come here and give me another hug. I won't break.' But she was still concerned. 'Where did you get the money for the air fare?'

'I had some I earned, and Karen lent me the rest.'

Karen swept into the room. 'Couldn't have a family party going on without Joe.' She raised her eyebrows at Annie. 'You have a satisfactory conversation with you know who?'

'Mum and Minty arrived before we got very far. I'm seeing him tomorrow.'

'Where is Gran?' Joe asked.

'Staying with Minty, in some stately home that belongs to a friend of hers. She gets about, your gran does. By the way, where are you staying?'

'At my sister's, with me,' Karen reassured her. 'Don't worry, it's all fixed.'

'Come on, Mum! Stop fussing. Aren't you going to take me to see her? Helena?'

Joe and Annie made their way to the nursery, and Joe stared at the baby, obviously taken aback by how small she was. After a few moments he gently put his finger beside her hand. 'Hello, Helena, I'm your big brother.'

'What do you think of her?'

Joe didn't reply. He kept looking at the baby.

'Is something the matter? Are you still angry with me?'

Joe pulled his gaze away and looked at Annie. 'I need to ask you something, Mum.'

'Ask away!' Annie braced herself for the dreaded paternity question.

'Can I come home, please? London was a big mistake.'

Chapter Fifty-Eight

The following morning Annie was packed and ready to go. She was being relocated to the accommodation provided for mothers with babies in the unit. While she waited for her bag of pills from the pharmacy, she leafed through the daily papers, kindly ordered by her office. She put one down and was about to pick up another when Joe and Karen arrived.

'We had to come and see you again before we left,' Karen explained. 'Plane's not till one, so can we have another peek at her before we go? I'm not sure when I'll see you next.'

'How long till you get her home?' They had decided that Joe's return was to coincide with this event.

'It'll be few weeks, Joe. As soon as I have an idea when, I promise I'll let you know, then you can hand in your notice.'

'Here's some mags for you.' Karen dumped *Hello!* and *Mother and Baby* on the bed. 'Couldn't decide between celeb gossip and remedies for sore nipples, so I got both.' She and Annie checked the cupboards and drawers.

Joe suddenly burst out laughing.

'What's so funny?' Annie enquired.

Joe, doubled up and, unable to speak, handed her the *Daily Scot*. Annie too became helpless with laughter.

'What is it? Show me?' Karen took the paper from Annie.

'"FIRST MINISTER IS A TWATT,"' read Karen, half horrified. 'Can they say that? Surely they can't say that, even if they think it.'

'Give it here, I need to read the rest.' Annie took back the paper and with herculean effort managed to compose herself. '"First Minister Marlene Watt is really a Twatt..."' She stopped again. Tears of laughter ran down her cheeks. 'My stitches...'

Karen continued in a newscaster's voice, '"Her grandfather John Twatt left Orkney in the 1930s in search of work in Glasgow. His children all had the surname Twatt, but by the time of Marlene's birth, the initial T had vanished and Marlene was registered as Watt. Twatt, from the old Norse, meaning a plot of land, is both an Orcadian and a Shetland surname. It is also the name of an area of Orkney, near to where Marlene's fore-bears originated." Look, here's a picture of Twatt church.' Karen pointed to a photo. '"Ivor Twatt, 68, from Windybreck, Birsay"... that sounds like a flatulence-inducing porridge ... "believes that he is Marlene Watt's second cousin. He told our reporter, "My grandfather's brother went to Glasgow, but we lost touch. I never realised I was related to the First Minister. I would love to meet her, as would all her second cousins. She'd get a big welcome from her relations in Orkney."'

Look – there's a picture of an old guy in a boiler suit leaning on a gate.'

Annie, still helpless with laughter, eventually found breath enough to speak. 'Bet *she* doesn't want to meet *them.*'

Colin was delighted with himself. Not only had he unearthed six Twatts worldwide, four of whom seemed to be direct relations of Marlene's, but his piece about Tarik for the *Sunday Saltire* was ready for publication. Unaware that both he and Morton Hunter had got their information from the Haunter, Colin was happy to have Morton confirm that Annie had had an Asian man in her hotel room the previous October. After all, Morton's sources were impeccable. Morton had also divulged another corker concerning the First Minister's dislike for Annie Cochrane, but it would keep for another day. In the meantime, Colin was employee of the month with the editor, especially as the paternity story, unlike the Twatt one, hadn't cost the paper a penny. He proofread what he had written one last time, and pressed *send.*

Lynn was also having a busy morning at her desk. She too had obtained further corroboration for her story. A second cup of coffee with her new best friend, Sandra's sister, had revealed that Annie Cochrane and her 'friend' Karen always seemed to be holding hands and hugging each other. Gerry Martin of the *Corrachan Times* had told her that he'd seen Annie and a female companion over the Easter weekend having a tête-a-tête dinner after having looked at buggies in the pram shop in

366

Strathperry, Lynn was cock-a-hoop. No need for smutty puns – she had decided on a headline that said what it meant: ANNIE COCHRANE MSP IN LESBIAN RELATIONSHIP. The article stated Annie's baby's father was unknown, and that the other mummy was Karen Warnock, an old friend from times past, who had been at Annie's side since labour commenced. She then related Karen's life story in remarkable detail. Lynn didn't worry about outing people – she'd done it several times before, believing that she was actually doing them a favour. As she sent her piece off for publication, she received a text telling her Connor Clarke had been charged with money laundering. It was time to go and get a comment from Ms Twatt.

Chapter Fifty-Nine

Alan, a temporary replacement for Morton, had been summoned by Marlene to help her draft a press statement. She was in full flow. 'I want to know where that journalist got his information. How dare he make me a laughing stock. It's puerile rubbish.' She paused. 'And anyway, it rhymes with Watt. It's a well-known Orkney name of Viking origin.'

'Did you know your father had changed his name?' Alan ventured.

'Of course I didn't!' This was not quite true. She had found her late father's birth certificate

367

amongst his papers.

'Do you think, perhaps, it might be good PR if we arranged a meeting with your cousins – family reunion, getting in touch with your roots, that sort of thing? A photo opportunity? A good-news story?' suggested Alan.

'No, I do *not*.'

Worried that she was about to assault him, Alan took a step backwards.

'This ludicrous and damaging story needs to be killed as soon as possible. Draft something which explains that this was news to me, but, on checking, it appears my father changed his name. Two sentences should be sufficient.' She challenged him with a look. 'What are you waiting for? Go away and get on with it.'

As he left the room, he heard her letting loose a stream of expletives, and the tinny thud as her metal wastepaper basket hit the wall at the far end of the office.

Later, when Marlene arrived at a fundraising fete at a primary school in her constituency, she managed to put on her genial public face. The press, initially gathered to elicit a Twatt response, now knew about Connor. The shouts started as she climbed out of the car.

'What do you think about Connor Clarke now?'

'When is he going to resign?'

'Did you know about his business activities?'

'Is it true he donated half a million to your party?'

Marlene ignored them and kept moving forwards, her smile fixed.

'Did you know you were a twat?'

368

That was a step too far. Marlene stopped, then, Thatcher-like, identified Lynn as the questioner.

'If you'll excuse me, I have constituency business to attend to.'

The head teacher somehow managed to thank Ms Watt for attending their event without bursting out laughing or mispronouncing their guest's name, unlike the gaggle of Primary 7 boys at the back of the hall. They had a field day. And their teachers didn't seem to be making any effort to curb their behaviour.

Marlene could deal with political attack, she could pass off unpopularity as ignorance, but she had never been able to cope with being laughed at. For the first time in many years, she couldn't wait to get home to Robert for some reassurance. She sank down into the back of the official car and closed her eyes against the barrage of flashing lights from the cameras.

Patrick dropped Marlene off at home and watched her make her way to the front door. She had said nothing all the way back. The Twatt story had obviously floored her and that surprised him. He hadn't thought anything got to Marlene. He started the engine and checked there was nothing coming. An hour to Edinburgh, then to the pub where Eoin was hosting a small party. This was turning out to be a good weekend.

Marlene turned her key in the lock and let herself in. The house was empty. A note on the kitchen table indicated that Stephanie had gone shopping. Jordan had long since stopped informing his mother of his whereabouts. Assuming

Robert was attending to his birds, she opened the back door and made her way across the lawn. The aviary was empty. An envelope with her name on it was propped up on a shelf. She ripped it open.

Deart Marlie,
So you have come looking for me. Perhaps you were wondering why your dinner wasn't ready or why your washing hasn't been done. Whatever the reason, you will see that the birds and I have flown. I realise my departure will cause some child-care difficulties, so I have arranged for my mother to come and stay till the end of June. Jordan is intending to leave school and I will discuss with you what is best for Stephanie. I am sure we can arrange to meet one evening, as I am now living in Edinburgh with Connie from the Caged Bird Society.
Best wishes,
Robert

Connie! That overweight nonentity with a squint and a personal freshness problem? How could he? Marlene was incandescent with rage. As she walked back up the garden, she saw Doris Keiller appear on the back step.

Now almost seventy, Doris looked much as she had when she retired from the prison service fifteen years earlier. Although she had enjoyed the kudos which went with Marlene's position, she had never warmed to her daughter-in-law. She nodded towards the letter in Marlene's hand. 'I see you've received his resignation.' She folded her arms. 'Your front door was unlocked, anyone

370

could have walked in. And where are the children? Their rooms are a disgrace! There will be no tea until things are tidy.'

Chapter Sixty

Annie, was standing outside the main door of the hospital, waiting for Andrew to pick her up. She doubted the track suit, however designer, was suitable for lunch out, but it would have to do. Despite a final nagging text from Karen, now in the departure lounge in Aberdeen airport, she still wasn't going to tell Andrew unless she had to. Let him think Tarik was the father for now and perhaps, sometime, she might tell him the truth. On the agenda today was her resignation. A political career finished, but she didn't care any more.

She took a deep breath. It was wonderful to be in the fresh air again but, despite the June sunshine, she was glad of her coat after two days in the overheated hospital. She felt inside her bag and found the card Eoin had sent her. It had arrived this morning and she wanted to show it to Andrew. Inside he had written *Congratulations! Hope you are both doing well. Eoin. PS My Orkney granny knows everything about everybody!* Annie smiled to herself. She hoped he had been sufficiently rewarded.

Andrew's car drew up beside her and she got in.

'Good turn-out at the dinner?' she asked as

they pulled out onto the main road.

'Mmm. About sixty.' He glanced at her. 'Baby all right this morning?'

'She's fine. She's got a name now – Helena Mary.'

'That's nice. A family name?' Andrew braked as the traffic lights turned to red.

'Mary is after Mum. Helena – Minty had a baby called Helena in the war. Also, I like the name.' There was a pause 'Where are we going for lunch?' She gestured at the tracksuit. 'I'm not sure I'm suitably dressed.'

'You are just fine. I thought we might be a bit conspicuous at the moment, so I've assembled a picnic. I thought we could park near the beach. Privacy and a view?' The lights changed and they were on the move again.

'Sounds good.' Annie looked out of the window for a few moments. 'Joe came to see me yesterday. He wants to come home.'

'That's great news.'

Silence again. They were running out of small talk. She needed to move to the point. 'I'm sorry you were out when I rang on Wednesday. I spoke to Pam. She sounds nice.' God strike her down as a liar. 'Have you known each other long?'

'Not long. She's a friend of my sister. A widow.'

'What does she do?'

'She doesn't have a job, if that's what you mean. Her late husband left her well provided for.'

Lucky her, Annie thought. 'Children?' she asked.

'Two. Thirteen and fifteen. I've not met them yet. They're at boarding school.'

This was not promising. Unless Pam was a very

372

late starter, she was probably young enough for an unpleasant surprise, but Annie was not going to admit defeat unless she had to. 'Has she been widowed long?'

'Eight years. She was only thirty-five when her husband died. She's had a tough time.' Not that tough if she has never had to work, Annie thought, but that was by the by. She had no option now. Easier to say it while the car was moving and they were looking straight ahead. Get it over with.

'Andrew, I don't really know how to tell you this...'

Chapter Sixty-One

With the press now intent on Marlene's downfall, certain people realised they had a valuable story to sell: the English teacher and headmaster at Jordan's school were keen to elaborate on Jordan's foul mouth and his mother's capacity to bully – off the record, of course; the girl on the check-in desk at Glasgow airport wanted to talk about Marlene's routine demand for upgrades; the housekeeper at her official residence let slip some interesting details about the use of the entertainment budget for personal parties; the Scottish Rugby Union official still bore a grudge about having to give up his seat; the pregnant au-pair told anybody who would listen that she might be carrying Marlene's grandchild; Patrick Liddell had a long list concerning the misuse of her ministerial car, including

373

the as-yet-unrecompensed cost of the specialist bird-poo stain-removal stuff, the proprietor of the Taj Mahal was happy to be photographed in front of his restaurant, holding the pile of unpaid bills for takeaway curries totalling £275.32; and Ally Bigswell finally found a use for his meticulous records of all that nocturnal blogging and the payments he'd received.

The First Minister didn't have to suffer for long. While Annie waited with growing excitement for her daughter to gain enough strength to come home, Marlene watched her reputation being tossed around, ridiculed and trashed. She had no choice but to step away from what had been – in so many ways – a remarkable political career.

Chapter Sixty-Two

Annie could hardly see for the driving November rain. The windscreen wipers were doing their best, but it wasn't quite good enough. She missed Eoin. Driving on narrow country roads in the winter was no fun.

She was on her way home from a day in Edinburgh. Life was much easier now. She only had to be at the Parliament a couple of days a week, and the rest could be done from her Corrachan office. Andrew kept her up to date with any news of Morton Hunter, Scotland's new and youngest-ever First Minister. Things were not, in fact, very different. No one called the ex First Minister anything but Marlene Twatt now. She had tried to cling to power while story after story about her murky past emerged, but when the *Top of the Form* story broke, she had no choice but to resign... *Top of the Form* – that benign, earnest kids' quiz show which had finally died a death in the mid-80s, and the reason for Marlene's unadulterated vitriol towards Annie. The press had a field day.

It was the day after she had brought month-old Helena home that Colin had contacted Annie, asking to come and see her.

'Were you ever a contestant on *Top of the Form*, the radio version?'

Annie laughed. That was a blast from the past. '*Yes*, but only by mistake.' She had been a reserve, called in at the last minute when the team captain had been concussed by a hockey ball half an hour before the recording. 'Why do you ask?'

'Do you remember the captain of the other team?'

'Yes, vaguely – she was all braid round the blazer and prefect badges. I can't even remember what school it was now.'

'What if I tell you her name was Marlene Watt.'

'*No! Marlene!*'

'The same!'

Annie remembered that day all too well. She'd been sitting with her friends in the back row of the school hall, waiting for the recording to start, making jokes about the team from the fee-paying school slumming it. Then the headmaster had beckoned her out of her seat to tell her she was now the team captain. She had laughed in his face, before realising he was serious. The rest of the team had spent every lunchtime for weeks creating questions to ask each other from every book on every shelf in the non-fiction section of the school library, while she had been smoking at the far end of the playing fields. The irony was that, although she'd been a near disaster, the second of only two correct answers she provided that day was the one that won the school the competition. 'So that was Marlene – the one who glared at me as if she wanted to kill me? Has she been bearing a grudge for over twenty-five years?'

'So I gather, but she only realised it was you when the *Sunday Clarion* article published that piece on where today's MSPs had gone to school – some time last February.'

Annie shook her head in disbelief. 'That would be about right. The serious bitching started just after that. So, how did you find out?'

'Shall we say *a source who used to be close to the First Minister?*'

Annie rolled her eyes. 'And did Morton tell you details about the final round?'

'No.'

Perhaps she shouldn't have told Colin, but once she had started it was a bit difficult to stop. It had been one of the high points in her school career.

'It was two points for a correct answer, one point for a bonus, and Marlene's team were two points ahead in the last round. Then it came to the final questions to the team captains. I had failed every question, so I expect she thought it was done and dusted. I remember it was on scientific words. The question master gave a definition and we had to say the word. Marlene went first – the definition was *a living thing which can't be seen by the naked eye*. Whether it was a slip of the tongue or whether she had led a more sheltered life than I had, I don't know, but she said *micro-orgasm* instead of *micro-organism*. The question master asked her to repeat it, which she duly did. The place erupted. They edited most of the laughter out for the broadcast but it was still audible. Anyway, I was offered the bonus, and as she had more or less given me the answer, I got the point. My word was *enzymes* – and we'd spent half the morning on them in biology. Complete fluke. So my school won – by one point. I do remember they were very bad losers.'

Colin loved a challenge, and he went off and tracked down an ancient recording of the episode. Before long it was on YouTube, and Marlene's resignation was announced soon thereafter. Had she been mean? Annie wondered, as she negotiated the final bend in the road home. Perhaps. But the woman was on her way out anyway and, in true Marlene-style, she had bounced back, negotiating a lucrative lecture tour of the States. It was rumoured that, like Annie, she would be standing down at the next election.

Annie turned into her driveway and switched off the engine. If she was lucky, she might have time for something to eat before Minty came to pick her up. She locked the car and made her way up the path, nearly losing her footing on some wet leaves. Joe was the limit. She had been asking him

377

to sweep them up for weeks. She unlocked the door, careful to lock it again behind her before putting the key back in her bag. It was the only way to stop her mother's escape attempts. The house was cosy and she could hear May chatting happily. Employing Jean McCafferty had been the best thing she could have done. She was wonderful with Helena, May was at ease with her, and she was a great cook. When Annie opened the kitchen door, she saw Helena in her high chair being spoon-fed by May. Joe was sitting at the table, holding out his plate for a second helping.

'Just in time!' said Jean cheerfully. 'Before Joe finishes your share too.'

'Hello, everyone!' Annie kissed the top of Helena's head, careful to avoid the baby rice which coated her face. 'Hello, my cherub, not quite got the hang of solids yet, have you?' She kissed her again. 'That one's from Daddy. He can't wait to see you tomorrow.'

Helena held her arms out to be picked up.

'I'll give you a cuddle when you've finished your tea.'

She gave her mother a kiss. 'How have you been today?'

May looked at her. 'Who are you?'

'I'm Annie, Mum.'

'This is my baby,' said May, waving a laden spoon in the direction of Helena's mouth. 'She's called Annie too.'

Annie looked at Jean. 'Bad day?'

'Not too bad. No escapes. She's fine with the baby stuff as long as I keep an eye. Have you got

378

time for some lasagne? When's Minty picking you up?'

'I'd love some. It smells delicious. I've got a few minutes.' She sat down next to Joe. 'You had a good day?'

There was no reply. She removed the earphone from the ear next to her. 'I said, have you had a good day?'

'Yeah, Mum, I've had a good day.' Joe put the earphone back in.

Annie accepted the plate from Jean. 'I shouldn't be too late tonight. The meeting won't go on and on. If Mum and Helena are asleep, Joe can manage. That would let you get off.'

Despite earphones, Joe heard that. 'I said I would go to Ellie's.'

'I'm happy to stay till you get back, don't worry.' Jean had her hands in the sink, attacking the washing up.

There was a long ring on the front doorbell.

Annie swallowed her mouthful. 'That'll be Minty!' She put down her knife and fork and went to give Helena another kiss. 'Big cuddles in the morning, honeybun.' She picked up her coat and bag. 'See you all later.'

'Perhaps not,' warned Joe. 'You have to have a death wish to let Minty drive you anywhere nowadays.'

Annie carefully made her way down the path to the road where Minty's car, with engine running, was rattling gently. She strapped herself in and they set off towards the centre of town on the wrong side of the road.

'I find it very difficult driving in the dark now,'

Minty informed her. 'This way, I can see the kerb on my side. Bit misty to my left.' Joe had a point.

'We can go back and take my car,' Annie suggested.

'No need. I've perfected this technique.' Minty swerved to avoid an oncoming car before returning to the right-hand side of the road. 'Now, tell me. Are you okay about tonight? After this, there's no going back.'

'I'm fine, Minty. After the new candidate is selected tonight, I only have to help make sure he or she gets elected next May, then I can move on. I've had enough of trailing back and fore to Edinburgh. I want to stay at home for a while and spend time with my family.'

'You might find you get bored, and, at the risk of being indelicate, there is the matter of money.' Minty repeated the swerving manoeuvre.

Annie's right foot stamped on the floor. 'You don't need to worry about that. We settled out of court last week, so money won't be a problem. Julia has been amazing. She sorted our case and Tarik's. Karen's mentally spent her compensation already. Being taken for a lesbian is the best thing to happen to her in years.'

Minty roared with laughter. 'And the boredom?'

'Something interesting and part-time will turn up. I used to think being a government minister was about the most important thing in my life, but it can't have been. I haven't missed it at all. Glad I did it, but glad it's gone. Letting go of the constituency bit will be the same.'

Now that they were in the centre of town where the street lighting was better, Minty was back to the correct side of the road. Annie relaxed a little, until Minty shot round the mini-roundabout in fourth gear and, much to the annoyance of the driver behind, turned sharp right without indicating, into the community centre car park. She came to an abrupt halt straddling two parking spaces, and yanked on the handbrake.

'And what about Andrew?'

'He'll be here tomorrow, as usual.'

Minty turned to face her. 'That wasn't what I meant. I know he's a besotted father. What about you and him?'

Annie looked straight ahead. 'He's keeping his options open. Poor guy doesn't have much choice at the moment, does he?' She laughed quietly. 'On the plus side, he's no longer seen as that dull and boring politician. The scandal has done amazing things for the party's standing in the opinion polls.'

'I'm not sure I'm a great believer in that "all publicity is good publicity" business,' said Minty. She paused, then said in a low voice, 'I would have expected Pam to have a termination.'

'She wants Andrew, Minty. It's as simple as that. And because Helena would bring him to me, she thinks she needs a baby too, to have any chance of keeping him. Extreme measures, perhaps, but she's probably right.'

'He can't accuse you of not being honest with him.'

'I was too late, wasn't I? What can go wrong, will go wrong. Can't expect to escape Sod's Law entirely.'

'Very unlucky,' Minty agreed.

Annie, however, wasn't as sanguine as she wanted to appear. 'His vasectomy must have been done by a medical student with a hangover, for goodness sake. He should sue. Maybe I'll get Julia onto it. It would pay for the child maintenance.'

'But will you get him in the end?'

Annie sighed and looked down at her hands. 'I'm not sure, Minty, but I have got a nine-month start in the baby stakes. It's not the traditional happy ending, but I feel better than I've felt in a long time.'

'But do you *want* to get him in the end?'

Annie hesitated. There was no point in trying to put Minty off, but she honestly couldn't answer that question.

'Pass!' she said finally. 'But whatever happens, I think it will be okay. For both of us.'

'For all of you,' said Minty, patting Annie's knee. 'That's the best way, you know. Just keep telling yourself, *All shall be well.* I've been doing it for nearly seventy years.' She undid her seat belt and fumbled on the floor for her handbag. 'Now, if we're not careful, we'll be late for the vote, and I know exactly who we need to put in place.'

Annie followed Minty up the steps into the hall. The old campaigner was right. All *shall* be well, she decided.

The publishers hope that this book has given you enjoyable reading. Large Print Books are especially designed to be as easy to see and hold as possible. If you wish a complete list of our books please ask at your local library or write directly to:

Magna Large Print Books
Magna House, Long Preston,
Skipton, North Yorkshire.
BD23 4ND

This Large Print Book for the partially sighted, who cannot read normal print, is published under the auspices of

THE ULVERSCROFT FOUNDATION